CUPCAKES of DOOM!

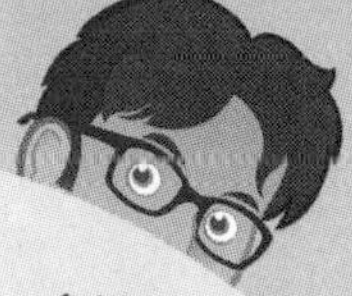

If you ever meet Ray Friesen, he'll sign this book for you! Even if you don't want him to!

Zone of Autographing

know your local pirates!

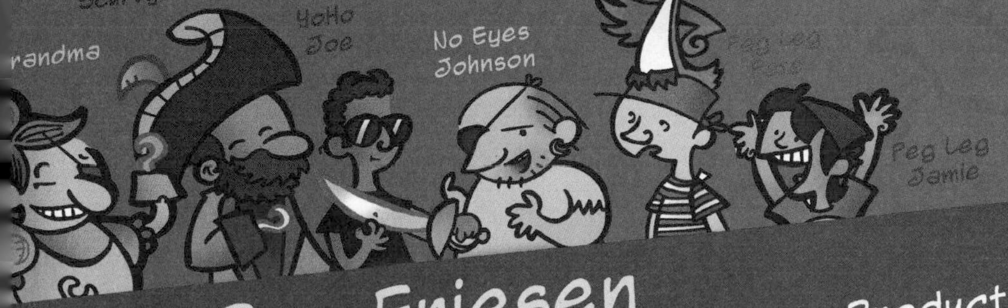

Lester
Captain Scurvybeard
YoHo Joe
randma
No Eyes Johnson
Peg Leg
Peg Leg Jamie

by Ray Friesen

Don't Eat Any Bugs Productions

Chapters

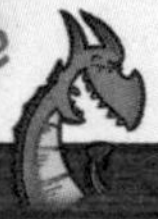

this book is dedicated to the thoroughly wonderful Rhianna Williams! xo

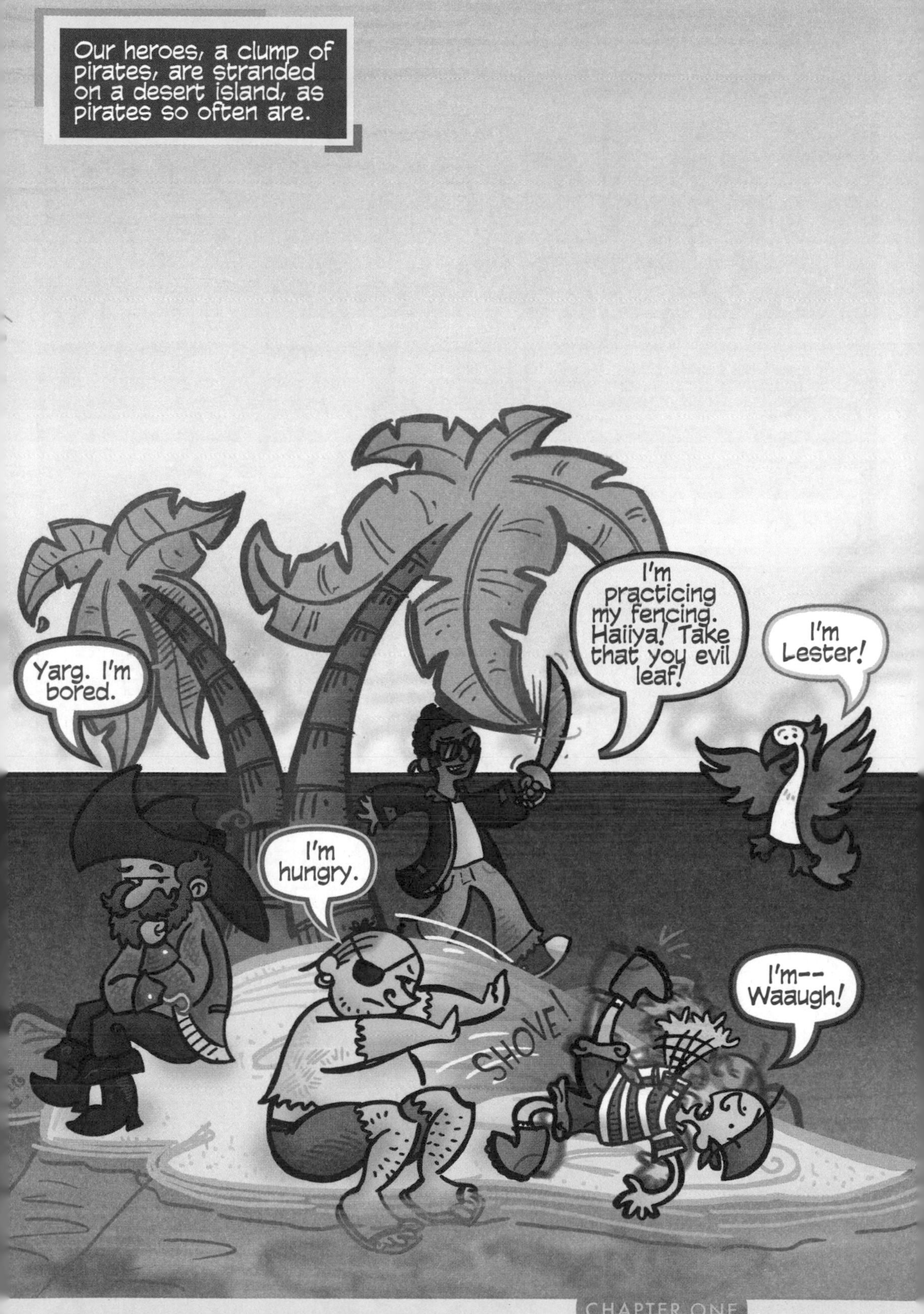
Our heroes, a clump of pirates, are stranded on a desert island, as pirates so often are.
Yarg. I'm bored.
I'm practicing my fencing. Haiiya! Take that you evil leaf!
I'm Lester!
I'm hungry.
SHOVE!
I'm-- Waaugh!

CHAPTER ONE

Abandon Coconut!

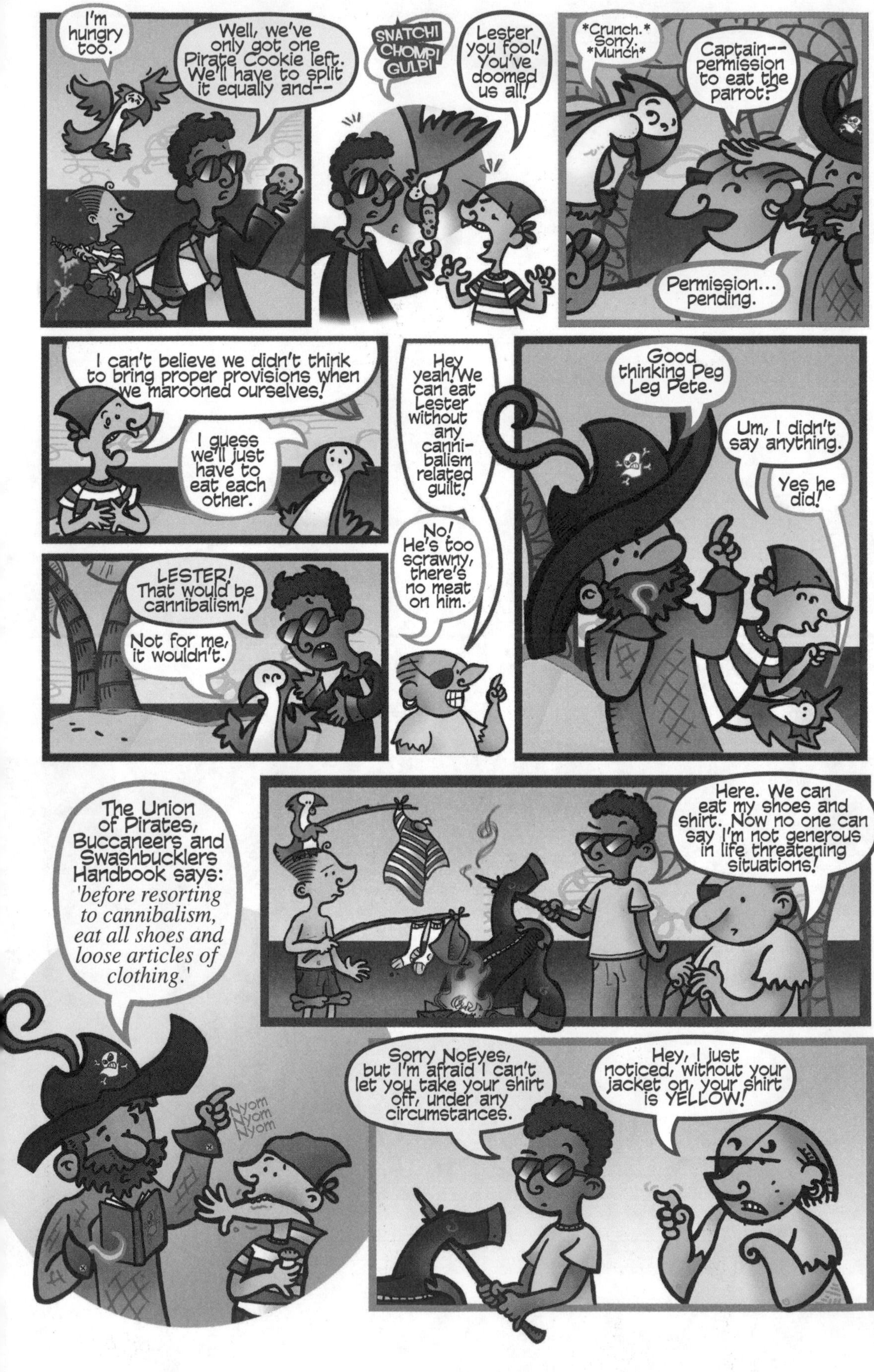
I'm hungry too.
Well, we've only got one Pirate Cookie left. We'll have to split it equally and--
SNATCH! CHOMP! GULP!
Lester you fool! You've doomed us all!
Crunch. Sorry. *Munch*
Captain-- permission to eat the parrot?
Permission... pending.
I can't believe we didn't think to bring proper provisions when we marooned ourselves!
I guess we'll just have to eat each other.
LESTER! That would be cannibalism!
Not for me, it wouldn't.
Hey yeah! We can eat Lester without any canni-balism related guilt!
No! He's too scrawny, there's no meat on him.
Good thinking Peg Leg Pete.
Um, I didn't say anything.
Yes he did!
The Union of Pirates, Buccaneers and Swashbucklers Handbook says: *'before resorting to cannibalism, eat all shoes and loose articles of clothing.'*
Nyom Nyom Nyom
Here. We can eat my shoes and shirt. Now no one can say I'm not generous in life threatening situations!
Sorry NoEyes, but I'm afraid I can't let you take your shirt off, under any circumstances.
Hey, I just noticed, without your jacket on, your shirt is YELLOW!

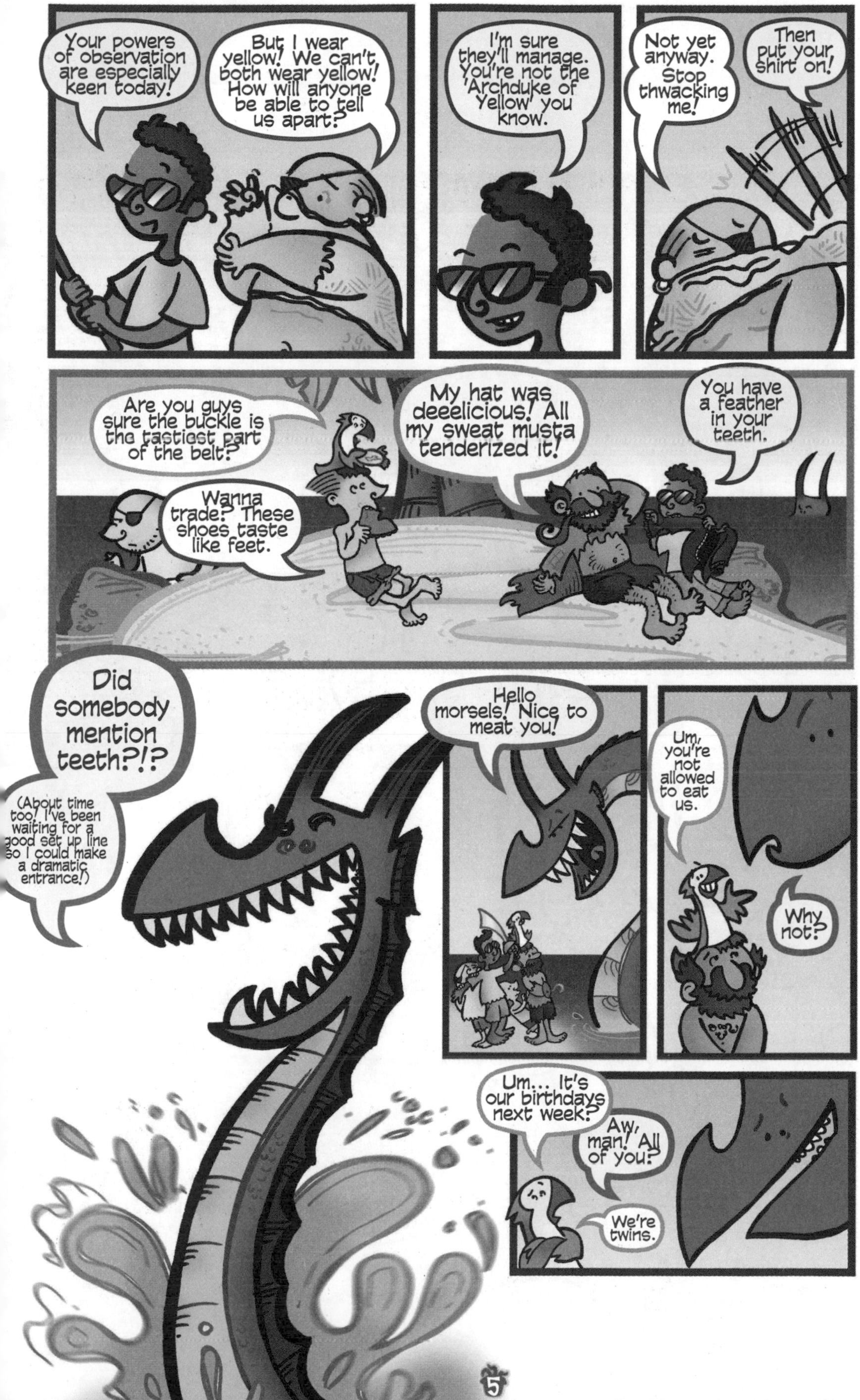
Your powers of observation are especially keen today!
But I wear yellow! We can't both wear yellow! How will anyone be able to tell us apart?
I'm sure they'll manage. You're not the 'Archduke of Yellow' you know.
Not yet anyway.
Stop thwacking me!
Then put your shirt on!
Are you guys sure the buckle is the tastiest part of the belt?
Wanna trade? These shoes taste like feet.
My hat was deeelicious! All my sweat musta tenderized it!
You have a feather in your teeth.
Did somebody mention teeth?!?
(About time too! I've been waiting for a good set up line so I could make a dramatic entrance!)
Hello morsels! Nice to meat you!
Um, you're not allowed to eat us.
Why not?
Um... It's our birthdays next week?
Aw, man! All of you?
We're twins.

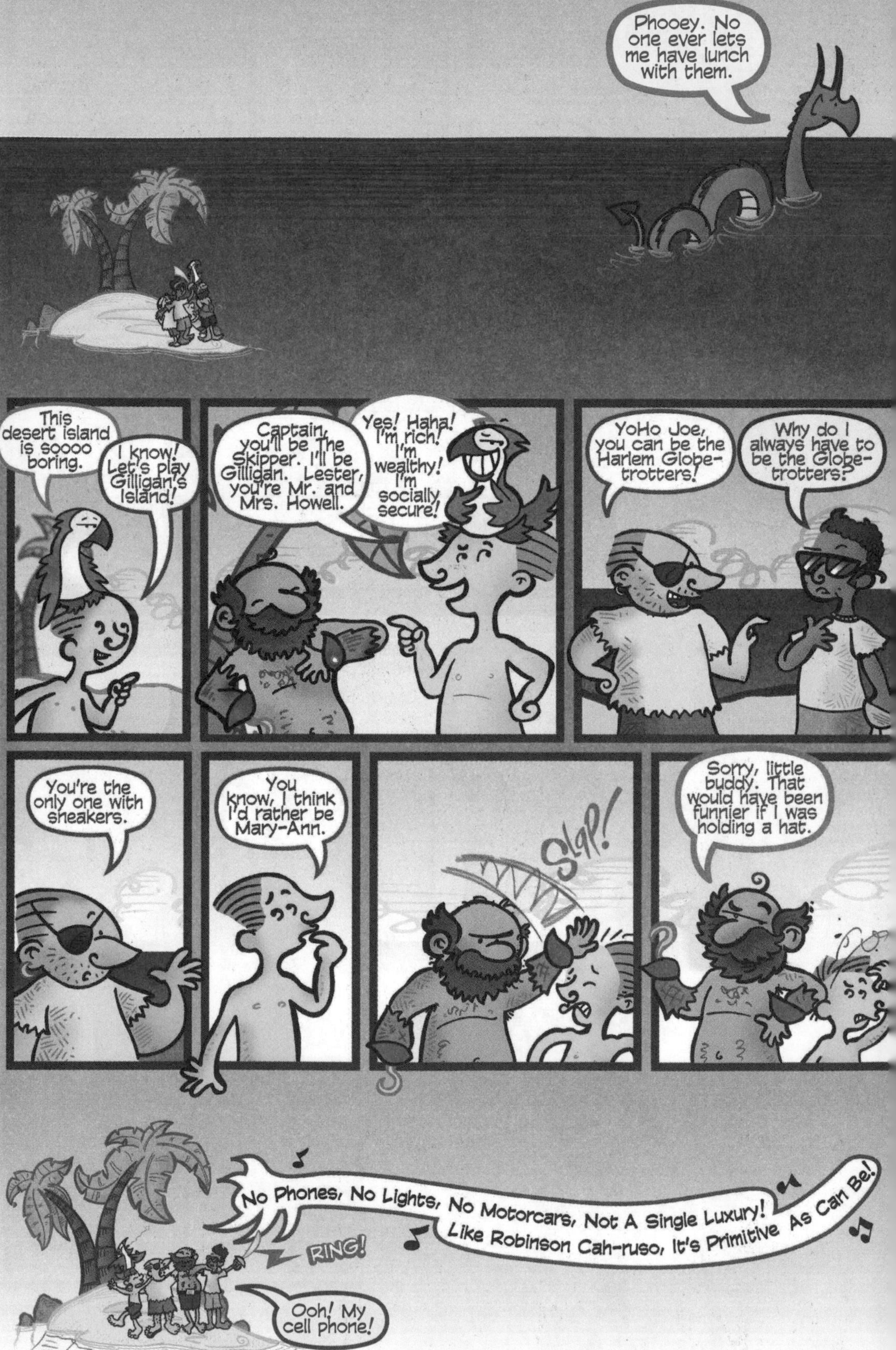
Phooey. No one ever lets me have lunch with them.
This desert island is soooo boring.
I know! Let's play Gilligan's Island!
Captain, you'll be The Skipper. I'll be Gilligan. Lester, you're Mr. and Mrs. Howell.
Yes! Haha! I'm rich! I'm wealthy! I'm socially secure!
YoHo Joe, you can be the Harlem Globe-trotters!
Why do I always have to be the Globe-trotters?
You're the only one with sneakers.
You know, I think I'd rather be Mary-Ann.
SLAP!
Sorry, little buddy. That would have been funnier if I was holding a hat.
No Phones, No Lights, No Motorcars, Not A Single Luxury!
Like Robinson Cah-ruso, It's Primitive As Can Be!
RING!
Ooh! My cell phone!

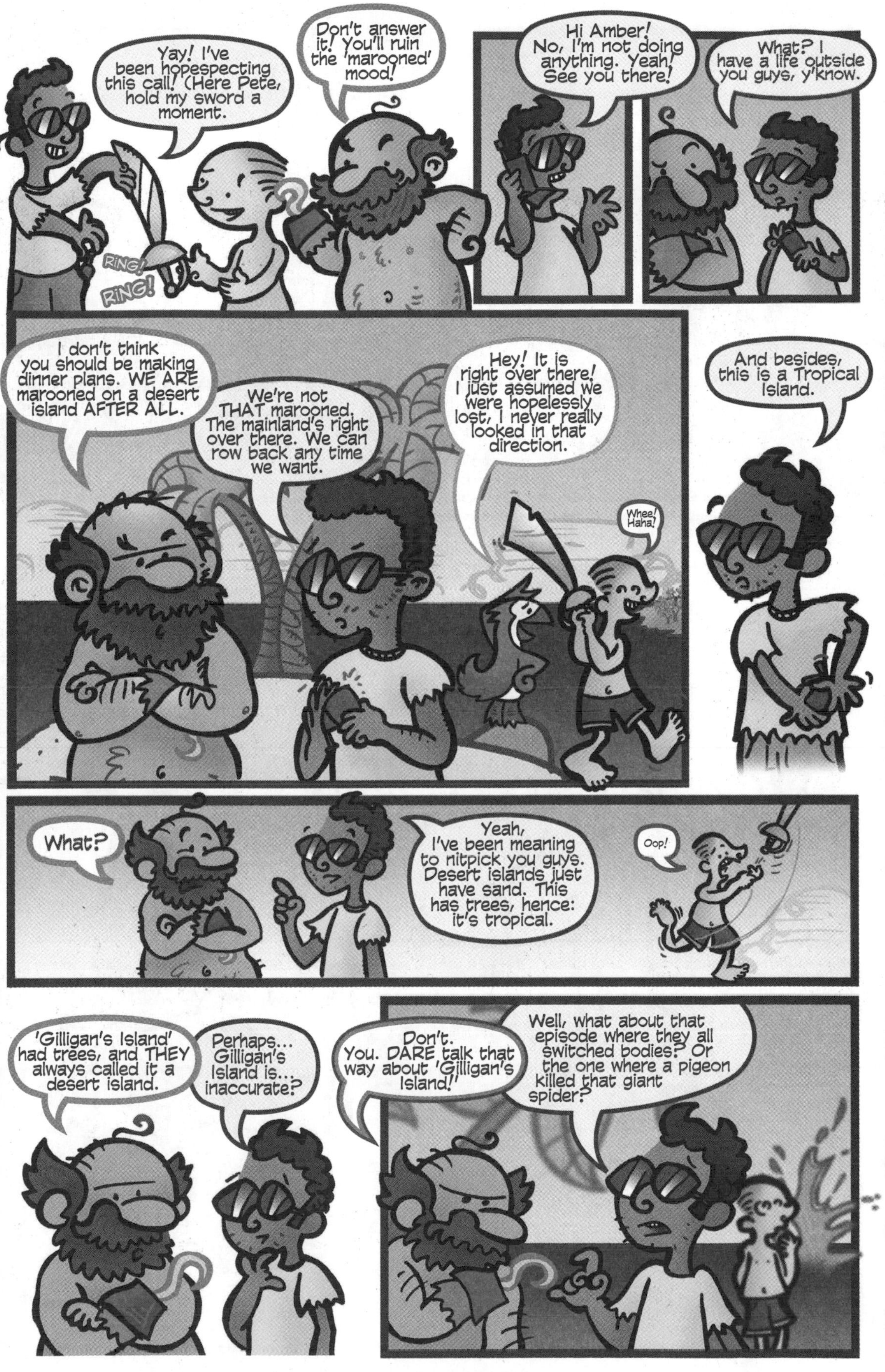
Yay! I've been hopespecting this call! (Here Pete, hold my sword a moment.
RING! RING!
Don't answer it! You'll ruin the 'marooned' mood!
Hi Amber! No, I'm not doing anything. Yeah! See you there!
What? I have a life outside you guys, y'know.
I don't think you should be making dinner plans. WE ARE marooned on a desert island AFTER ALL.
We're not THAT marooned. The mainland's right over there. We can row back any time we want.
Hey! It is right over there! I just assumed we were hopelessly lost, I never really looked in that direction.
Whee! Haha!
And besides, this is a Tropical Island.
What?
Yeah, I've been meaning to nitpick you guys. Desert islands just have sand. This has trees, hence: it's tropical.
Oop!
'Gilligan's Island' had trees, and THEY always called it a desert island.
Perhaps... Gilligan's Island is... inaccurate?
Don't. You. DARE talk that way about 'Gilligan's Island!'
Well, what about that episode where they all switched bodies? Or the one where a pigeon killed that giant spider?

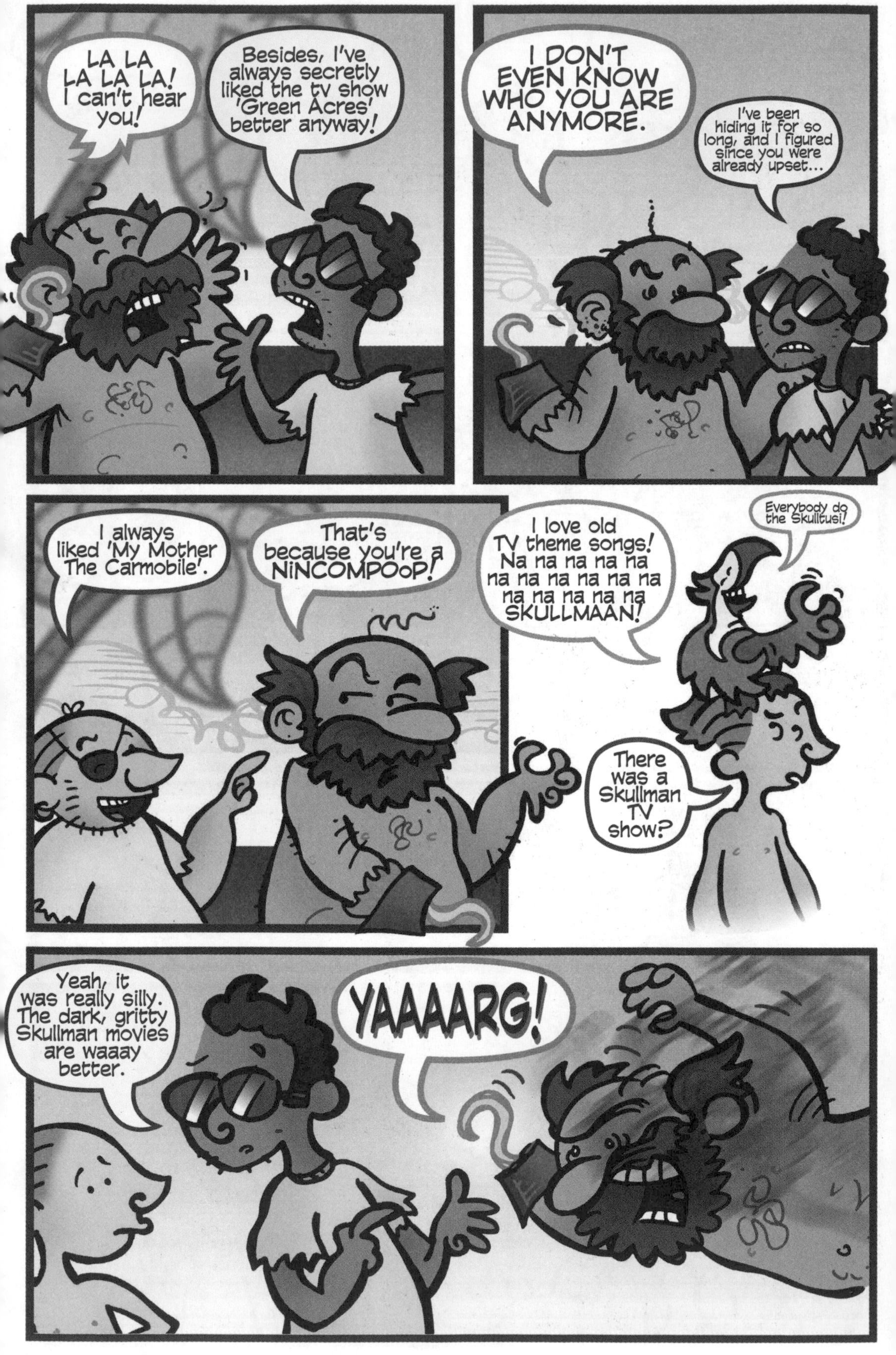
LA LA
LA LA LA!
I can't hear
you!
Besides, I've
always secretly
liked the tv show
'Green Acres'
better anyway!
I DON'T
EVEN KNOW
WHO YOU ARE
ANYMORE.
I've been
hiding it for so
long, and I figured
since you were
already upset...
I always
liked 'My Mother
The Carmobile'.
That's
because you're a
NiNCOMPOoP!
I love old
TV theme songs!
Na na na na na
na na na na na na
na na na na na
SKULLMAAN!
Everybody do
the Skulltusi!
There
was a
Skullman
TV
show?
Yeah, it
was really silly.
The dark, gritty
Skullman movies
are waaay
better.
YAAAARG!

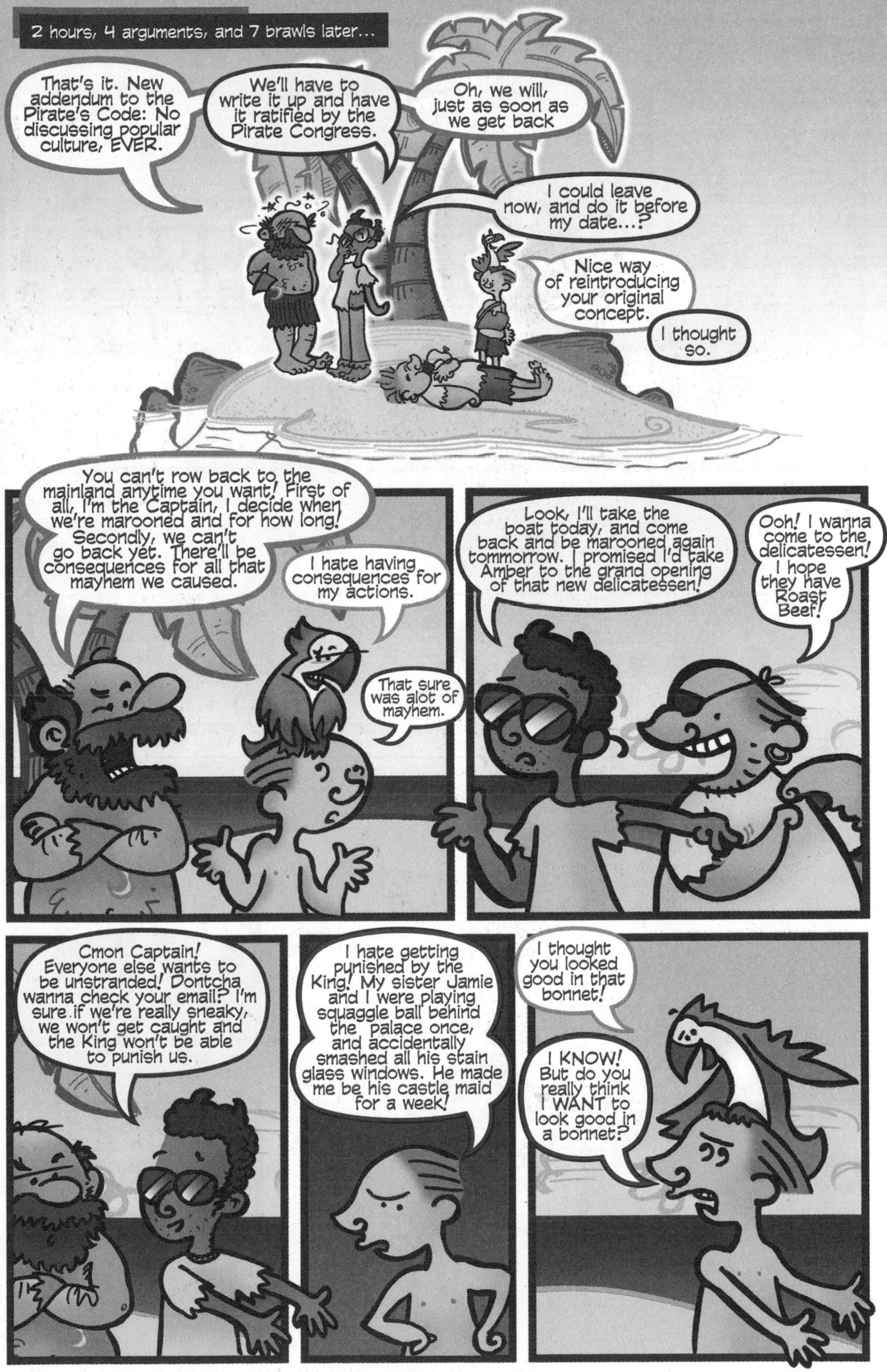
2 hours, 4 arguments, and 7 brawls later...
That's it. New addendum to the Pirate's Code: No discussing popular culture, EVER.
We'll have to write it up and have it ratified by the Pirate Congress.
Oh, we will, just as soon as we get back
I could leave now, and do it before my date...?
Nice way of reintroducing your original concept.
I thought so.
You can't row back to the mainland anytime you want! First of all, I'm the Captain, I decide when we're marooned and for how long! Secondly, we can't go back yet. There'll be consequences for all that mayhem we caused.
I hate having consequences for my actions.
That sure was alot of mayhem.
Look, I'll take the boat today, and come back and be marooned again tommorrow. I promised I'd take Amber to the grand opening of that new delicatessen!
Ooh! I wanna come to the delicatessen! I hope they have Roast Beef!
Cmon Captain! Everyone else wants to be unstranded! Dontcha wanna check your email? I'm sure if we're really sneaky, we won't get caught and the King won't be able to punish us.
I hate getting punished by the King! My sister Jamie and I were playing squaggle ball behind the palace once, and accidentally smashed all his stain glass windows. He made me be his castle maid for a week!
I thought you looked good in that bonnet!
I KNOW! But do you really think I WANT to look good in a bonnet?

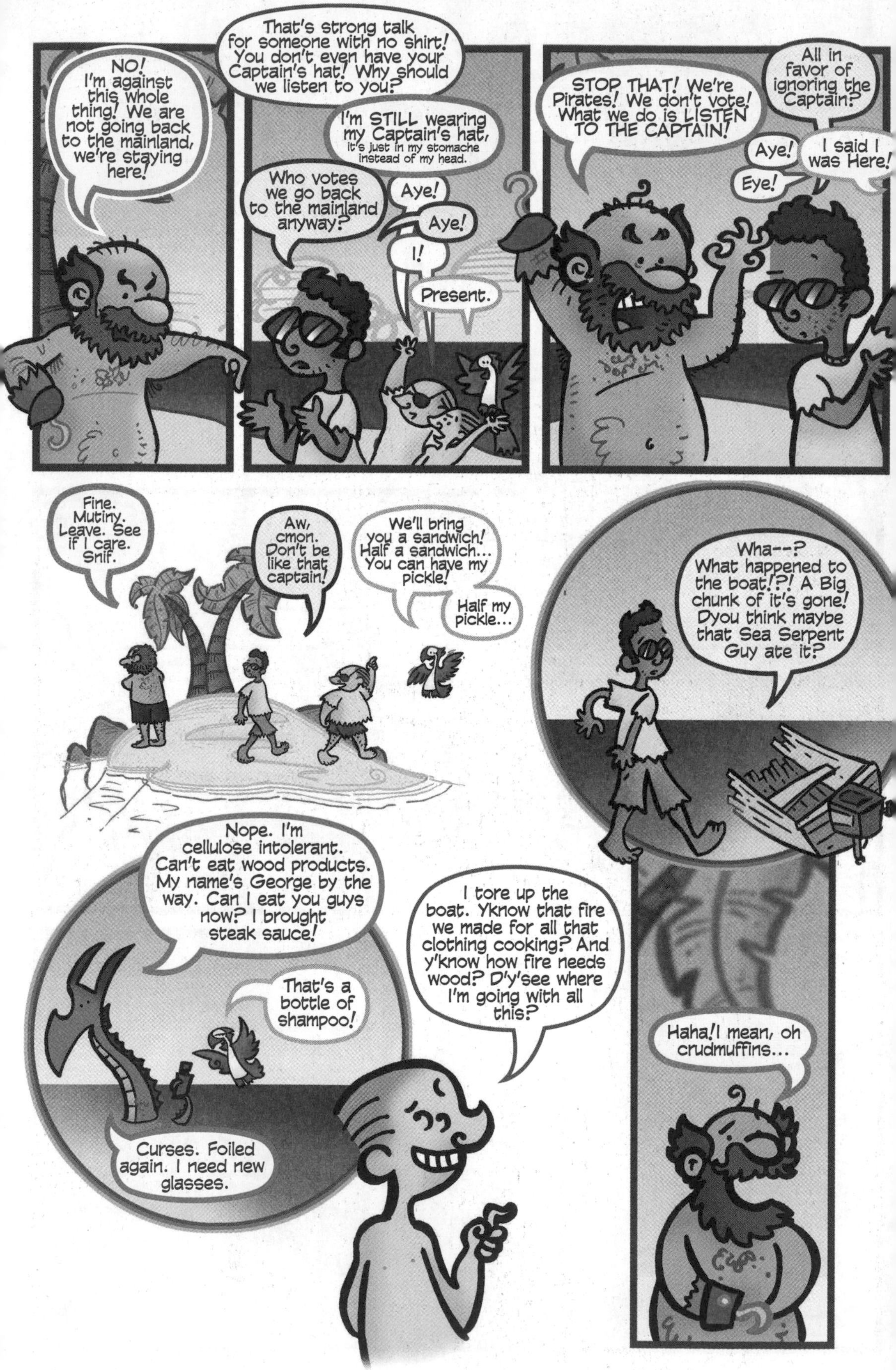
NO! I'm against this whole thing! We are not going back to the mainland, we're staying here!
That's strong talk for someone with no shirt! You don't even have your Captain's hat! Why should we listen to you?
I'm STILL wearing my Captain's hat, it's just in my stomache instead of my head.
Who votes we go back to the mainland anyway?
Aye!
Aye!
I!
Present.
STOP THAT! We're Pirates! We don't vote! What we do is LISTEN TO THE CAPTAIN!
All in favor of ignoring the Captain?
Aye!
I said I was Here!
Eye!
Fine. Mutiny. Leave. See if I care. Snif.
Aw, cmon. Don't be like that captain!
We'll bring you a sandwich! Half a sandwich... You can have my pickle!
Half my pickle...
Wha--? What happened to the boat!?! A Big chunk of it's gone! Dyou think maybe that Sea Serpent Guy ate it?
Nope. I'm cellulose intolerant. Can't eat wood products. My name's George by the way. Can I eat you guys now? I brought steak sauce!
That's a bottle of shampoo!
Curses. Foiled again. I need new glasses.
I tore up the boat. Yknow that fire we made for all that clothing cooking? And y'know how fire needs wood? D'y'see where I'm going with all this?
Haha! I mean, oh crudmuffins...

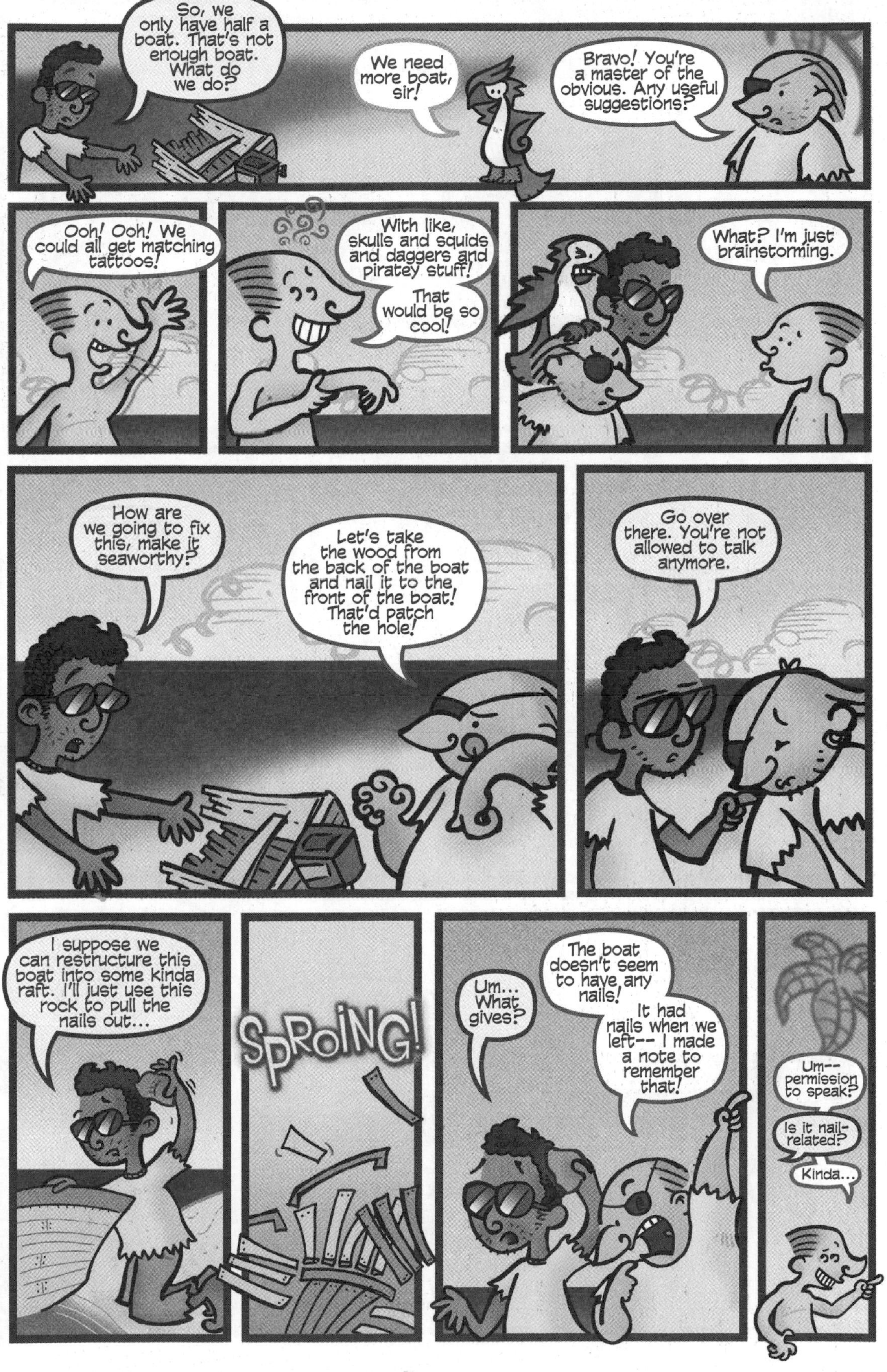
So, we only have half a boat. That's not enough boat. What do we do?
We need more boat, sir!
Bravo! You're a master of the obvious. Any useful suggestions?
Ooh! Ooh! We could all get matching tattoos!
With like, skulls and squids and daggers and piratey stuff!
That would be so cool!
What? I'm just brainstorming.
How are we going to fix this, make it seaworthy?
Let's take the wood from the back of the boat and nail it to the front of the boat! That'd patch the hole!
Go over there. You're not allowed to talk anymore.
I suppose we can restructure this boat into some kinda raft. I'll just use this rock to pull the nails out...
SPROING!
Um... What gives?
The boat doesn't seem to have any nails!
It had nails when we left-- I made a note to remember that!
Um-- permission to speak?
Is it nail-related?
Kinda...

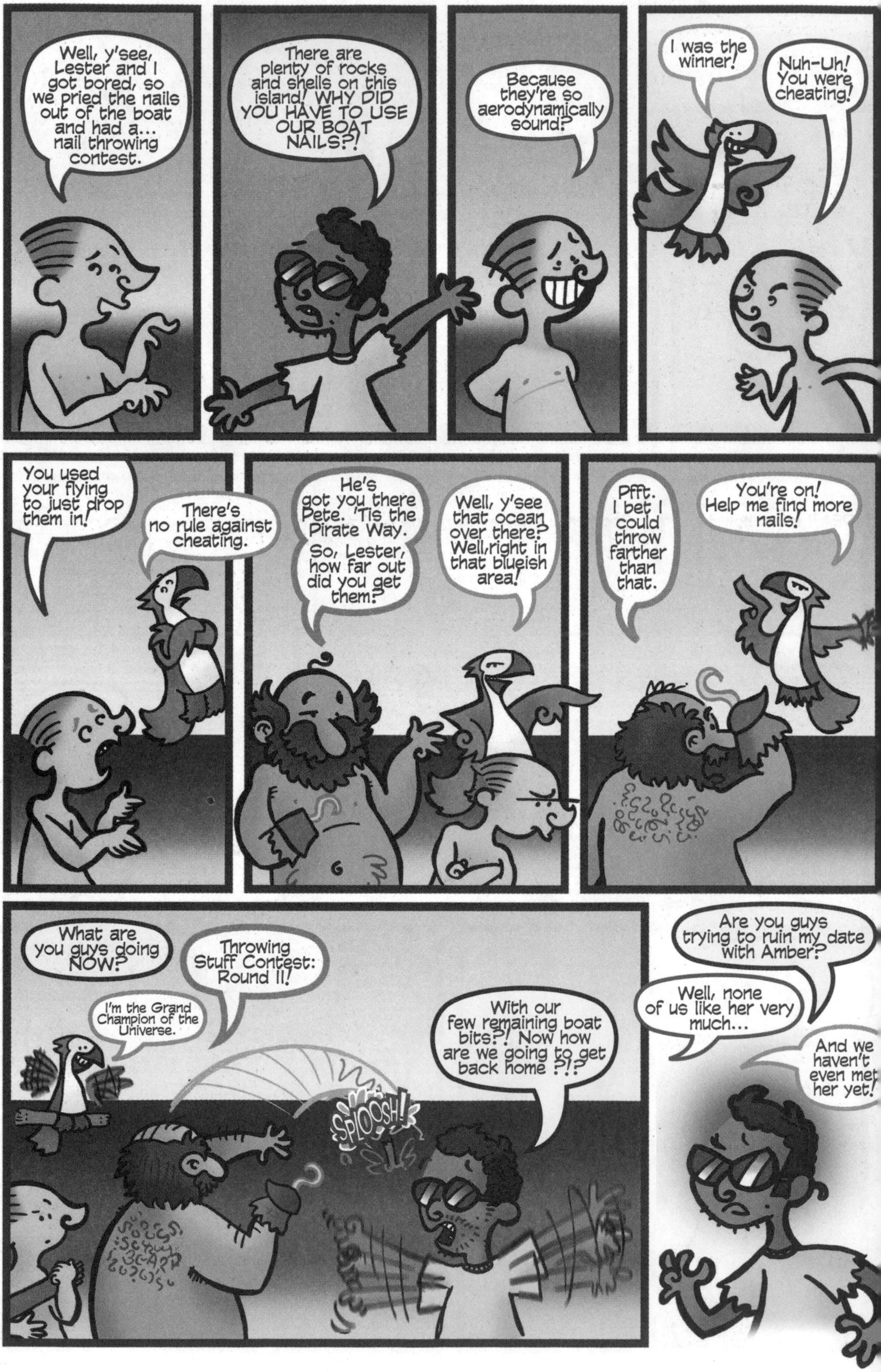
Well, y'see, Lester and I got bored, so we pried the nails out of the boat and had a... nail throwing contest.
There are plenty of rocks and shells on this island! WHY DID YOU HAVE TO USE OUR BOAT NAILS?!
Because they're so aerodynamically sound?
I was the winner!
Nuh-Uh! You were cheating!
You used your flying to just drop them in!
There's no rule against cheating.
He's got you there Pete. 'Tis the Pirate Way.
So, Lester, how far out did you get them?
Well, y'see that ocean over there? Well, right in that blueish area!
Pfft. I bet I could throw farther than that.
You're on! Help me find more nails!
What are you guys doing NOW?
Throwing Stuff Contest: Round II!
I'm the Grand Champion of the Universe.
SPLOOSH!
With our few remaining boat bits?! Now how are we going to get back home ?!?
Are you guys trying to ruin my date with Amber?
Well, none of us like her very much...
And we haven't even met her yet!

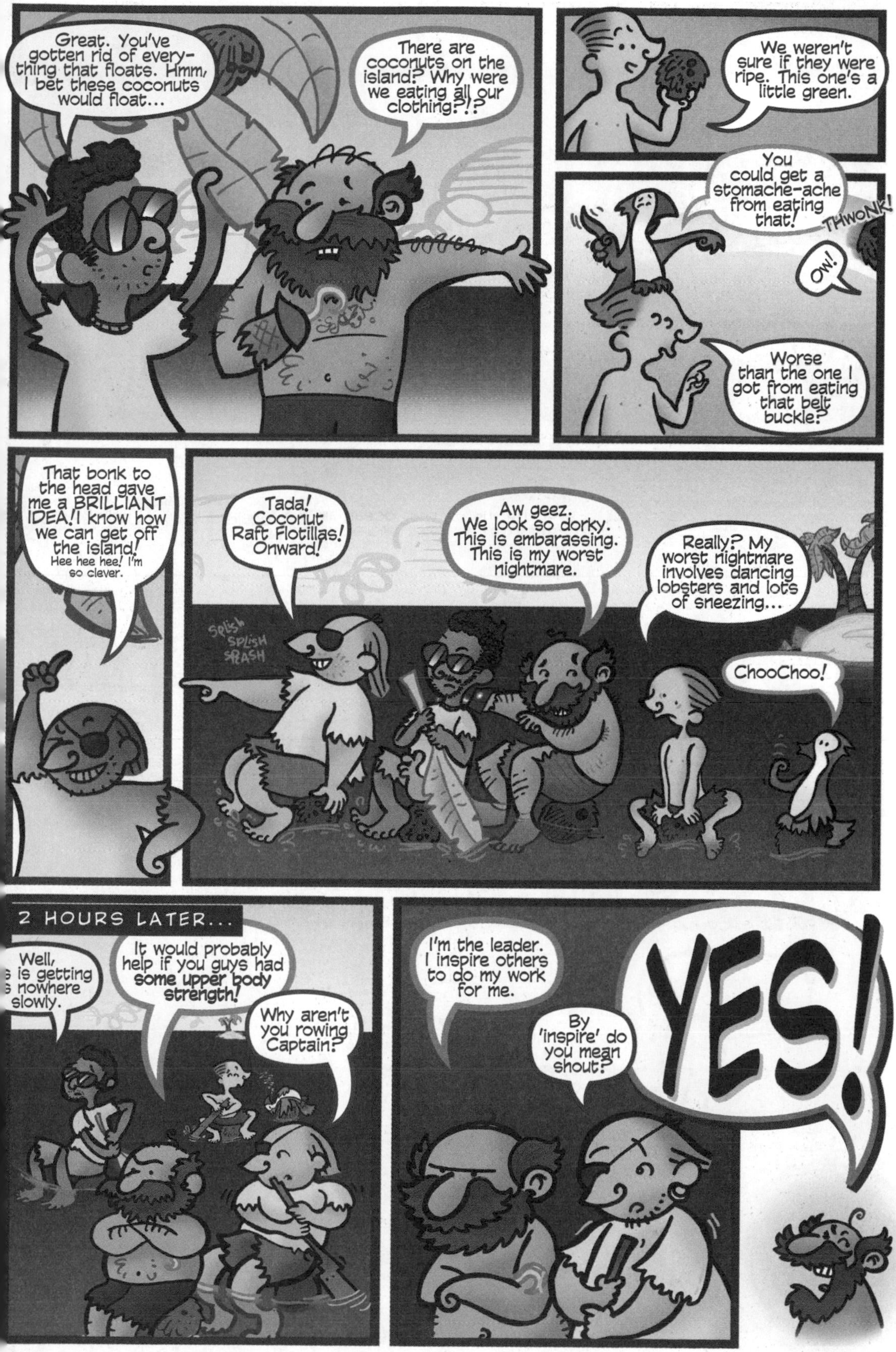
Great. You've gotten rid of everything that floats. Hmm, I bet these coconuts would float...
There are coconuts on the island? Why were we eating all our clothing?!?
We weren't sure if they were ripe. This one's a little green.
You could get a stomache-ache from eating that!
THWONK!
OW!
Worse than the one I got from eating that belt buckle?
That bonk to the head gave me a BRILLIANT IDEA! I know how we can get off the island! Hee hee hee! I'm so clever.
Tada! Coconut Raft Flotillas! Onward!
SPLISH SPLISH SPLASH
Aw geez. We look so dorky. This is embarassing. This is my worst nightmare.
Really? My worst nightmare involves dancing lobsters and lots of sneezing...
ChooChoo!
2 HOURS LATER...
Well, s is getting s nowhere slowly.
It would probably help if you guys had some upper body strength!
Why aren't you rowing Captain?
I'm the leader. I inspire others to do my work for me.
By 'inspire' do you mean shout?
YES!

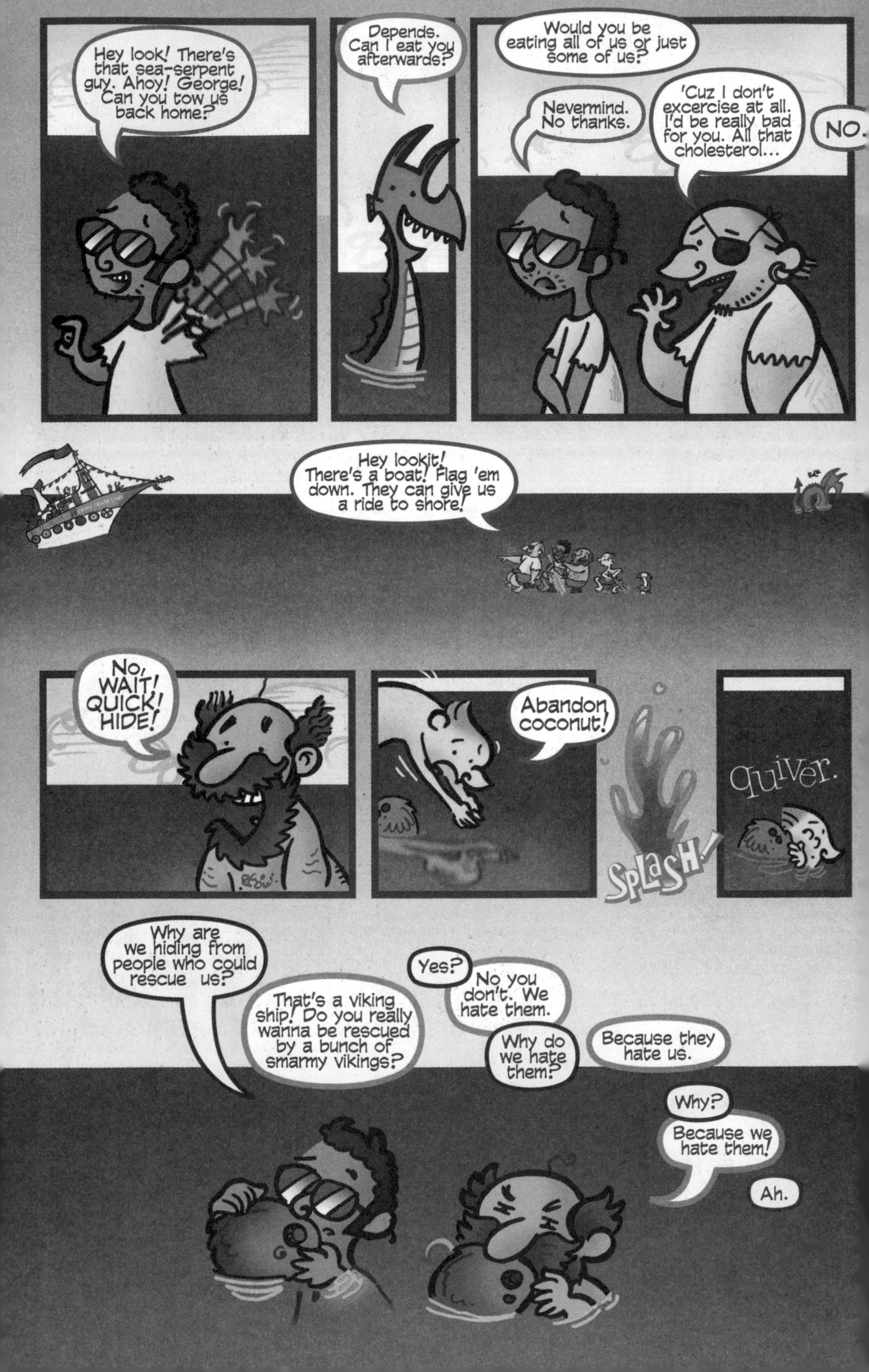
Hey look! There's that sea-serpent guy. Ahoy! George! Can you tow us back home?
Depends. Can I eat you afterwards?
Would you be eating all of us or just some of us?
'Cuz I don't excercise at all. I'd be really bad for you. All that cholesterol...
Nevermind. No thanks.
NO.
Hey lookit! There's a boat! Flag 'em down. They can give us a ride to shore!
No, WAIT! QUICK! HIDE!
Abandon coconut!
SPLASH!
quiver.
Why are we hiding from people who could rescue us?
That's a viking ship! Do you really wanna be rescued by a bunch of smarmy vikings?
Yes?
No you don't. We hate them.
Why do we hate them?
Because they hate us.
Why?
Because we hate them!
Ah.

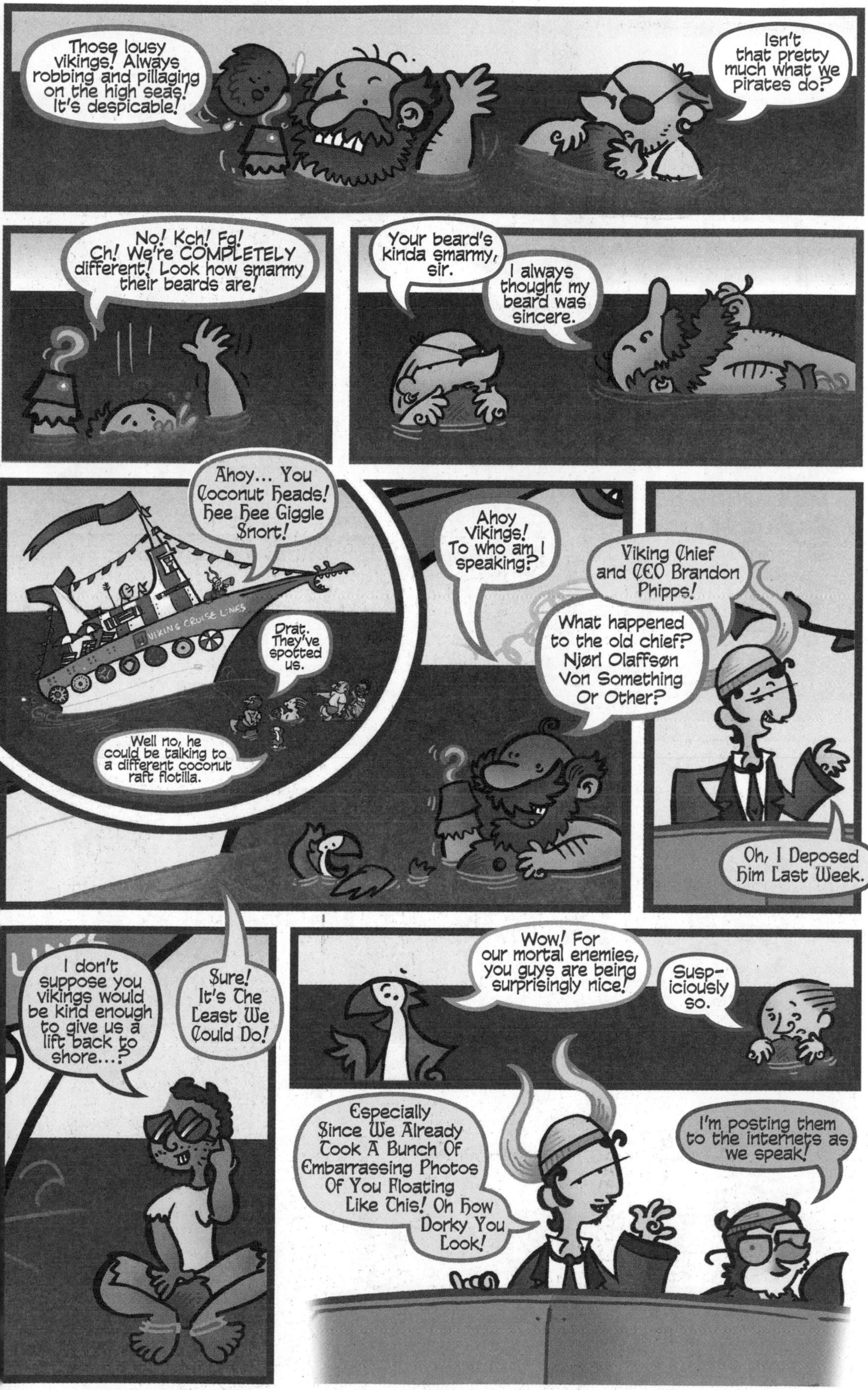
Those lousy vikings! Always robbing and pillaging on the high seas! It's despicable!
Isn't that pretty much what we pirates do?
No! Kch! Fg! Ch! We're COMPLETELY different! Look how smarmy their beards are!
Your beard's kinda smarmy, sir.
I always thought my beard was sincere.
Ahoy... You Coconut Heads! Hee Hee Giggle Snort!
VIKING CRUISE LINES
Drat. They've spotted us.
Well no, he could be talking to a different coconut raft flotilla.
Ahoy Vikings! To who am I speaking?
Viking Chief and CEO Brandon Phipps!
What happened to the old chief? Njørl Olaffsøn Von Something Or Other?
Oh, I Deposed Him Last Week.
I don't suppose you vikings would be kind enough to give us a lift back to shore...?
Sure! It's The Least We Could Do!
Wow! For our mortal enemies, you guys are being surprisingly nice!
Susp-iciously so.
Especially Since We Already Took A Bunch Of Embarrassing Photos Of You Floating Like This! Oh How Dorky You Look!
I'm posting them to the internets as we speak!

CHAPTER TWO
Lousy Vikings!

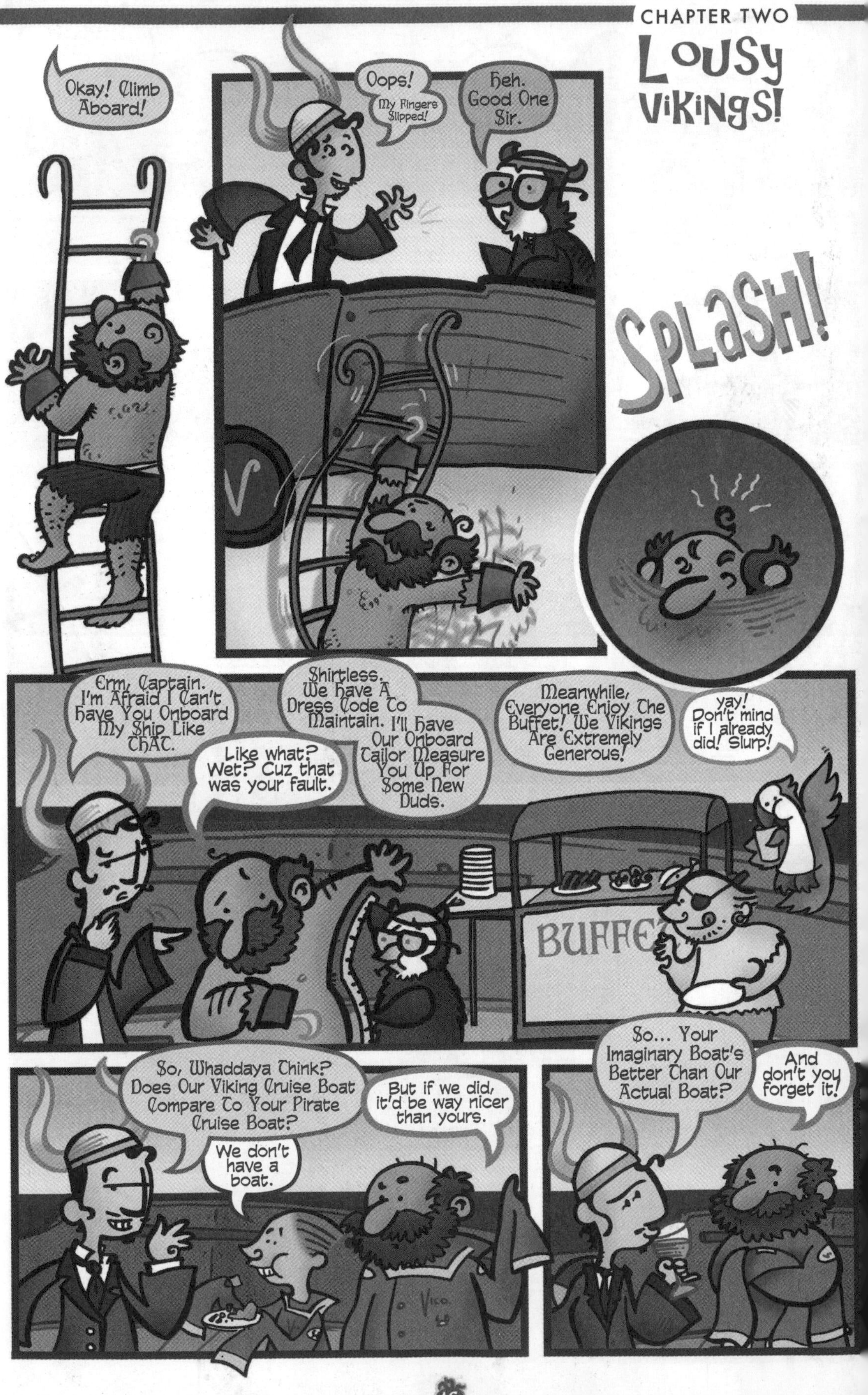
Okay! Climb Aboard!
Oops!
My Fingers Slipped!
Heh. Good One Sir.
SPLASH!
Erm, Captain. I'm Afraid I Can't Have You Onboard My Ship Like THAT.
Like what? Wet? Cuz that was your fault.
Shirtless. We Have A Dress Code To Maintain. I'll Have Our Onboard Tailor Measure You Up For Some New Duds.
Meanwhile, Everyone Enjoy The Buffet! We Vikings Are Extremely Generous!
yay! Don't mind if I already did! Slurp!
BUFFE
So, Whaddaya Think? Does Our Viking Cruise Boat Compare To Your Pirate Cruise Boat?
We don't have a boat.
But if we did, it'd be way nicer than yours.
So... Your Imaginary Boat's Better Than Our Actual Boat?
And don't you forget it!

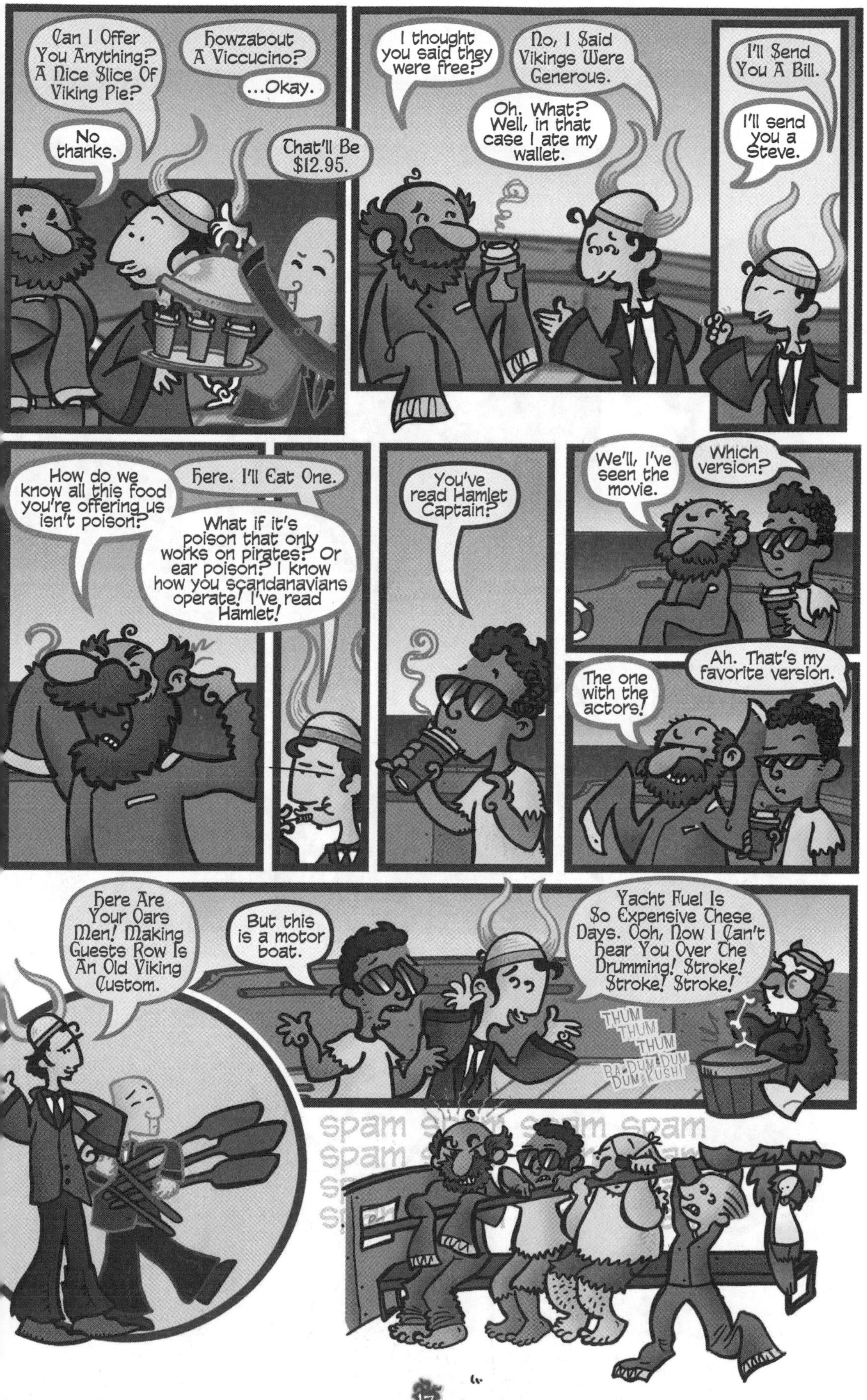
Can I Offer You Anything? A Nice Slice Of Viking Pie?
No thanks.
Howzabout A Viccucino?
...Okay.
That'll Be $12.95.
I thought you said they were free?
No, I Said Vikings Were Generous.
Oh. What? Well, in that case I ate my wallet.
I'll Send You A Bill.
I'll send you a Steve.
How do we know all this food you're offering us isn't poison?
Here. I'll Eat One.
What if it's poison that only works on pirates? Or ear poison? I know how you scandanavians operate! I've read Hamlet!
You've read Hamlet Captain?
We'll, I've seen the movie.
Which version?
The one with the actors!
Ah. That's my favorite version.
Here Are Your Oars Men! Making Guests Row Is An Old Viking Custom.
But this is a motor boat.
Yacht Fuel Is So Expensive These Days. Ooh, Now I Can't Hear You Over The Drumming! Stroke! Stroke! Stroke!
THUM THUM THUM
BA-DUM-DUM DUM KUSH!
spam spam spam spam
spam spam

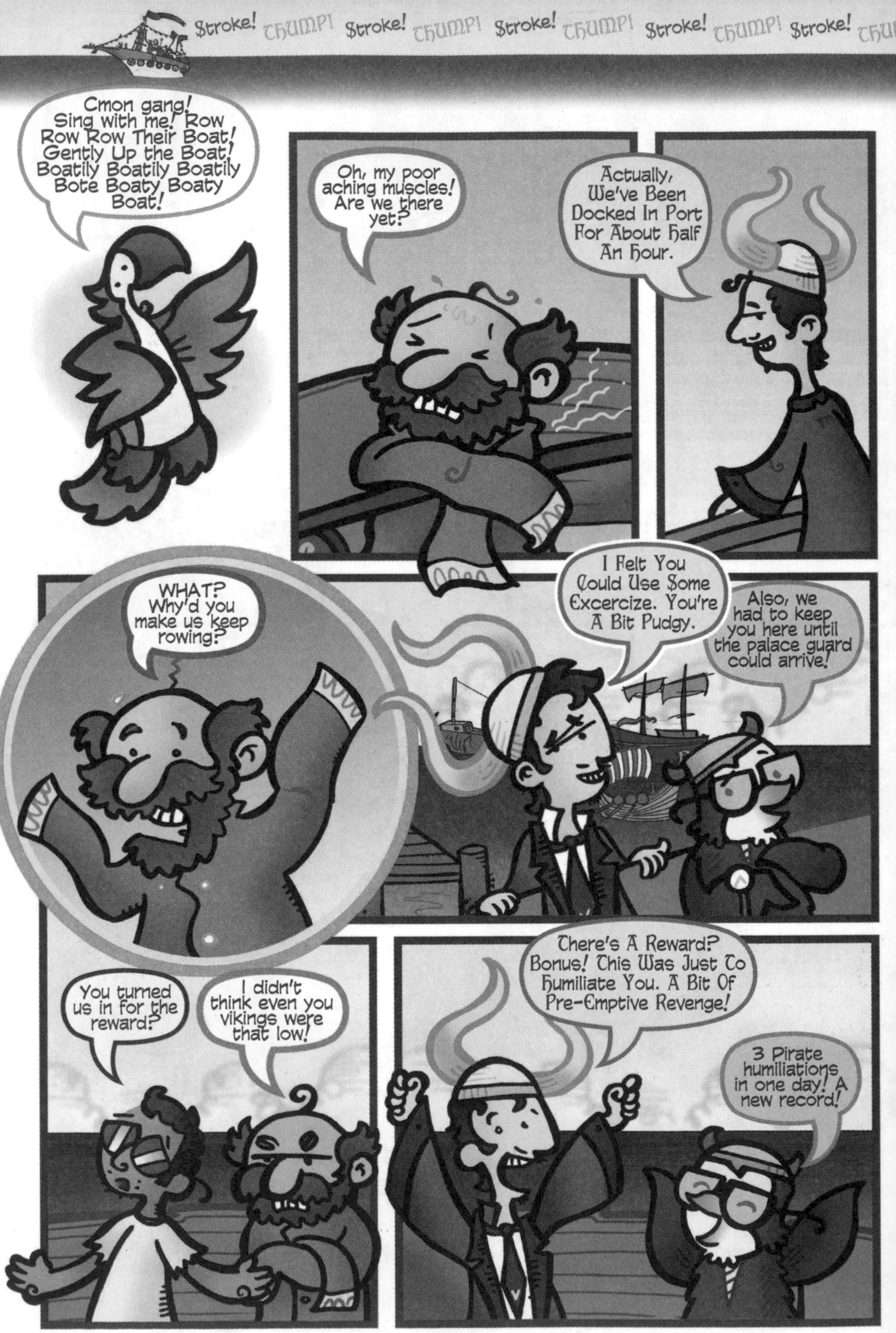
Stroke! THUMP! Stroke! THUMP! Stroke! THUMP! Stroke! THUMP! Stroke!
Cmon gang! Sing with me! Row Row Row Their Boat! Gently Up the Boat! Boatily Boatily Boatily Bote Boaty Boaty Boat!
Oh, my poor aching muscles! Are we there yet?
Actually, We've Been Docked In Port For About Half An Hour.
WHAT? Why'd you make us keep rowing?
I Felt You Could Use Some Excercize. You're A Bit Pudgy.
Also, we had to keep you here until the palace guard could arrive!
You turned us in for the reward?
I didn't think even you vikings were that low!
There's A Reward? Bonus! This Was Just To Humiliate You. A Bit Of Pre-Emptive Revenge!
3 Pirate humiliations in one day! A new record!

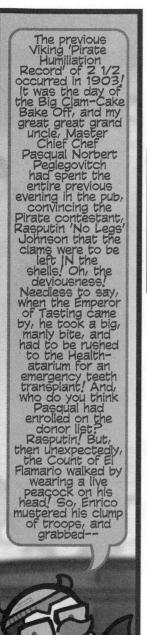

The previous Viking 'Pirate Humiliation Record' of 2 1/2 occurred in 1903! It was the day of the Big Clam-Cake Bake Off, and my great great grand uncle, Master Chief Chef Pasqual Norbert Peglegovitch had spent the entire previous evening in the pub, convincing the Pirate contestant, Rasputin 'No Legs' Johnson that the clams were to be left IN the shells! Oh, the deviousness! Needless to say, when the Emperor of Tasting came by, he took a big, manly bite, and had to be rushed to the Health-atarium for an emergency teeth transplant! And, who do you think Pasqual had enrolled on the donor list? Rasputin! But, then unexpectedly, the Count of El Flamario walked by wearing a live peacock on his head! So, Enrico mustered his clump of troops, and grabbed--

Quiet Minion! You're Interrupting My Gloating!

How many times must I tell you, MY NAME IS MINESTRONE! Like the soup!

I Don't Have Time To Go Around Remembering Your Name! I Call You Minion Because Your Job Is To Do Whatever I Say. Now I'm Bored Of You. Butler? Remove Him.

Bored of me? But... I'm so fascinating!

You can't do this to me! Well, I guess you are, but I wish you wouldn't!! You've made a powerful enemy today Chief Brandon! Not powerful physically, but.... You'll live to regret this! Tyrants always sow the seeds of their own downfall!

Those who don't study history are doomed to repeat it! I'm not sure how exactly. Maybe time travel's involved! Oh, dear Thor, I sure hope you don't get a time machine!

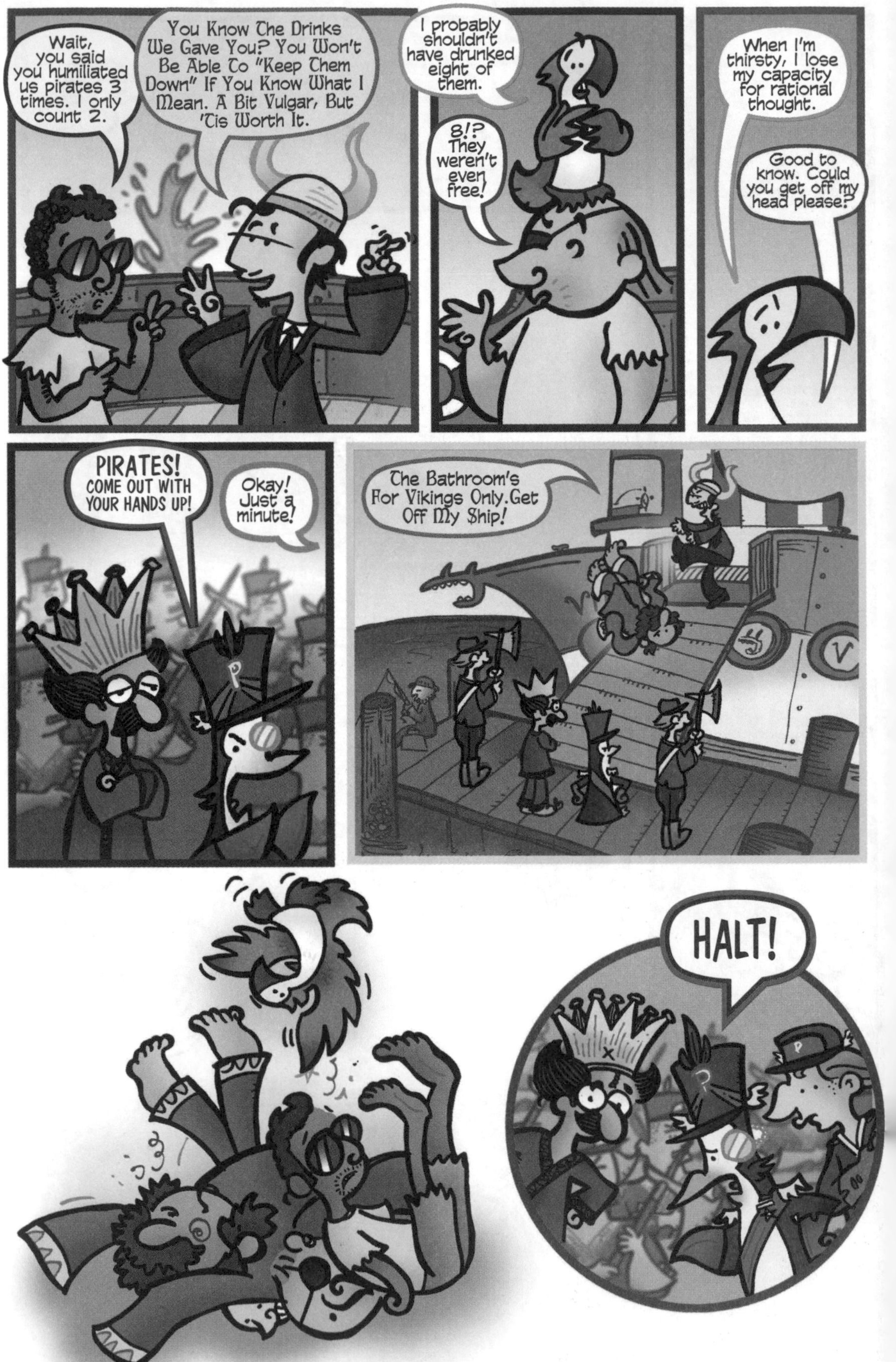

Wait, you said you humiliated us pirates 3 times. I only count 2.
You Know The Drinks We Gave You? You Won't Be Able To "Keep Them Down" If You Know What I Mean. A Bit Vulgar, But 'Tis Worth It.
I probably shouldn't have drunked eight of them.
8!? They weren't even free!
When I'm thirsty, I lose my capacity for rational thought.
Good to know. Could you get off my head please?
PIRATES! COME OUT WITH YOUR HANDS UP!
Okay! Just a minute!
The Bathroom's For Vikings Only. Get Off My Ship!
HALT!

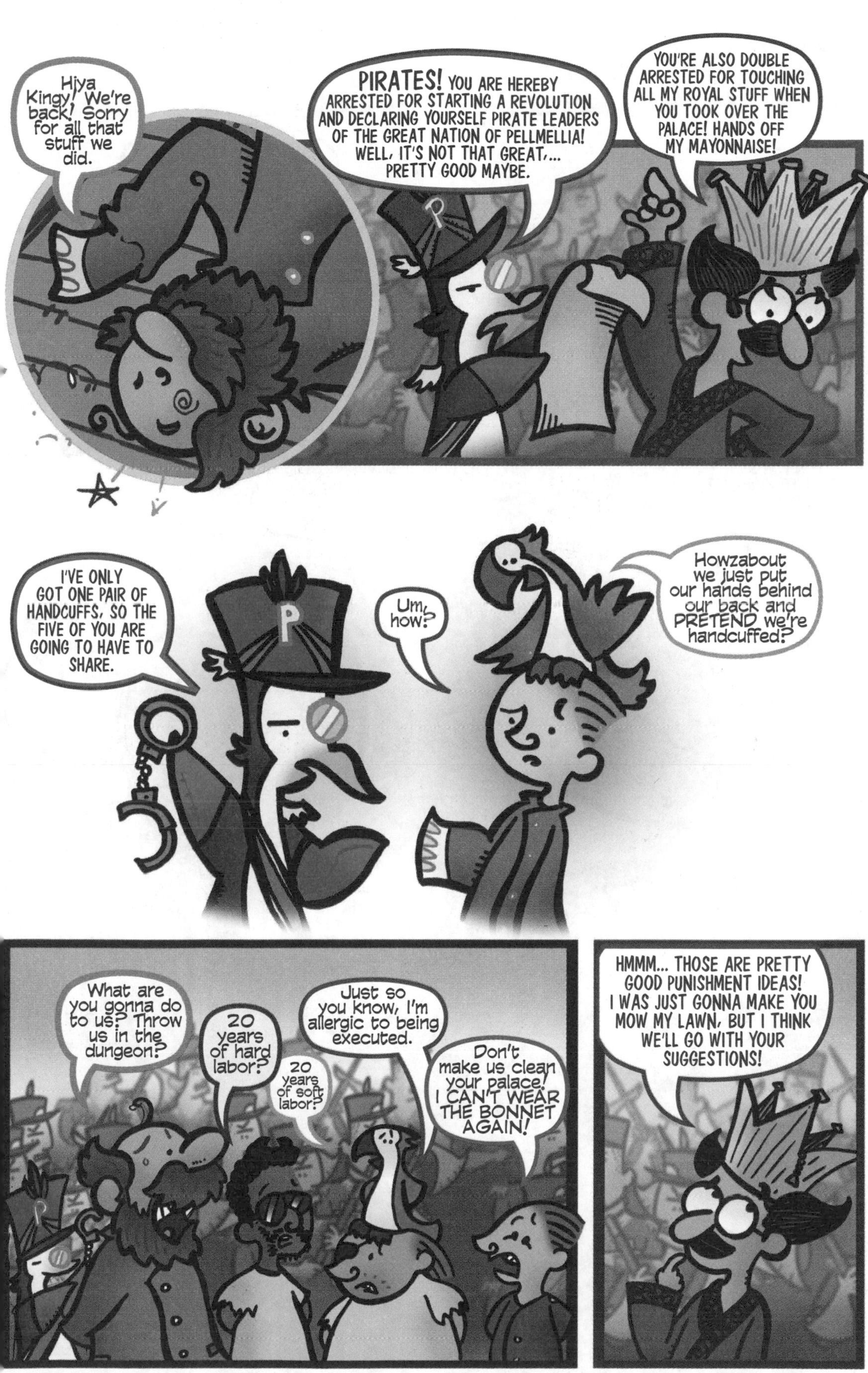

Hiya Kingy! We're back! Sorry for all that stuff we did.
PIRATES! YOU ARE HEREBY ARRESTED FOR STARTING A REVOLUTION AND DECLARING YOURSELF PIRATE LEADERS OF THE GREAT NATION OF PELLMELLIA! WELL, IT'S NOT THAT GREAT,... PRETTY GOOD MAYBE.
YOU'RE ALSO DOUBLE ARRESTED FOR TOUCHING ALL MY ROYAL STUFF WHEN YOU TOOK OVER THE PALACE! HANDS OFF MY MAYONNAISE!
I'VE ONLY GOT ONE PAIR OF HANDCUFFS, SO THE FIVE OF YOU ARE GOING TO HAVE TO SHARE.
Um, how?
Howzabout we just put our hands behind our back and PRETEND we're handcuffed?
What are you gonna do to us? Throw us in the dungeon?
20 years of hard labor?
20 years of soft labor?
Just so you know, I'm allergic to being executed.
Don't make us clean your palace! I CAN'T WEAR THE BONNET AGAIN!
HMMM... THOSE ARE PRETTY GOOD PUNISHMENT IDEAS! I WAS JUST GONNA MAKE YOU MOW MY LAWN, BUT I THINK WE'LL GO WITH YOUR SUGGESTIONS!

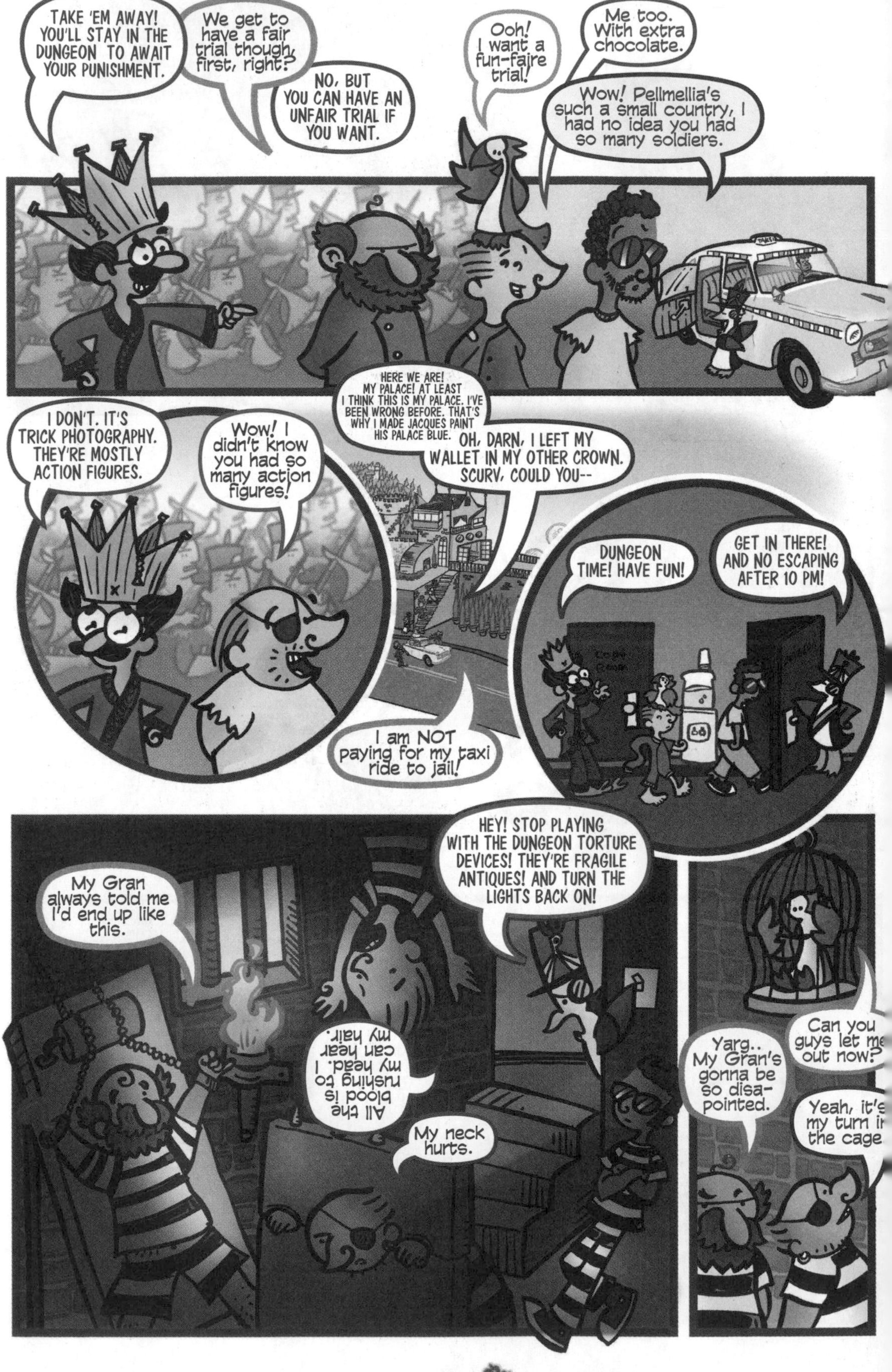
TAKE 'EM AWAY! YOU'LL STAY IN THE DUNGEON TO AWAIT YOUR PUNISHMENT.
We get to have a fair trial though, first, right?
NO, BUT YOU CAN HAVE AN UNFAIR TRIAL IF YOU WANT.
Ooh! I want a fun-faire trial!
Me too. With extra chocolate.
Wow! Pellmellia's such a small country, I had no idea you had so many soldiers.
I DON'T. IT'S TRICK PHOTOGRAPHY. THEY'RE MOSTLY ACTION FIGURES.
Wow! I didn't know you had so many action figures!
HERE WE ARE! MY PALACE! AT LEAST I THINK THIS IS MY PALACE. I'VE BEEN WRONG BEFORE. THAT'S WHY I MADE JACQUES PAINT HIS PALACE BLUE.
OH, DARN, I LEFT MY WALLET IN MY OTHER CROWN. SCURV, COULD YOU--
I am NOT paying for my taxi ride to jail!
DUNGEON TIME! HAVE FUN!
GET IN THERE! AND NO ESCAPING AFTER 10 PM!
My Gran always told me I'd end up like this.
HEY! STOP PLAYING WITH THE DUNGEON TORTURE DEVICES! THEY'RE FRAGILE ANTIQUES! AND TURN THE LIGHTS BACK ON!
All the blood is rushing to my head. I can hear my hair.
My neck hurts.
Yarg.. My Gran's gonna be so disa-pointed.
Can you guys let me out now?
Yeah, it's my turn in the cage.

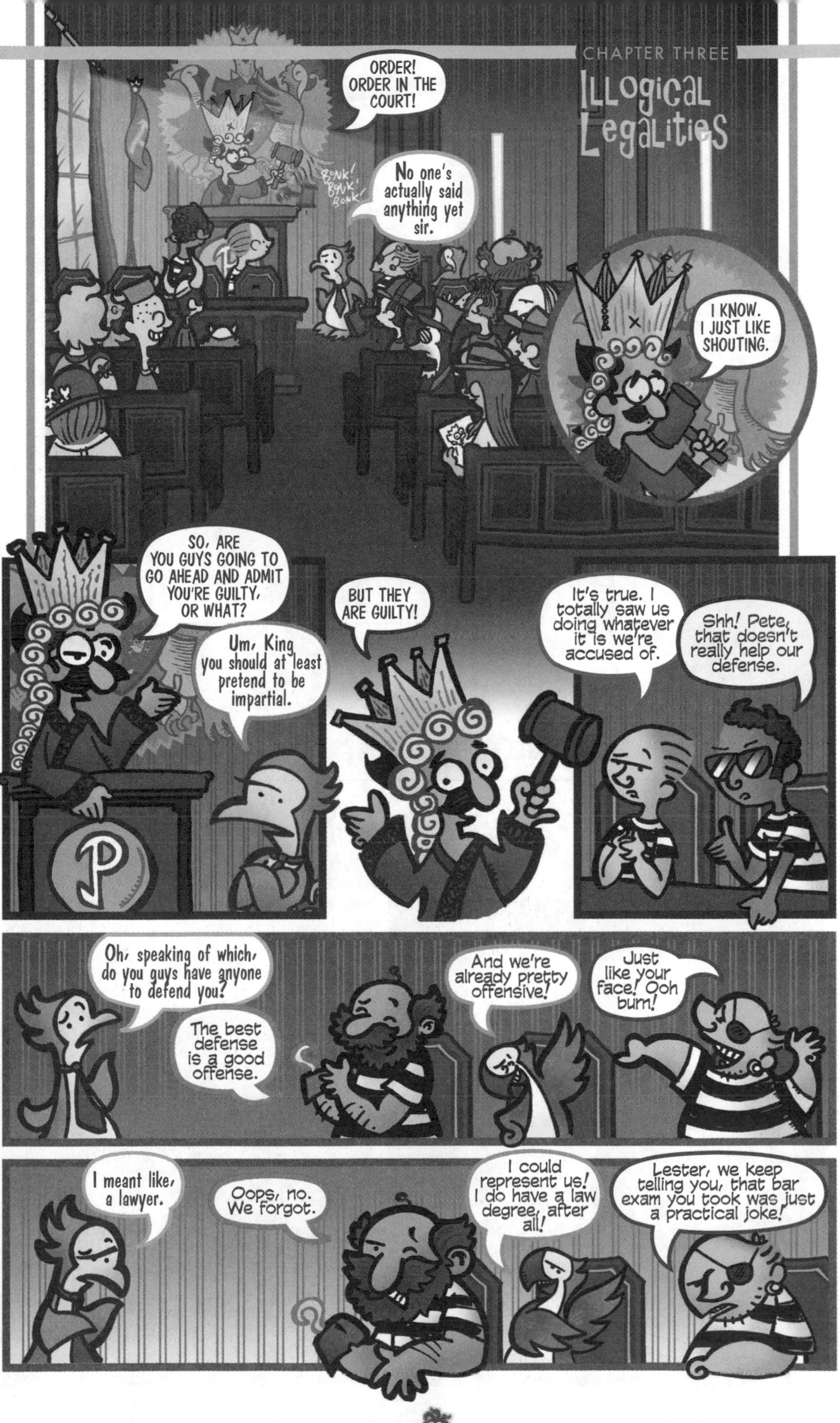
CHAPTER THREE
Illogical Legalities
ORDER! ORDER IN THE COURT!
BONK! BONK! BONK!
No one's actually said anything yet sir.
I KNOW. I JUST LIKE SHOUTING.
SO, ARE YOU GUYS GOING TO GO AHEAD AND ADMIT YOU'RE GUILTY, OR WHAT?
Um, King you should at least pretend to be impartial.
BUT THEY ARE GUILTY!
It's true. I totally saw us doing whatever it is we're accused of.
Shh! Pete, that doesn't really help our defense.
Oh, speaking of which, do you guys have anyone to defend you?
The best defense is a good offense.
And we're already pretty offensive!
Just like your face! Ooh burn!
I meant like, a lawyer.
Oops, no. We forgot.
I could represent us! I do have a law degree, after all!
Lester, we keep telling you, that bar exam you took was just a practical joke!

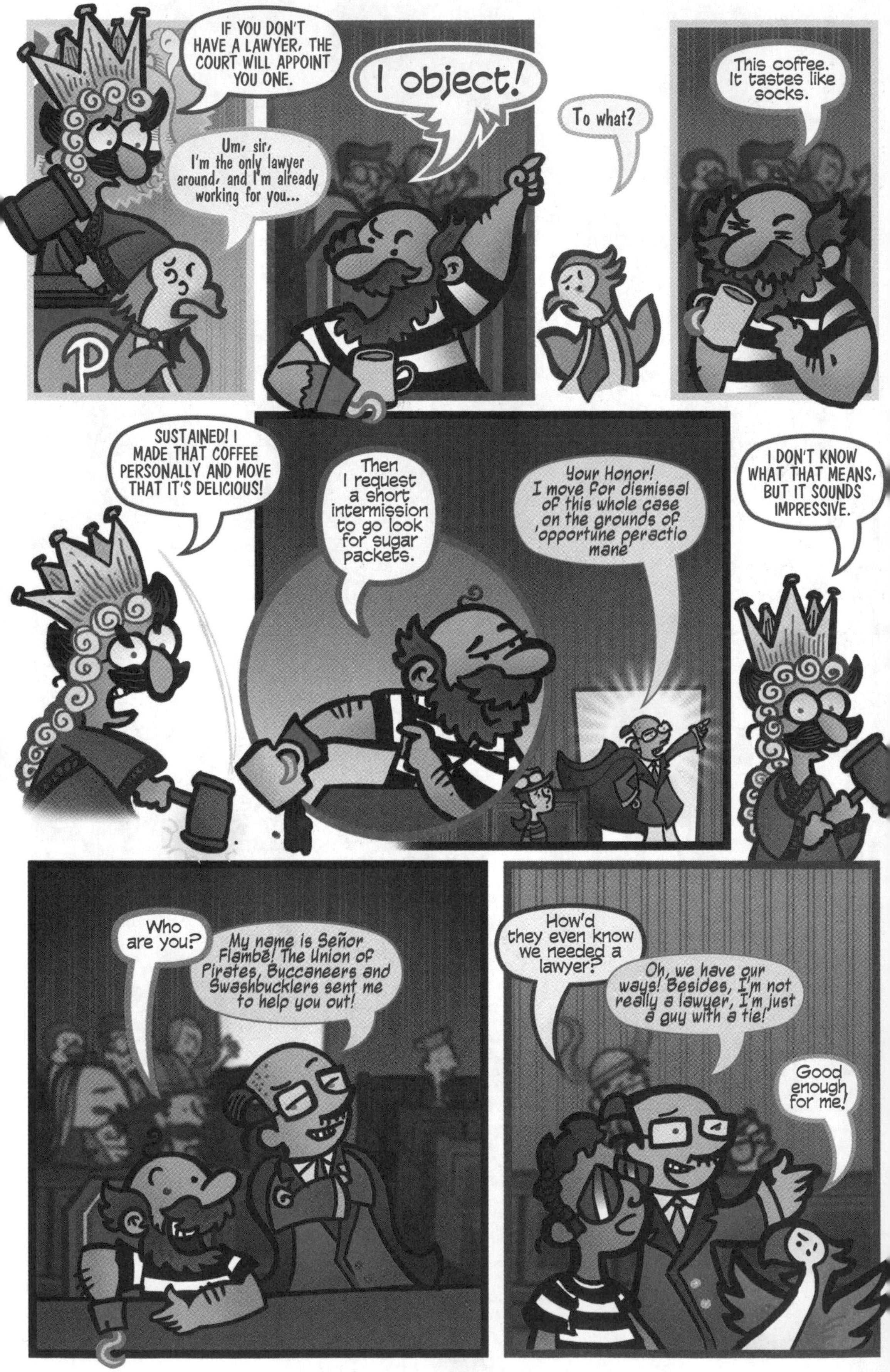
IF YOU DON'T HAVE A LAWYER, THE COURT WILL APPOINT YOU ONE.
Um, sir, I'm the only lawyer around, and I'm already working for you...
I object!
To what?
This coffee. It tastes like socks.
SUSTAINED! I MADE THAT COFFEE PERSONALLY AND MOVE THAT IT'S DELICIOUS!
Then I request a short intermission to go look for sugar packets.
Your Honor! I move for dismissal of this whole case on the grounds of 'opportune peractio mane'
I DON'T KNOW WHAT THAT MEANS, BUT IT SOUNDS IMPRESSIVE.
Who are you?
My name is Señor Flambé! The Union of Pirates, Buccaneers and Swashbucklers sent me to help you out!
How'd they even know we needed a lawyer?
Oh, we have our ways! Besides, I'm not really a lawyer, I'm just a guy with a tie!
Good enough for me!

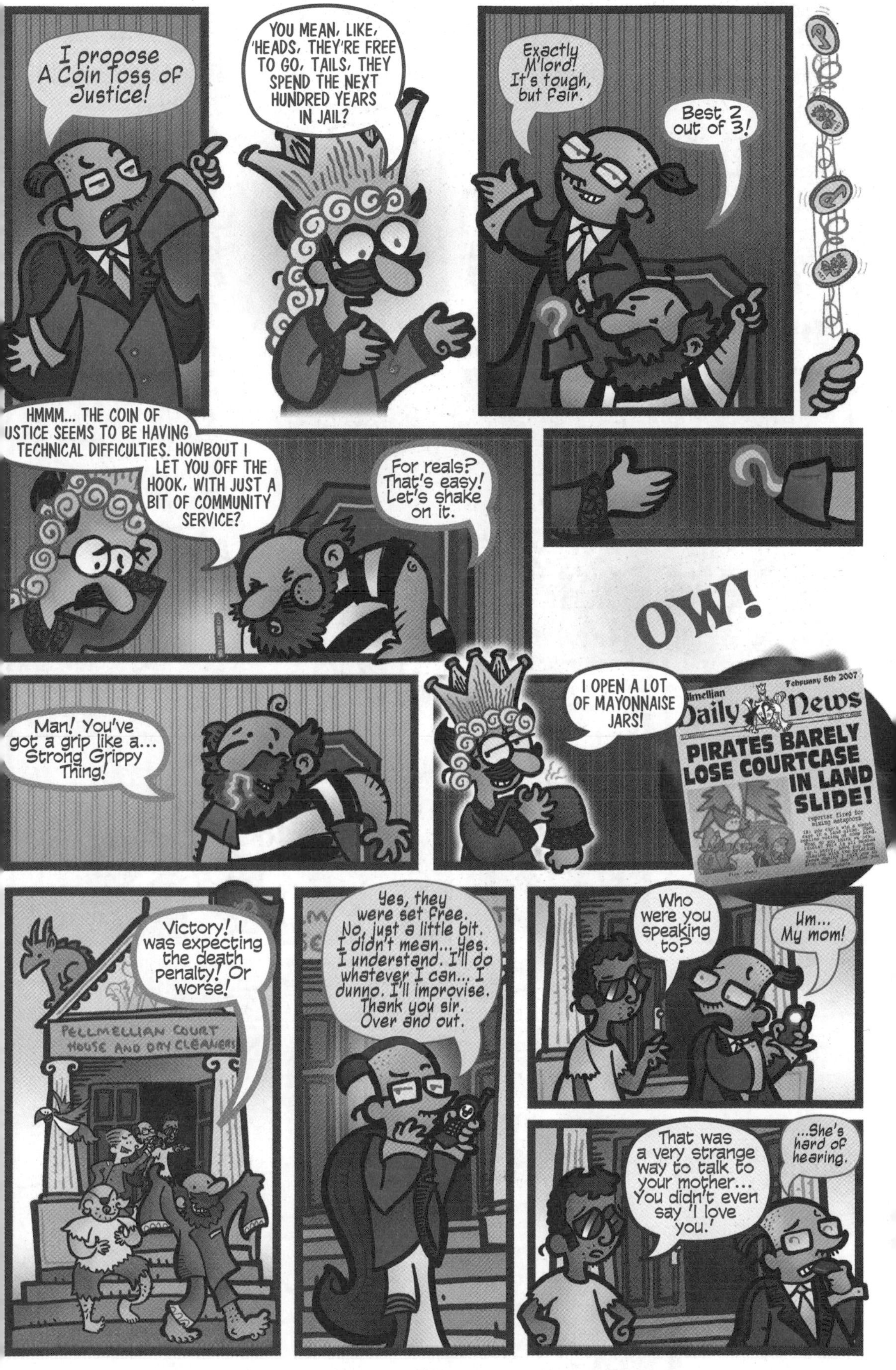
I propose A Coin Toss of Justice!
YOU MEAN, LIKE, 'HEADS, THEY'RE FREE TO GO, TAILS, THEY SPEND THE NEXT HUNDRED YEARS IN JAIL?
Exactly M'lord! It's tough, but fair.
Best 2 out of 3!
HMMM... THE COIN OF USTICE SEEMS TO BE HAVING TECHNICAL DIFFICULTIES. HOWBOUT I LET YOU OFF THE HOOK, WITH JUST A BIT OF COMMUNITY SERVICE?
For reals? That's easy! Let's shake on it.
OW!
Man! You've got a grip like a... Strong Grippy Thing!
I OPEN A LOT OF MAYONNAISE JARS!
February 5th 2007
llmellian Daily News
PIRATES BARELY LOSE COURTCASE IN LAND SLIDE!
reporter fired for mixing metaphors
PELLMELLIAN COURT HOUSE AND DRY CLEANERS
Victory! I was expecting the death penalty! Or worse!
Yes, they were set free. No, just a little bit. I didn't mean... Yes. I understand. I'll do whatever I can... I dunno. I'll improvise. Thank you sir. Over and out.
Who were you speaking to?
Um... My mom!
That was a very strange way to talk to your mother... You didn't even say 'I love you.'
...She's hard of hearing.

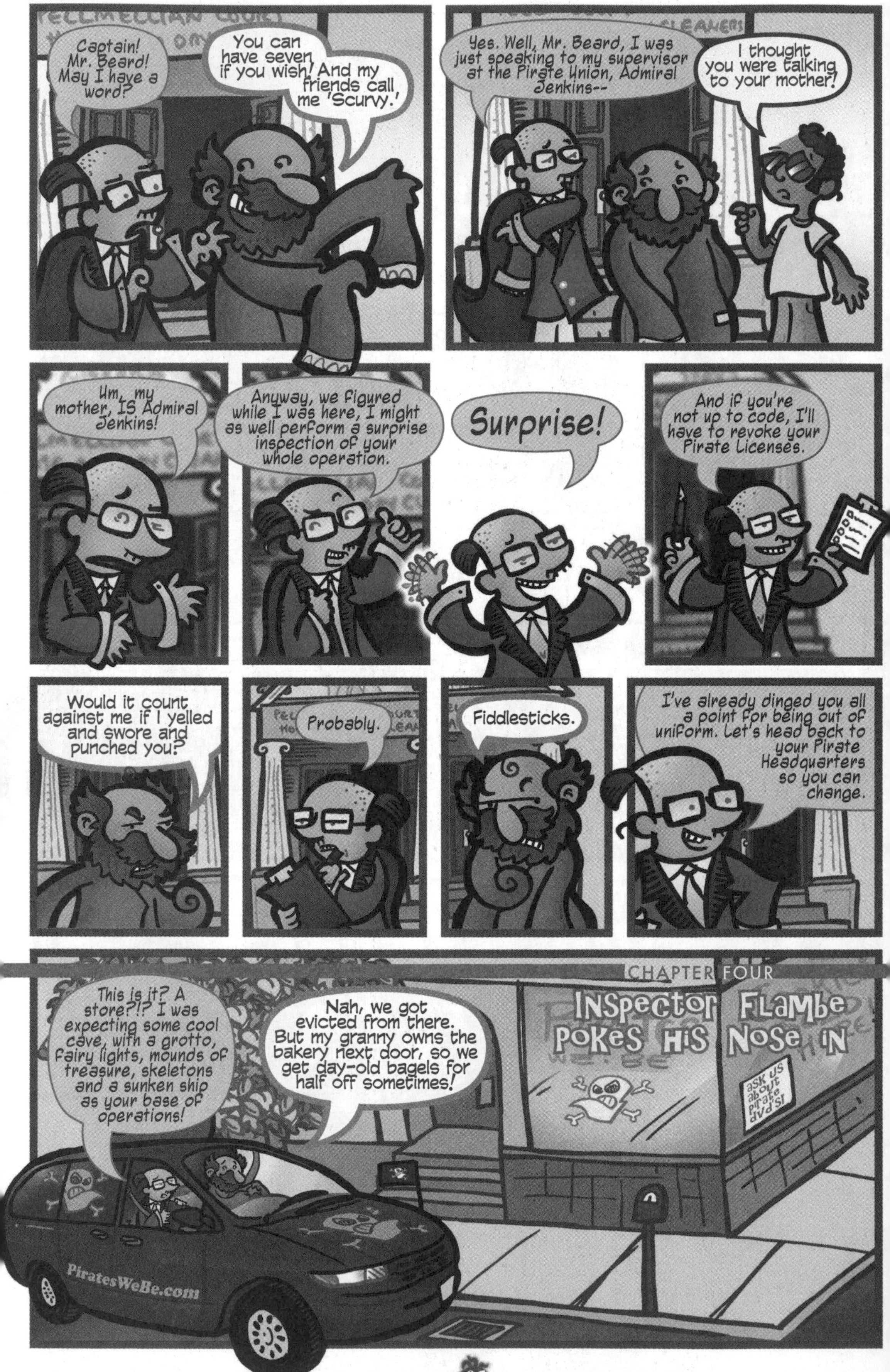
Captain! Mr. Beard! May I have a word?
You can have seven if you wish! And my friends call me 'Scurvy.'
CLEANERS
Yes. Well, Mr. Beard, I was just speaking to my supervisor at the Pirate Union, Admiral Jenkins--
I thought you were talking to your mother!
Um, my mother, IS Admiral Jenkins!
Anyway, we figured while I was here, I might as well perform a surprise inspection of your whole operation.
Surprise!
And if you're not up to code, I'll have to revoke your Pirate Licenses.
Would it count against me if I yelled and swore and punched you?
Probably.
Fiddlesticks.
I've already dinged you all a point for being out of uniform. Let's head back to your Pirate Headquarters so you can change.
CHAPTER FOUR
INSPECTOR FLAMBE POKES HIS NOSE IN
This is it? A store?!? I was expecting some cool cave, with a grotto, fairy lights, mounds of treasure, skeletons and a sunken ship as your base of operations!
Nah, we got evicted from there. But my granny owns the bakery next door, so we get day-old bagels for half off sometimes!
ask us about pirate dvd's!
PiratesWeBe.com

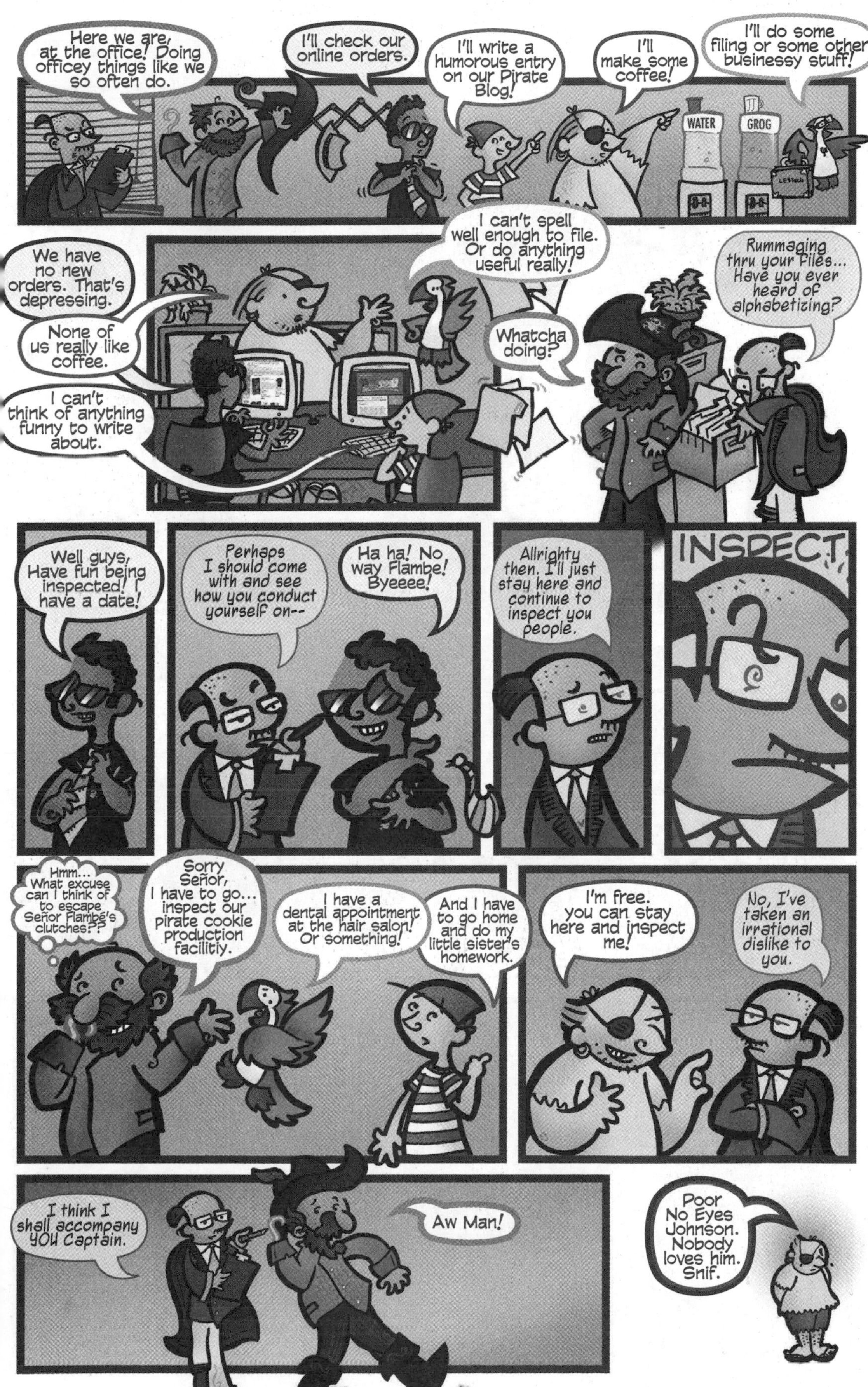

Here we are, at the office! Doing officey things like we so often do.
I'll check our online orders.
I'll write a humorous entry on our Pirate Blog!
I'll make some coffee!
I'll do some filing or some other businessy stuff!
WATER
GROG
We have no new orders. That's depressing.
None of us really like coffee.
I can't think of anything funny to write about.
I can't spell well enough to file. Or do anything useful really!
Whatcha doing?
Rummaging thru your files... Have you ever heard of alphabetizing?
Well guys, Have fun being inspected! I have a date!
Perhaps I should come with and see how you conduct yourself on--
Ha ha! No way Flambe! Byeeee!
Allrighty then. I'll just stay here and continue to inspect you people.
INSPECT.
Hmm... What excuse can I think of to escape Señor Flambé's clutches??
Sorry Señor, I have to go... inspect our pirate cookie production facilitiy.
I have a dental appointment at the hair salon! Or something!
And I have to go home and do my little sister's homework.
I'm free. you can stay here and inspect me!
No, I've taken an irrational dislike to you.
I think I shall accompany YOU Captain.
Aw Man!
Poor No Eyes Johnson. Nobody loves him. Snif.

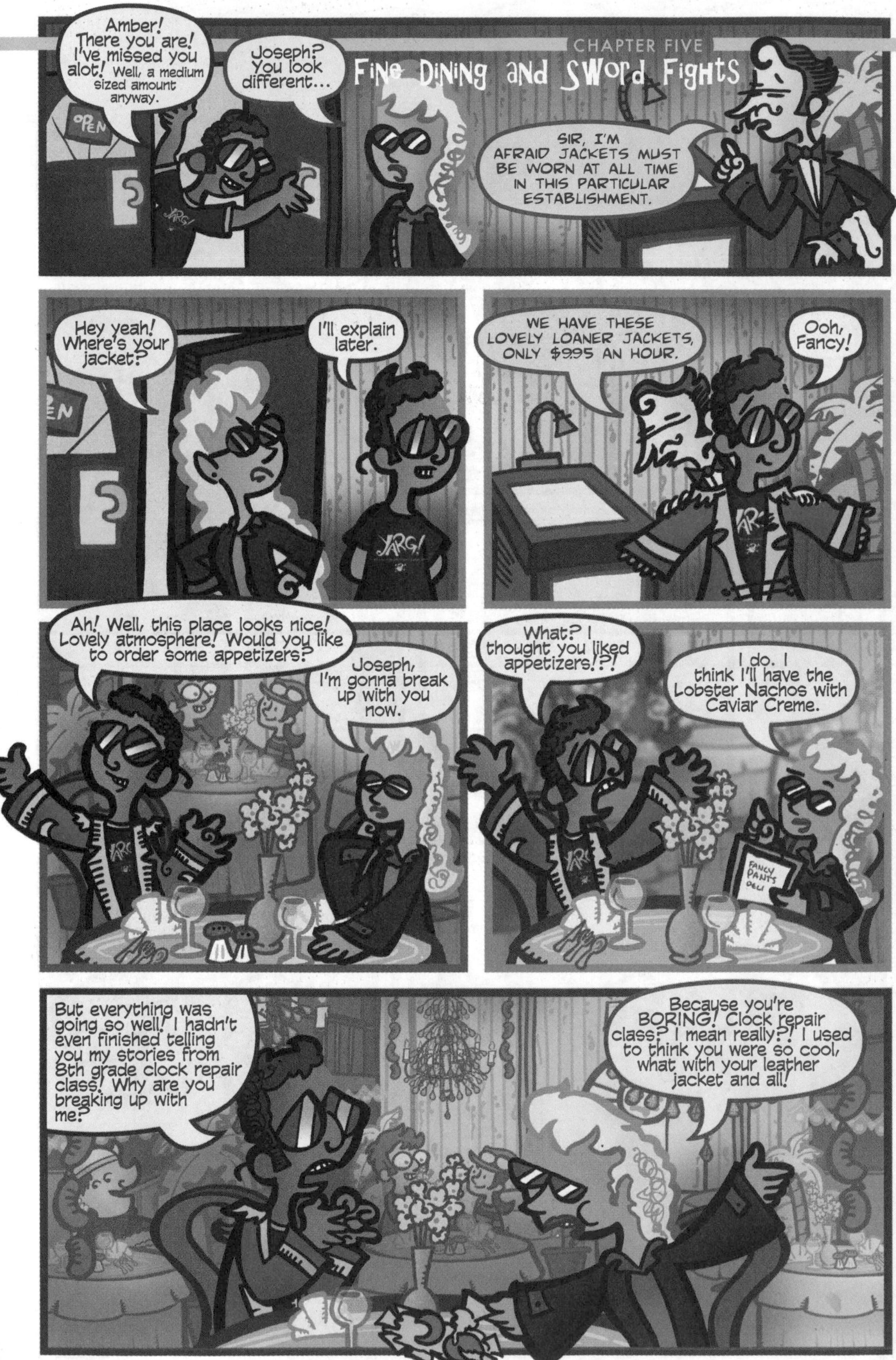
Amber! There you are! I've missed you alot! Well, a medium sized amount anyway.
Joseph? You look different...
CHAPTER FIVE
Fine Dining and Sword Fights
OPEN
YARG!
SIR, I'M AFRAID JACKETS MUST BE WORN AT ALL TIME IN THIS PARTICULAR ESTABLISHMENT.
Hey yeah! Where's your jacket?
I'll explain later.
YARG!
WE HAVE THESE LOVELY LOANER JACKETS, ONLY $9.95 AN HOUR.
Ooh, Fancy!
Ah! Well, this place looks nice! Lovely atmosphere! Would you like to order some appetizers?
Joseph, I'm gonna break up with you now.
What? I thought you liked appetizers!?!
I do. I think I'll have the Lobster Nachos with Caviar Creme.
FANCY PANTS DELI
But everything was going so well! I hadn't even finished telling you my stories from 8th grade clock repair class! Why are you breaking up with me?
Because you're BORING! Clock repair class? I mean really?! I used to think you were so cool, what with your leather jacket and all!

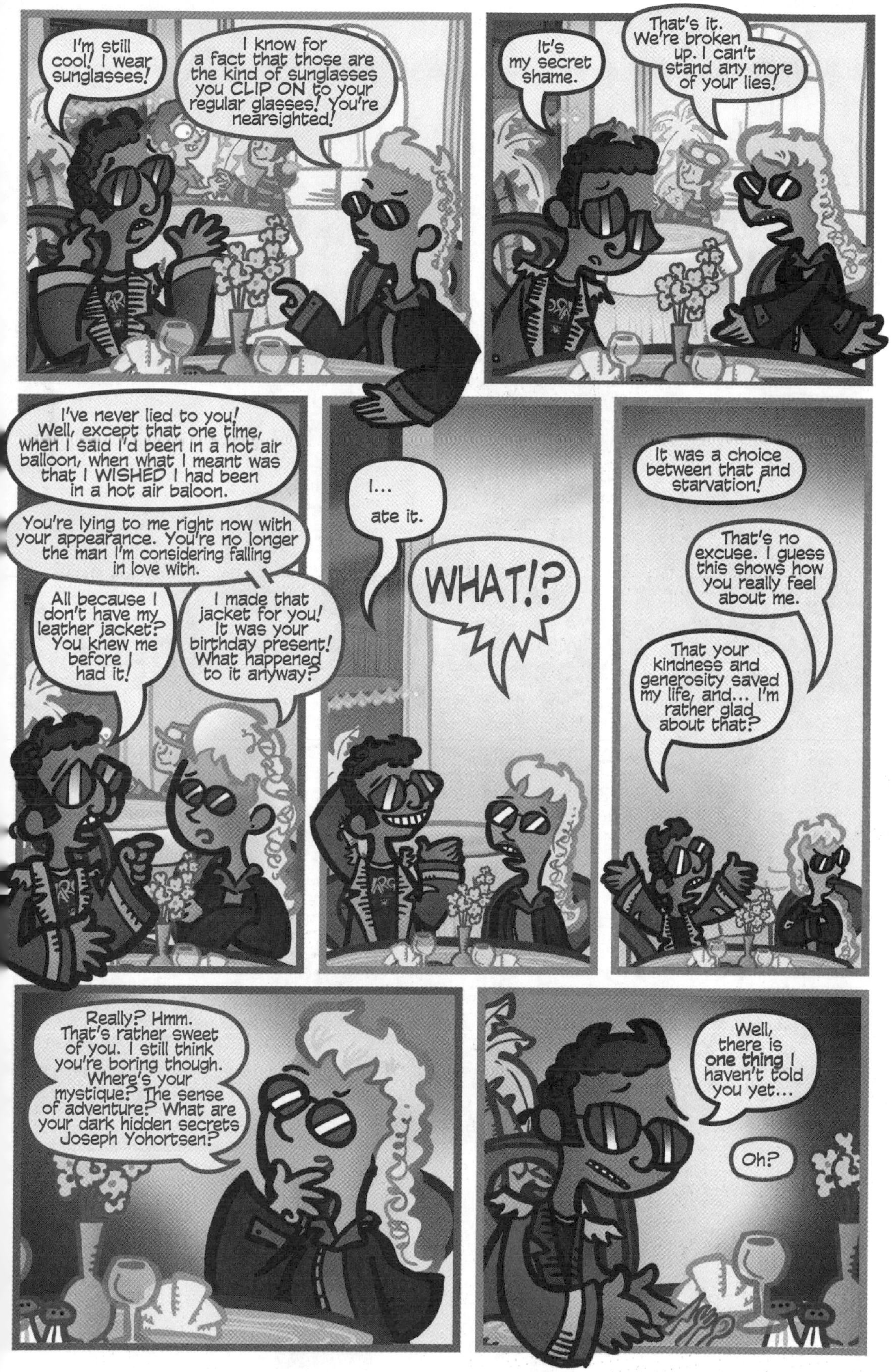
I'm still cool! I wear sunglasses!
I know for a fact that those are the kind of sunglasses you CLIP ON to your regular glasses! You're nearsighted!
It's my secret shame.
That's it. We're broken up. I can't stand any more of your lies!
I've never lied to you! Well, except that one time, when I said I'd been in a hot air balloon, when what I meant was that I WISHED I had been in a hot air baloon.
You're lying to me right now with your appearance. You're no longer the man I'm considering falling in love with.
All because I don't have my leather jacket? You knew me before I had it!
I made that jacket for you! It was your birthday present! What happened to it anyway?
I... ate it.
WHAT!?
It was a choice between that and starvation!
That's no excuse. I guess this shows how you really feel about me.
That your kindness and generosity saved my life, and... I'm rather glad about that?
Really? Hmm. That's rather sweet of you. I still think you're boring though. Where's your mystique? The sense of adventure? What are your dark hidden secrets Joseph Yohortsen?
Well, there is one thing I haven't told you yet...
Oh?

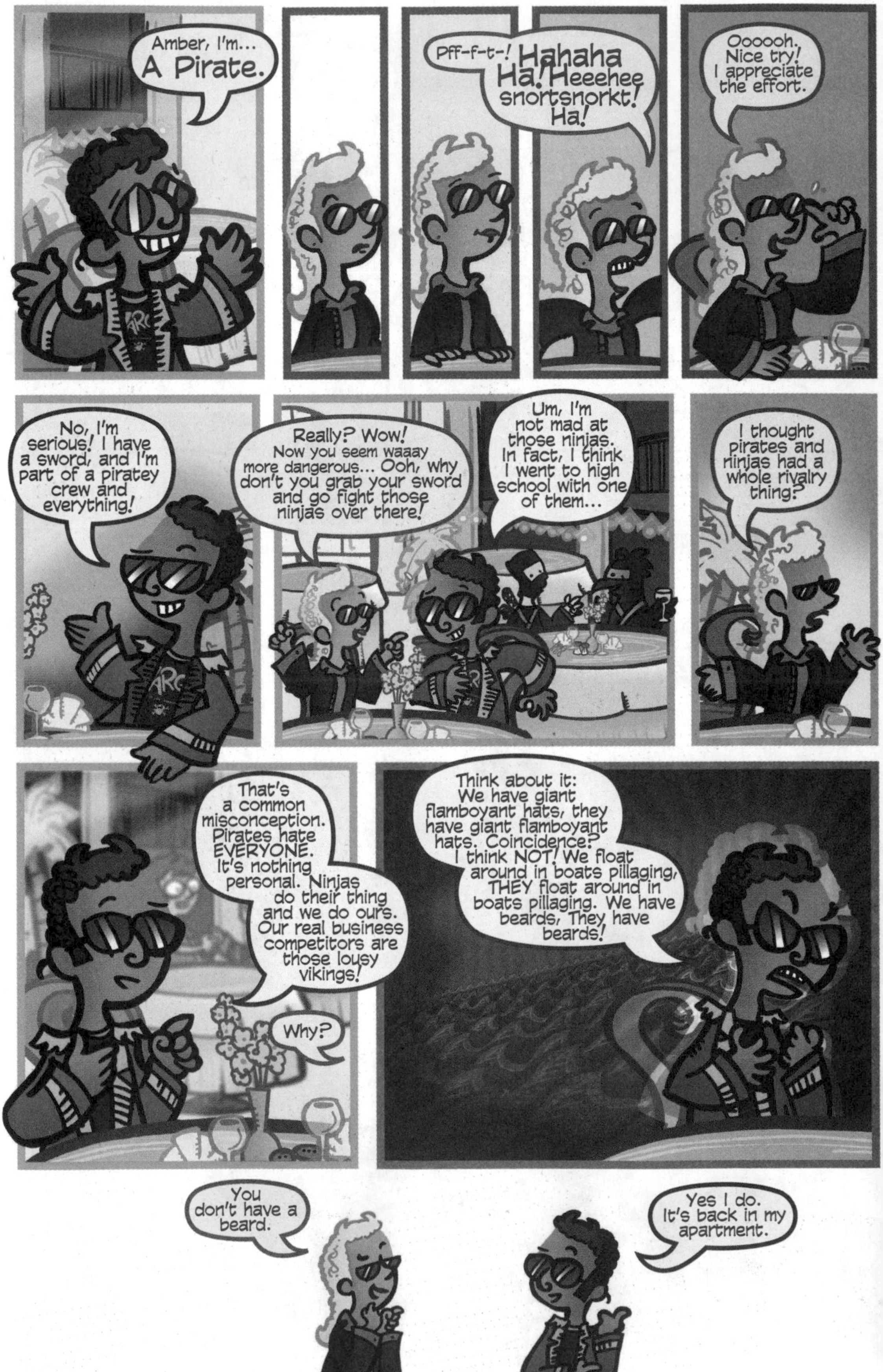
Amber, I'm... A Pirate.
Pff-f-t-! Hahaha Ha! Heeehee snortsnorkt! Ha!
Oooooh. Nice try! I appreciate the effort.
No, I'm serious! I have a sword, and I'm part of a piratey crew and everything!
Really? Wow! Now you seem waaay more dangerous... Ooh, why don't you grab your sword and go fight those ninjas over there!
Um, I'm not mad at those ninjas. In fact, I think I went to high school with one of them...
I thought pirates and ninjas had a whole rivalry thing?
That's a common misconception. Pirates hate EVERYONE. It's nothing personal. Ninjas do their thing and we do ours. Our real business competitors are those lousy vikings!
Why?
Think about it: We have giant flamboyant hats, they have giant flamboyant hats. Coincidence? I think NOT! We float around in boats pillaging, THEY float around in boats pillaging. We have beards, They have beards!
You don't have a beard.
Yes I do. It's back in my apartment.

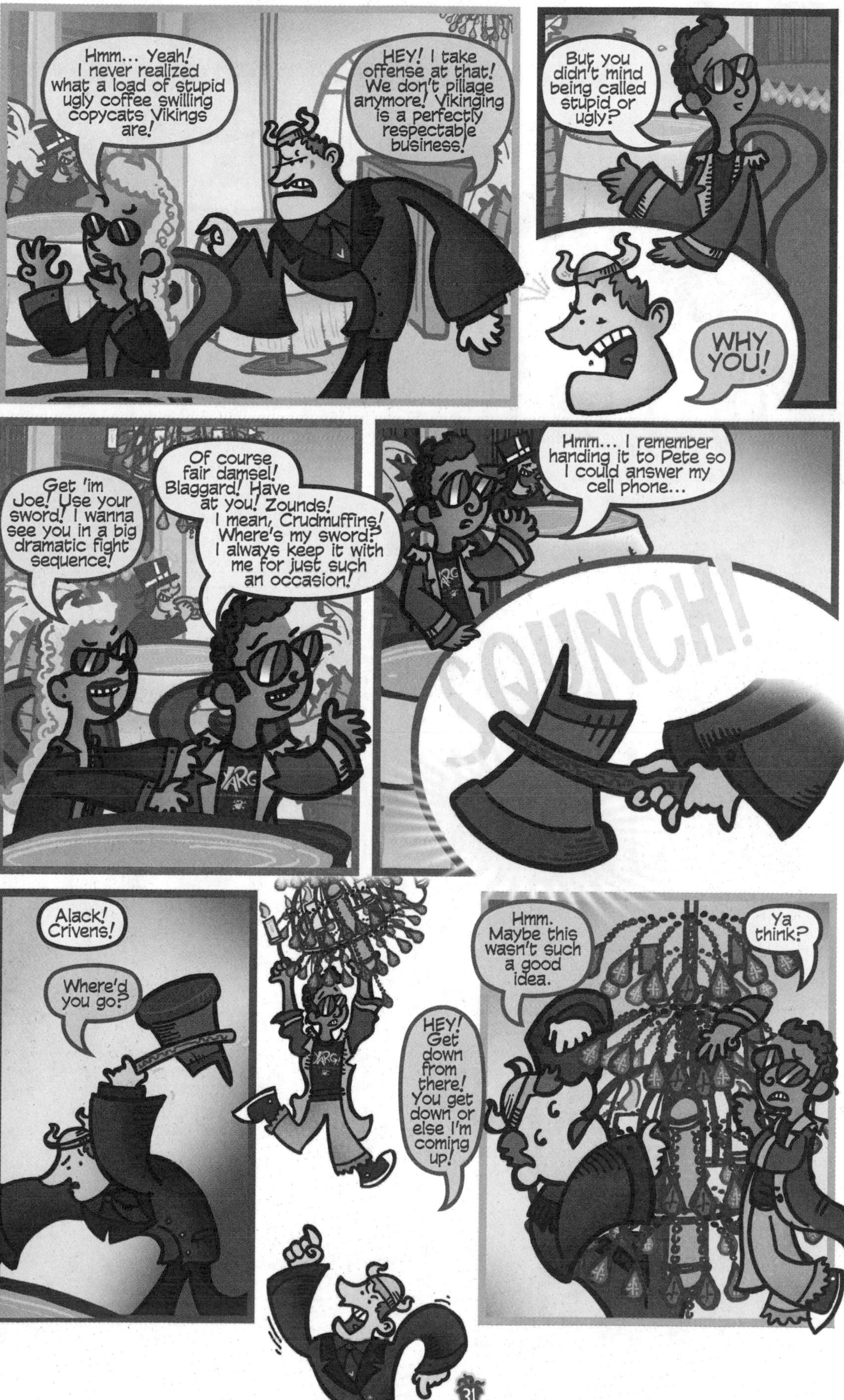

Hmm... Yeah! I never realized what a load of stupid ugly coffee swilling copycats Vikings are!
HEY! I take offense at that! We don't pillage anymore! Vikinging is a perfectly respectable business!
But you didn't mind being called stupid or ugly?
WHY YOU!
Get 'im Joe! Use your sword! I wanna see you in a big dramatic fight sequence!
Of course fair damsel! Blaggard! Have at you! Zounds! I mean, Crudmuffins! Where's my sword? I always keep it with me for just such an occasion!
Hmm... I remember handing it to Pete so I could answer my cell phone...
SQUNCH!
Alack! Crivens!
Where'd you go?
HEY! Get down from there! You get down or else I'm coming up!
Hmm. Maybe this wasn't such a good idea.
Ya think?

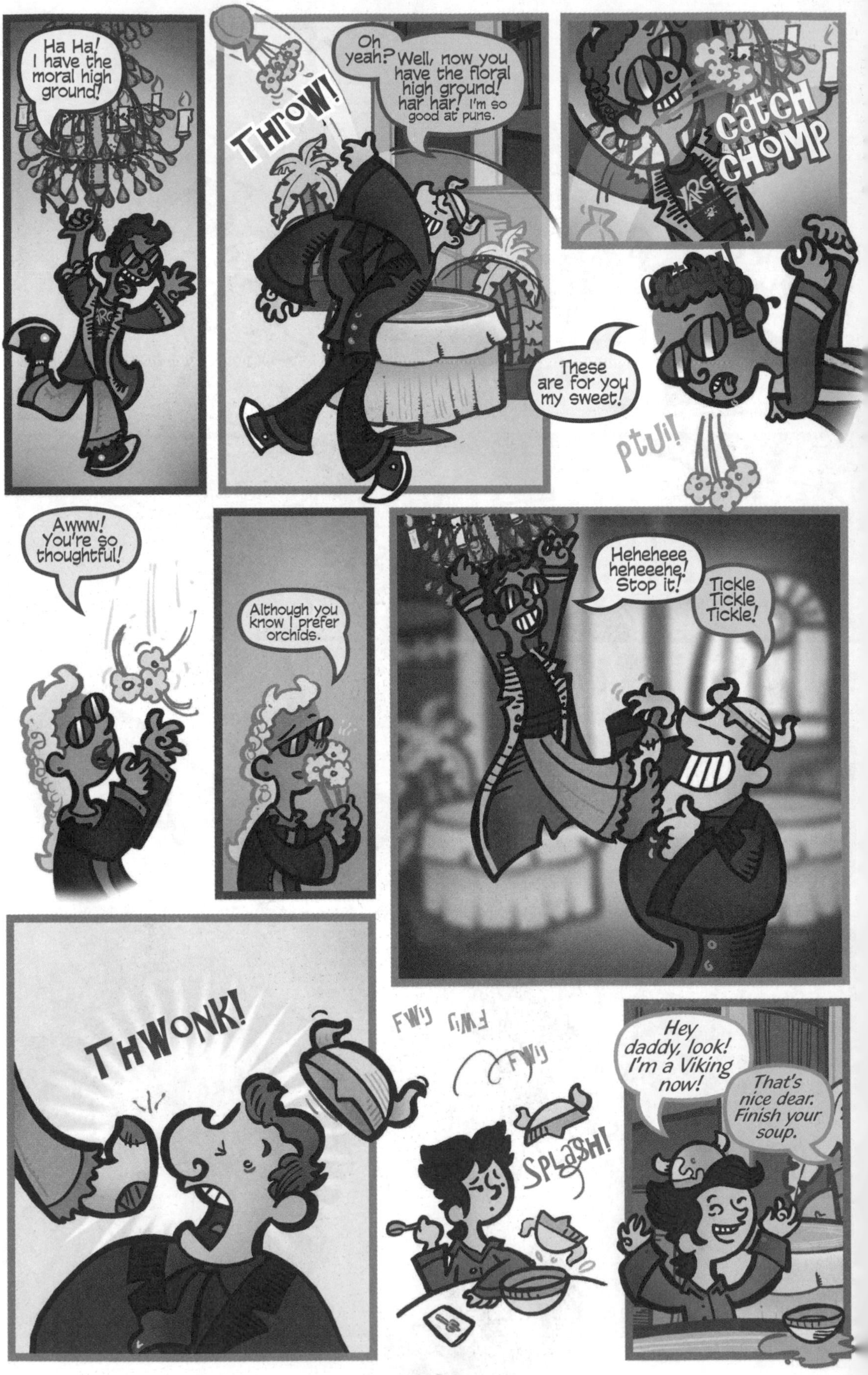
Ha Ha! I have the moral high ground!
THROW!
Oh yeah? Well, now you have the floral high ground! har har! I'm so good at puns.
CATCH
CHOMP
These are for you my sweet!
PTUI!
Awww! You're so thoughtful!
Although you know I prefer orchids.
Heheheee heheeehe! Stop it!
Tickle Tickle Tickle!
THWONK!
FWIJ
FWIJ
FWIJ
SPLASH!
Hey daddy, look! I'm a Viking now!
That's nice dear. Finish your soup.

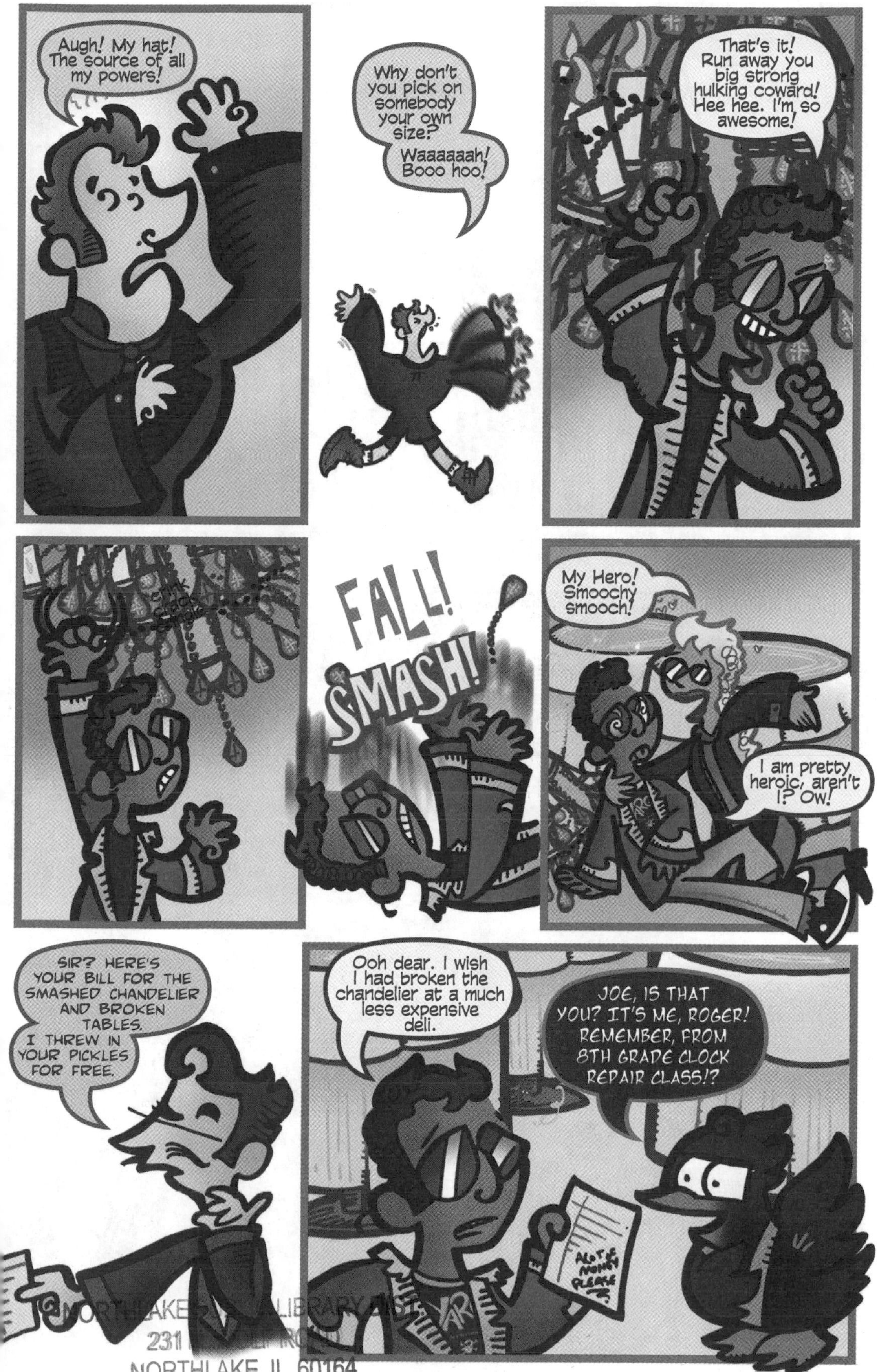

Augh! My hat! The source of all my powers!
Why don't you pick on somebody your own size?
Waaaaaah! Booo hoo!
That's it! Run away you big strong hulking coward! Hee hee. I'm so awesome!
crink crack crackle
FALL!
SMASH!
My Hero! Smoochy smooch!
I am pretty heroic, aren't I? Ow!
SIR? HERE'S YOUR BILL FOR THE SMASHED CHANDELIER AND BROKEN TABLES. I THREW IN YOUR PICKLES FOR FREE.
Ooh dear. I wish I had broken the chandelier at a much less expensive deli.
JOE, IS THAT YOU? IT'S ME, ROGER! REMEMBER, FROM 8TH GRADE CLOCK REPAIR CLASS!?

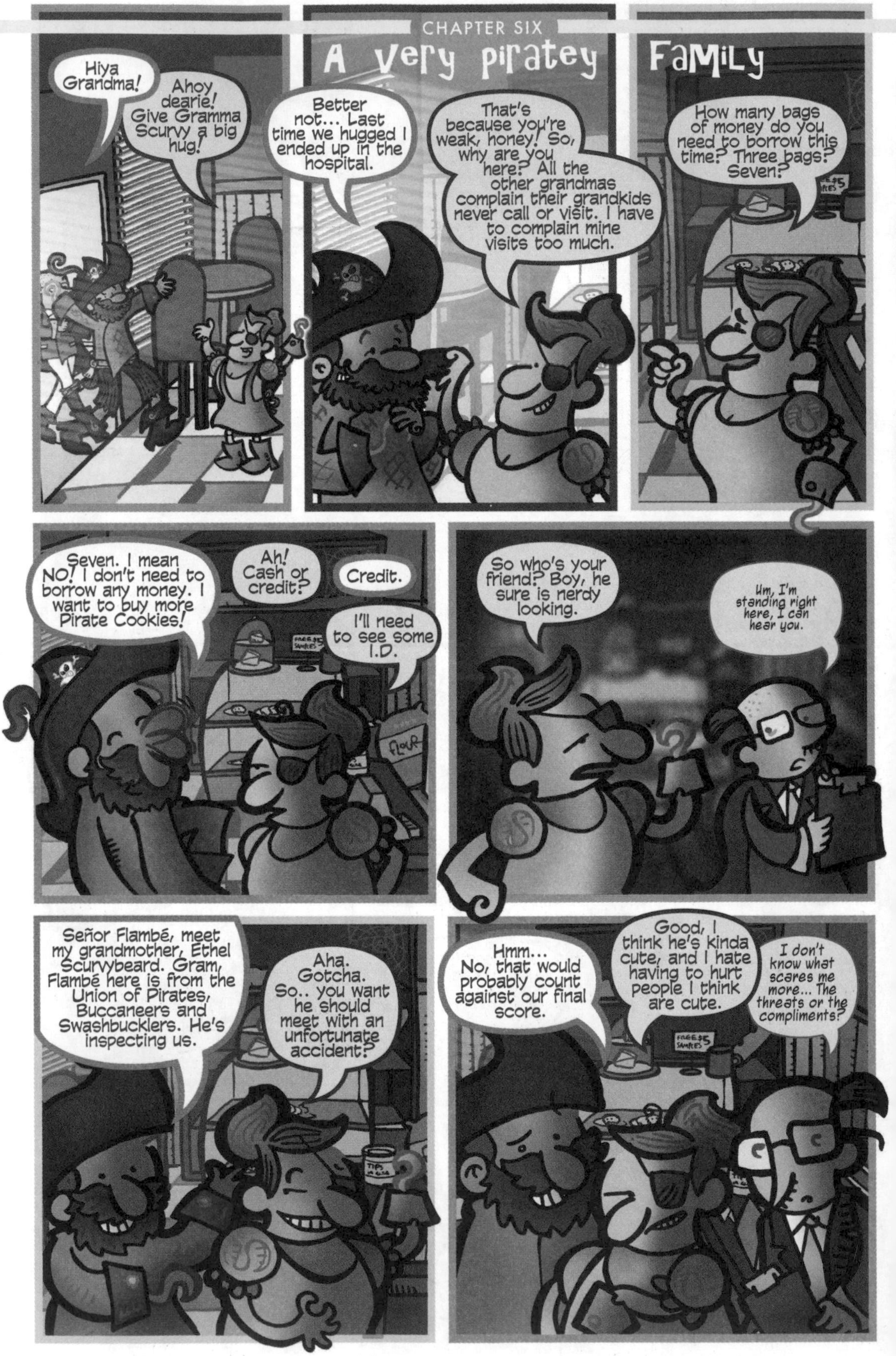
CHAPTER SIX
A very piratey Family
Hiya Grandma!
Ahoy dearie! Give Gramma Scurvy a big hug!
Better not... Last time we hugged I ended up in the hospital.
That's because you're weak, honey! So, why are you here? All the other grandmas complain their grandkids never call or visit. I have to complain mine visits too much.
How many bags of money do you need to borrow this time? Three bags? Seven?
Seven. I mean NO! I don't need to borrow any money. I want to buy more Pirate Cookies!
Ah! Cash or credit?
Credit.
I'll need to see some I.D.
FLOUR
So who's your friend? Boy, he sure is nerdy looking.
Um, I'm standing right here, I can hear you.
Señor Flambé, meet my grandmother, Ethel Scurvybeard. Gram, Flambé here is from the Union of Pirates, Buccaneers and Swashbucklers. He's inspecting us.
Aha. Gotcha. So.. you want he should meet with an unfortunate accident?
Hmm... No, that would probably count against our final score.
Good, I think he's kinda cute, and I hate having to hurt people I think are cute.
I don't know what scares me more... The threats or the compliments?
FREE $5 SAMPLES

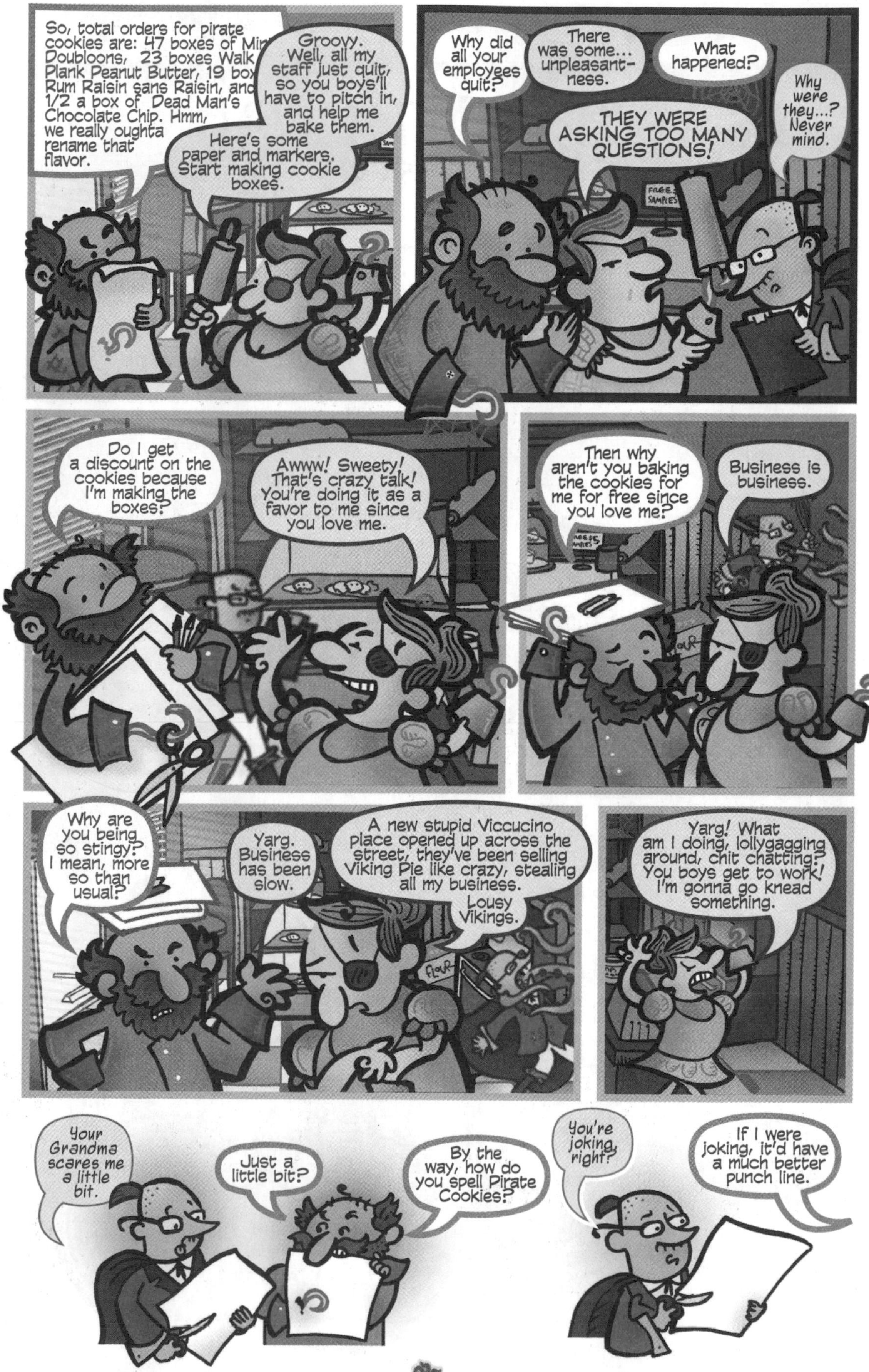

So, total orders for pirate cookies are: 47 boxes of Min Doubloons, 23 boxes Walk Plank Peanut Butter, 19 box Rum Raisin sans Raisin, and 1/2 a box of Dead Man's Chocolate Chip. Hmm, we really oughta rename that flavor.
Groovy. Well, all my staff just quit, so you boys'll have to pitch in, and help me bake them.
Here's some paper and markers. Start making cookie boxes.
Why did all your employees quit?
There was some... unpleasant-ness.
What happened?
THEY WERE ASKING TOO MANY QUESTIONS!
Why were they...? Never mind.
FREE SAMPLES
Do I get a discount on the cookies because I'm making the boxes?
Awww! Sweety! That's crazy talk! You're doing it as a favor to me since you love me.
Then why aren't you baking the cookies for me for free since you love me?
Business is business.
Why are you being so stingy? I mean, more so than usual?
Yarg. Business has been slow.
A new stupid Viccucino place opened up across the street, they've been selling Viking Pie like crazy, stealing all my business.
Lousy Vikings.
FLOUR
Yarg! What am I doing, lollygagging around, chit chatting? You boys get to work! I'm gonna go knead something.
Your Grandma scares me a little bit.
Just a little bit?
By the way, how do you spell Pirate Cookies?
You're joking, right?
If I were joking, it'd have a much better punch line.

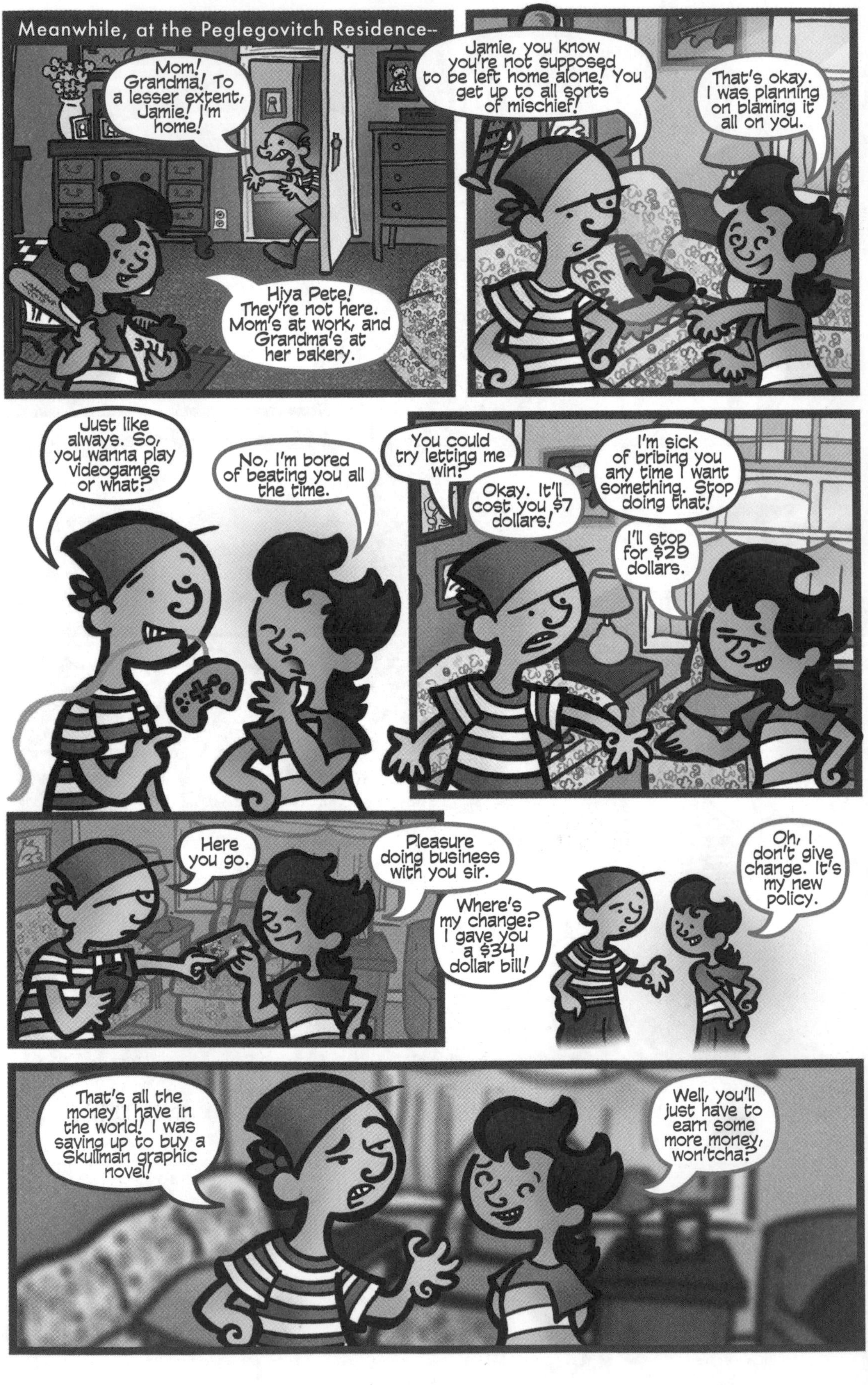
Meanwhile, at the Peglegovitch Residence--
Mom! Grandma! To a lesser extent, Jamie! I'm home!
Hiya Pete! They're not here. Mom's at work, and Grandma's at her bakery.
Jamie, you know you're not supposed to be left home alone! You get up to all sorts of mischief!
That's okay. I was planning on blaming it all on you.
ICE CREAM
Just like always. So, you wanna play videogames or what?
No, I'm bored of beating you all the time.
You could try letting me win?
Okay. It'll cost you $7 dollars!
I'm sick of bribing you any time I want something. Stop doing that!
I'll stop for $29 dollars.
Here you go.
Pleasure doing business with you sir.
Where's my change? I gave you a $34 dollar bill!
Oh, I don't give change. It's my new policy.
That's all the money I have in the world! I was saving up to buy a Skullman graphic novel!
Well, you'll just have to earn some more money, won'tcha?

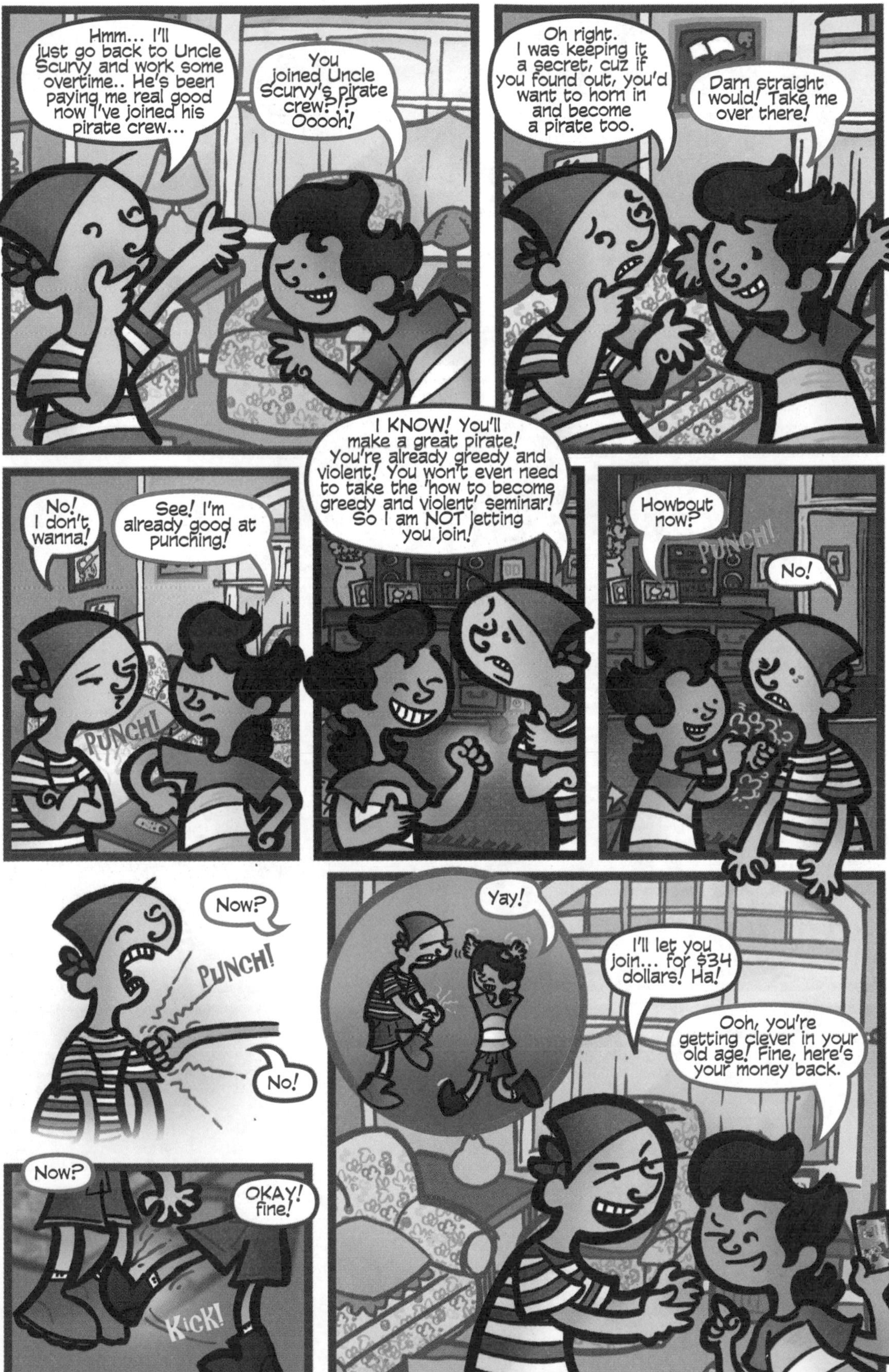
Hmm... I'll just go back to Uncle Scurvy and work some overtime.. He's been paying me real good now I've joined his pirate crew...
You joined Uncle Scurvy's pirate crew?!? Ooooh!
Oh right. I was keeping it a secret, cuz if you found out, you'd want to horn in and become a pirate too.
Darn straight I would! Take me over there!
No! I don't wanna!
See! I'm already good at punching!
PUNCH!
I KNOW! You'll make a great pirate! You're already greedy and violent! You won't even need to take the 'how to become greedy and violent' seminar! So I am NOT letting you join!
Howbout now?
PUNCH!
No!
Now?
PUNCH!
No!
Now?
OKAY! fine!
KICK!
Yay!
I'll let you join... for $34 dollars! Ha!
Ooh, you're getting clever in your old age! Fine, here's your money back.

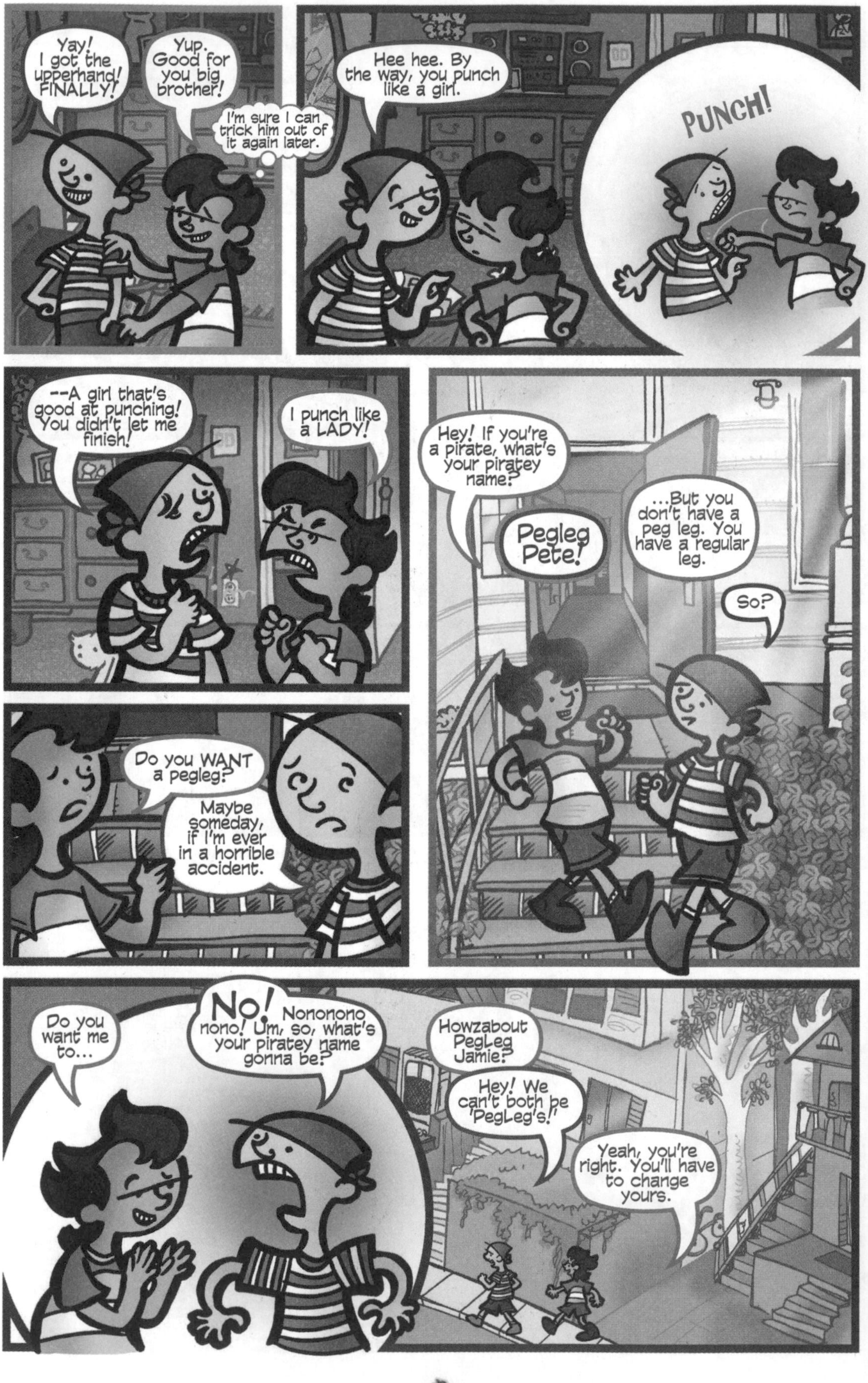

Yay! I got the upperhand! FINALLY!
Yup. Good for you big brother!
I'm sure I can trick him out of it again later.
Hee hee. By the way, you punch like a girl.
PUNCH!
--A girl that's good at punching! You didn't let me finish!
I punch like a LADY!
Hey! If you're a pirate, what's your piratey name?
Pegleg Pete!
...But you don't have a peg leg. You have a regular leg.
So?
Do you WANT a pegleg?
Maybe someday, if I'm ever in a horrible accident.
Do you want me to...
No! Nonononono nono! Um, so, what's your piratey name gonna be?
Howzabout PegLeg Jamie?
Hey! We can't both be 'PegLeg's!'
Yeah, you're right. You'll have to change yours.

CHAPTER SEVEN

Math is Pirate Kryptonite

also, Spelling. Pirates aren't very Smart.

except For the Smart ones.

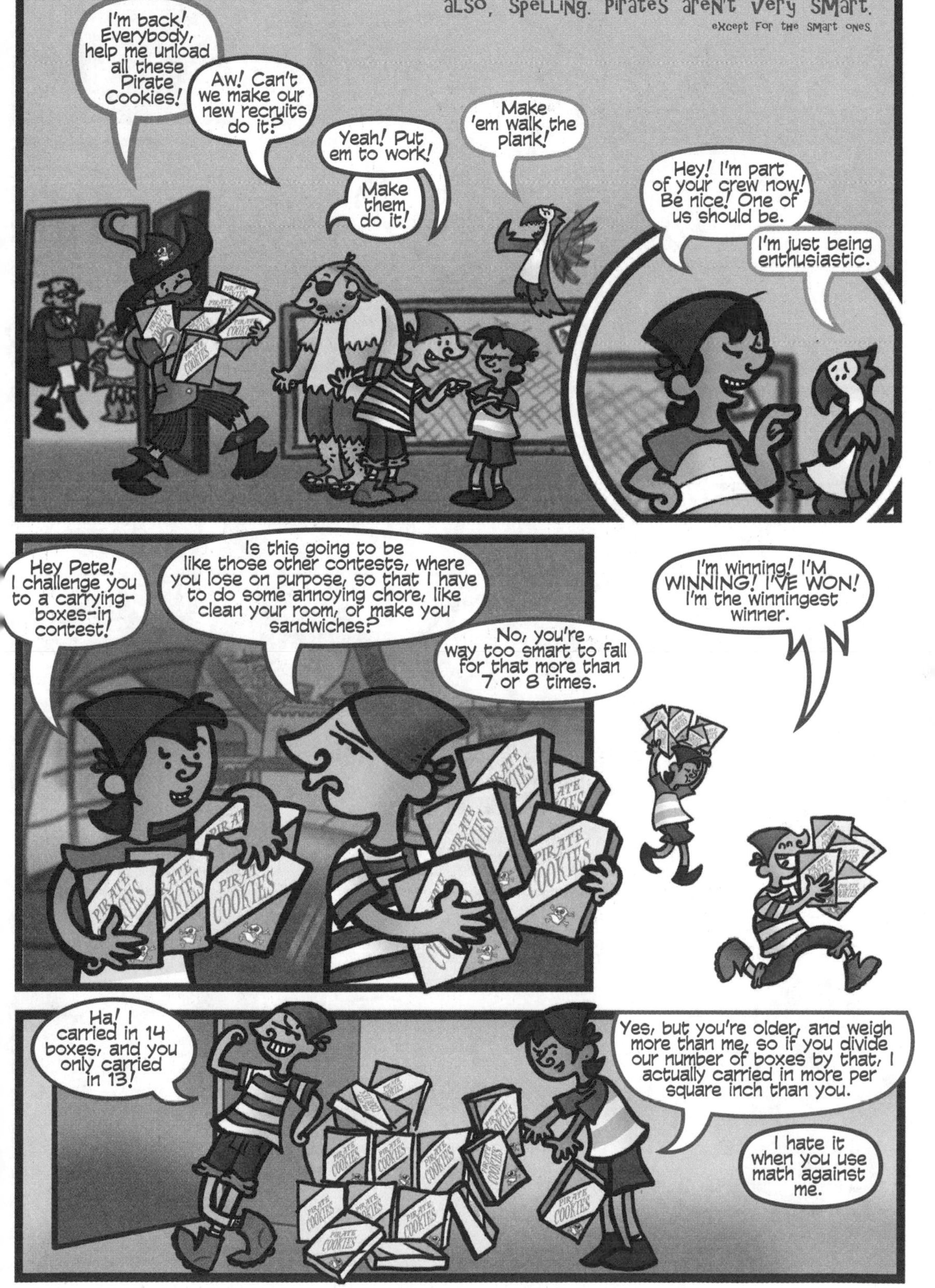

I'm back! Everybody, help me unload all these Pirate Cookies!
Aw! Can't we make our new recruits do it?
Yeah! Put em to work!
Make them do it!
Make 'em walk the plank!
Hey! I'm part of your crew now! Be nice! One of us should be.
I'm just being enthusiastic.
Hey Pete! I challenge you to a carrying-boxes-in contest!
Is this going to be like those other contests, where you lose on purpose, so that I have to do some annoying chore, like clean your room, or make you sandwiches?
No, you're way too smart to fall for that more than 7 or 8 times.
I'm winning! I'M WINNING! I'VE WON! I'm the winningest winner.
Ha! I carried in 14 boxes, and you only carried in 13!
Yes, but you're older, and weigh more than me, so if you divide our number of boxes by that, I actually carried in more per square inch than you.
I hate it when you use math against me.

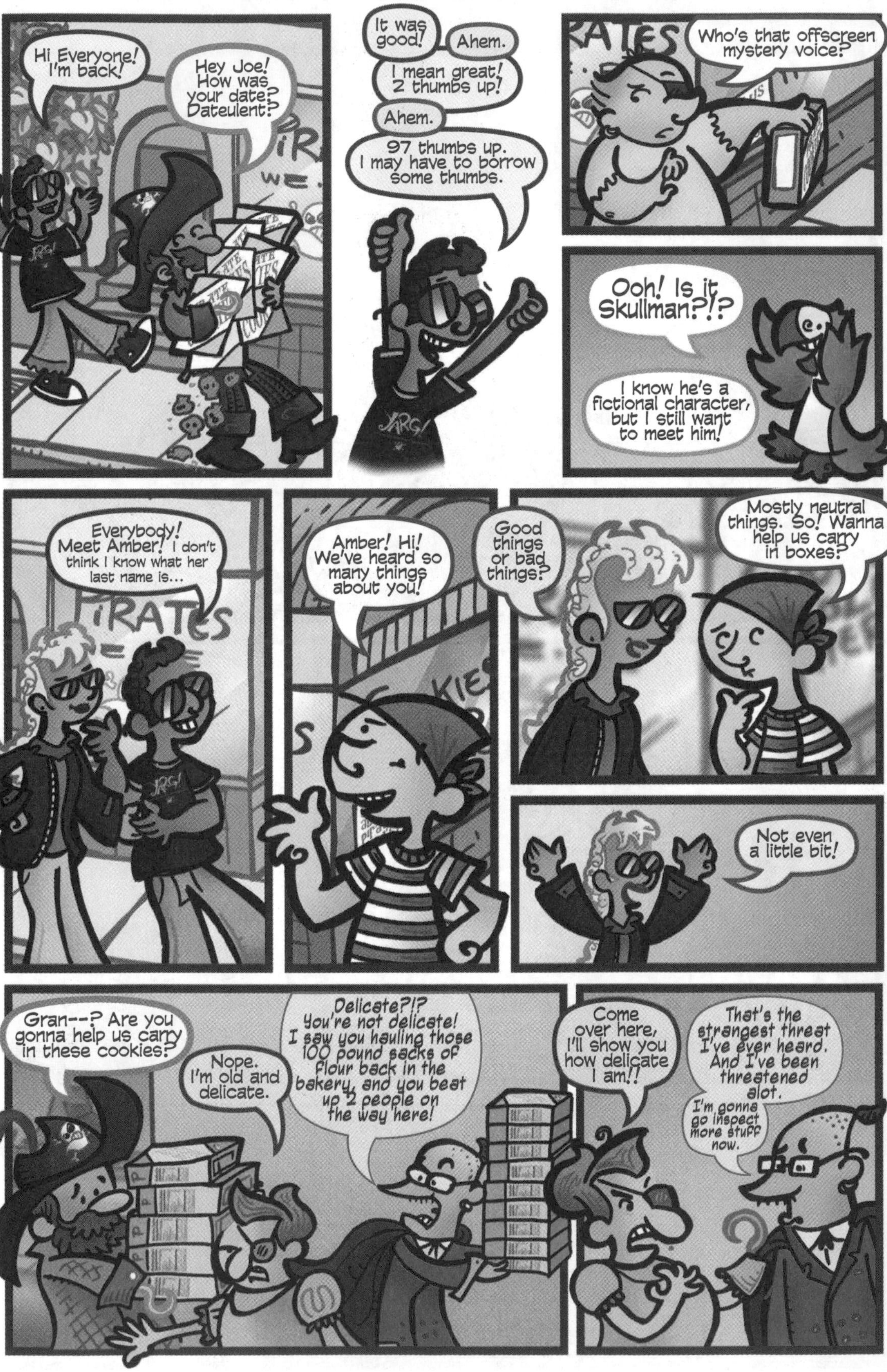
Hi Everyone! I'm back!
Hey Joe! How was your date? Dateulent?
It was good!
Ahem.
I mean great! 2 thumbs up!
Ahem.
97 thumbs up. I may have to borrow some thumbs.
Who's that offscreen mystery voice?
Ooh! Is it Skullman?!?
I know he's a fictional character, but I still want to meet him!
Everybody! Meet Amber! I don't think I know what her last name is...
PiRATES
Amber! Hi! We've heard so many things about you!
Good things or bad things?
Mostly neutral things. So! Wanna help us carry in boxes?
Not even a little bit!
Gran--? Are you gonna help us carry in these cookies?
Nope. I'm old and delicate.
Delicate?!? You're not delicate! I saw you hauling those 100 pound sacks of flour back in the bakery, and you beat up 2 people on the way here!
Come over here, I'll show you how delicate I am!!
That's the strangest threat I've ever heard. And I've been threatened alot.
I'm gonna go inspect more stuff now.

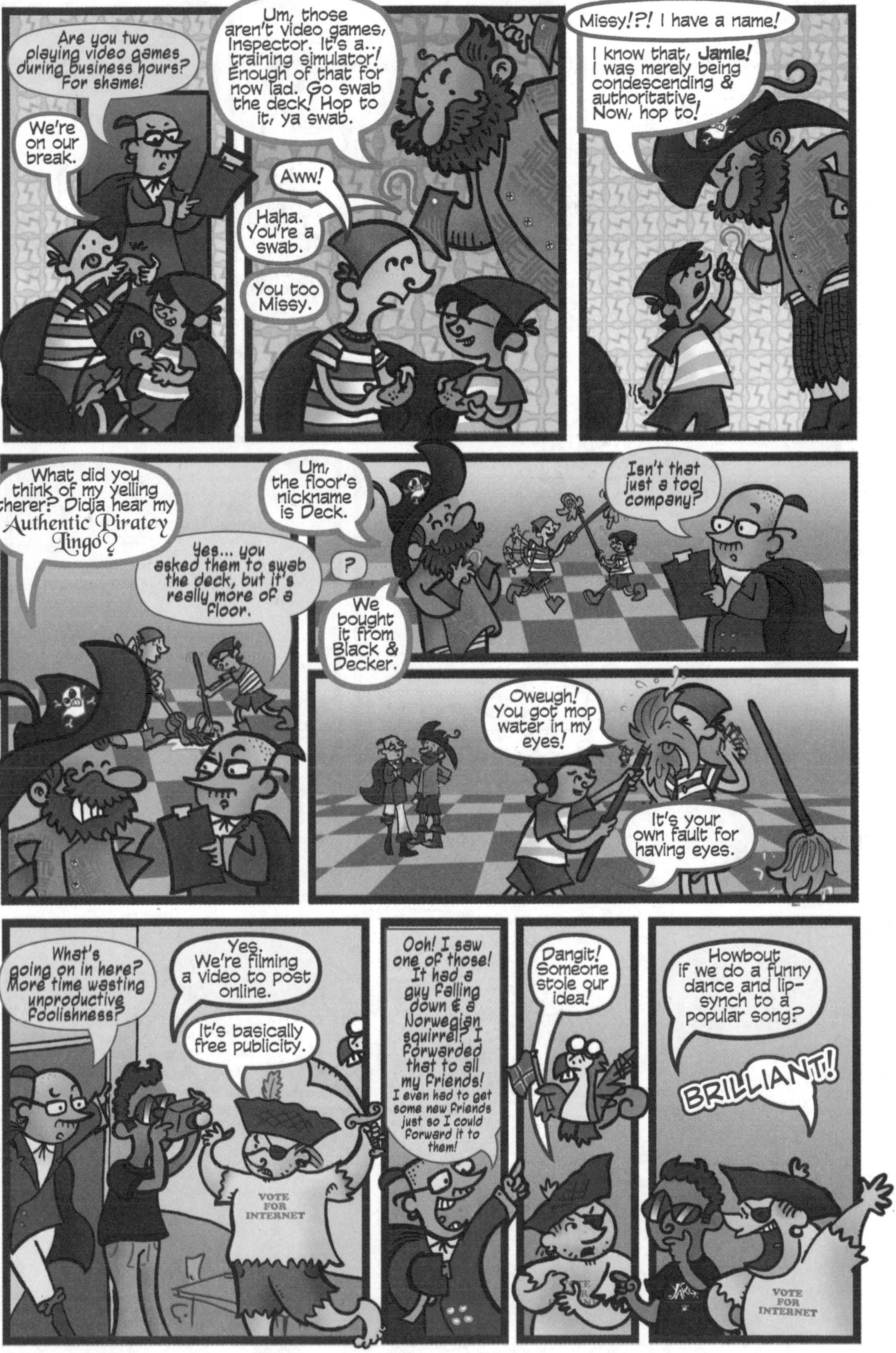
Are you two playing video games during business hours? For shame!
We're on our break.
Um, those aren't video games, Inspector. It's a.. training simulator! Enough of that for now lad. Go swab the deck! Hop to it, ya swab.
Aww!
Haha. You're a swab.
You too Missy.
Missy!?! I have a name!
I know that, Jamie! I was merely being condescending & authoritative. Now, hop to!
What did you think of my yelling therer? Didja hear my Authentic Piratey Lingo?
Yes... you asked them to swab the deck, but it's really more of a floor.
Um, the floor's nickname is Deck.
?
We bought it from Black & Decker.
Isn't that just a tool company?
Oweugh! You got mop water in my eyes!
It's your own fault for having eyes.
What's going on in here? More time wasting unproductive foolishness?
Yes. We're filming a video to post online.
It's basically free publicity.
VOTE FOR INTERNET
Ooh! I saw one of those! It had a guy falling down & a Norwegian squirrel! I forwarded that to all my friends! I even had to get some new friends just so I could forward it to them!
Dangit! Someone stole our idea!
Howbout if we do a funny dance and lip-synch to a popular song?
BRILLIANT!
VOTE FOR INTERNET

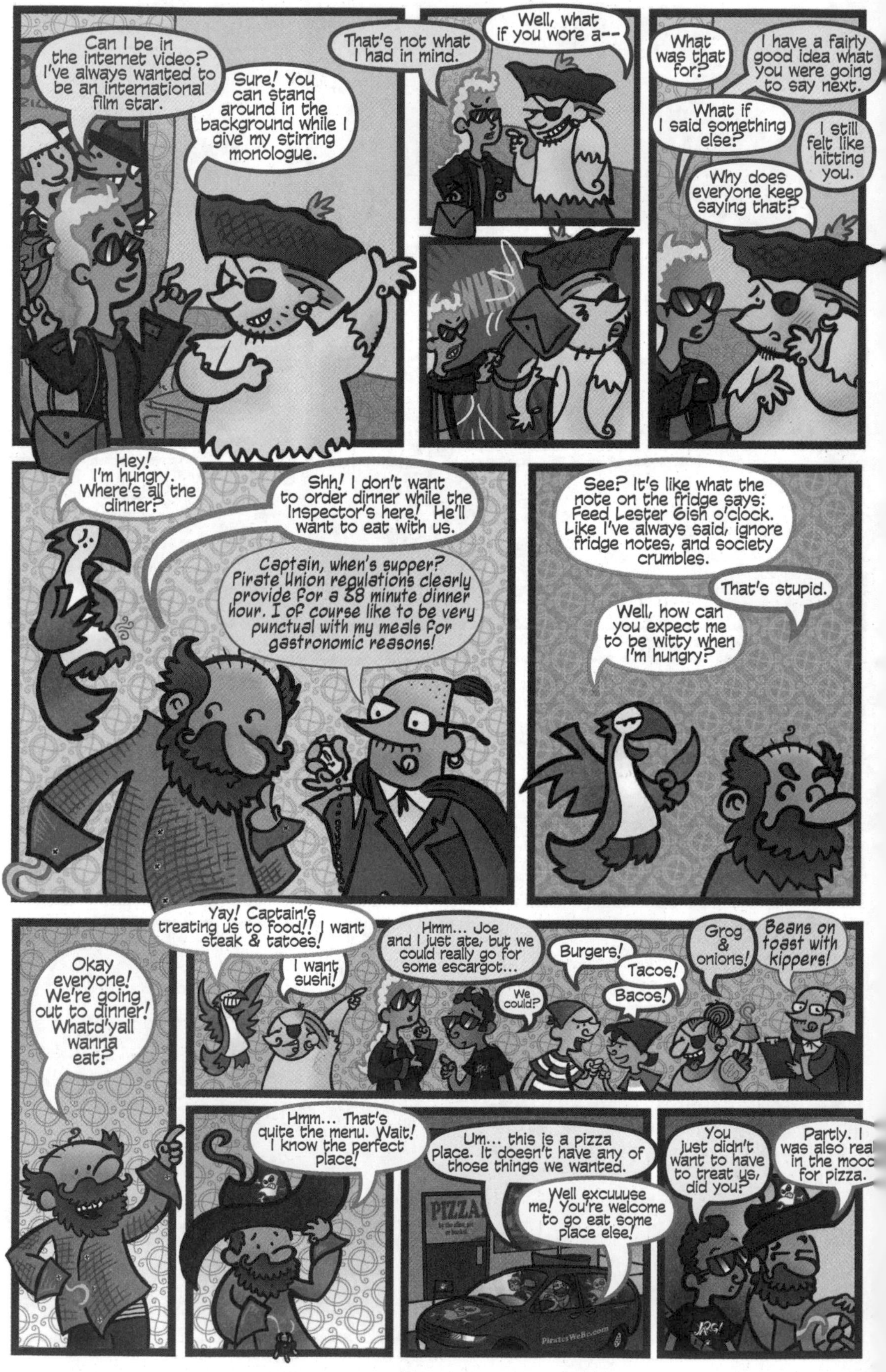
Can I be in the internet video? I've always wanted to be an international film star.
Sure! You can stand around in the background while I give my stirring monologue.
That's not what I had in mind.
Well, what if you wore a--
What was that for?
I have a fairly good idea what you were going to say next.
What if I said something else?
I still felt like hitting you.
Why does everyone keep saying that?
Hey! I'm hungry. Where's all the dinner?
Shh! I don't want to order dinner while the Inspector's here! He'll want to eat with us.
Captain, when's supper? Pirate Union regulations clearly provide for a 38 minute dinner hour. I of course like to be very punctual with my meals for gastronomic reasons!
See? It's like what the note on the fridge says: Feed Lester 6ish o'clock. Like I've always said, ignore fridge notes, and society crumbles.
That's stupid.
Well, how can you expect me to be witty when I'm hungry?
Okay everyone! We're going out to dinner! Whatd'yall wanna eat?
Yay! Captain's treating us to food!! I want steak & tatoes!
I want sushi!
Hmm... Joe and I just ate, but we could really go for some escargot...
We could?
Burgers!
Tacos!
Bacos!
Grog & onions!
Beans on toast with kippers!
Hmm... That's quite the menu. Wait! I know the perfect place!
Um... this is a pizza place. It doesn't have any of those things we wanted.
PIZZA
Well excuuuse me! You're welcome to go eat some place else!
You just didn't want to have to treat us, did you?
Partly. I was also rea in the mooc for pizza.

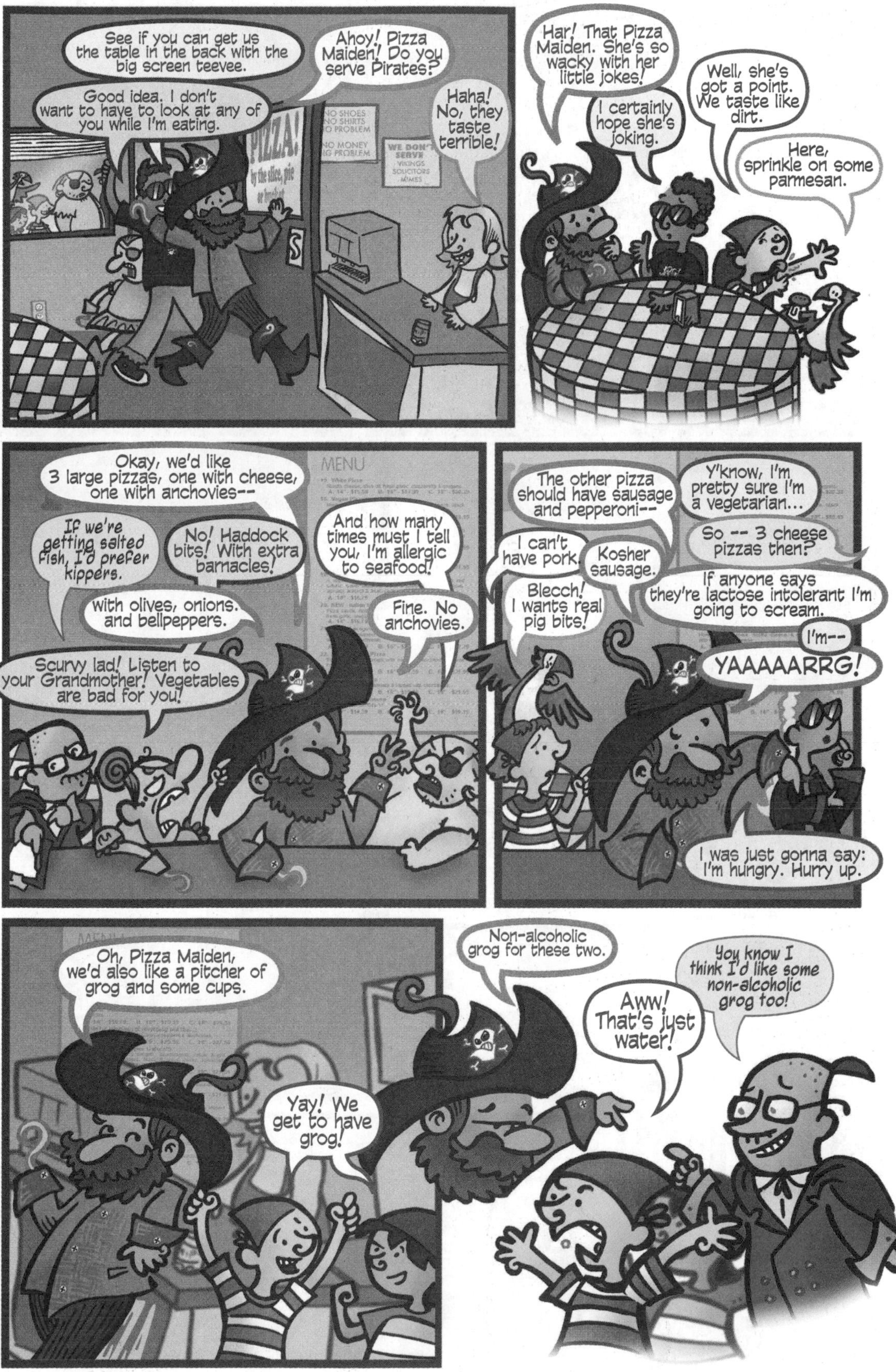
See if you can get us the table in the back with the big screen teevee.
Good idea. I don't want to have to look at any of you while I'm eating.
Ahoy! Pizza Maiden! Do you serve Pirates?
PIZZA!
WE DON'T SERVE VIKINGS SOLICITORS MIMES
Haha! No, they taste terrible!
Har! That Pizza Maiden. She's so wacky with her little jokes!
I certainly hope she's joking.
Well, she's got a point. We taste like dirt.
Here, sprinkle on some parmesan.
MENU
Okay, we'd like 3 large pizzas, one with cheese, one with anchovies--
If we're getting salted fish, I'd prefer kippers.
No! Haddock bits! With extra barnacles!
And how many times must I tell you, I'm allergic to seafood!
with olives, onions. and bellpeppers.
Fine. No anchovies.
Scurvy lad! Listen to your Grandmother! Vegetables are bad for you!
The other pizza should have sausage and pepperoni--
Y'know, I'm pretty sure I'm a vegetarian...
I can't have pork.
Kosher sausage.
So -- 3 cheese pizzas then?
Blecch! I wants real pig bits!
If anyone says they're lactose intolerant I'm going to scream.
I'm--
YAAAAARRG!
I was just gonna say: I'm hungry. Hurry up.
Oh, Pizza Maiden, we'd also like a pitcher of grog and some cups.
Non-alcoholic grog for these two.
Yay! We get to have grog!
Aww! That's just water!
You know I think I'd like some non-alcoholic grog too!

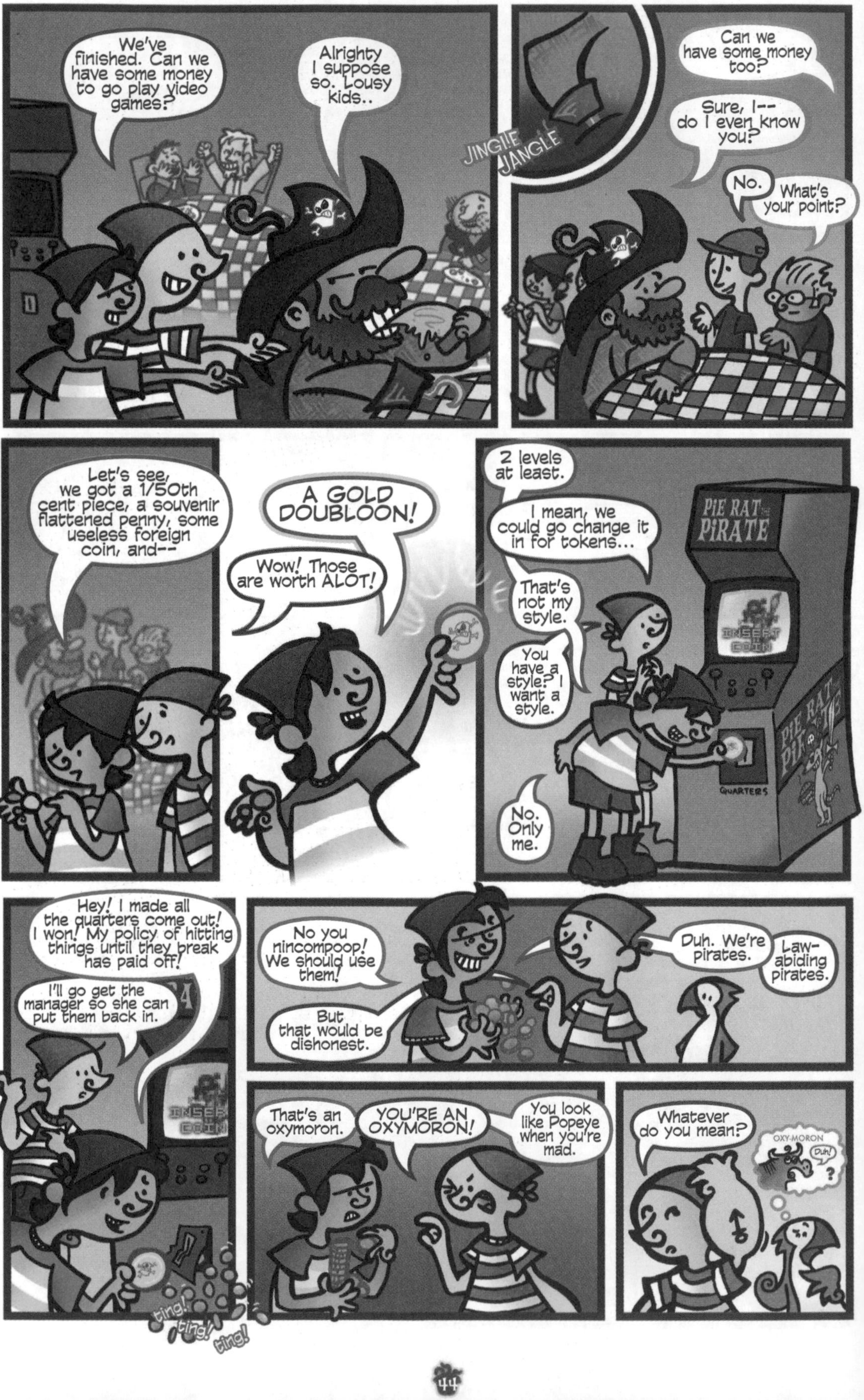
We've finished. Can we have some money to go play video games?
Alrighty I suppose so. Lousy kids..
JINGLE JANGLE
Can we have some money too?
Sure, I-- do I even know you?
No.
What's your point?
Let's see, we got a 1/50th cent piece, a souvenir flattened penny, some useless foreign coin, and--
A GOLD DOUBLOON!
Wow! Those are worth ALOT!
2 levels at least.
I mean, we could go change it in for tokens...
That's not my style.
You have a style? I want a style.
No. Only me.
PIE RAT THE PIRATE
INSERT COIN
QUARTERS
Hey! I made all the quarters come out! I won! My policy of hitting things until they break has paid off!
I'll go get the manager so she can put them back in.
ting! ting! ting!
No you nincompoop! We should use them!
But that would be dishonest.
Duh. We're pirates.
Law-abiding pirates.
That's an oxymoron.
YOU'RE AN OXYMORON!
You look like Popeye when you're mad.
Whatever do you mean?
OXY-MORON
Duh!

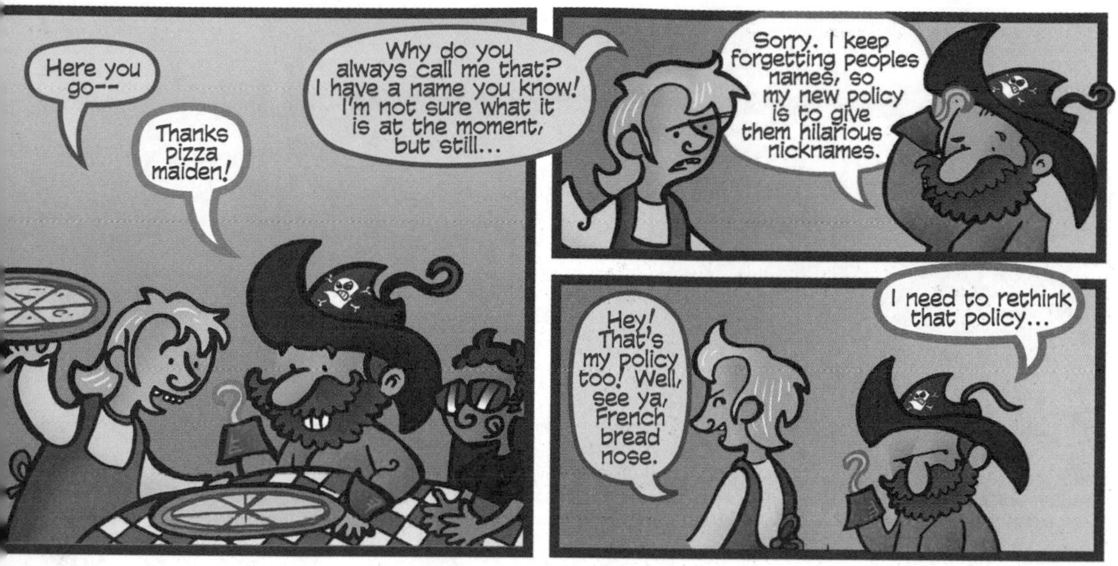
Here you go--
Thanks pizza maiden!
Why do you always call me that? I have a name you know! I'm not sure what it is at the moment, but still...
Sorry. I keep forgetting peoples names, so my new policy is to give them hilarious nicknames.
Hey! That's my policy too! Well, see ya, French bread nose.
I need to rethink that policy...

and now a brief, strange interlude

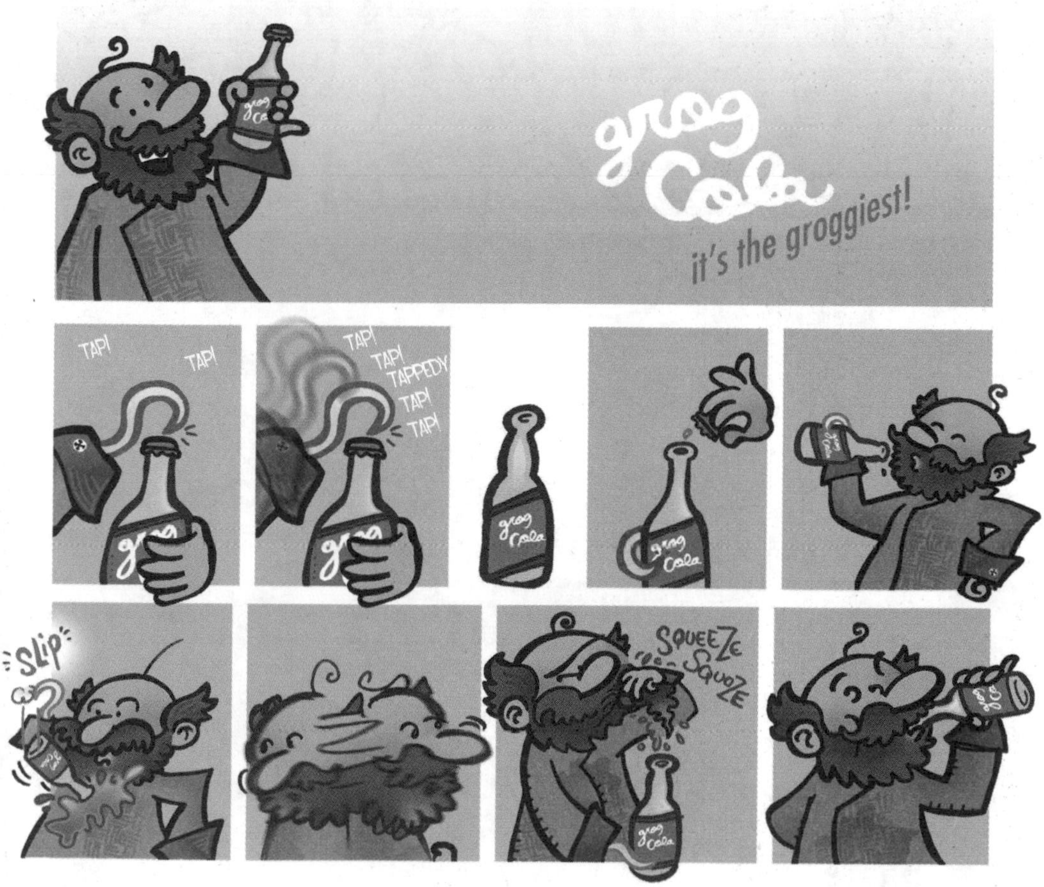
grog Cola
it's the groggiest!
TAP!
TAP!
TAP!
TAP!
TAPPEDY
TAP!
TAP!
SLIP
SQUEEZE
SQUOZE

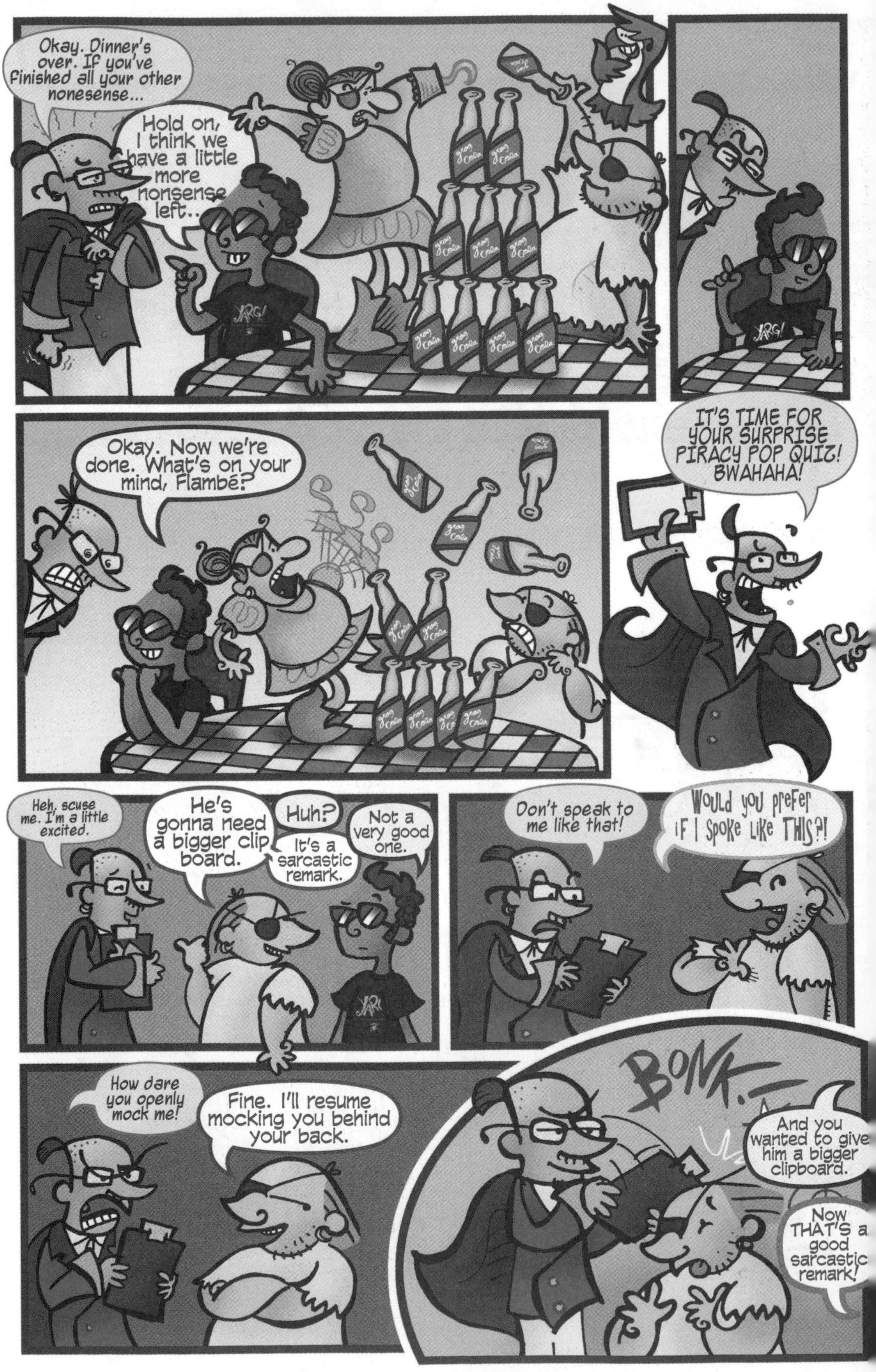

Okay. Dinner's over. If you've finished all your other nonesense...
Hold on, I think we have a little more nonsense left..
Okay. Now we're done. What's on your mind, Flambé?
IT'S TIME FOR YOUR SURPRISE PIRACY POP QUIZ! BWAHAHA!
Heh, scuse me. I'm a little excited.
He's gonna need a bigger clip board.
Huh?
It's a sarcastic remark.
Not a very good one.
Don't speak to me like that!
Would you prefer if I spoke like THIS?!
How dare you openly mock me!
Fine. I'll resume mocking you behind your back.
BONK
And you wanted to give him a bigger clipboard.
Now THAT'S a good sarcastic remark!

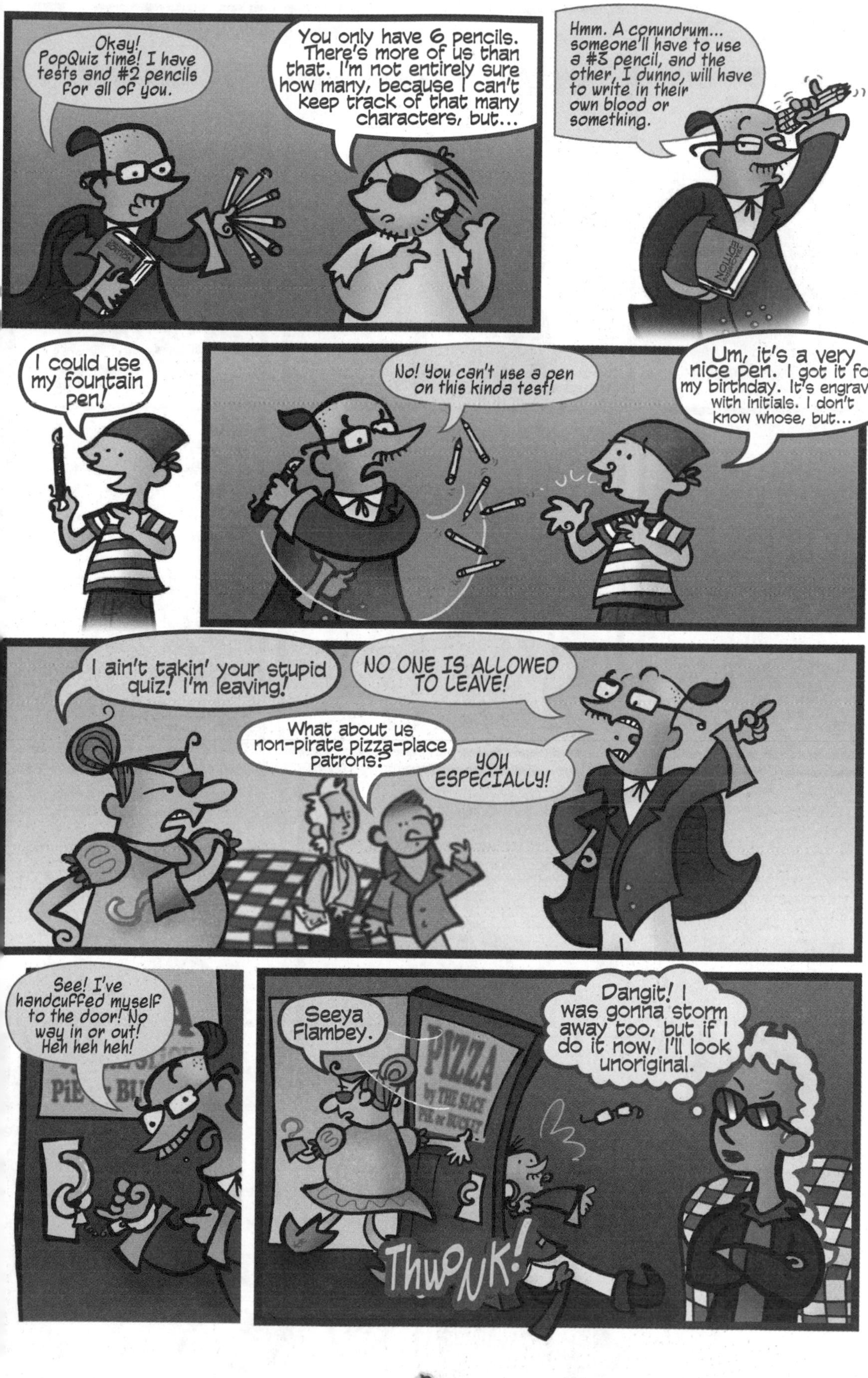
Okay! PopQuiz time! I have tests and #2 pencils for all of you.
You only have 6 pencils. There's more of us than that. I'm not entirely sure how many, because I can't keep track of that many characters, but...
Hmm. A conundrum... someone'll have to use a #3 pencil, and the other, I dunno, will have to write in their own blood or something.
I could use my fountain pen!
No! You can't use a pen on this kinda test!
Um, it's a very nice pen. I got it for my birthday. It's engraved with initials. I don't know whose, but...
I ain't takin' your stupid quiz! I'm leaving!
NO ONE IS ALLOWED TO LEAVE!
What about us non-pirate pizza-place patrons?
YOU ESPECIALLY!
See! I've handcuffed myself to the door! No way in or out! Heh heh heh!
Seeya Flambey.
PIZZA by THE SLICE PIE or BUCKET
Dangit! I was gonna storm away too, but if I do it now, I'll look unoriginal.
THWONK!

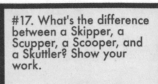

Okay, to renew your piracy licenses, please sit the following exam. Cheating's not only allowed, it's mandatory. Go!

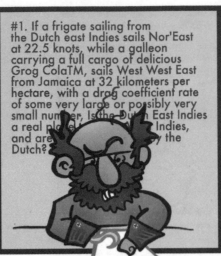

#1. If a frigate sailing from the Dutch east Indies sails Nor'East at 22.5 knots, while a galleon carrying a full cargo of delicious Grog ColaTM, sails West West East from Jamaica at 32 kilometers per hectare, with a drag coefficient rate of some very large or possibly very small number. Is the Dutch East Indies a real pl... ...... Indies, and are ....y the Dutch?

#17. What's the difference between a Skipper, a Scupper, a Scooper, and a Skuttler? Show your work.

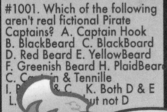

66. Draw the Spanish Armada. Points will be deducted for inaccuracy.

#101. Who played the Pirate King in the first production of the Pirates of Penzance?
A. Federici   B. Sir Brocolini
C. Leicester Tunks

Hmm... I dunno. I better just choose the person with the funniest name. Gee, this is gonna be hard.

#313. What kind of treasure is best? A. Gold   B. Spices C. Doubloons D. Triploons E. Fine Silks

What? They don't tell you how much of each... there's no exchange rate. It's almost as if they want us to fail...

#1001. Which of the following aren't real fictional Pirate Captains? A. Captain Hook B. BlackBeard C. BlackBoard D. Red Beard E. YellowBeard F. Greenish Beard H. PlaidBeard C. Ca...in & Tennille I. B... & C   K. Both D & E L. ....ut not D

Why am I doing this? I went to Harvard for crying out loud.

Essay Question: Who is the best actor to ever play a pirate? Obviously, this is an opinion, so you'll have to guess the opinion of whoever's grading your test.

ZzzZz

#1 (cont.) I mean, is it the Dutch East Indies or Dutch West Indies, or British East West Indies, or what? I mean, this isn't a trick question, but we are trying to confuse you. Is it working?
GRR!

Alrighty then. You'll have your results in 4-6 weeks.

Does that mean we get rid of you for 4-6 weeks?

No, I've got abunch more nitpicking to do. While we wait.

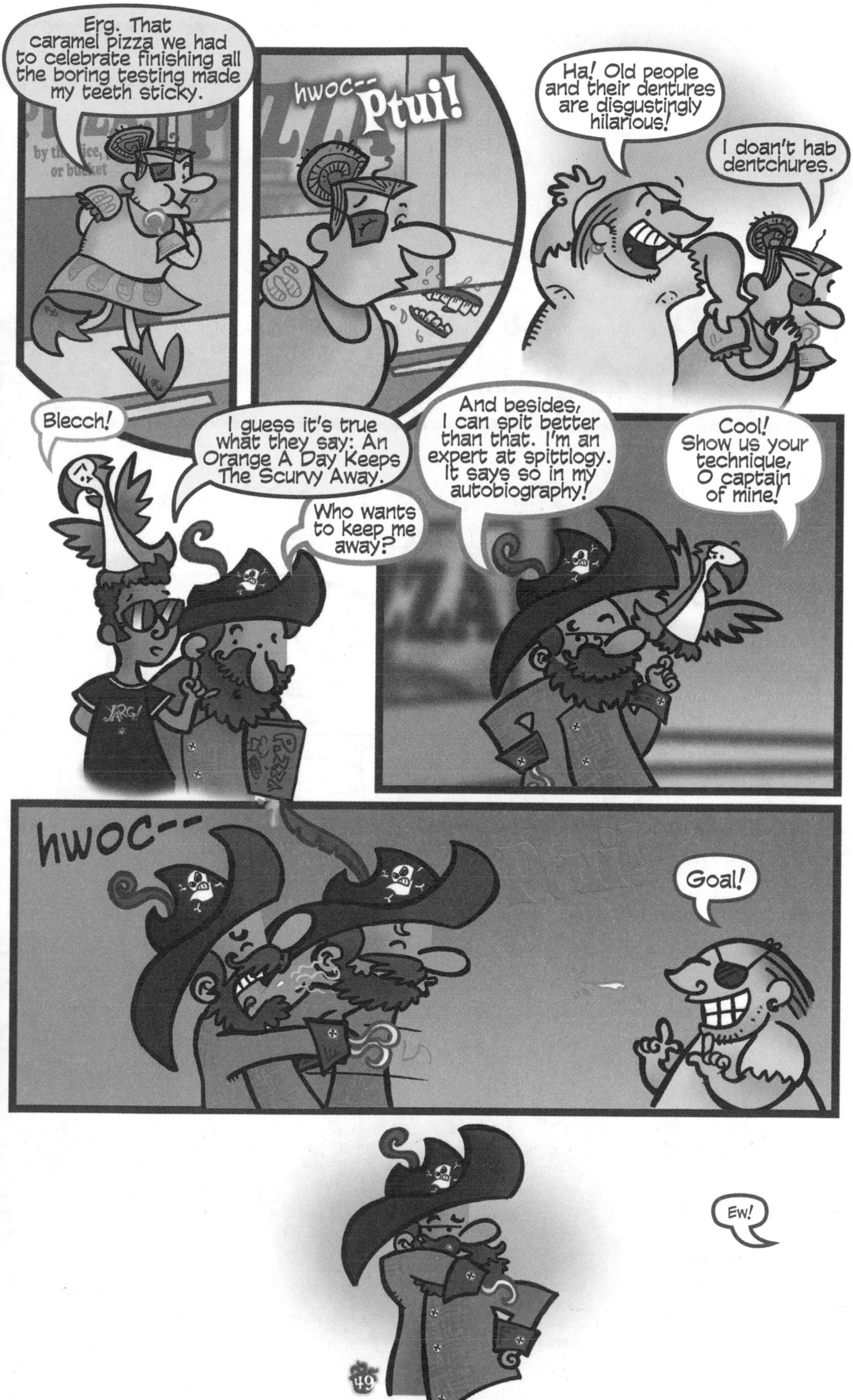
Erg. That caramel pizza we had to celebrate finishing all the boring testing made my teeth sticky.
hwoc-- Ptui!
Ha! Old people and their dentures are disgustingly hilarious!
I doan't hab dentchures.
Blecch!
I guess it's true what they say: An Orange A Day Keeps The Scurvy Away.
Who wants to keep me away?
YARG!
And besides, I can spit better than that. I'm an expert at spittlogy. It says so in my autobiography!
Cool! Show us your technique, O captain of mine!
hwoc--
Ptui!
Goal!
Ew!

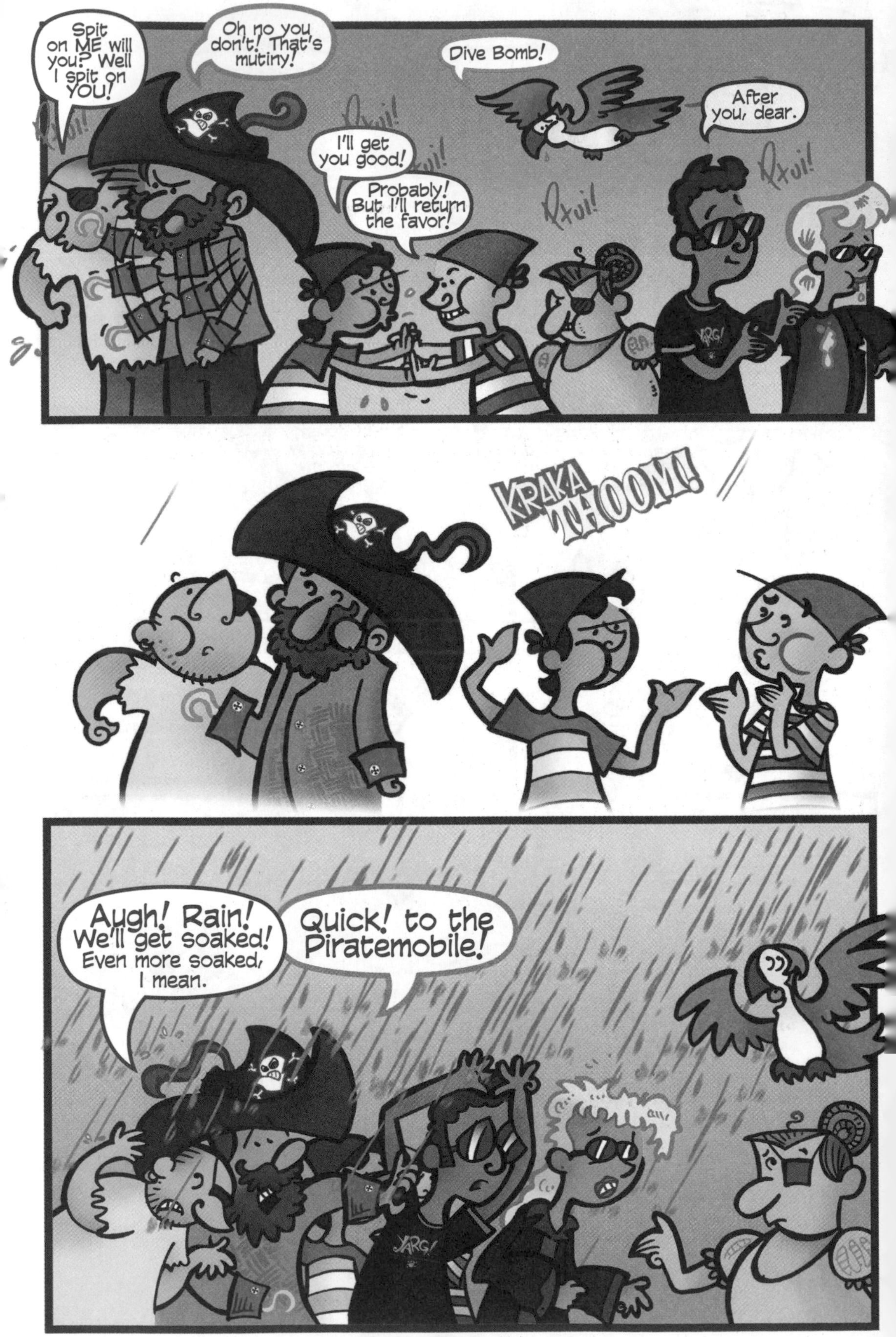
Spit on ME will you? Well I spit on YOU!
Ptui!
Oh no you don't! That's mutiny!
Ptui!
I'll get you good!
Ptui!
Probably! But I'll return the favor!
Dive Bomb!
Ptui!
After you, dear.
Ptui!
YARG!
KRAKA THOOM!
Augh! Rain! We'll get soaked! Even more soaked, I mean.
Quick! to the Piratemobile!
YARG!

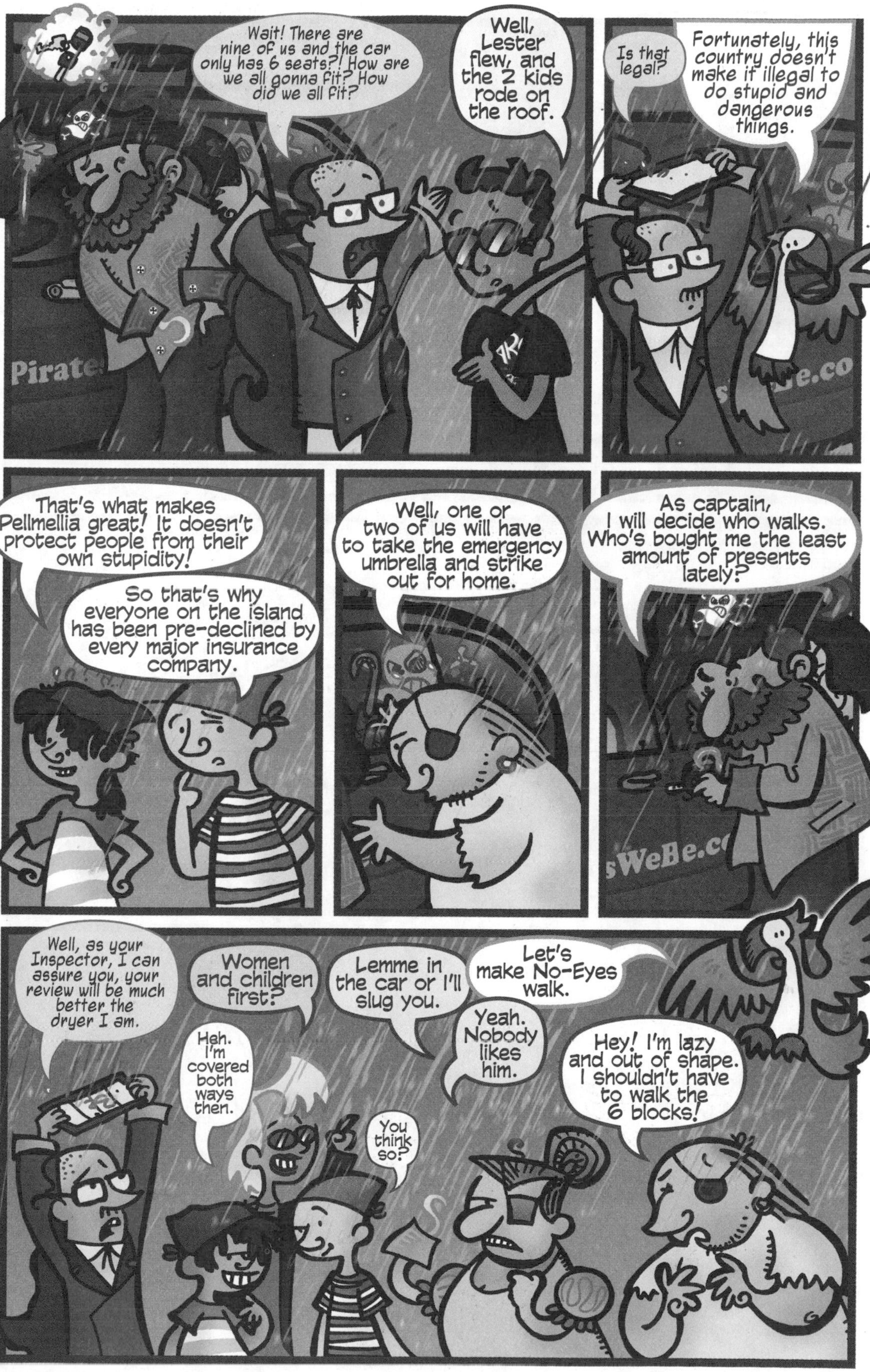

Wait! There are nine of us and the car only has 6 seats?! How are we all gonna fit? How did we all fit?
Well, Lester flew, and the 2 kids rode on the roof.
Is that legal?
Fortunately, this country doesn't make it illegal to do stupid and dangerous things.
Pirate
sWeBe.co
That's what makes Pellmellia great! It doesn't protect people from their own stupidity!
So that's why everyone on the island has been pre-declined by every major insurance company.
Well, one or two of us will have to take the emergency umbrella and strike out for home.
As captain, I will decide who walks. Who's bought me the least amount of presents lately?
sWeBe.co
Well, as your Inspector, I can assure you, your review will be much better the dryer I am.
Women and children first?
Lemme in the car or I'll slug you.
Let's make No-Eyes walk.
Heh. I'm covered both ways then.
Yeah. Nobody likes him.
Hey! I'm lazy and out of shape. I shouldn't have to walk the 6 blocks!
You think so?

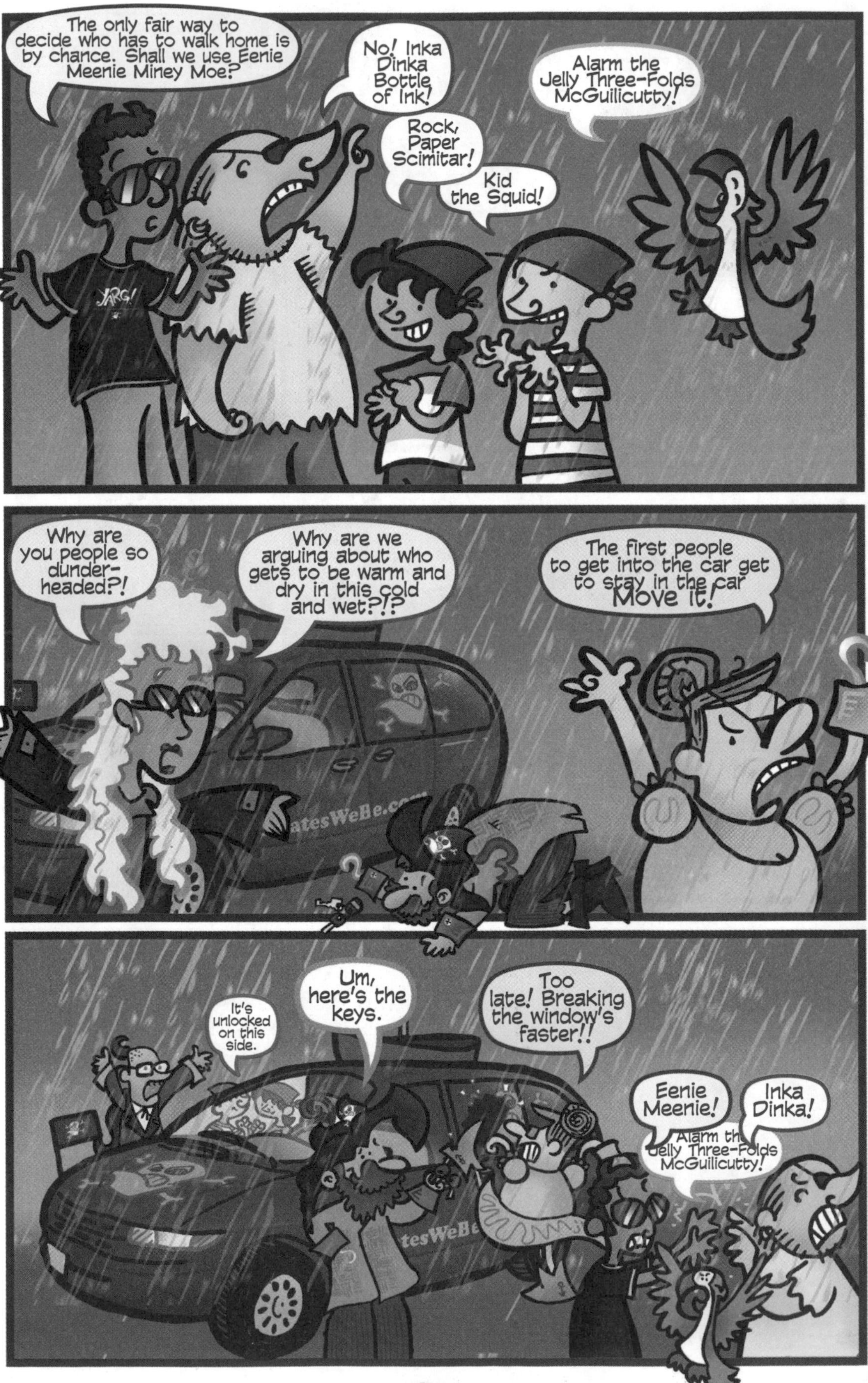
The only fair way to decide who has to walk home is by chance. Shall we use Eenie Meenie Miney Moe?
No! Inka Dinka Bottle of Ink!
Rock, Paper Scimitar!
Kid the Squid!
Alarm the Jelly Three-Folds McGuilicutty!
YARG!
Why are you people so dunder-headed?!
Why are we arguing about who gets to be warm and dry in this cold and wet?!?
The first people to get into the car get to stay in the car
Move it!
It's unlocked on this side.
Um, here's the keys.
Too late! Breaking the window's faster!!
Eenie Meenie!
Inka Dinka!
Alarm th
Jelly Three-Folds McGuilicutty!

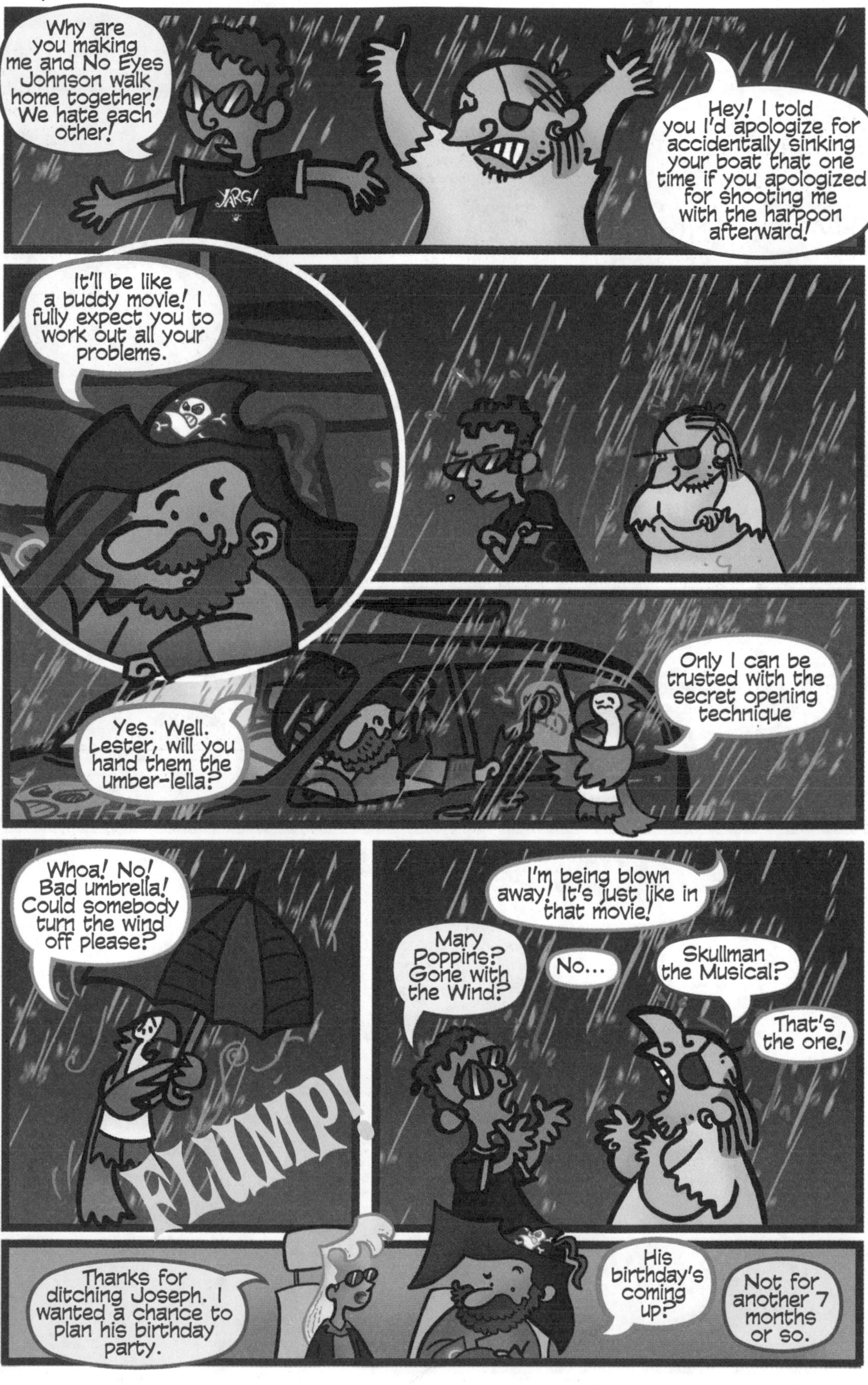
Why are you making me and No Eyes Johnson walk home together! We hate each other!
YARG!
Hey! I told you I'd apologize for accidentally sinking your boat that one time if you apologized for shooting me with the harpoon afterward!
It'll be like a buddy movie! I fully expect you to work out all your problems.
Yes. Well. Lester, will you hand them the umber-lella?
Only I can be trusted with the secret opening technique
Whoa! No! Bad umbrella! Could somebody turn the wind off please?
FLUMP!
I'm being blown away! It's just like in that movie!
Mary Poppins? Gone with the Wind?
No...
Skullman the Musical?
That's the one!
Thanks for ditching Joseph. I wanted a chance to plan his birthday party.
His birthday's coming up?
Not for another 7 months or so.

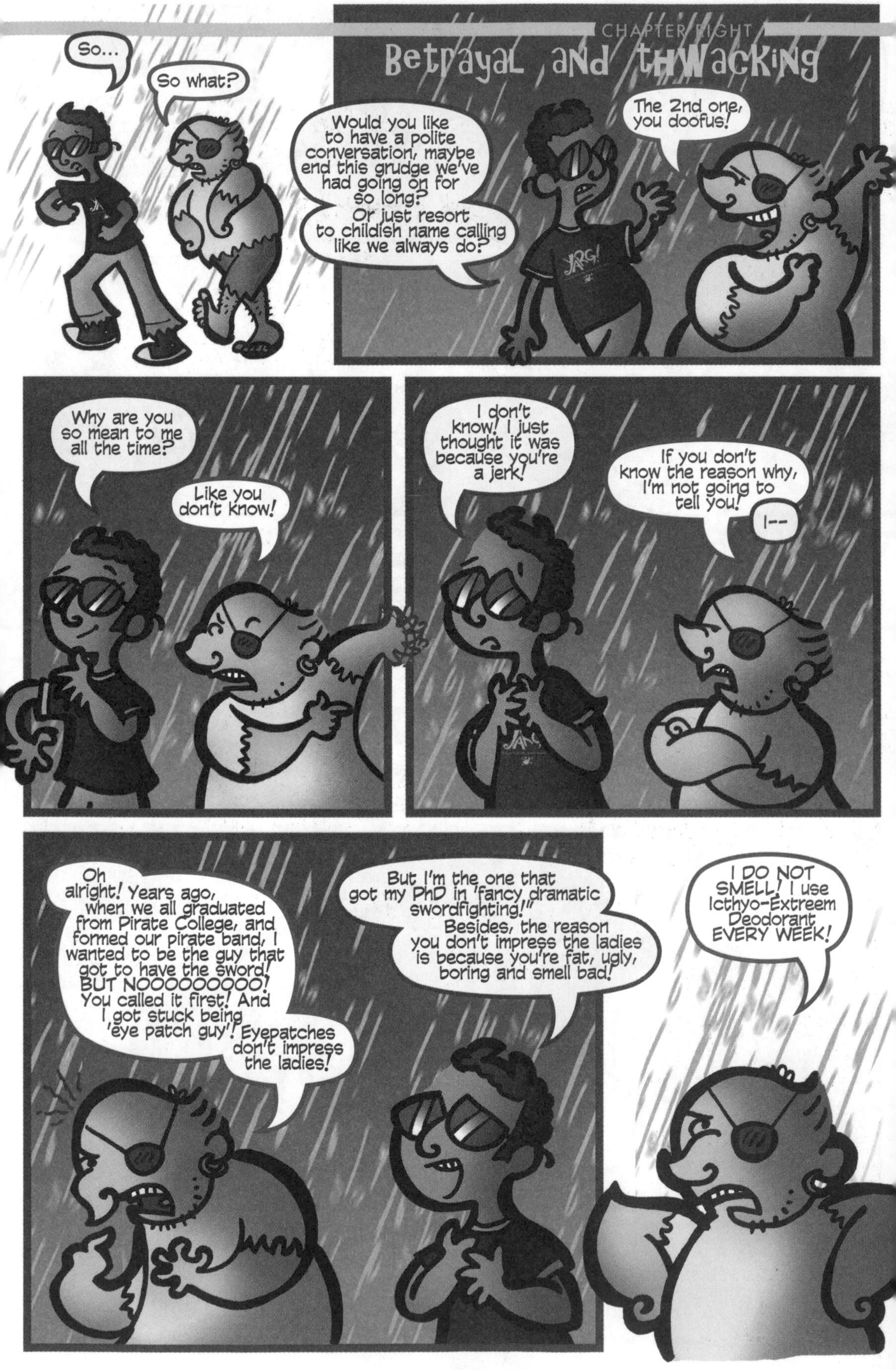
CHAPTER EIGHT
Betrayal and Thwacking
So...
So what?
Would you like to have a polite conversation, maybe end this grudge we've had going on for so long? Or just resort to childish name calling like we always do?
The 2nd one, you doofus!
Why are you so mean to me all the time?
Like you don't know!
I don't know! I just thought it was because you're a jerk!
If you don't know the reason why, I'm not going to tell you!
I--
Oh alright! Years ago, when we all graduated from Pirate College, and formed our pirate band, I wanted to be the guy that got to have the sword! BUT NOOOOOOOOO! You called it first! And I got stuck being 'eye patch guy'! Eyepatches don't impress the ladies!
But I'm the one that got my PhD in 'fancy dramatic swordfighting!" Besides, the reason you don't impress the ladies is because you're fat, ugly, boring and smell bad!
I DO NOT SMELL! I use Icthyo-Extreem Deodorant EVERY WEEK!

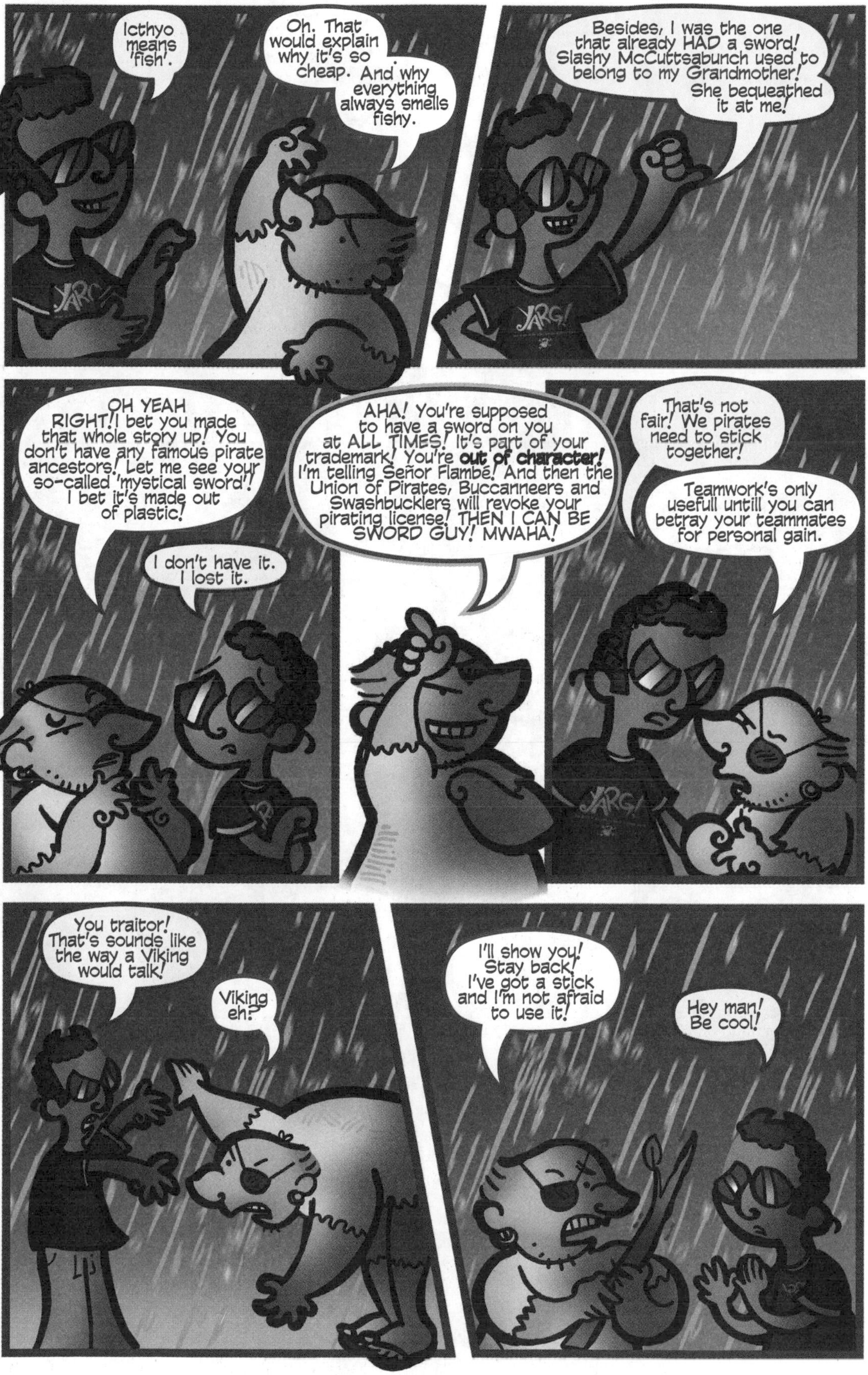
Icthyo means 'fish'.
Oh. That would explain why it's so cheap. And why everything always smells fishy.
Besides, I was the one that already HAD a sword! Slashy McCuttsabunch used to belong to my Grandmother!
She bequeathed it at me!
OH YEAH RIGHT! I bet you made that whole story up! You don't have any famous pirate ancestors! Let me see your so-called 'mystical sword'! I bet it's made out of plastic!
I don't have it. I lost it.
AHA! You're supposed to have a sword on you at ALL TIMES! It's part of your trademark! You're **out of character!** I'm telling Señor Flambé! And then the Union of Pirates, Buccanneers and Swashbucklers will revoke your pirating license! THEN I CAN BE SWORD GUY! MWAHA!
That's not fair! We pirates need to stick together!
Teamwork's only usefull untill you can betray your teammates for personal gain.
You traitor! That's sounds like the way a Viking would talk!
Viking eh?
I'll show you! Stay back! I've got a stick and I'm not afraid to use it!
Hey man! Be cool!

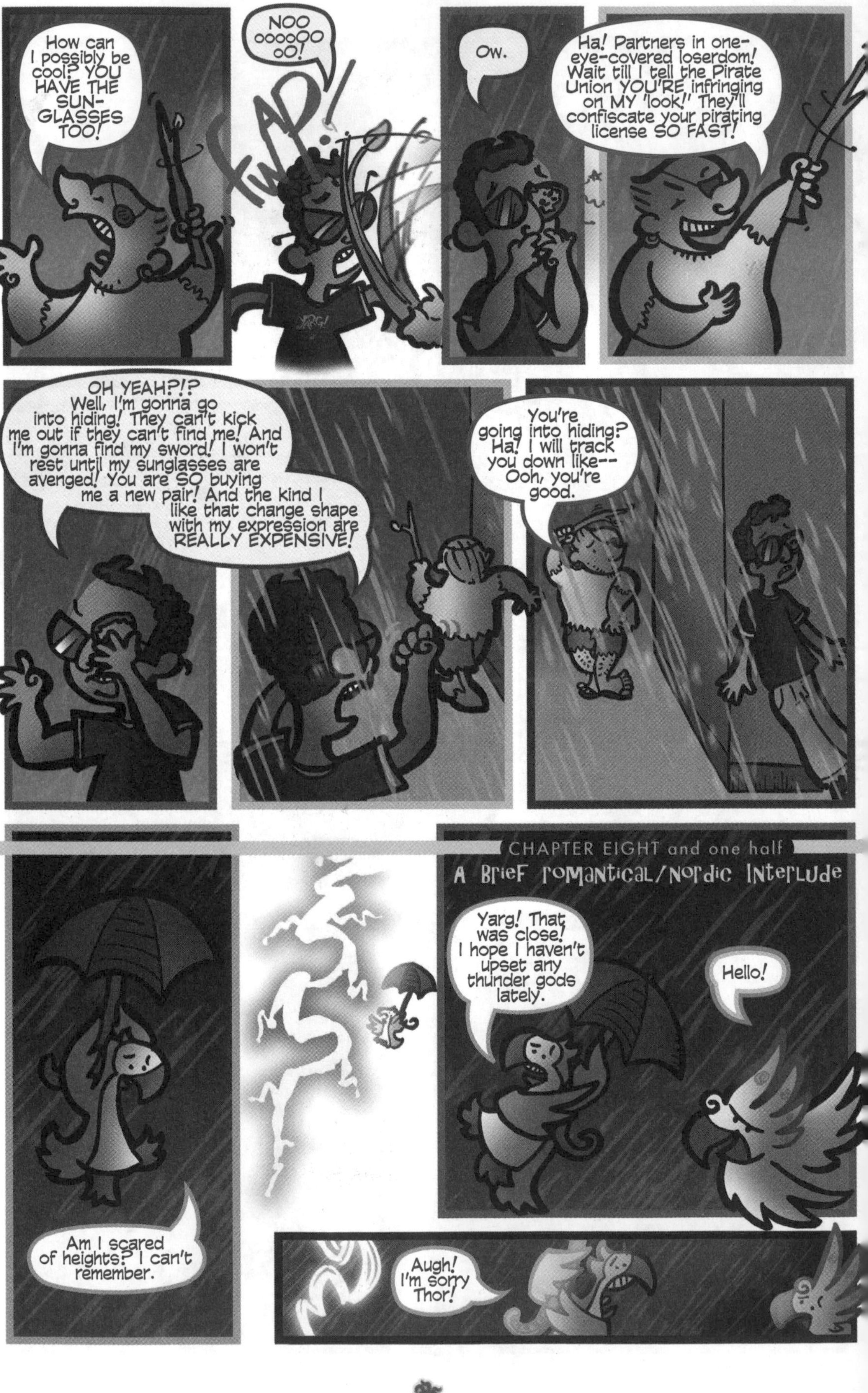
How can I possibly be cool? YOU HAVE THE SUN-GLASSES TOO!
NOOOOOOOOOO!
Ow.
Ha! Partners in one-eye-covered loserdom! Wait till I tell the Pirate Union YOU'RE infringing on MY 'look!' They'll confiscate your pirating license SO FAST!
OH YEAH?!? Well, I'm gonna go into hiding! They can't kick me out if they can't find me! And I'm gonna find my sword! I won't rest until my sunglasses are avenged! You are SO buying me a new pair! And the kind I like that change shape with my expression are REALLY EXPENSIVE!
You're going into hiding? Ha! I will track you down like-- Ooh, you're good.
Am I scared of heights? I can't remember.
CHAPTER EIGHT and one half
A Brief romantical/Nordic Interlude
Yarg! That was close! I hope I haven't upset any thunder gods lately.
Hello!
Augh! I'm sorry Thor!

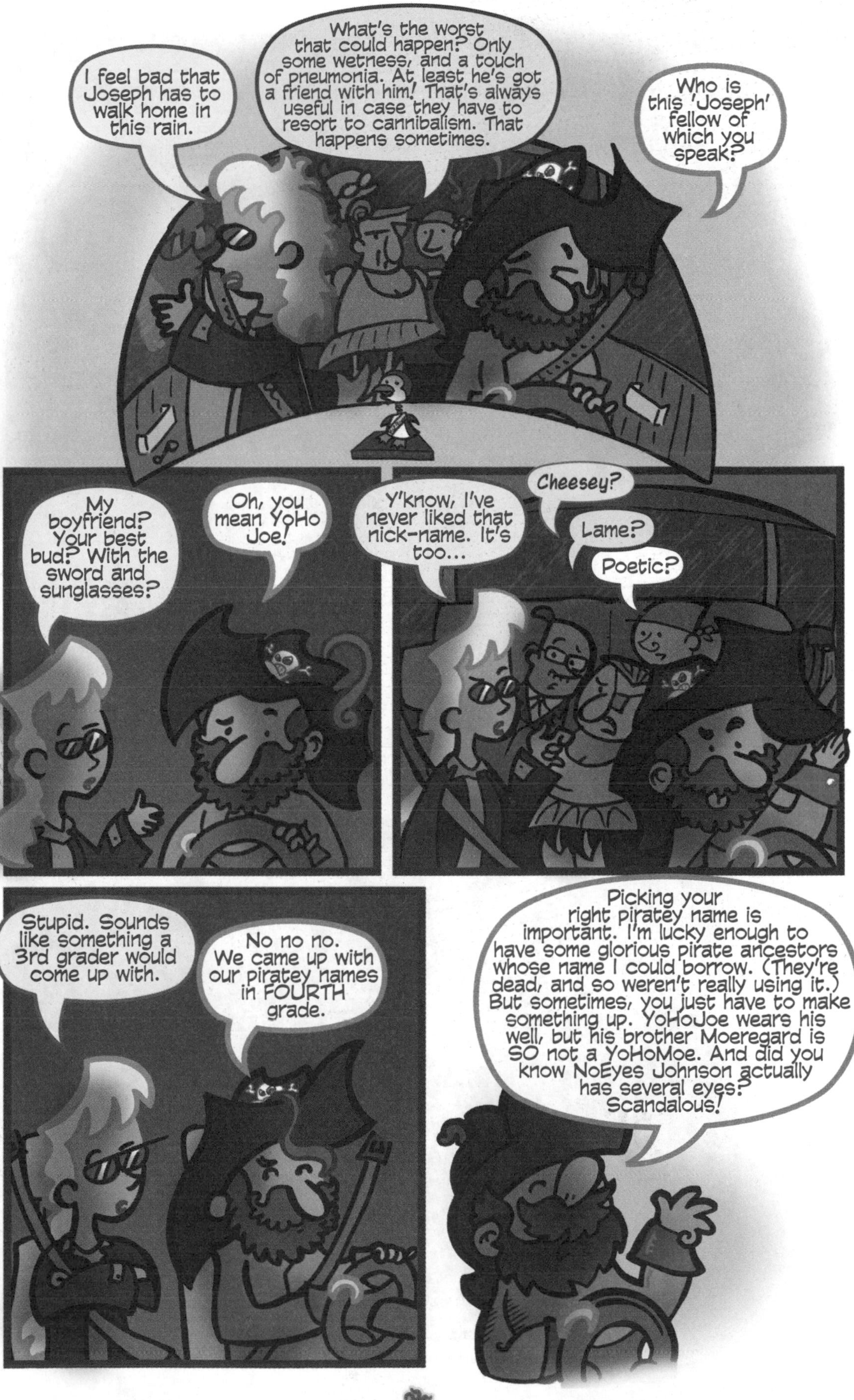
I feel bad that Joseph has to walk home in this rain.
What's the worst that could happen? Only some wetness, and a touch of pneumonia. At least he's got a friend with him! That's always useful in case they have to resort to cannibalism. That happens sometimes.
Who is this 'Joseph' fellow of which you speak?
My boyfriend? Your best bud? With the sword and sunglasses?
Oh, you mean YoHo Joe!
Y'know, I've never liked that nick-name. It's too...
Cheesey?
Lame?
Poetic?
Stupid. Sounds like something a 3rd grader would come up with.
No no no. We came up with our piratey names in FOURTH grade.
Picking your right piratey name is important. I'm lucky enough to have some glorious pirate ancestors whose name I could borrow. (They're dead, and so weren't really using it.) But sometimes, you just have to make something up. YoHoJoe wears his well, but his brother Moeregard is SO not a YoHoMoe. And did you know NoEyes Johnson actually has several eyes? Scandalous!

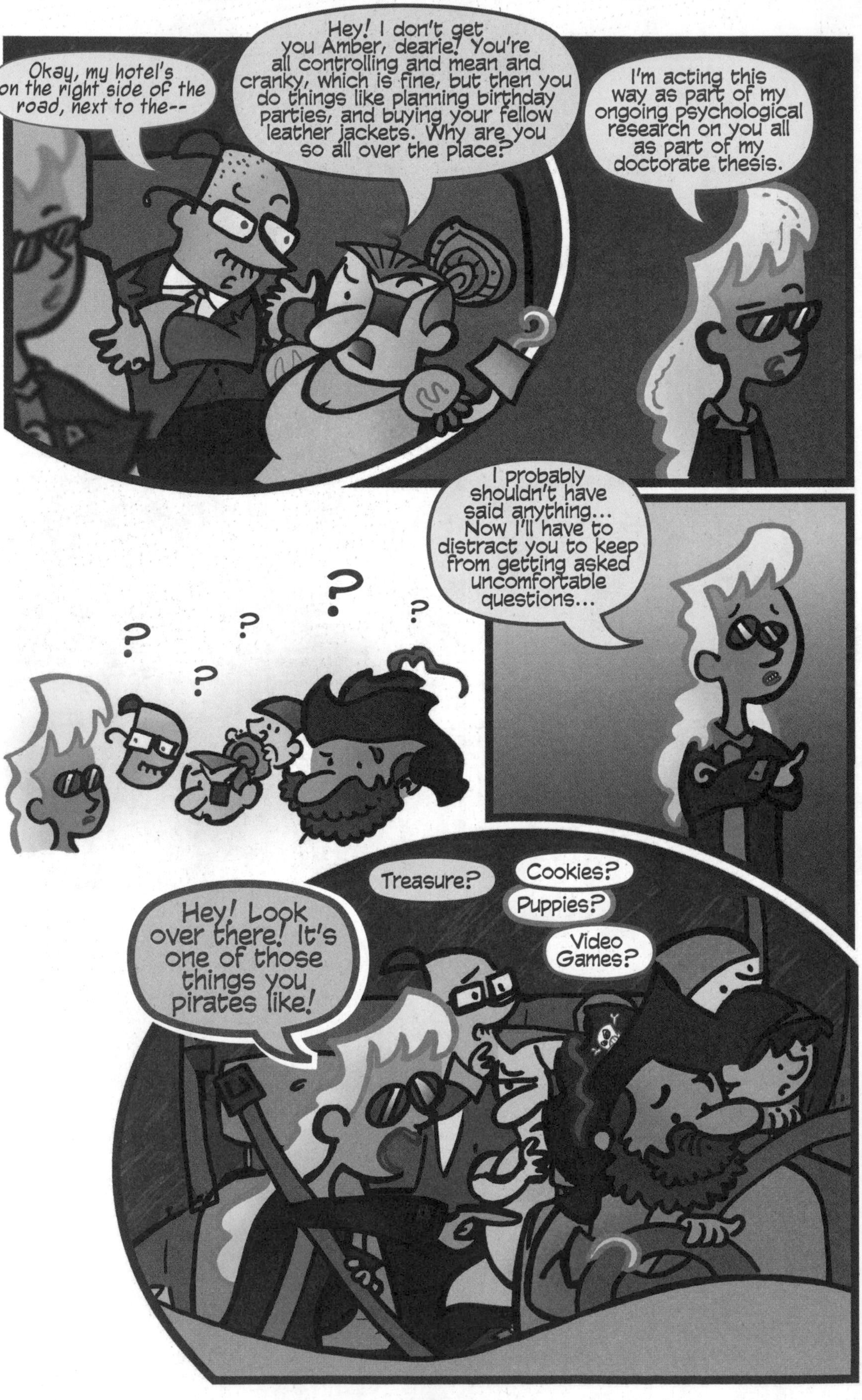
Okay, my hotel's on the right side of the road, next to the--
Hey! I don't get you Amber, dearie! You're all controlling and mean and cranky, which is fine, but then you do things like planning birthday parties, and buying your fellow leather jackets. Why are you so all over the place?
I'm acting this way as part of my ongoing psychological research on you all as part of my doctorate thesis.
I probably shouldn't have said anything... Now I'll have to distract you to keep from getting asked uncomfortable questions...
?
?
?
?
?
Hey! Look over there! It's one of those things you pirates like!
Treasure?
Cookies?
Puppies?
Video Games?

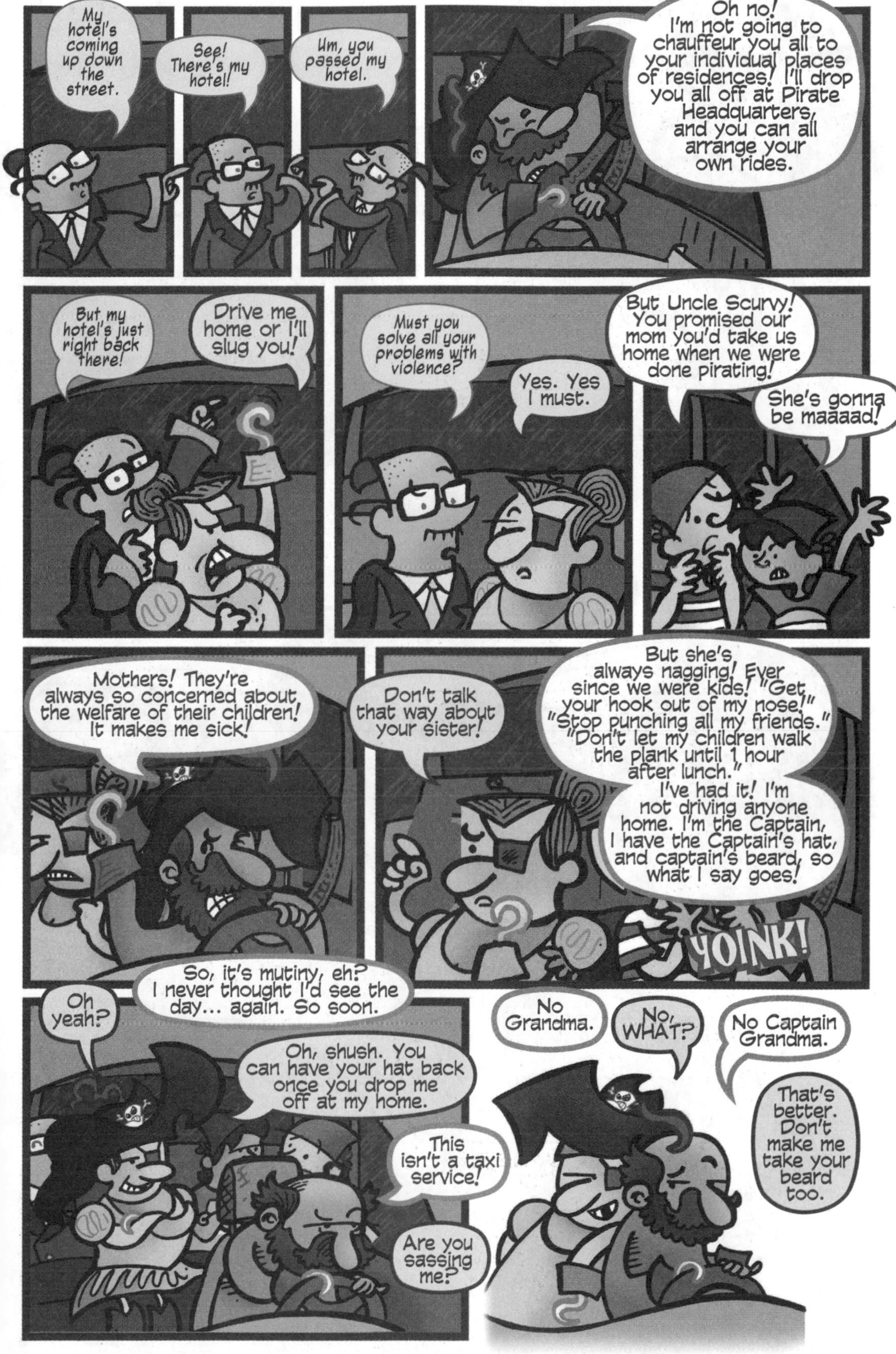
My hotel's coming up down the street.
See! There's my hotel!
Um, you passed my hotel.
Oh no! I'm not going to chauffeur you all to your individual places of residences! I'll drop you all off at Pirate Headquarters, and you can all arrange your own rides.
But my hotel's just right back there!
Drive me home or I'll slug you!
Must you solve all your problems with violence?
Yes. Yes I must.
But Uncle Scurvy! You promised our mom you'd take us home when we were done pirating!
She's gonna be maaaad!
Mothers! They're always so concerned about the welfare of their children! It makes me sick!
Don't talk that way about your sister!
But she's always nagging! Ever since we were kids! "Get your hook out of my nose!" "Stop punching all my friends." "Don't let my children walk the plank until 1 hour after lunch."
I've had it! I'm not driving anyone home. I'm the Captain, I have the Captain's hat, and captain's beard, so what I say goes!
YOINK!
Oh yeah?
So, it's mutiny, eh? I never thought I'd see the day... again. So soon.
Oh, shush. You can have your hat back once you drop me off at my home.
This isn't a taxi service!
Are you sassing me?
No Grandma.
No, WHAT?
No Captain Grandma.
That's better. Don't make me take your beard too.

CHAPTER NINE

MisUnderReMeMbered

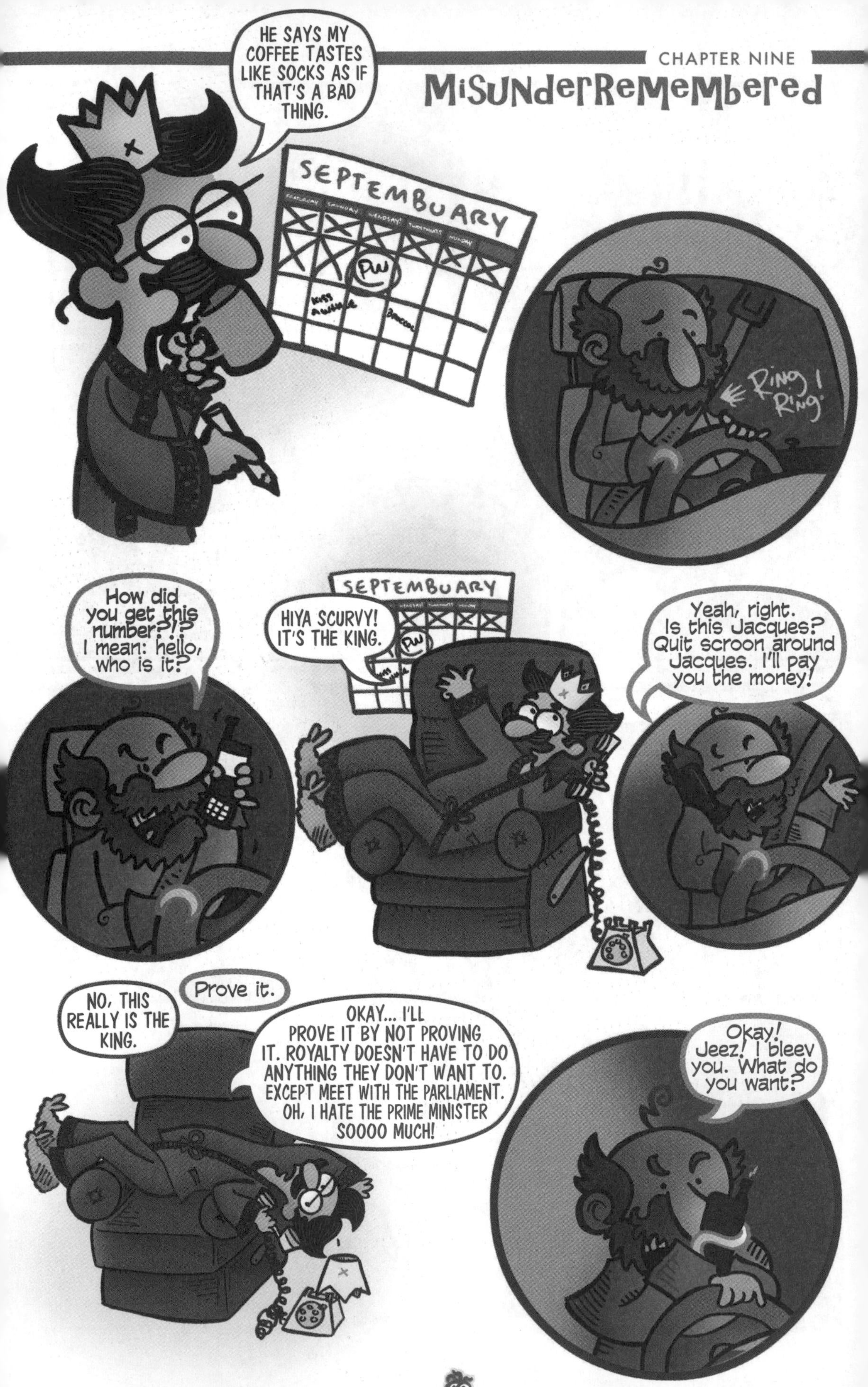
HE SAYS MY COFFEE TASTES LIKE SOCKS AS IF THAT'S A BAD THING.
SEPTEMBUARY
PW
Ring! Ring!
How did you get this number?!? I mean: hello, who is it?
HIYA SCURVY! IT'S THE KING.
Yeah, right. Is this Jacques? Quit scroon around Jacques. I'll pay you the money!
NO, THIS REALLY IS THE KING.
Prove it.
OKAY... I'LL PROVE IT BY NOT PROVING IT. ROYALTY DOESN'T HAVE TO DO ANYTHING THEY DON'T WANT TO. EXCEPT MEET WITH THE PARLIAMENT. OH, I HATE THE PRIME MINISTER SOOOO MUCH!
Okay! Jeez! I bleev you. What do you want?

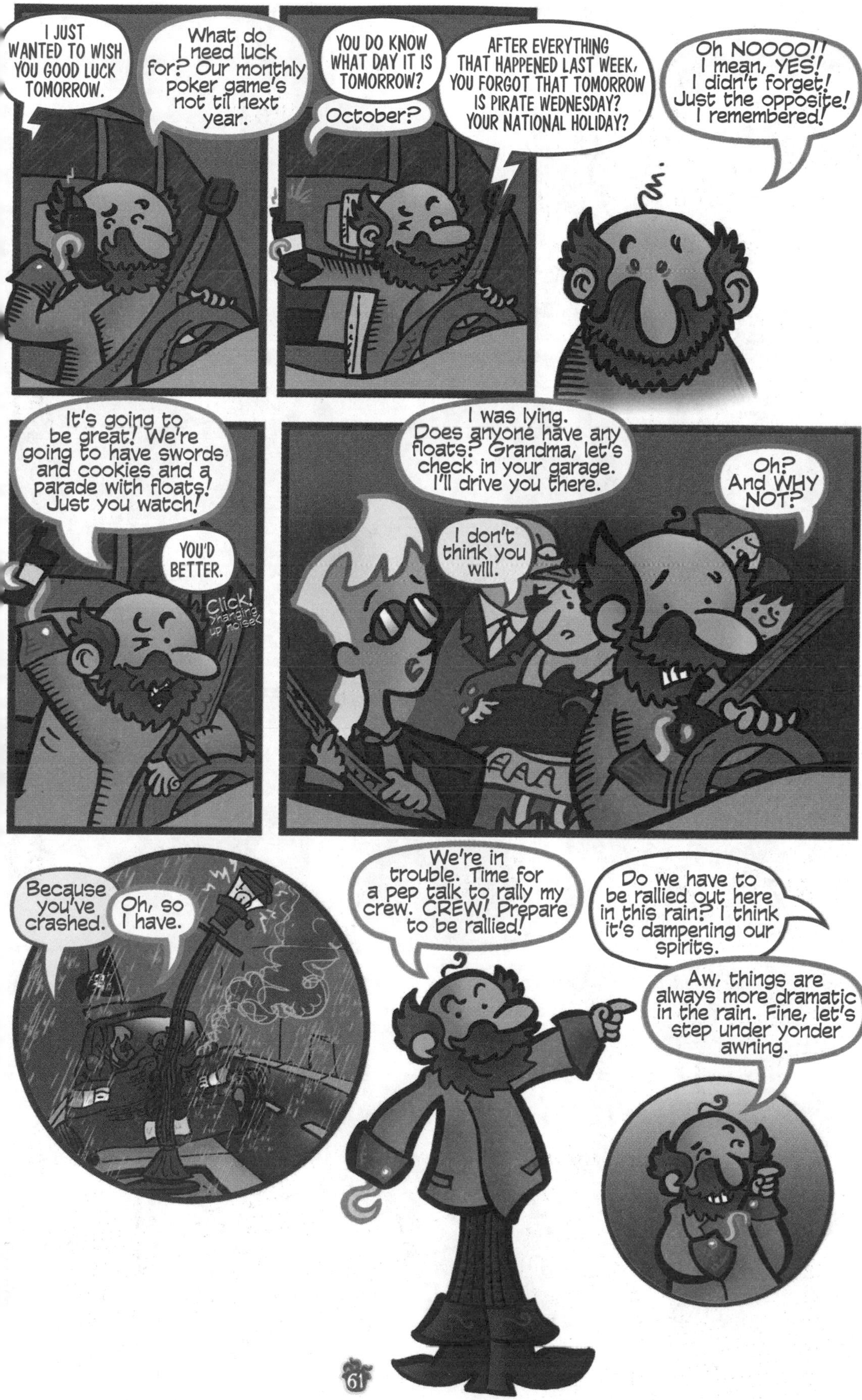
I JUST WANTED TO WISH YOU GOOD LUCK TOMORROW.
What do I need luck for? Our monthly poker game's not til next year.
YOU DO KNOW WHAT DAY IT IS TOMORROW?
October?
AFTER EVERYTHING THAT HAPPENED LAST WEEK, YOU FORGOT THAT TOMORROW IS PIRATE WEDNESDAY? YOUR NATIONAL HOLIDAY?
Oh NOOOO!! I mean, YES! I didn't forget! Just the opposite! I remembered!
It's going to be great! We're going to have swords and cookies and a parade with floats! Just you watch!
YOU'D BETTER.
Click! >hanging up noise<
I was lying. Does anyone have any floats? Grandma, let's check in your garage. I'll drive you there.
I don't think you will.
Oh? And WHY NOT?
Because you've crashed.
Oh, so I have.
We're in trouble. Time for a pep talk to rally my crew. CREW! Prepare to be rallied!
Do we have to be rallied out here in this rain? I think it's dampening our spirits.
Aw, things are always more dramatic in the rain. Fine, let's step under yonder awning.

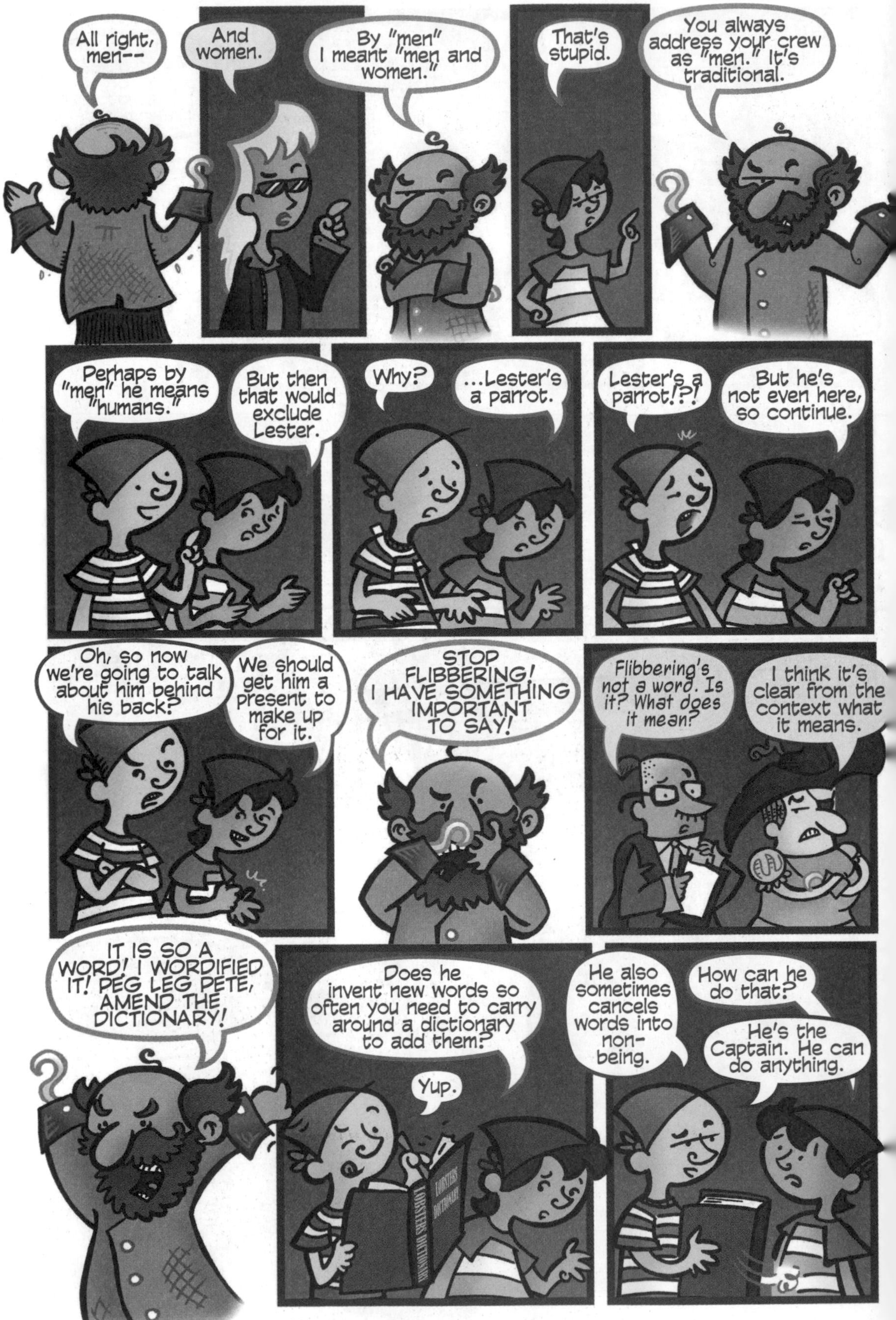
All right, men--
And women.
By "men" I meant "men and women."
That's stupid.
You always address your crew as "men." It's traditional.
Perhaps by "men" he means "humans."
But then that would exclude Lester.
Why?
...Lester's a parrot.
Lester's a parrot!?!
But he's not even here, so continue.
Oh, so now we're going to talk about him behind his back?
We should get him a present to make up for it.
STOP FLIBBERING! I HAVE SOMETHING IMPORTANT TO SAY!
Flibbering's not a word. Is it? What does it mean?
I think it's clear from the context what it means.
IT IS SO A WORD! I WORDIFIED IT! PEG LEG PETE, AMEND THE DICTIONARY!
Does he invent new words so often you need to carry around a dictionary to add them?
Yup.
He also sometimes cancels words into non-being.
How can he do that?
He's the Captain. He can do anything.

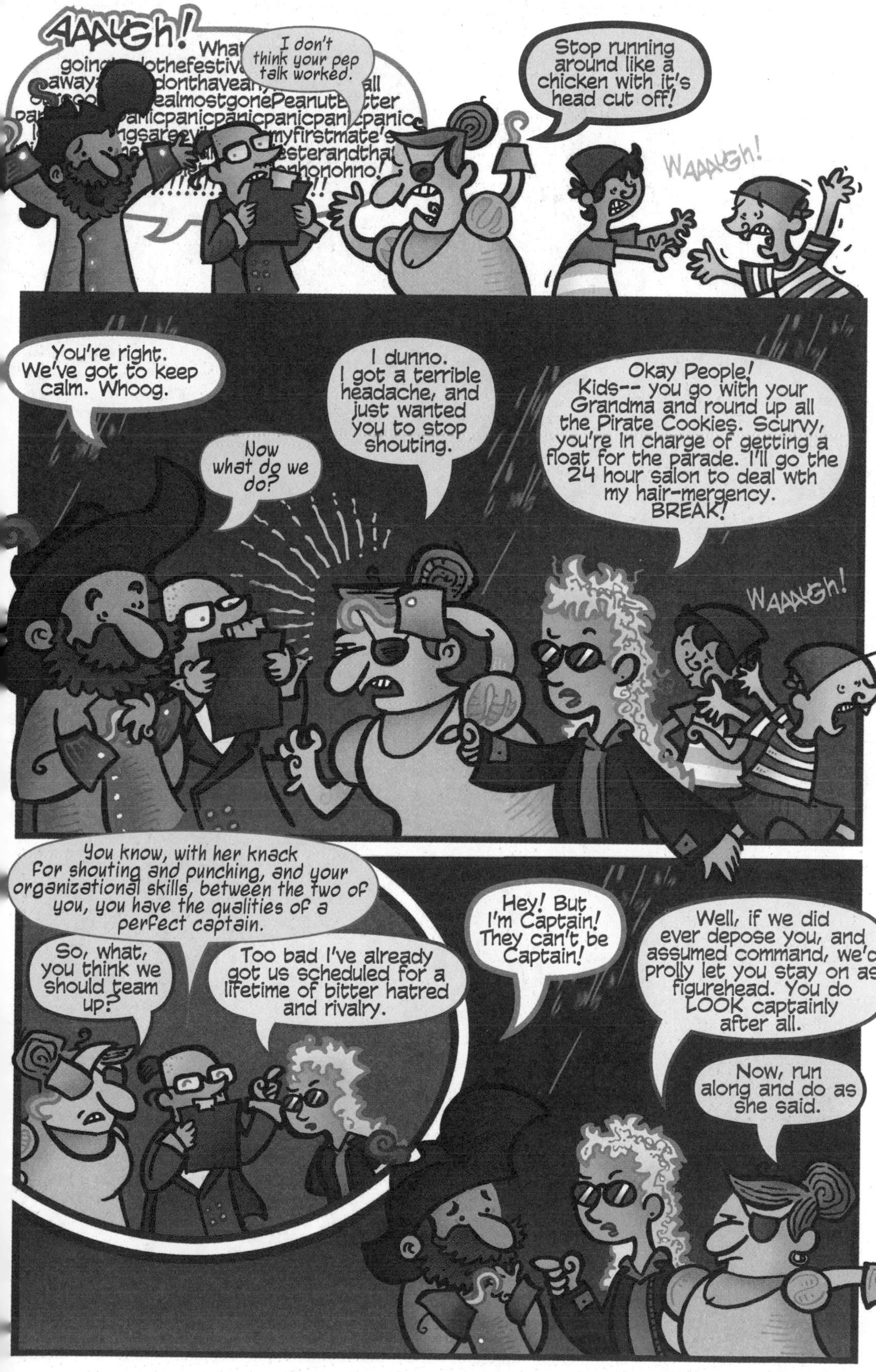
AAAUGh!
I don't think your pep talk worked.
Stop running around like a chicken with it's head cut off!
WAAAUGh!
You're right. We've got to keep calm. Whoog.
Now what do we do?
I dunno. I got a terrible headache, and just wanted you to stop shouting.
Okay People! Kids-- you go with your Grandma and round up all the Pirate Cookies. Scurvy, you're in charge of getting a float for the parade. I'll go the 24 hour salon to deal wth my hair-mergency. BREAK!
WAAAUGh!
You know, with her knack for shouting and punching, and your organizational skills, between the two of you, you have the qualities of a perfect captain.
So, what, you think we should team up?
Too bad I've already got us scheduled for a lifetime of bitter hatred and rivalry.
Hey! But I'm Captain! They can't be Captain!
Well, if we did ever depose you, and assumed command, we'd prolly let you stay on as figurehead. You do LOOK captainly after all.
Now, run along and do as she said.

Attack of the Things

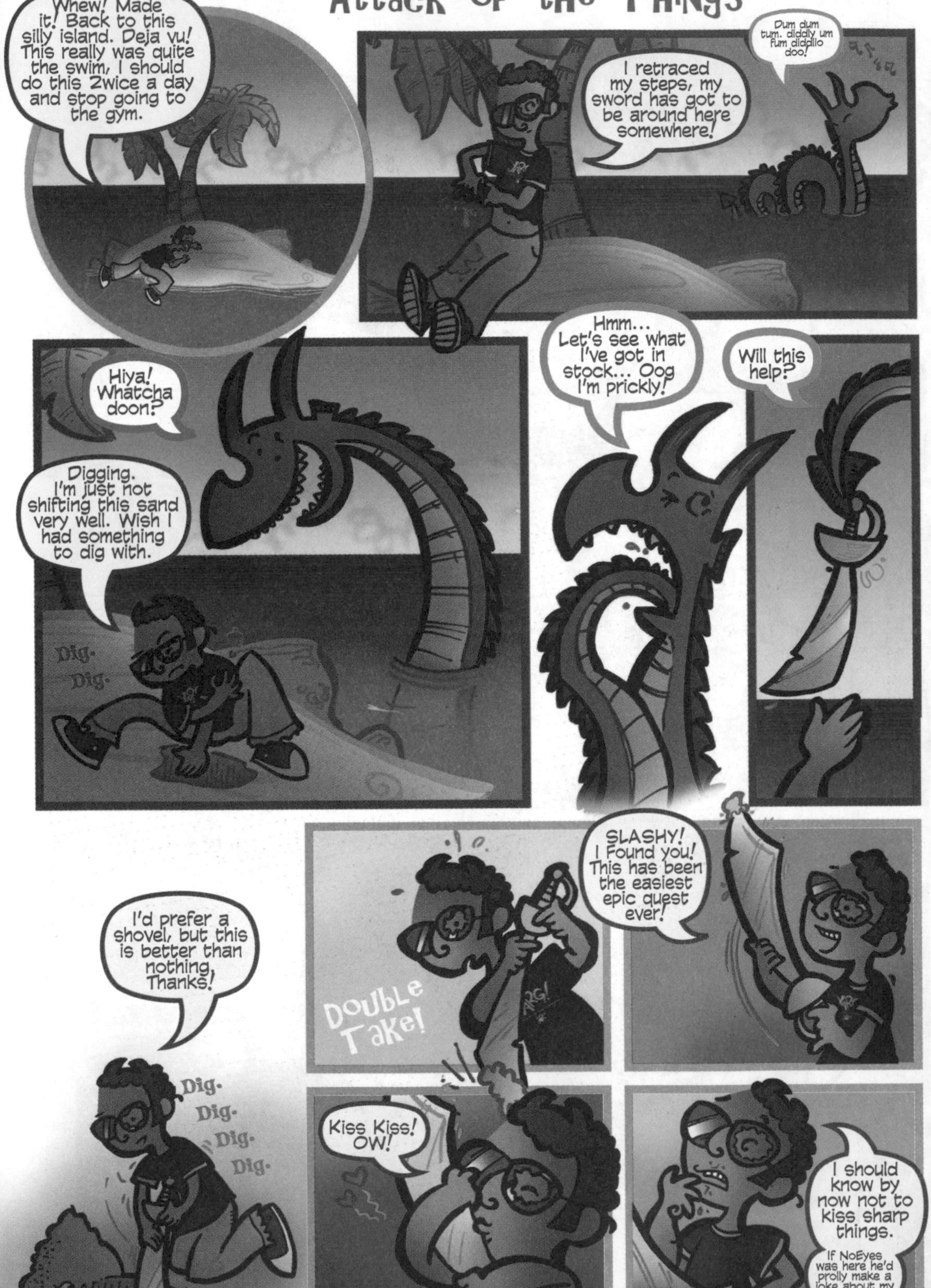
Whew! Made it! Back to this silly island. Deja vu! This really was quite the swim, I should do this 2wice a day and stop going to the gym.
I retraced my steps, my sword has got to be around here somewhere!
Dum dum tum. diddly um fum diddlio doo!
Hiya! Whatcha doon?
Digging. I'm just not shifting this sand very well. Wish I had something to dig with.
Dig. Dig.
Hmm... Let's see what I've got in stock... Oog I'm prickly!
Will this help?
I'd prefer a shovel, but this is better than nothing. Thanks!
Dig. Dig. Dig. Dig.
Clunk
DOUBLE TAKE!
SLASHY! I Found you! This has been the easiest epic quest ever!
Kiss Kiss! OW!
I should know by now not to kiss sharp things.
If NoEyes was here he'd prolly make a joke about my girlfriend.

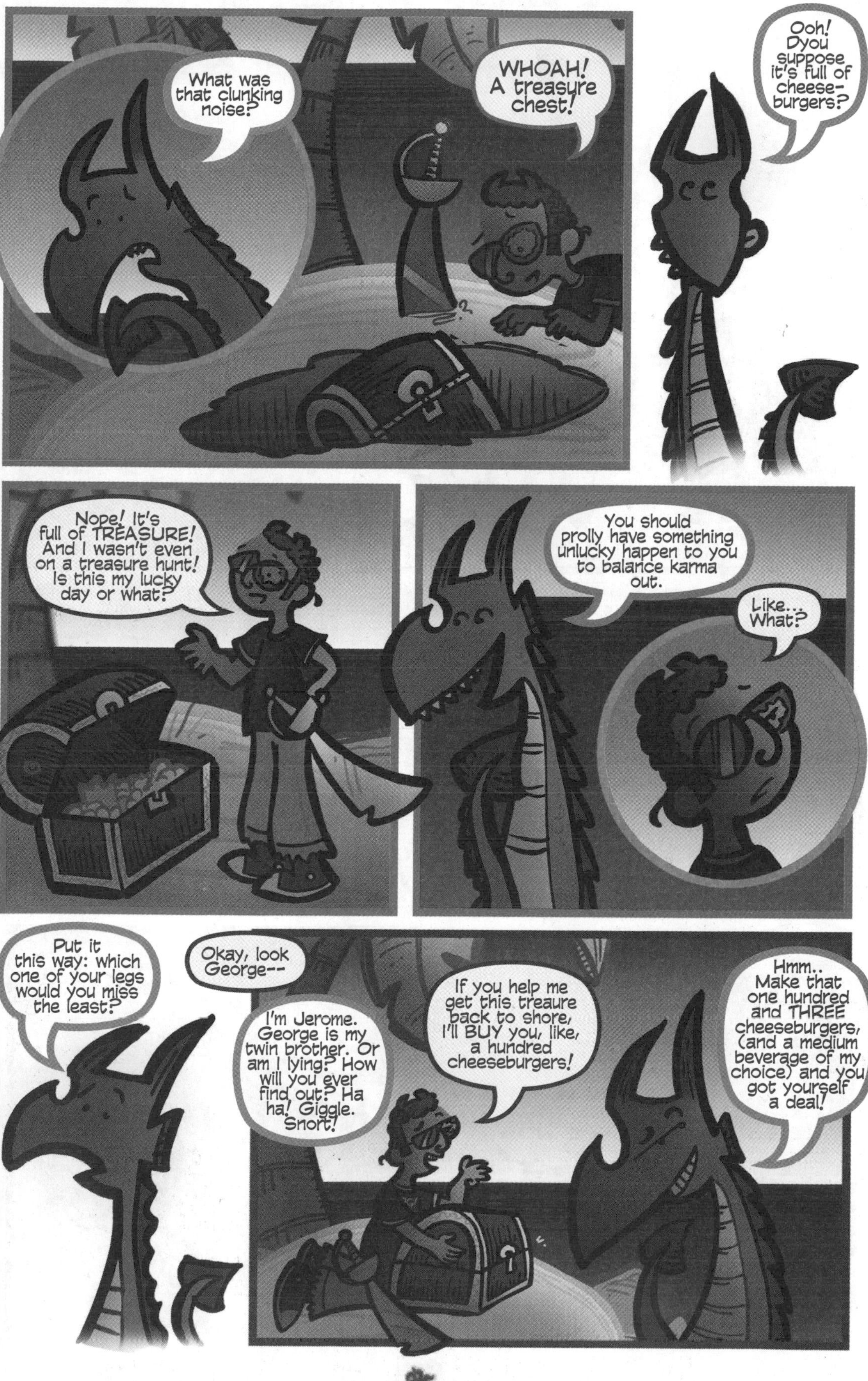
What was that clunking noise?
WHOAH! A treasure chest!
Ooh! Dyou suppose it's full of cheese-burgers?
Nope! It's full of TREASURE! And I wasn't even on a treasure hunt! Is this my lucky day or what?
You should prolly have something unlucky happen to you to balance karma out.
Like... What?
Put it this way: which one of your legs would you miss the least?
Okay, look George--
I'm Jerome. George is my twin brother. Or am I lying? How will you ever find out? Ha ha! Giggle. Snort!
If you help me get this treaure back to shore, I'll BUY you, like, a hundred cheeseburgers!
Hmm.. Make that one hundred and THREE cheeseburgers, (and a medium beverage of my choice) and you got yourself a deal!

CHAPTER ELEVEN

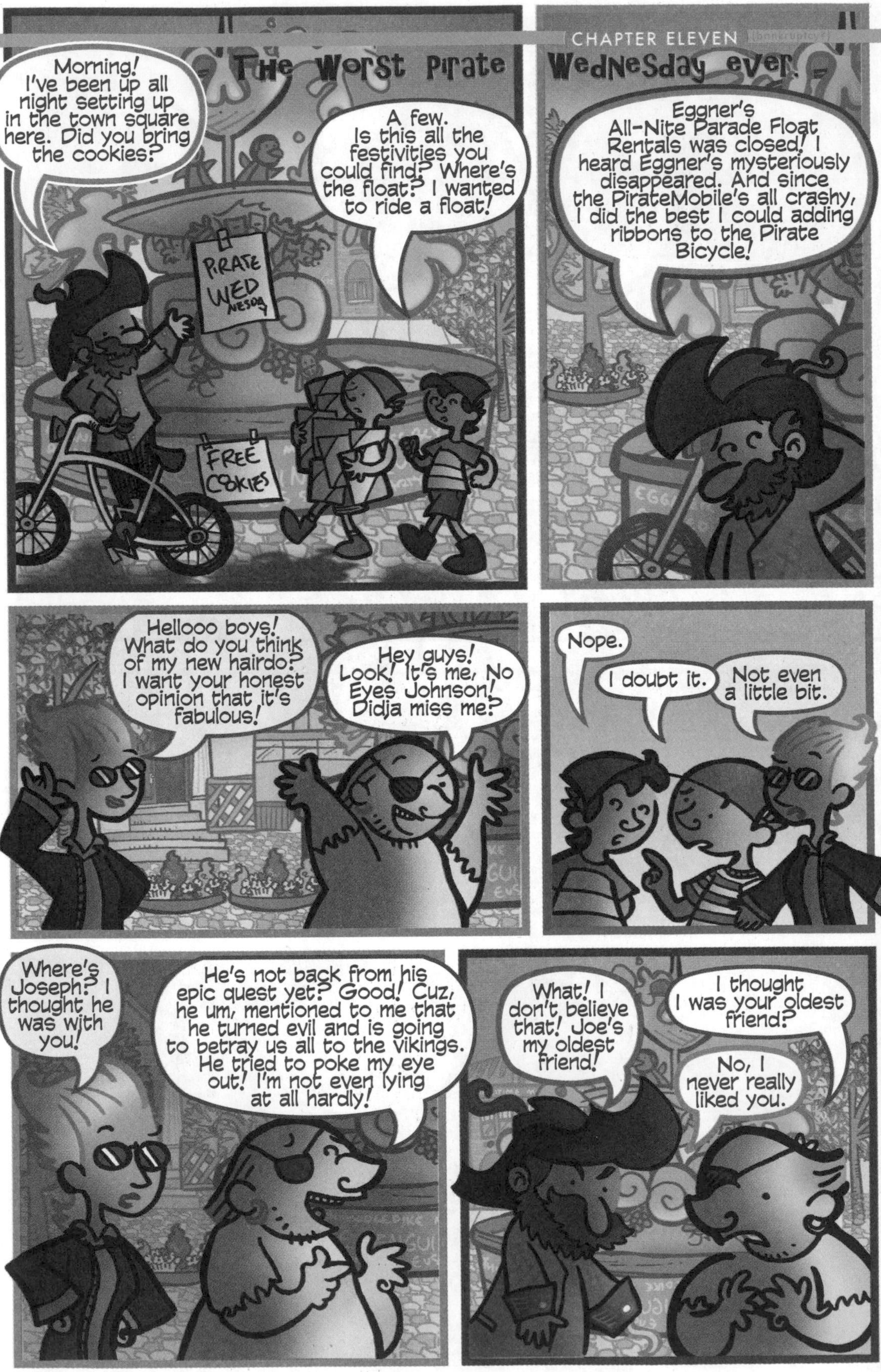
The Worst Pirate Wednesday ever!
Morning! I've been up all night setting up in the town square here. Did you bring the cookies?
PIRATE WEDNESDAY
FREE COOKIES
A few. Is this all the festivities you could find? Where's the float? I wanted to ride a float!
Eggner's All-Nite Parade Float Rentals was closed! I heard Eggner's mysteriously disappeared. And since the PirateMobile's all crashy, I did the best I could adding ribbons to the Pirate Bicycle!
Hellooo boys! What do you think of my new hairdo? I want your honest opinion that it's fabulous!
Hey guys! Look! It's me, No Eyes Johnson! Didja miss me?
Nope.
I doubt it.
Not even a little bit.
Where's Joseph? I thought he was with you!
He's not back from his epic quest yet? Good! Cuz, he um, mentioned to me that he turned evil and is going to betray us all to the vikings. He tried to poke my eye out! I'm not even lying at all hardly!
What! I don't believe that! Joe's my oldest friend!
I thought I was your oldest friend?
No, I never really liked you.

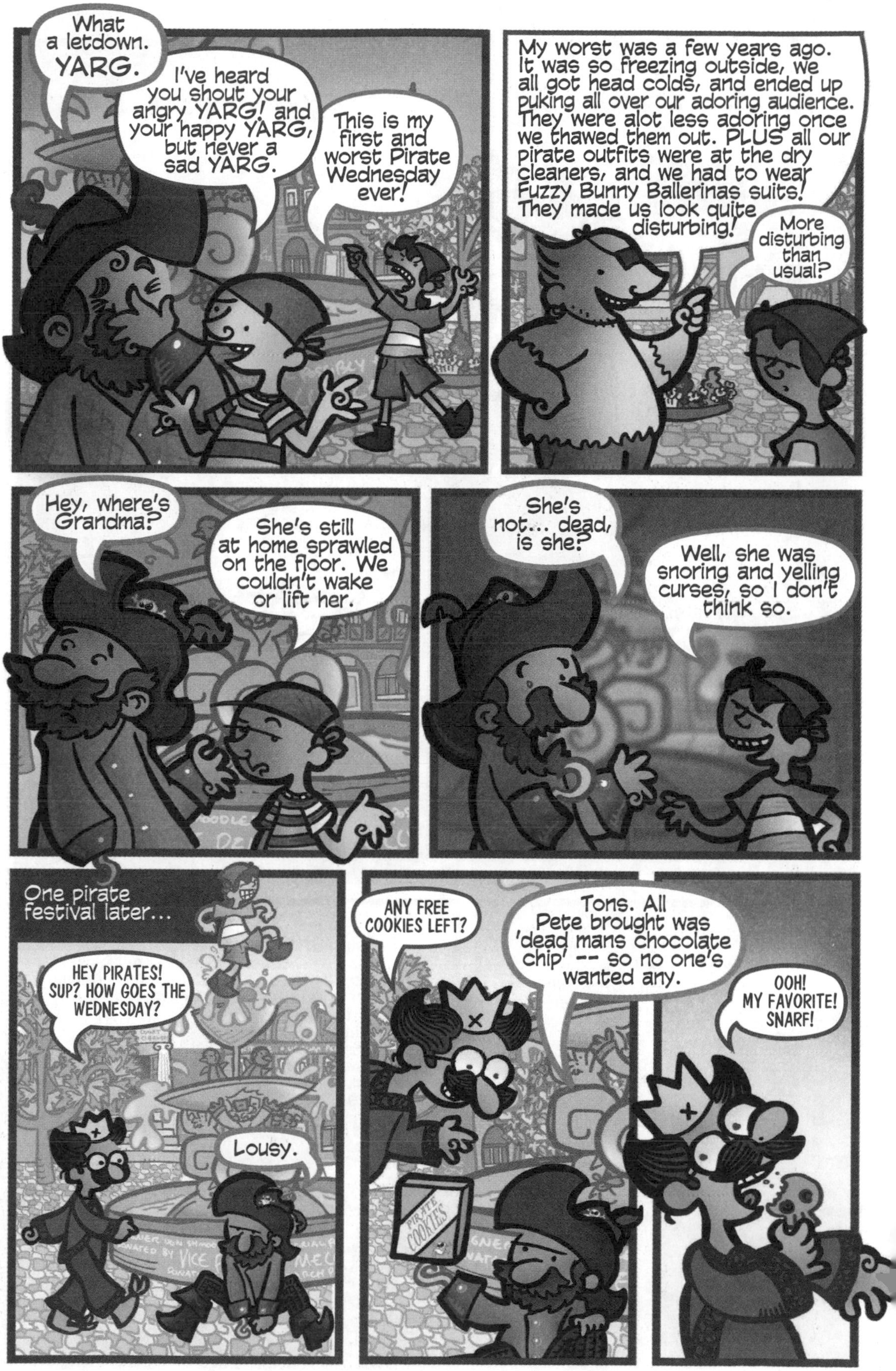
What a letdown. YARG.
I've heard you shout your angry YARG! and your happy YARG, but never a sad YARG.
This is my first and worst Pirate Wednesday ever!
My worst was a few years ago. It was so freezing outside, we all got head colds, and ended up puking all over our adoring audience. They were alot less adoring once we thawed them out. PLUS all our pirate outfits were at the dry cleaners, and we had to wear Fuzzy Bunny Ballerinas suits! They made us look quite disturbing!
More disturbing than usual?
Hey, where's Grandma?
She's still at home sprawled on the floor. We couldn't wake or lift her.
She's not... dead, is she?
Well, she was snoring and yelling curses, so I don't think so.
One pirate festival later...
HEY PIRATES! SUP? HOW GOES THE WEDNESDAY?
Lousy.
ANY FREE COOKIES LEFT?
Tons. All Pete brought was 'dead mans chocolate chip' -- so no one's wanted any.
PIRATE COOKIES
OOH! MY FAVORITE! SNARF!

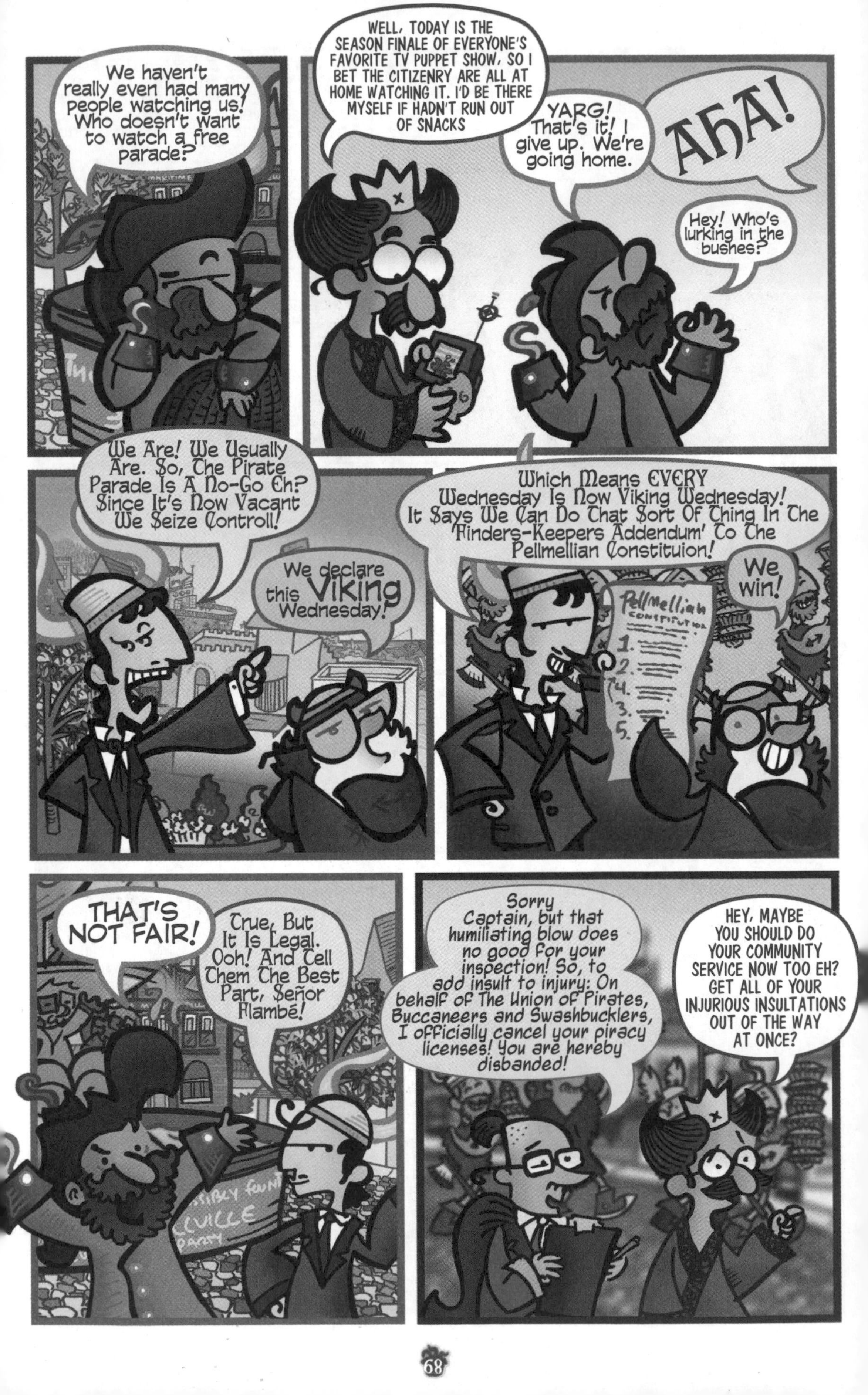
We haven't really even had many people watching us! Who doesn't want to watch a free parade?
WELL, TODAY IS THE SEASON FINALE OF EVERYONE'S FAVORITE TV PUPPET SHOW, SO I BET THE CITIZENRY ARE ALL AT HOME WATCHING IT. I'D BE THERE MYSELF IF HADN'T RUN OUT OF SNACKS
YARG! That's it! I give up. We're going home.
AHA!
Hey! Who's lurking in the bushes?
We Are! We Usually Are. So, The Pirate Parade Is A No-Go Eh? Since It's Now Vacant We Seize Controll!
We declare this Viking Wednesday!
Which Means EVERY Wednesday Is Now Viking Wednesday! It Says We Can Do That Sort Of Thing In The 'Finders-Keepers Addendum' To The Pellmellian Constituion!
We win!
Pellmellian Constitution
THAT'S NOT FAIR!
True, But It Is Legal. Ooh! And Tell Them The Best Part, Señor Flambé!
Sorry Captain, but that humiliating blow does no good for your inspection! So, to add insult to injury: On behalf of The Union of Pirates, Buccaneers and Swashbucklers, I officially cancel your piracy licenses! You are hereby disbanded!
HEY, MAYBE YOU SHOULD DO YOUR COMMUNITY SERVICE NOW TOO EH? GET ALL OF YOUR INJURIOUS INSULTATIONS OUT OF THE WAY AT ONCE?

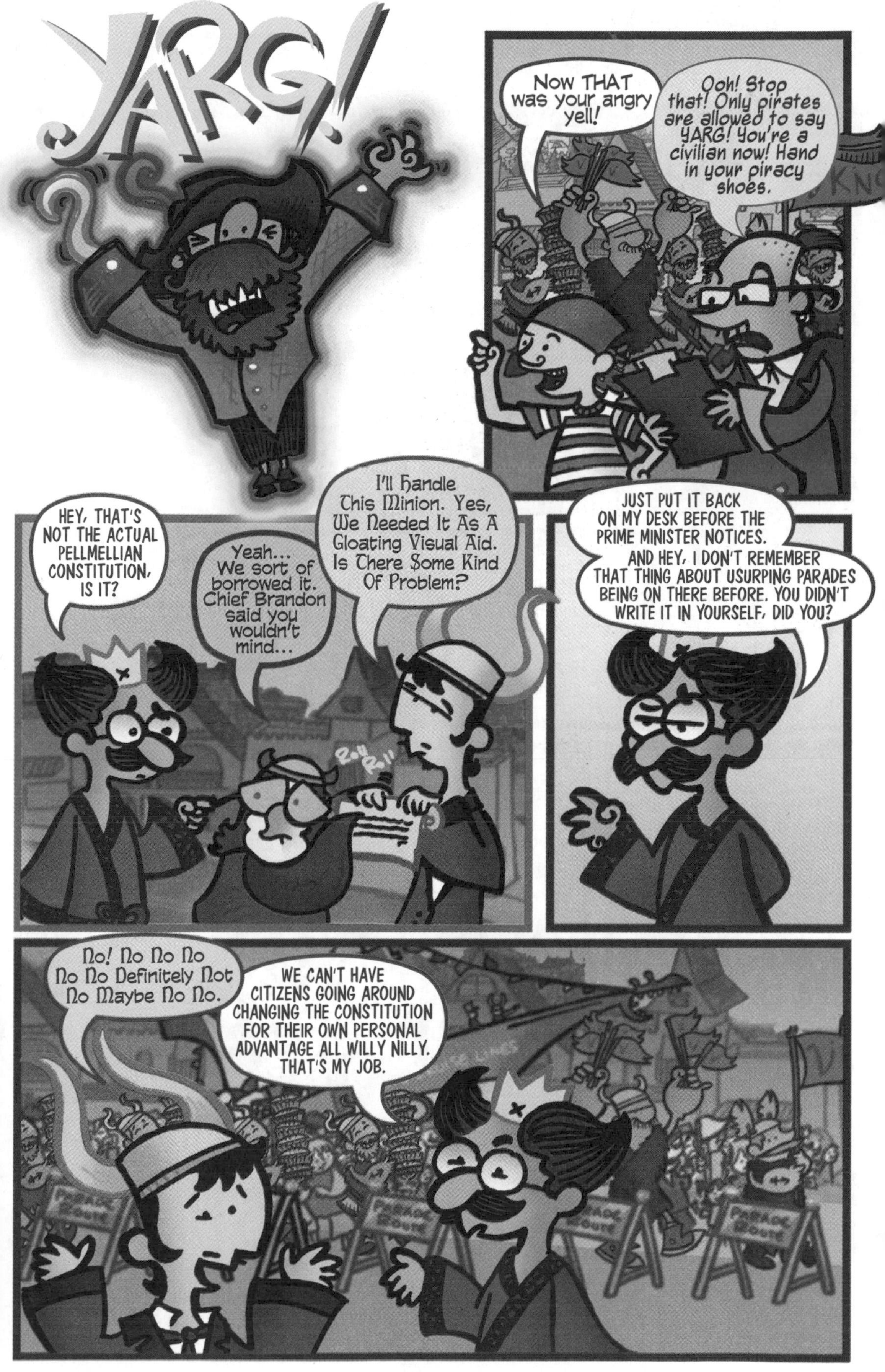
YARG!
Now THAT was your angry yell!
Ooh! Stop that! Only pirates are allowed to say YARG! You're a civilian now! Hand in your piracy shoes.
HEY, THAT'S NOT THE ACTUAL PELLMELLIAN CONSTITUTION, IS IT?
Yeah... We sort of borrowed it. Chief Brandon said you wouldn't mind...
I'll Handle This Minion. Yes, We Needed It As A Gloating Visual Aid. Is There Some Kind Of Problem?
JUST PUT IT BACK ON MY DESK BEFORE THE PRIME MINISTER NOTICES.
AND HEY, I DON'T REMEMBER THAT THING ABOUT USURPING PARADES BEING ON THERE BEFORE. YOU DIDN'T WRITE IT IN YOURSELF, DID YOU?
No! No No No No No Definitely Not No Maybe No No.
WE CAN'T HAVE CITIZENS GOING AROUND CHANGING THE CONSTITUTION FOR THEIR OWN PERSONAL ADVANTAGE ALL WILLY NILLY. THAT'S MY JOB.
PARADE ROUTE
PARADE ROUTE
PARADE ROUTE
PARADE ROUTE

CMON SCURV. I'LL GET YOU STARTED ON THAT COMMUNITY SERVICE. I GOTS JUST THE THING FOR YOU...

Goodbye all! I must find Joseph!

I'm leaving too. I know when I'm not wanted. lousy pirates. Grumble.

Now what do we do?

Hi guys! I'm back! And I'm front!

Lester! Where have you been? So much has happened!

Yeah yeah yeah. Your boring news later.

Guess what! I met someone! A girl someone! Allow me to introduce my brand new serious long-term sweety René!

Hiya!

She's just like me, only smarter and nicer and prettier!

Nice to meetcha!

Lester, we're in trouble! Señor Flambé disbanded us!

We're not allowed to be pirates anymore! Captain Scurvybeard's doing community service newhere're Wednes can the Viking ve ta everythin with usly ev Viking Pie.

Lester?

Smooch Smooch Clonk! Ow!

Ew! Gross!

Mmph. Stop. What was that about pie?

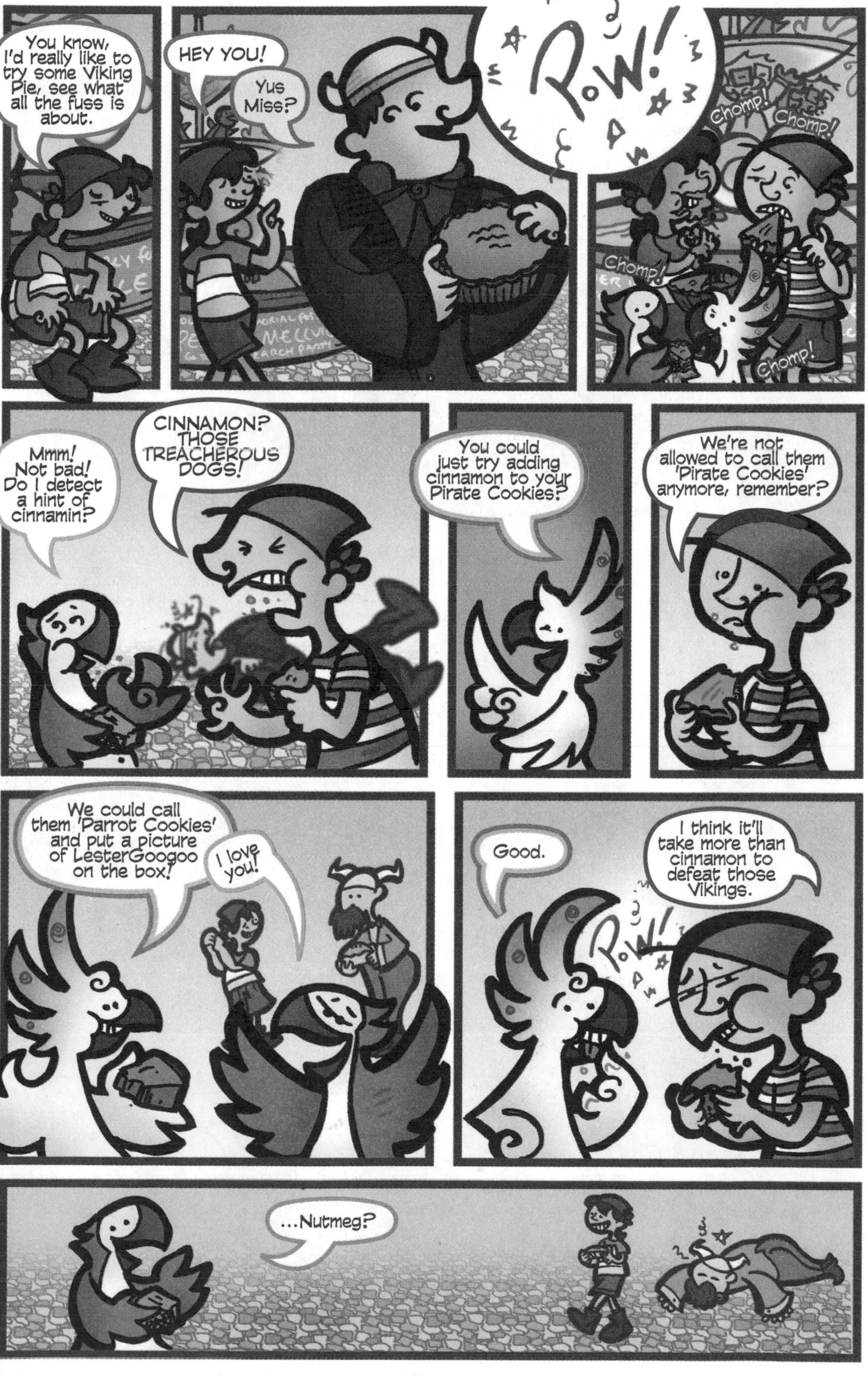
You know, I'd really like to try some Viking Pie, see what all the fuss is about.
HEY YOU!
Yus Miss?
PoW!
Chomp!
Chomp!
Chomp!
Chomp!
Mmm! Not bad! Do I detect a hint of cinnamin?
CINNAMON? THOSE TREACHEROUS DOGS!
You could just try adding cinnamon to your Pirate Cookies?
We're not allowed to call them 'Pirate Cookies' anymore, remember?
We could call them 'Parrot Cookies' and put a picture of LesterGoogoo on the box!
I love you!
Good.
I think it'll take more than cinnamon to defeat those Vikings.
PoW!
...Nutmeg?

CHAPTER TWELVE

The Cookbook of Destruction

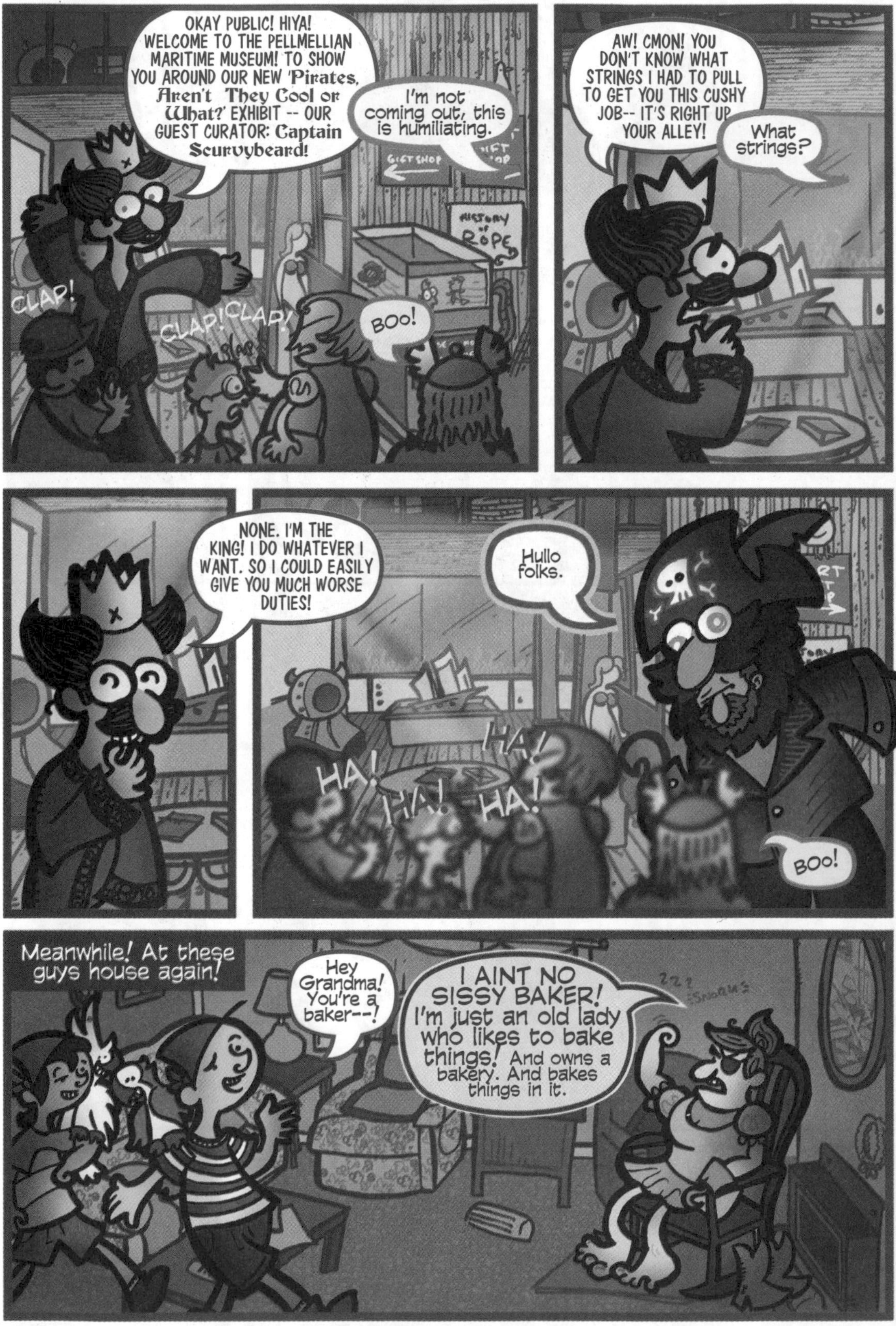
OKAY PUBLIC! HIYA! WELCOME TO THE PELLMELLIAN MARITIME MUSEUM! TO SHOW YOU AROUND OUR NEW 'Pirates, Aren't They Cool or What?' EXHIBIT -- OUR GUEST CURATOR: Captain Scurvybeard!
I'm not coming out, this is humiliating.
GIFT SHOP
HISTORY of ROPE
CLAP!
CLAP! CLAP!
BOO!
AW! CMON! YOU DON'T KNOW WHAT STRINGS I HAD TO PULL TO GET YOU THIS CUSHY JOB-- IT'S RIGHT UP YOUR ALLEY!
What strings?
NONE. I'M THE KING! I DO WHATEVER I WANT. SO I COULD EASILY GIVE YOU MUCH WORSE DUTIES!
Hullo folks.
HA!
HA!
HA!
HA!
BOO!
Meanwhile! At these guys house again!
Hey Grandma! You're a baker--!
I AINT NO SISSY BAKER! I'm just an old lady who likes to bake things! And owns a bakery. And bakes things in it.

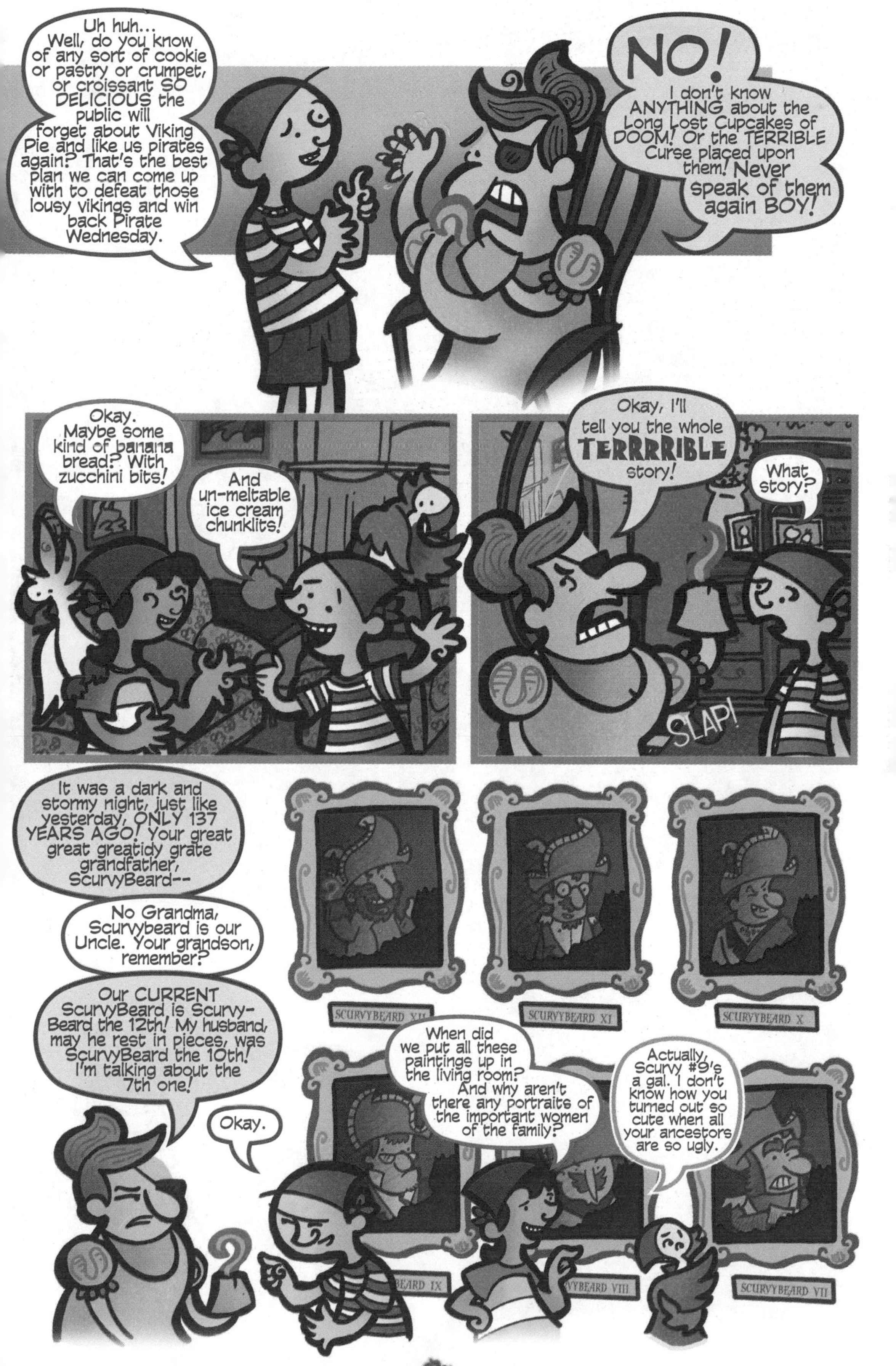

Uh huh... Well, do you know of any sort of cookie or pastry or crumpet, or croissant SO DELICIOUS the public will forget about Viking Pie and like us pirates again? That's the best plan we can come up with to defeat those lousy vikings and win back Pirate Wednesday.
NO! I don't know ANYTHING about the Long Lost Cupcakes of DOOM! Or the TERRIBLE Curse placed upon them! Never speak of them again BOY!
Okay. Maybe some kind of banana bread? With zucchini bits!
And un-meltable ice cream chunklits!
Okay, I'll tell you the whole TERRRRIBLE story!
What story?
SLAP!
It was a dark and stormy night, just like yesterday, ONLY 137 YEARS AGO! Your great great greatidy grate grandfather, ScurvyBeard--
No Grandma, Scurvybeard is our Uncle. Your grandson, remember?
Our CURRENT ScurvyBeard is Scurvy-Beard the 12th! My husband, may he rest in pieces, was ScurvyBeard the 10th! I'm talking about the 7th one!
Okay.
SCURVYBEARD XII
SCURVYBEARD XI
SCURVYBEARD X
When did we put all these paintings up in the living room? And why aren't there any portraits of the important women of the family?
Actually, Scurvy #9's a gal. I don't know how you turned out so cute when all your ancestors are so ugly.
BEARD IX
VYBEARD VIII
SCURVYBEARD VII

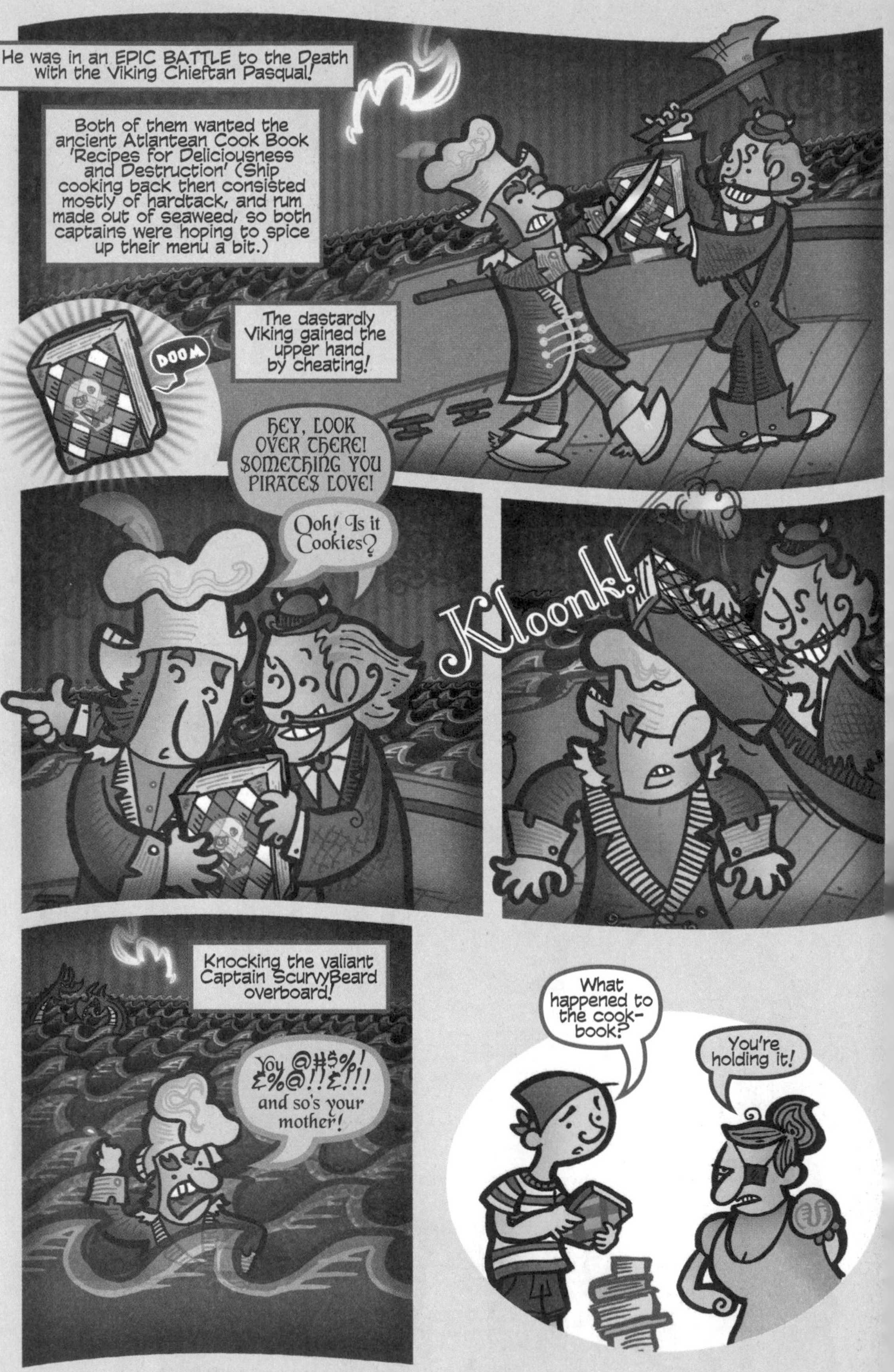
He was in an EPIC BATTLE to the Death with the Viking Chieftan Pasqual!
Both of them wanted the ancient Atlantean Cook Book 'Recipes for Deliciousness and Destruction' (Ship cooking back then consisted mostly of hardtack, and rum made out of seaweed, so both captains were hoping to spice up their menu a bit.)
DOOM
The dastardly Viking gained the upper hand by cheating!
HEY, LOOK OVER THERE! SOMETHING YOU PIRATE$ LOVE!
Ooh! Is it Cookies?
Kloonk!
Knocking the valiant Captain ScurvyBeard overboard!
You @#$%! £%@!!£!!! and so's your mother!
What happened to the cook-book?
You're holding it!

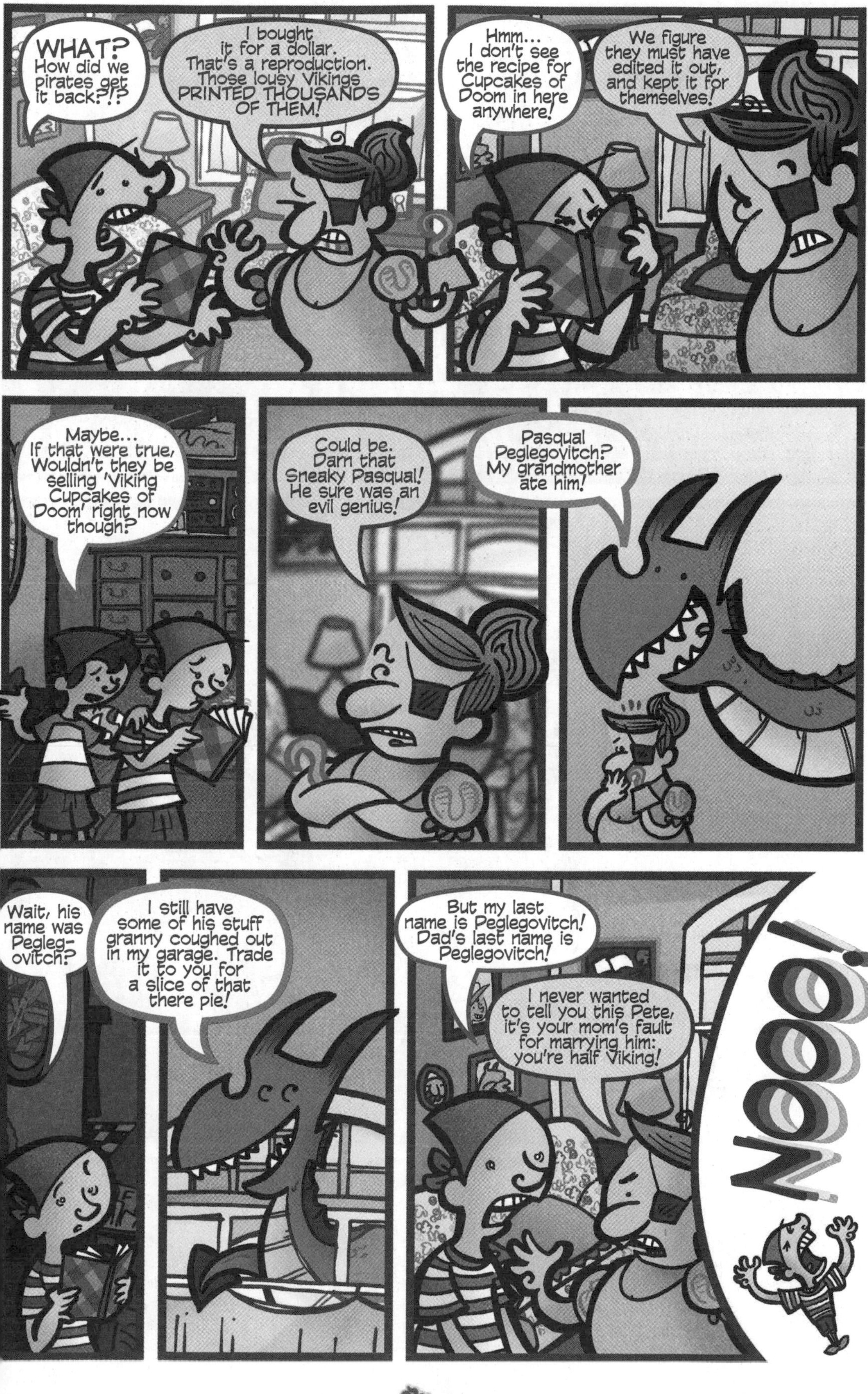
WHAT? How did we pirates get it back?!?
I bought it for a dollar. That's a reproduction. Those lousy Vikings PRINTED THOUSANDS OF THEM!
Hmm... I don't see the recipe for Cupcakes of Doom in here anywhere!
We figure they must have edited it out, and kept it for themselves!
Maybe... If that were true, Wouldn't they be selling 'Viking Cupcakes of Doom' right now though?
Could be. Darn that Sneaky Pasqual! He sure was an evil genius!
Pasqual Peglegovitch? My grandmother ate him!
Wait, his name was Pegleg-ovitch?
I still have some of his stuff granny coughed out in my garage. Trade it to you for a slice of that there pie!
But my last name is Peglegovitch! Dad's last name is Peglegovitch!
I never wanted to tell you this Pete, it's your mom's fault for marrying him: you're half Viking!
NOOO!!

So of course, your sister is too.

Here you go! Pasqual's shoe, his keys, his skull, and his book. Now pie me!

So that's where she gets all her evil from!

Ha! Ha! Ha! Ha! Ha! Ha!

LEMME SEE THAT THERE BOOK!

Hot diggety! IT IS the original Cookbook of Destruction!

AND There's a page that's been ripped out! I'll bet you anything it's the Cupcakes of Doom page!

GRILLED CHEESE RELATED MISHAP

MR. T SANDWICH CALAMITY

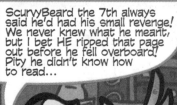

ScurvyBeard the 7th always said he'd had his small revenge! We never knew what he meant, but I bet HE ripped that page out before he fell overboard! Pity he didn't know how to read...

What do you mean you knew Scurvybeard the 7th? He lived over a century ago!

Um, I'm actually older than I look. I used to be HIS parrot.

Phew! I was wondering how I was gonna tell you I'm actually 146 years old!

Whoo! I'm 145! I'm younger!

Yeah, but I'm cuter.

Well DUH. I'm still pretty dam cute tho.

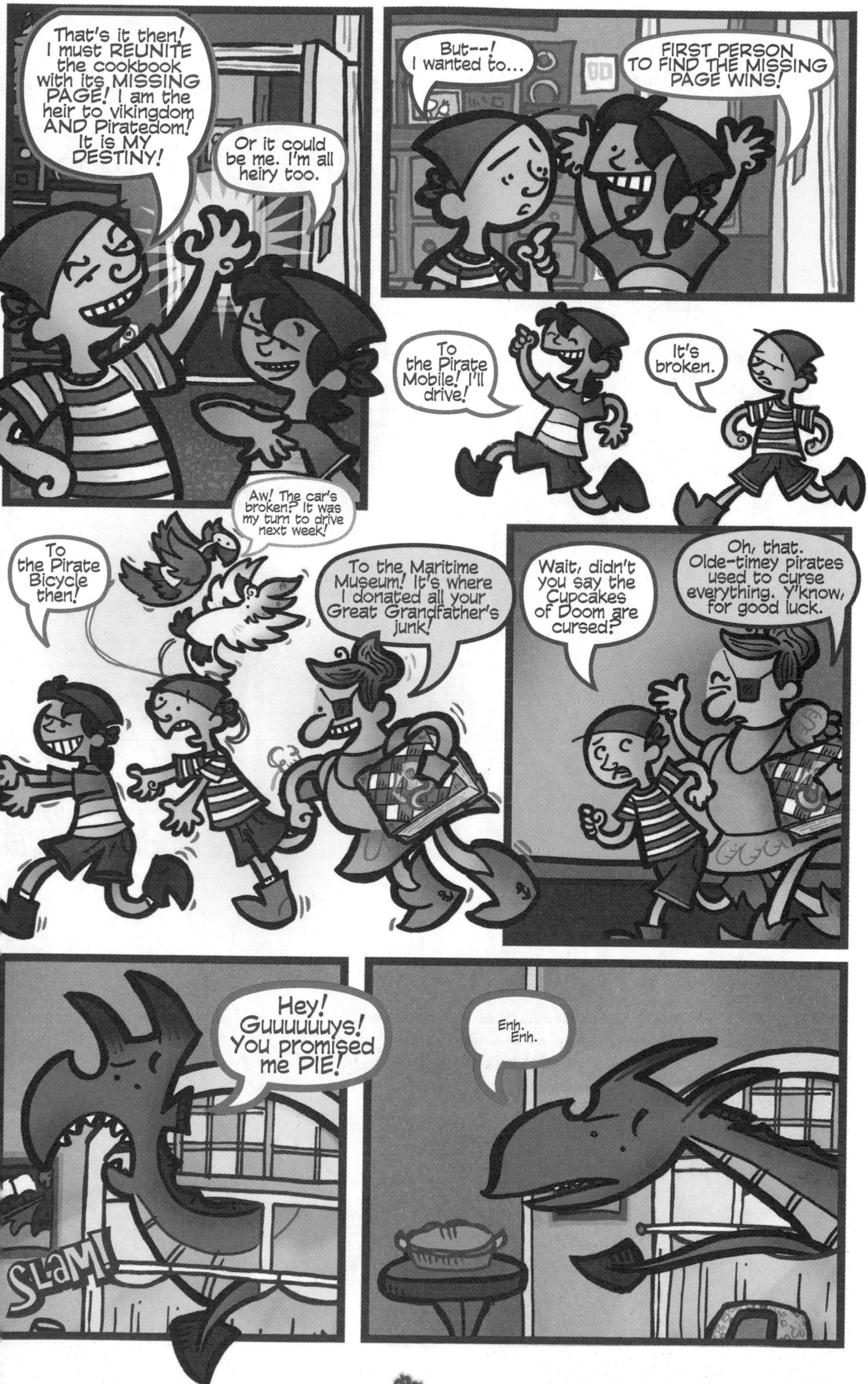
That's it then! I must REUNITE the cookbook with its MISSING PAGE! I am the heir to vikingdom AND Piratedom! It is MY DESTINY!
Or it could be me. I'm all heiry too.
But--! I wanted to...
FIRST PERSON TO FIND THE MISSING PAGE WINS!
To the Pirate Mobile! I'll drive!
It's broken.
To the Pirate Bicycle then!
Aw! The car's broken? It was my turn to drive next week!
To the Maritime Museum! It's where I donated all your Great Grandfather's junk!
Wait, didn't you say the Cupcakes of Doom are cursed?
Oh, that. Olde-timey pirates used to curse everything. Y'know, for good luck.
Hey! Guuuuuuys! You promised me PIE!
SLAM!
Enh. Enh.

CHAPTER THIRTEEN

SHOWDOWN TIME (3:00)

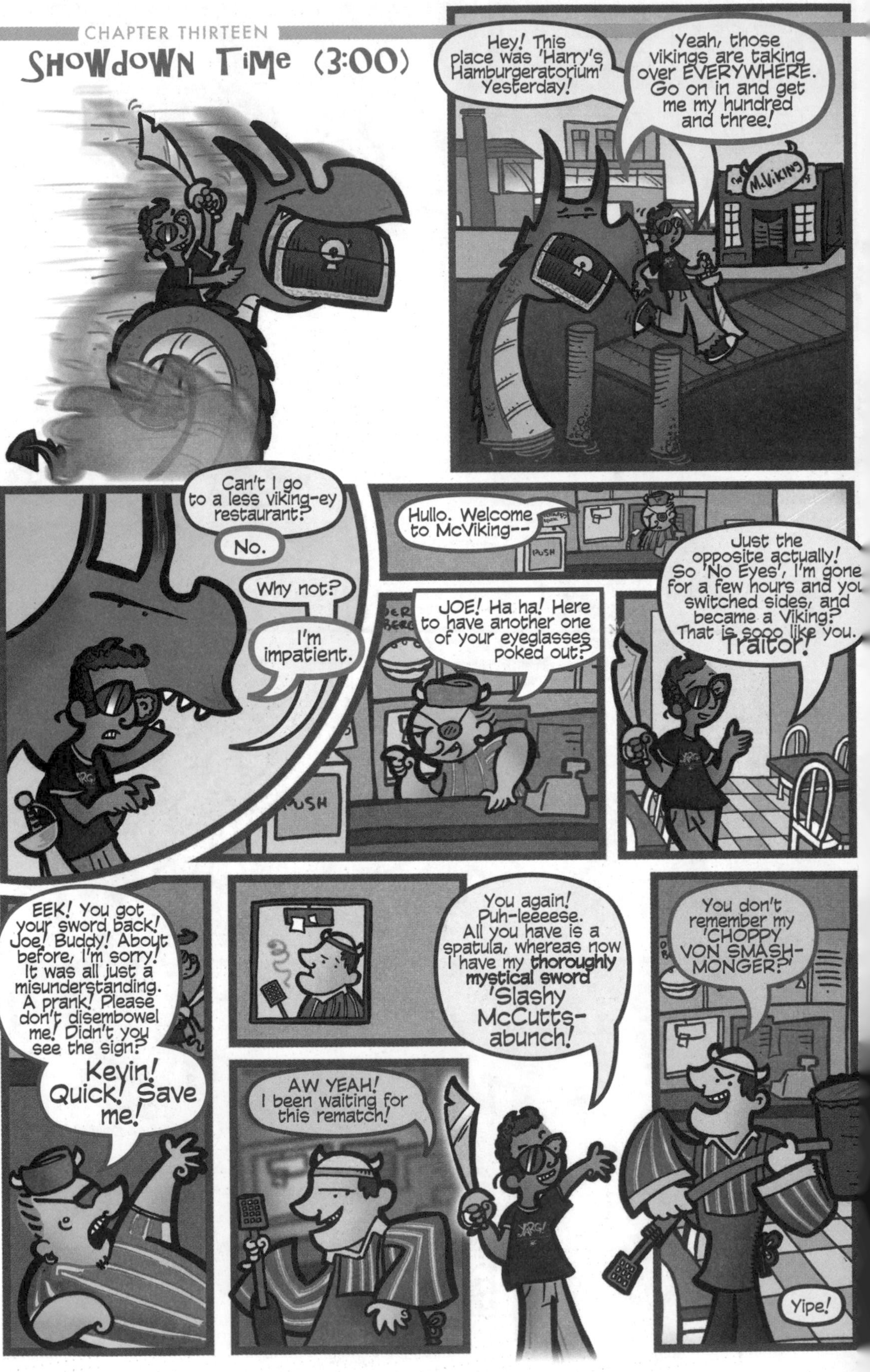
Hey! This place was 'Harry's Hamburgeratorium' Yesterday!
Yeah, those vikings are taking over EVERYWHERE. Go on in and get me my hundred and three!
McViking
Can't I go to a less viking-ey restaurant?
No.
Why not?
I'm impatient.
Hullo. Welcome to McViking--
PUSH
JOE! Ha ha! Here to have another one of your eyeglasses poked out?
PUSH
Just the opposite actually! So 'No Eyes', I'm gone for a few hours and you switched sides, and became a Viking? That is sooo like you. Traitor!
EEK! You got your sword back! Joe! Buddy! About before, I'm sorry! It was all just a misunderstanding. A prank! Please don't disembowel me! Didn't you see the sign? Kevin! Quick! Save me!
AW YEAH! I been waiting for this rematch!
You again! Puh-leeeese. All you have is a spatula, whereas now I have my thoroughly mystical sword 'Slashy McCutts-abunch!
You don't remember my 'CHOPPY VON SMASH-MONGER?'
Yipe!

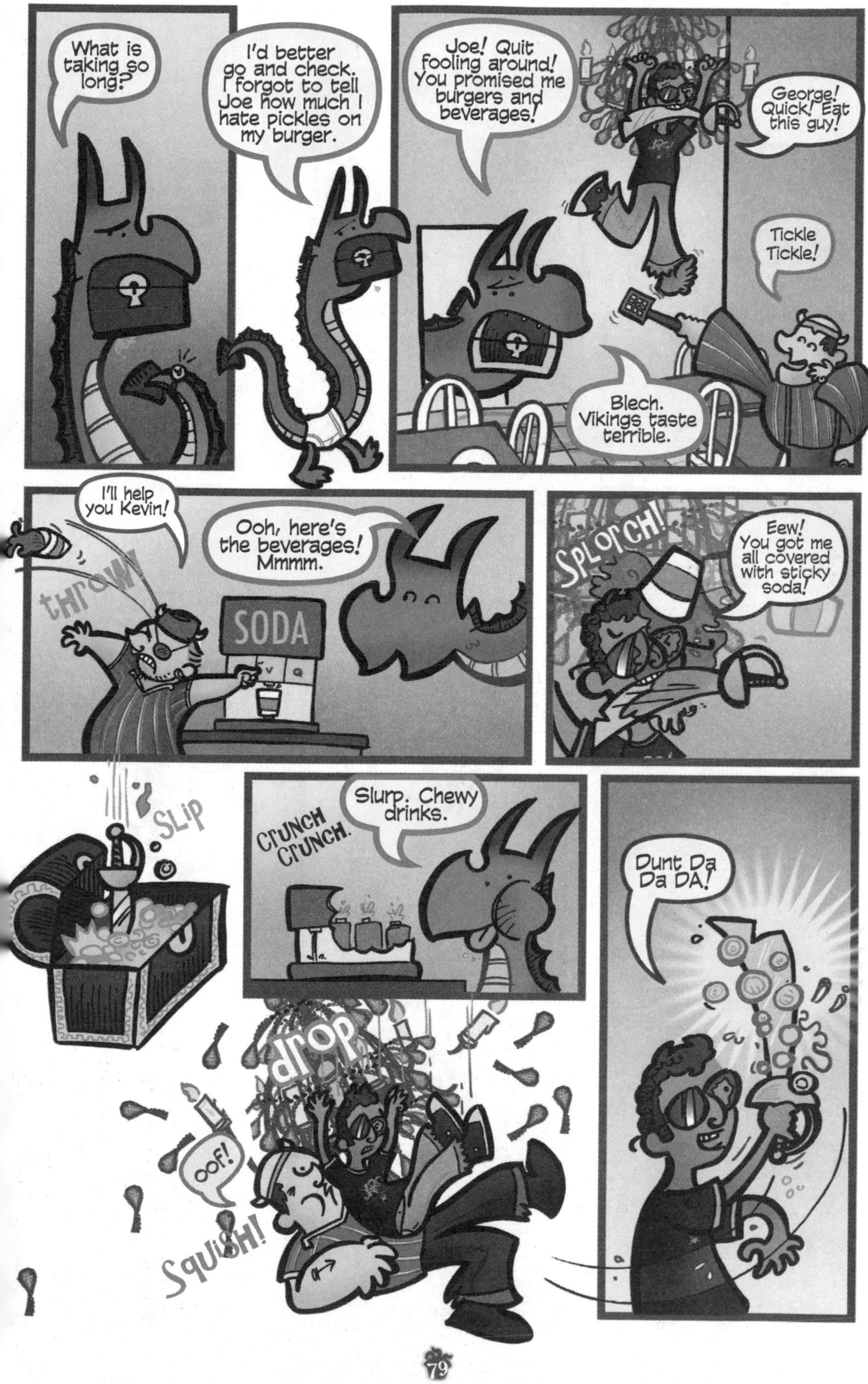
What is taking so long?
I'd better go and check. I forgot to tell Joe how much I hate pickles on my burger.
Joe! Quit fooling around! You promised me burgers and beverages!
George! Quick! Eat this guy!
Tickle Tickle!
Blech. Vikings taste terrible.
I'll help you Kevin!
THROW!
Ooh, here's the beverages! Mmmm.
SODA
SPLORCH!
Eew! You got me all covered with sticky soda!
SLIP
CRUNCH CRUNCH.
Slurp. Chewy drinks.
Dunt Da Da DA!
drop
oof!
SQUISH!

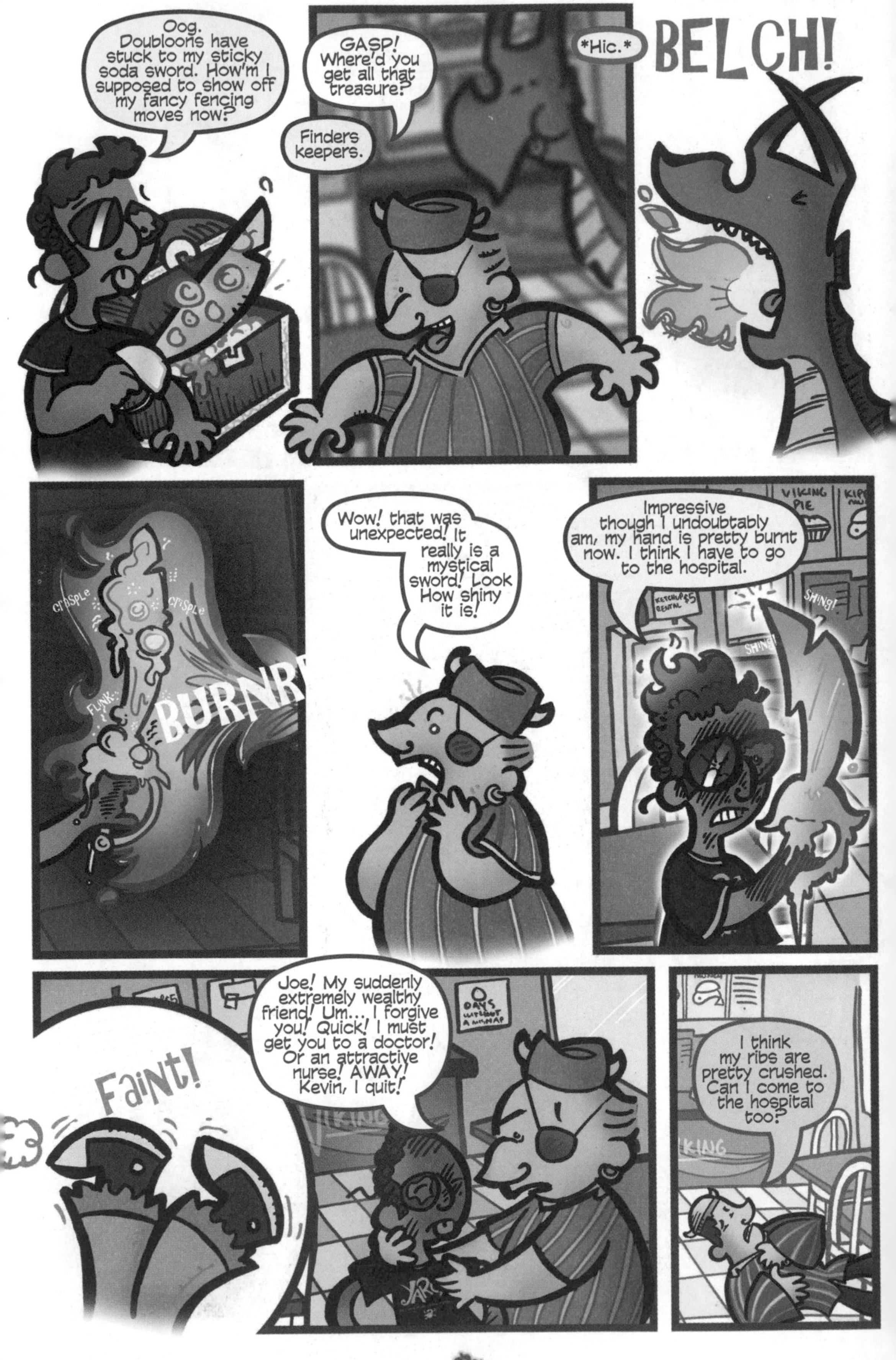
Oog. Doubloons have stuck to my sticky soda sword. How'm I supposed to show off my fancy fencing moves now?
GASP! Where'd you get all that treasure?
Finders keepers.
Hic.
BELCH!
crispLe
crispLe
FUNK
BURNR
Wow! that was unexpected! It really is a mystical sword! Look How shiny it is!
Impressive though I undoubtably am, my hand is pretty burnt now. I think I have to go to the hospital.
VIKING PIE
KETCHUP RENTAL $5
SHING!
SHING!
Faint!
Joe! My suddenly extremely wealthy friend! Um... I forgive you! Quick! I must get you to a doctor! Or an attractive nurse! AWAY! Kevin, I quit!
YAR!
I think my ribs are pretty crushed. Can I come to the hospital too?

Secrecy, Motorcycles & Lampposts

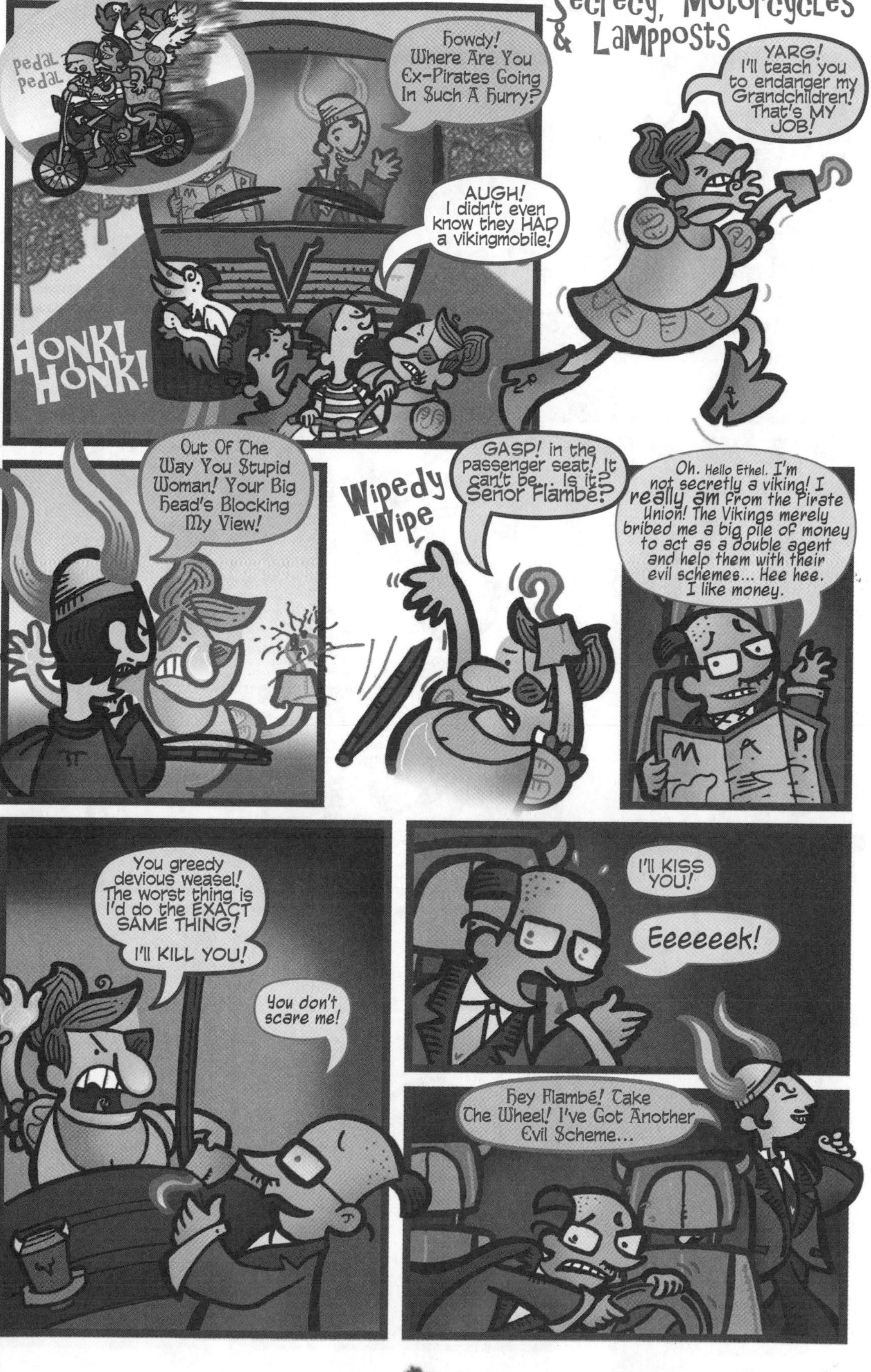
pedal pedal
Howdy! Where Are You Ex-Pirates Going In Such A Hurry?
YARG! I'll teach you to endanger my Grandchildren! That's MY JOB!
AUGH! I didn't even know they HAD a vikingmobile!
HONK! HONK!
Out Of The Way You Stupid Woman! Your Big Head's Blocking My View!
Wipedy Wipe
GASP! in the passenger seat! It can't be... is it? Senor Flambé?
Oh. Hello Ethel. I'm not secretly a viking! I really am from the Pirate Union! The Vikings merely bribed me a big pile of money to act as a double agent and help them with their evil schemes... Hee hee. I like money.
M A P
You greedy devious weasel! The worst thing is I'd do the EXACT SAME THING!
I'll KILL YOU!
You don't scare me!
I'll KISS YOU!
Eeeeeek!
Hey Flambé! Take The Wheel! I've Got Another Evil Scheme...

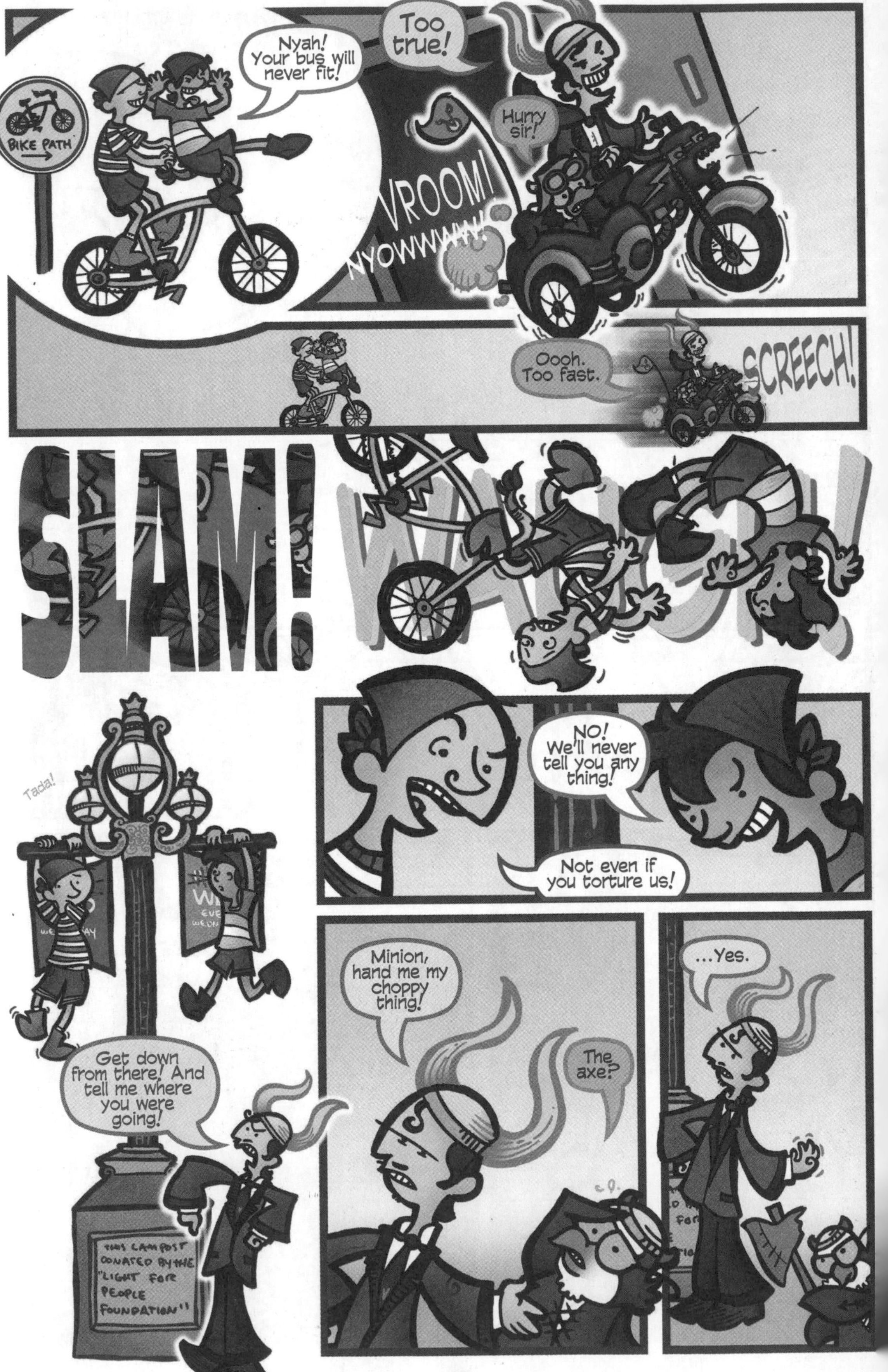
BIKE PATH
Nyah! Your bus will never fit!
Too true!
Hurry sir!
VROOM!
NYOWWWN!
Oooh. Too fast.
SCREECH!
SLAM!
Tada!
NO! We'll never tell you any thing!
Not even if you torture us!
Get down from there! And tell me where you were going!
THIS LAMPOST DONATED BY THE "LIGHT FOR PEOPLE FOUNDATION"
Minion, hand me my choppy thing!
The axe?
...Yes.

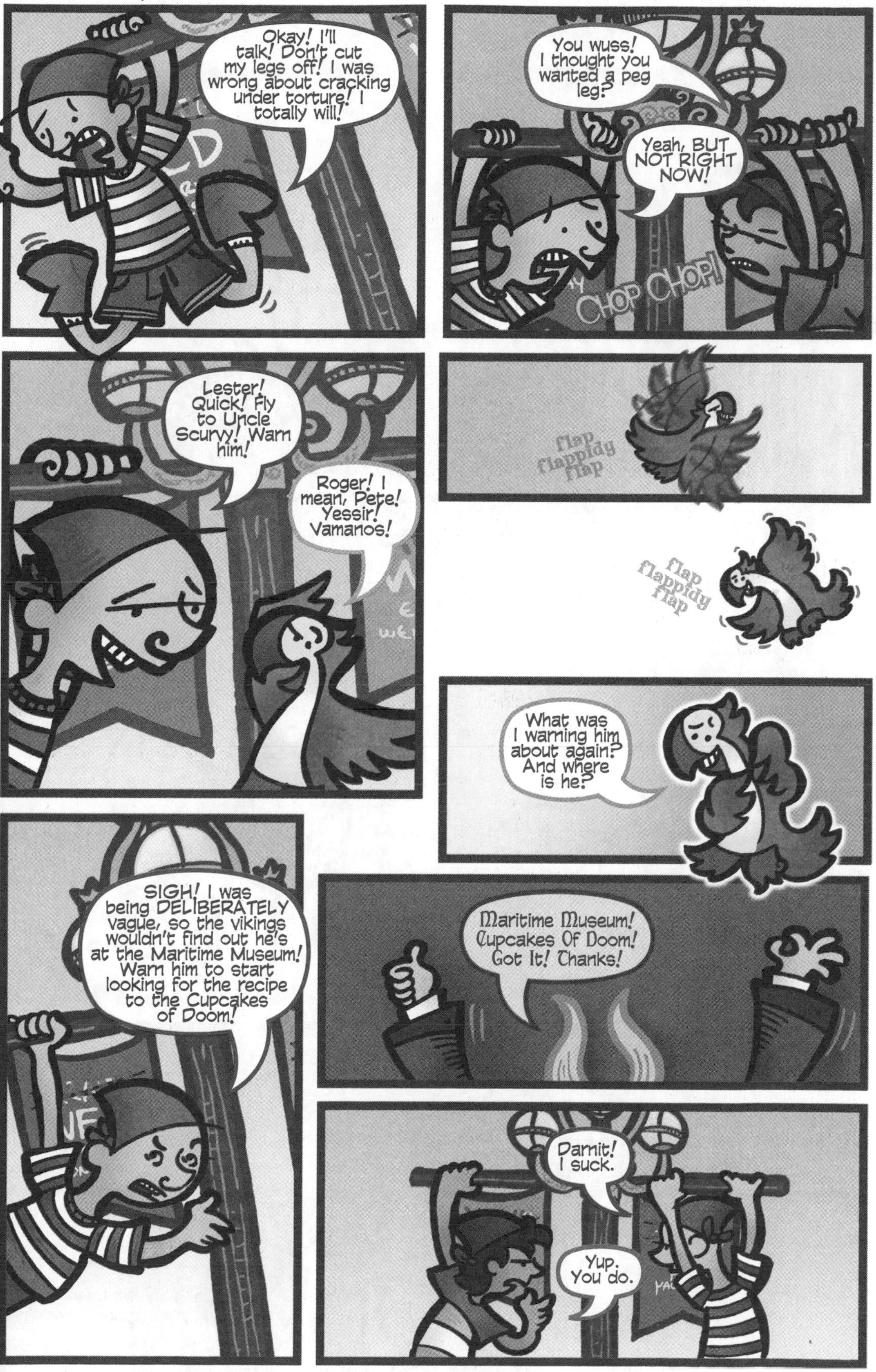
Okay! I'll talk! Don't cut my legs off! I was wrong about cracking under torture! I totally will!
You wuss! I thought you wanted a peg leg?
Yeah, BUT NOT RIGHT NOW!
CHOP CHOP!
Lester! Quick! Fly to Uncle Scurvy! Warn him!
Roger! I mean, Pete! Yessir! Vamanos!
flap flappidy flap
flap flappidy flap
What was I warning him about again? And where is he?
SIGH! I was being DELIBERATELY vague, so the vikings wouldn't find out he's at the Maritime Museum! Warn him to start looking for the recipe to the Cupcakes of Doom!
Maritime Museum! Cupcakes Of Doom! Got It! Thanks!
Darnit! I suck.
Yup. You do.

Minion! Fly After Those Parrots! Stop Them From Warning the Pirate Captain Whilst I Drive Ahead And Get That Recipe!

Sir, I can't fly.

I'M A PENGUIN.

I Thunk You Were A Pelican!

Ugh! I wouldn't be caught DEAD being a pelican! They're so ugly!

I Always Thought You Were Pretty Ugly...

HEY!

I Know! Why Don't You Drink, Like, 87 Vikkucinos! That'll Give You Enough Caffeine Power To Take Off!

Naw, I've tried that before. It just gives me heart palpitations.

Crudmuffins.

Ooh! I could always use the Emergency Viking Jetpack!

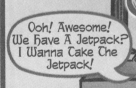

Ooh! Awesome! We Have A Jetpack? I Wanna Take The Jetpack!

NO. I forgot, we don't HAVE a jetpack anymore. You said it wasn't in our budget and made me return it to the Steampunkatorium.

I think they've forgotten about us.

How rude! I should always be the center of attention.

84

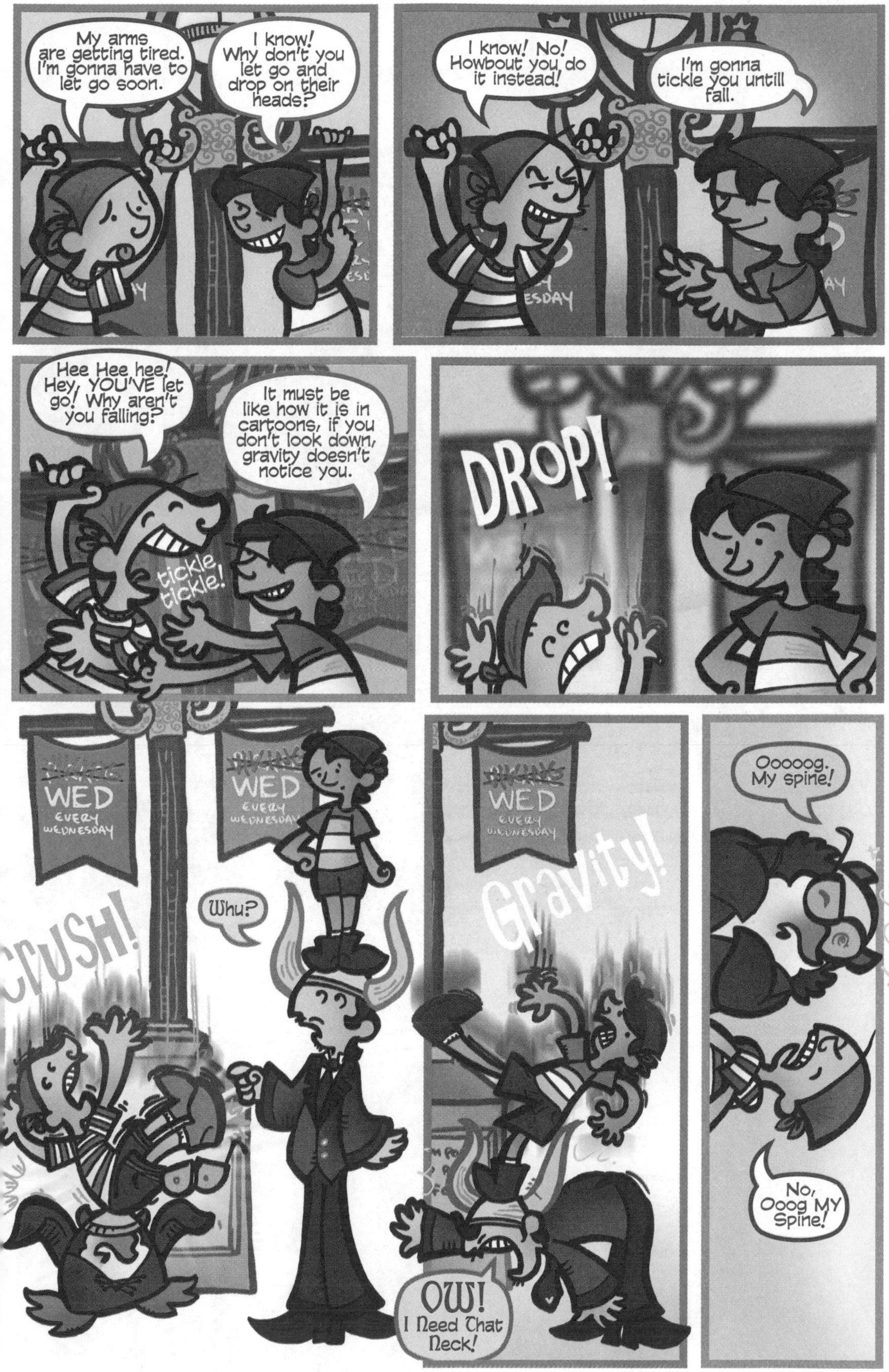
My arms are getting tired. I'm gonna have to let go soon.
I know! Why don't you let go and drop on their heads?
I know! No! Howbout you do it instead!
I'm gonna tickle you untill fall.
Hee Hee hee! Hey, YOU'VE let go! Why aren't you falling?
It must be like how it is in cartoons, if you don't look down, gravity doesn't notice you.
tickle tickle!
DROP!
WED
EVERY WEDNESDAY
WED
EVERY WEDNESDAY
Whu?
CRUSH!
WED
EVERY WEDNESDAY
Gravity!
OW! I Need That Neck!
Oooooog. My spine!
No, Ooog MY Spine!

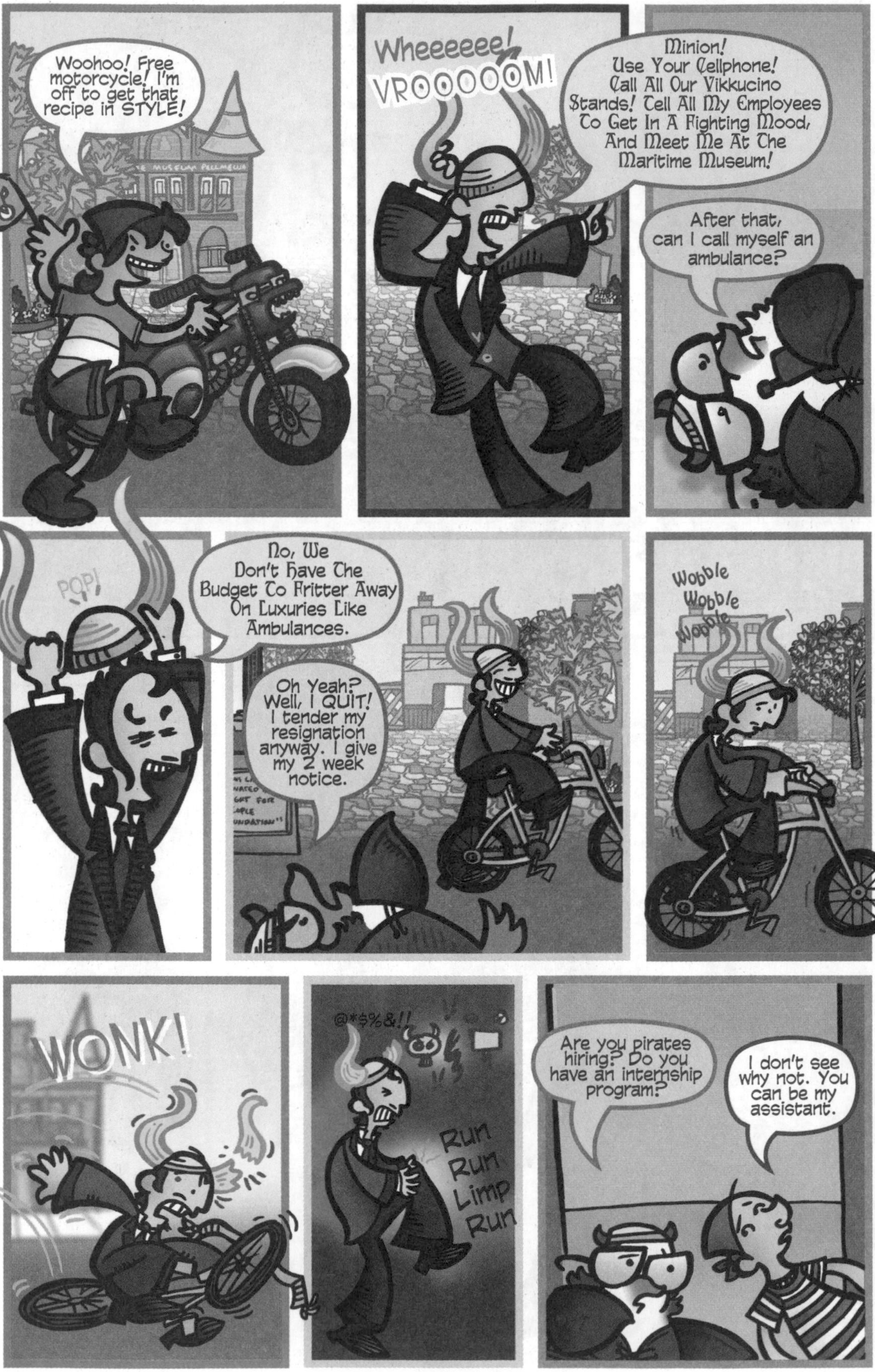
Woohoo! Free motorcycle! I'm off to get that recipe in STYLE!
Wheeeeee!
VROOOOOM!
Minion! Use Your Cellphone! Call All Our Vikkucino Stands! Tell All My Employees To Get In A Fighting Mood, And Meet Me At The Maritime Museum!
After that, can I call myself an ambulance?
POP!
No, We Don't Have The Budget To Fritter Away On Luxuries Like Ambulances.
Oh Yeah? Well, I QUIT! I tender my resignation anyway. I give my 2 week notice.
Wobble
Wobble
Wobble
WONK!
@*$%&!!
Run
Run
Limp
Run
Are you pirates hiring? Do you have an internship program?
I don't see why not. You can be my assistant.

CHAPTER FIFTEEN
Pillage and Plunder

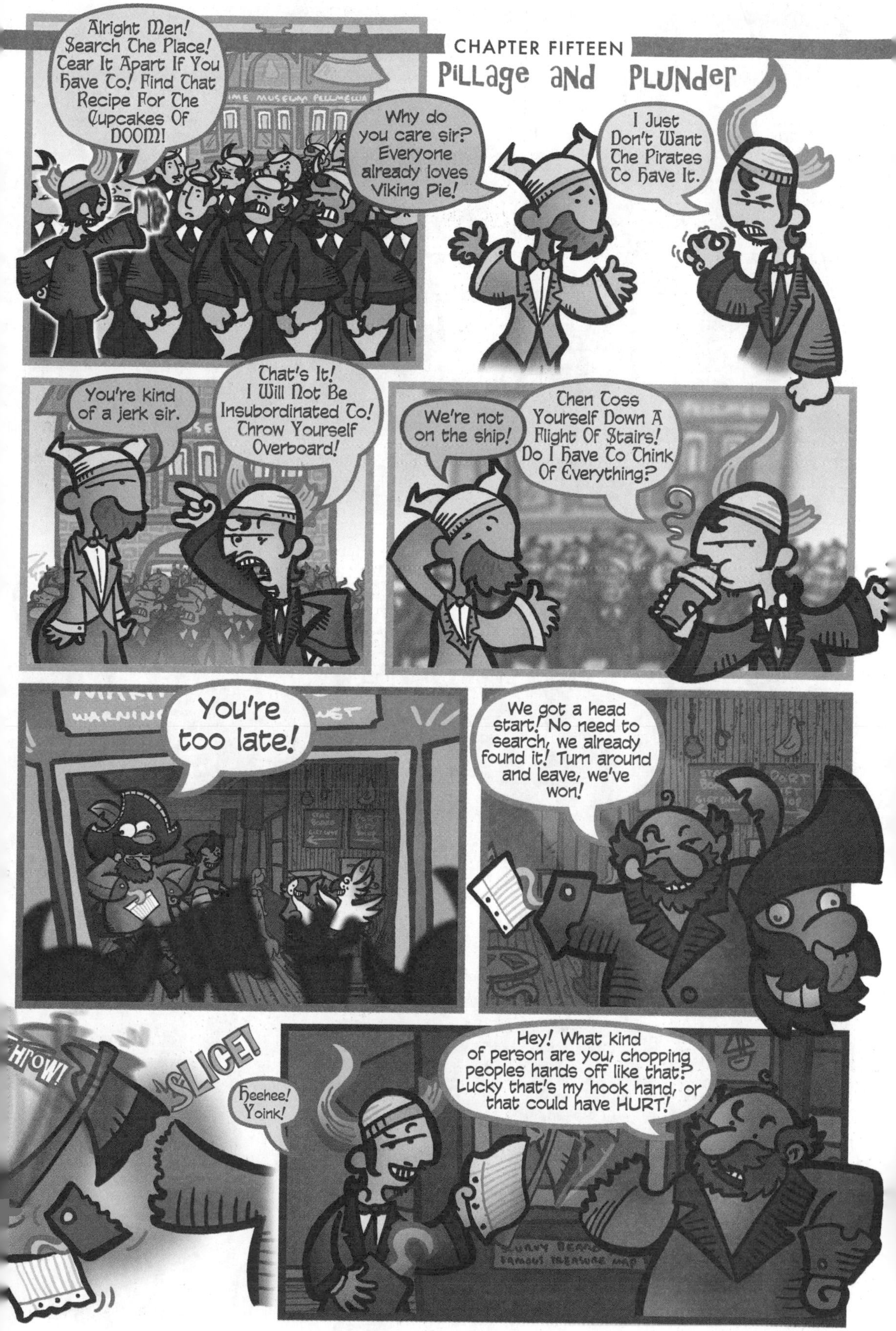

Alright Men! Search The Place! Tear It Apart If You Have To! Find That Recipe For The Cupcakes Of DOOM!
Why do you care sir? Everyone already loves Viking Pie!
I Just Don't Want The Pirates To Have It.
You're kind of a jerk sir.
That's It! I Will Not Be Insubordinated To! Throw Yourself Overboard!
We're not on the ship!
Then Toss Yourself Down A Flight Of Stairs! Do I Have To Think Of Everything?
You're too late!
We got a head start! No need to search, we already found it! Turn around and leave, we've won!
SLICE!
Heehee! Yoink!
Hey! What kind of person are you, chopping peoples hands off like that? Lucky that's my hook hand, or that could have HURT!

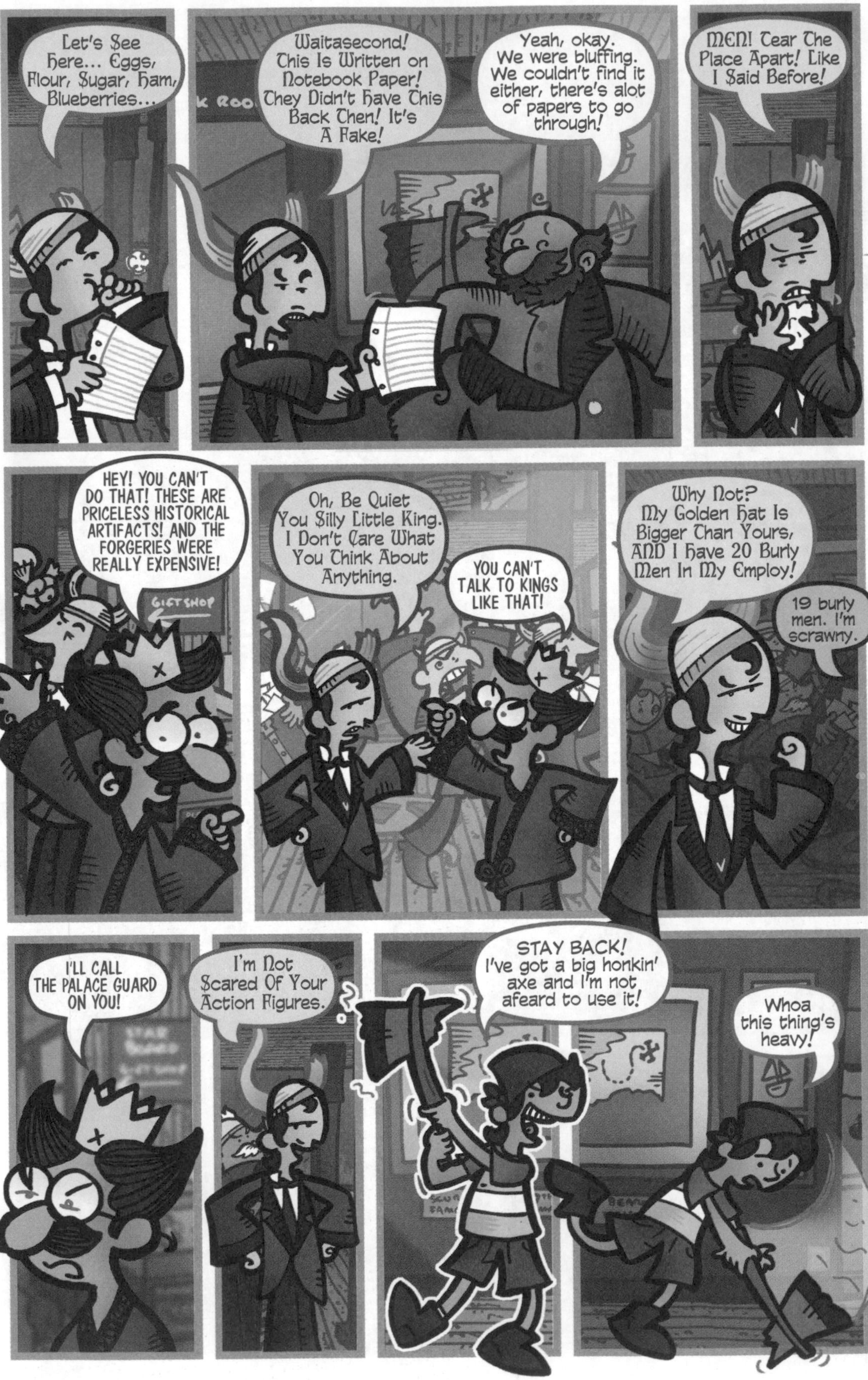
Let's See Here... Eggs, Flour, Sugar, Ham, Blueberries...
Waitasecond! This Is Written on Notebook Paper! They Didn't Have This Back Then! It's A Fake!
Yeah, okay. We were bluffing. We couldn't find it either, there's alot of papers to go through!
MEN! Tear The Place Apart! Like I Said Before!
HEY! YOU CAN'T DO THAT! THESE ARE PRICELESS HISTORICAL ARTIFACTS! AND THE FORGERIES WERE REALLY EXPENSIVE!
GIFT SHOP
Oh, Be Quiet You Silly Little King. I Don't Care What You Think About Anything.
YOU CAN'T TALK TO KINGS LIKE THAT!
Why Not? My Golden Hat Is Bigger Than Yours, AND I Have 20 Burly Men In My Employ!
19 burly men. I'm scrawny.
I'LL CALL THE PALACE GUARD ON YOU!
I'm Not Scared Of Your Action Figures.
STAY BACK! I've got a big honkin' axe and I'm not afeard to use it!
Whoa this thing's heavy!

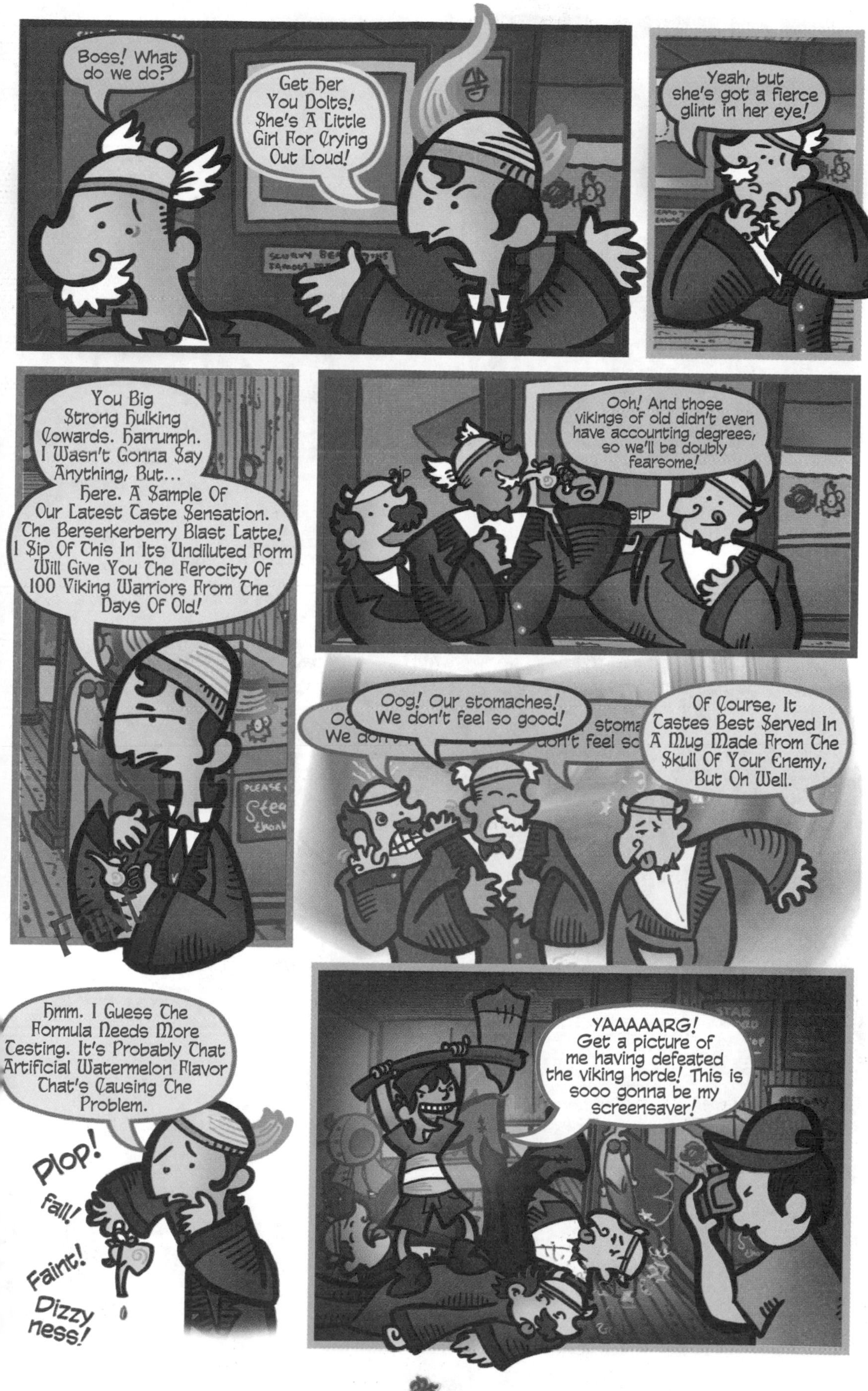
Boss! What do we do?
Get Her You Dolts! She's A Little Girl For Crying Out Loud!
Yeah, but she's got a fierce glint in her eye!
You Big Strong Hulking Cowards. Harrumph. I Wasn't Gonna Say Anything, But... Here. A Sample Of Our Latest Taste Sensation. The Berserkerberry Blast Latte! 1 Sip Of This In Its Undiluted Form Will Give You The Ferocity Of 100 Viking Warriors From The Days Of Old!
sip
sip
Ooh! And those vikings of old didn't even have accounting degrees, so we'll be doubly fearsome!
Oog! Our stomaches! We don't feel so good!
Of Course, It Tastes Best Served In A Mug Made From The Skull Of Your Enemy, But Oh Well.
Hmm. I Guess The Formula Needs More Testing. It's Probably That Artificial Watermelon Flavor That's Causing The Problem.
Plop!
fall!
Faint!
Dizzy ness!
YAAAAARG! Get a picture of me having defeated the viking horde! This is sooo gonna be my screensaver!

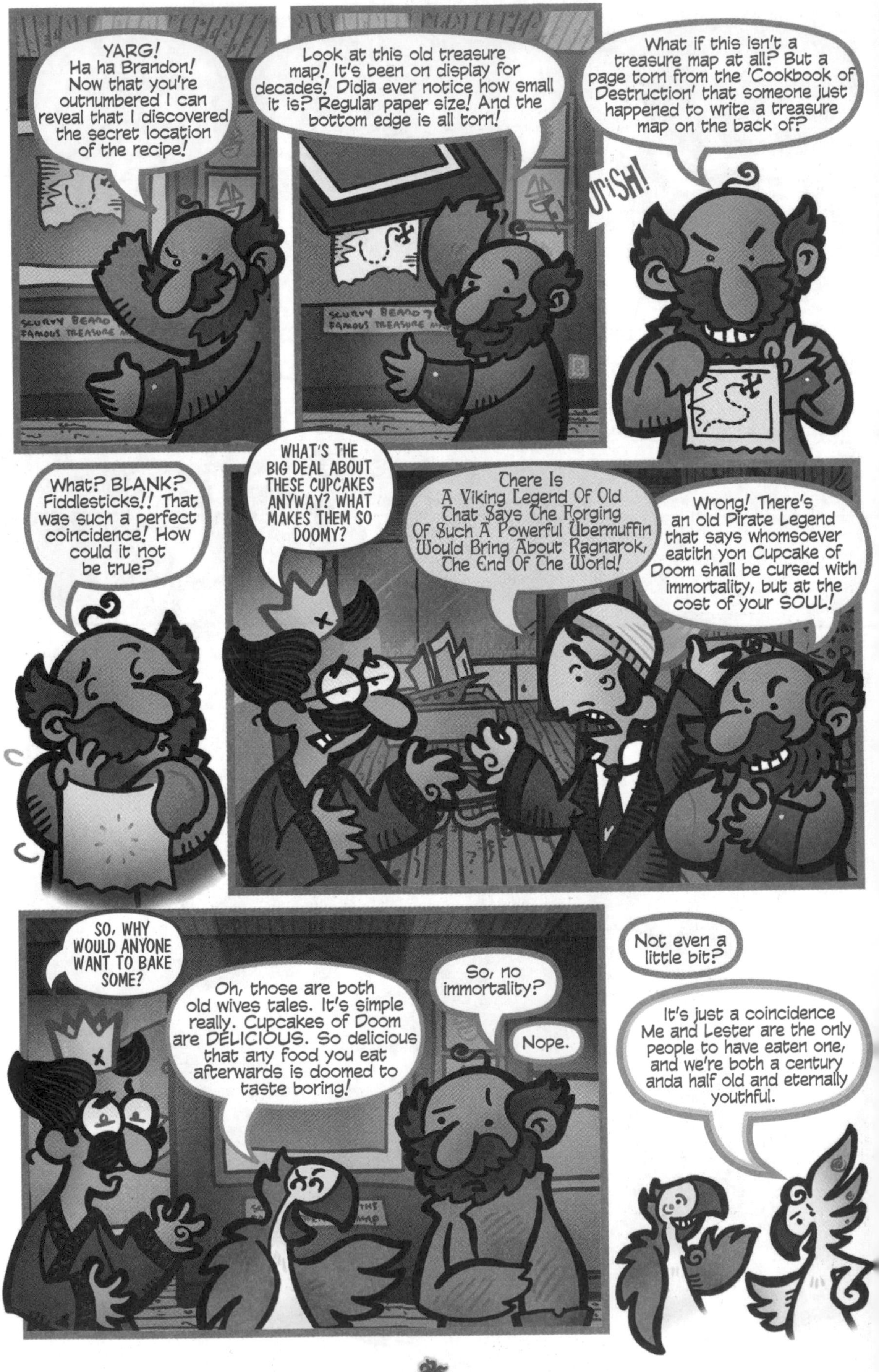
YARG! Ha ha Brandon! Now that you're outnumbered I can reveal that I discovered the secret location of the recipe!
SCURVY BEARD FAMOUS TREASURE
Look at this old treasure map! It's been on display for decades! Didja ever notice how small it is? Regular paper size! And the bottom edge is all torn!
What if this isn't a treasure map at all? But a page torn from the 'Cookbook of Destruction' that someone just happened to write a treasure map on the back of?
FLOURISH!
What? BLANK? Fiddlesticks!! That was such a perfect coincidence! How could it not be true?
WHAT'S THE BIG DEAL ABOUT THESE CUPCAKES ANYWAY? WHAT MAKES THEM SO DOOMY?
There Is A Viking Legend Of Old That Says The Forging Of Such A Powerful Übermuffin Would Bring About Ragnarok, The End Of The World!
Wrong! There's an old Pirate Legend that says whomsoever eatith yon Cupcake of Doom shall be cursed with immortality, but at the cost of your SOUL!
SO, WHY WOULD ANYONE WANT TO BAKE SOME?
Oh, those are both old wives tales. It's simple really. Cupcakes of Doom are DELICIOUS. So delicious that any food you eat afterwards is doomed to taste boring!
So, no immortality?
Nope.
Not even a little bit?
It's just a coincidence Me and Lester are the only people to have eaten one, and we're both a century anda half old and eternally youthful.

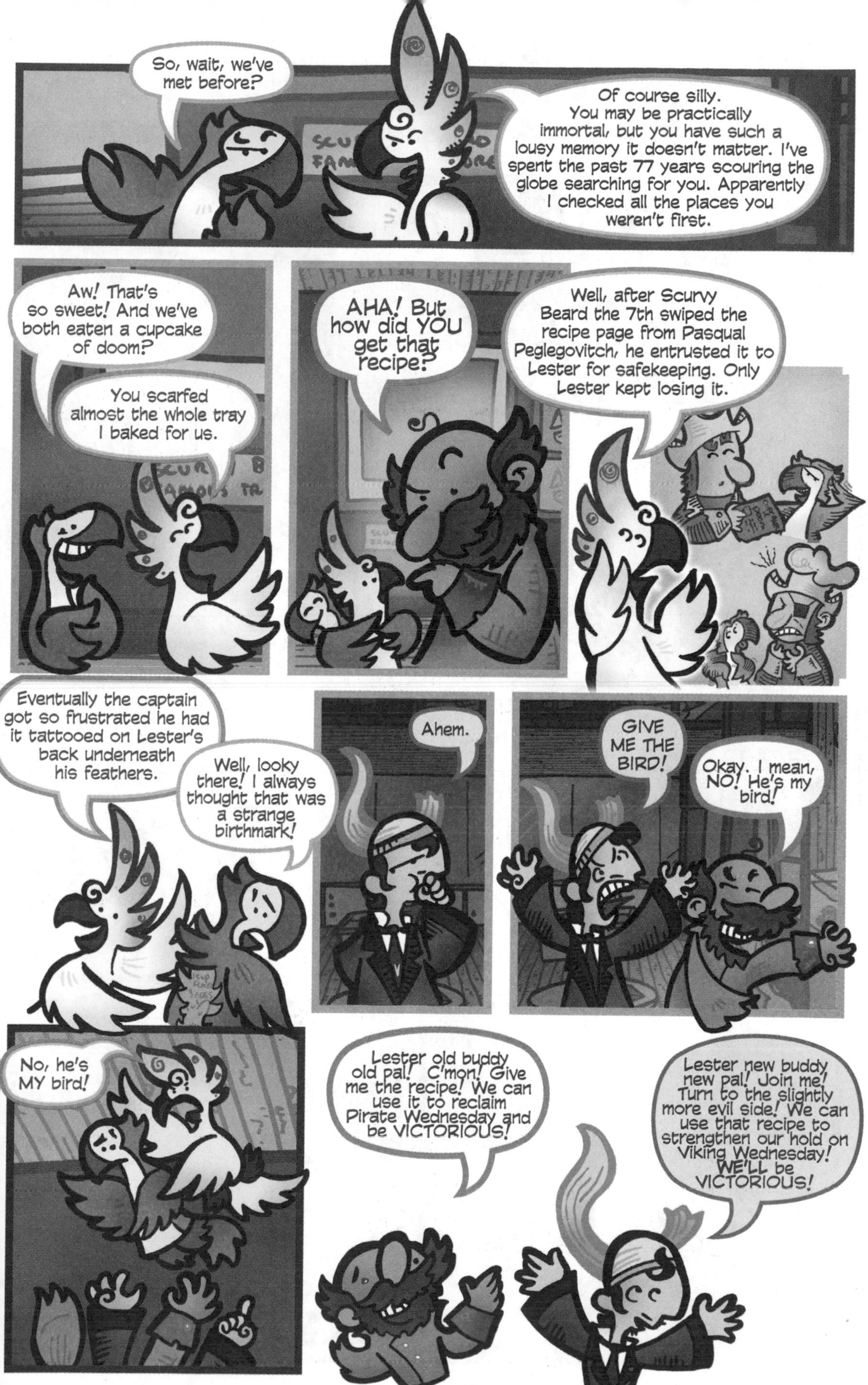
So, wait, we've met before?
Of course silly. You may be practically immortal, but you have such a lousy memory it doesn't matter. I've spent the past 77 years scouring the globe searching for you. Apparently I checked all the places you weren't first.
Aw! That's so sweet! And we've both eaten a cupcake of doom?
You scarfed almost the whole tray I baked for us.
AHA! But how did YOU get that recipe?
Well, after Scurvy Beard the 7th swiped the recipe page from Pasqual Peglegovitch, he entrusted it to Lester for safekeeping. Only Lester kept losing it.
Eventually the captain got so frustrated he had it tattooed on Lester's back underneath his feathers.
Well, looky there! I always thought that was a strange birthmark!
Ahem.
GIVE ME THE BIRD!
Okay. I mean, NO! He's my bird!
No, he's MY bird!
Lester old buddy old pal! C'mon! Give me the recipe! We can use it to reclaim Pirate Wednesday and be VICTORIOUS!
Lester new buddy new pal! Join me! Turn to the slightly more evil side! We can use that recipe to strengthen our hold on Viking Wednesday! WE'LL be VICTORIOUS!

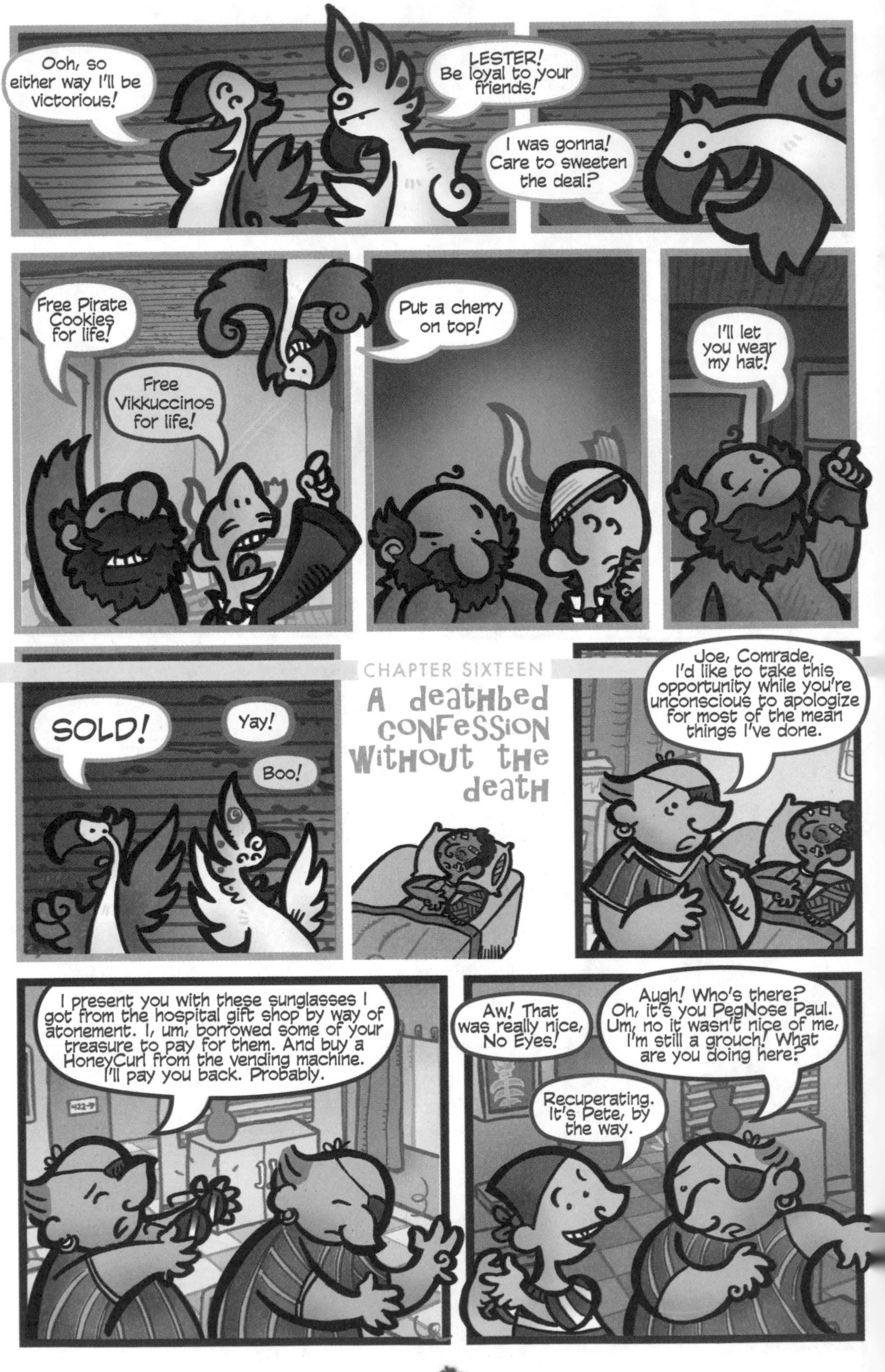
Ooh, so either way I'll be victorious!
LESTER! Be loyal to your friends!
I was gonna! Care to sweeten the deal?
Free Pirate Cookies for life!
Free Vikkuccinos for life!
Put a cherry on top!
I'll let you wear my hat!
SOLD!
Yay!
Boo!
CHAPTER SIXTEEN
A deathbed confession without the death
Joe, Comrade, I'd like to take this opportunity while you're unconscious to apologize for most of the mean things I've done.
I present you with these sunglasses I got from the hospital gift shop by way of atonement. I, um, borrowed some of your treasure to pay for them. And buy a HoneyCurl from the vending machine. I'll pay you back. Probably.
Aw! That was really nice, No Eyes!
Augh! Who's there? Oh, it's you PegNose Paul. Um, no it wasn't nice of me, I'm still a grouch! What are you doing here?
Recuperating. It's Pete, by the way.

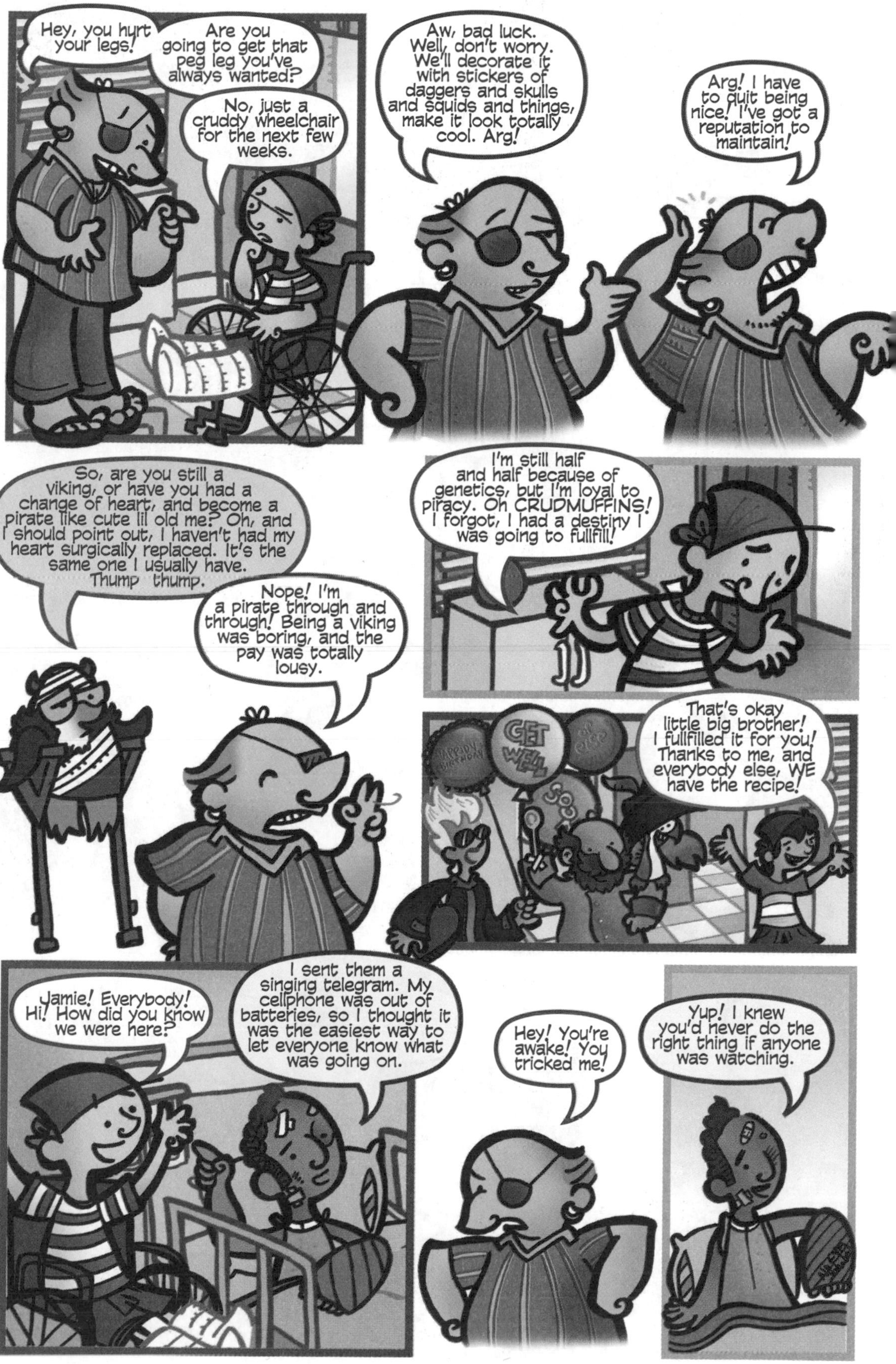
Hey, you hurt your legs!
Are you going to get that peg leg you've always wanted?
No, just a cruddy wheelchair for the next few weeks.
Aw, bad luck. Well, don't worry. We'll decorate it with stickers of daggers and skulls and squids and things, make it look totally cool. Arg!
Arg! I have to quit being nice! I've got a reputation to maintain!
So, are you still a viking, or have you had a change of heart, and become a pirate like cute lil old me? Oh, and I should point out, I haven't had my heart surgically replaced. It's the same one I usually have. Thump thump.
Nope! I'm a pirate through and through! Being a viking was boring, and the pay was totally lousy.
I'm still half and half because of genetics, but I'm loyal to piracy. Oh CRUDMUFFINS! I forgot, I had a destiny I was going to fullfill!
GET WELL
That's okay little big brother! I fullfilled it for you! Thanks to me, and everybody else, WE have the recipe!
Jamie! Everybody! Hi! How did you know we were here?
I sent them a singing telegram. My cellphone was out of batteries, so I thought it was the easiest way to let everyone know what was going on.
Hey! You're awake! You tricked me!
Yup! I knew you'd never do the right thing if anyone was watching.

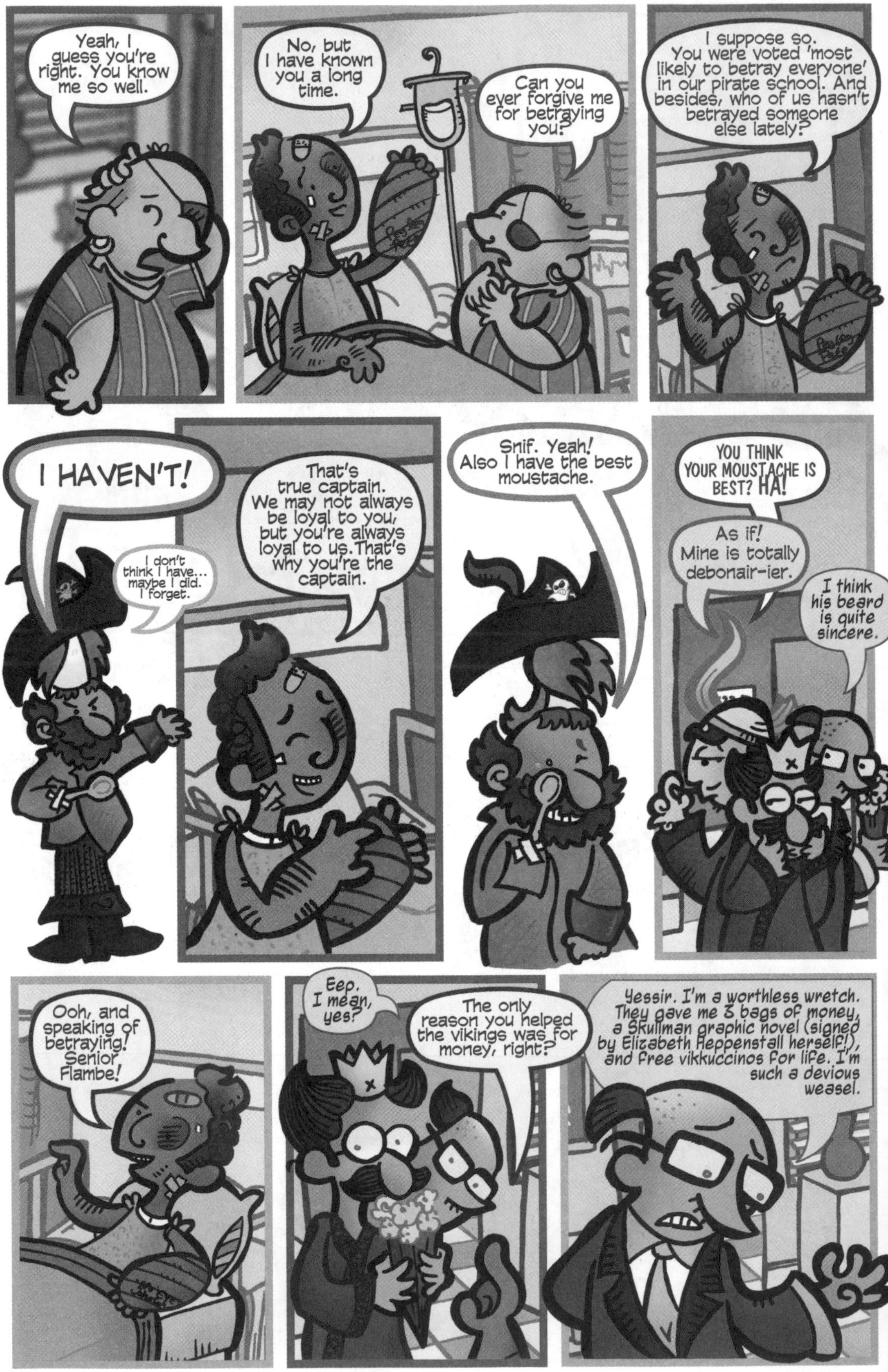

Yeah, I guess you're right. You know me so well.
No, but I have known you a long time.
Can you ever forgive me for betraying you?
I suppose so. You were voted 'most likely to betray everyone' in our pirate school. And besides, who of us hasn't betrayed someone else lately?
I HAVEN'T!
I don't think I have... maybe I did. I forget.
That's true captain. We may not always be loyal to you, but you're always loyal to us. That's why you're the captain.
Snif. Yeah! Also I have the best moustache.
YOU THINK YOUR MOUSTACHE IS BEST? HA!
As if! Mine is totally debonair-ier.
I think his beard is quite sincere.
Ooh, and speaking of betraying! Senior Flambe!
Eep. I mean, yes?
The only reason you helped the vikings was for money, right?
Yessir. I'm a worthless wretch. They gave me 3 bags of money, a Skullman graphic novel (signed by Elizabeth Heppenstall herself!), and free vikkuccinos for life. I'm such a devious weasel.

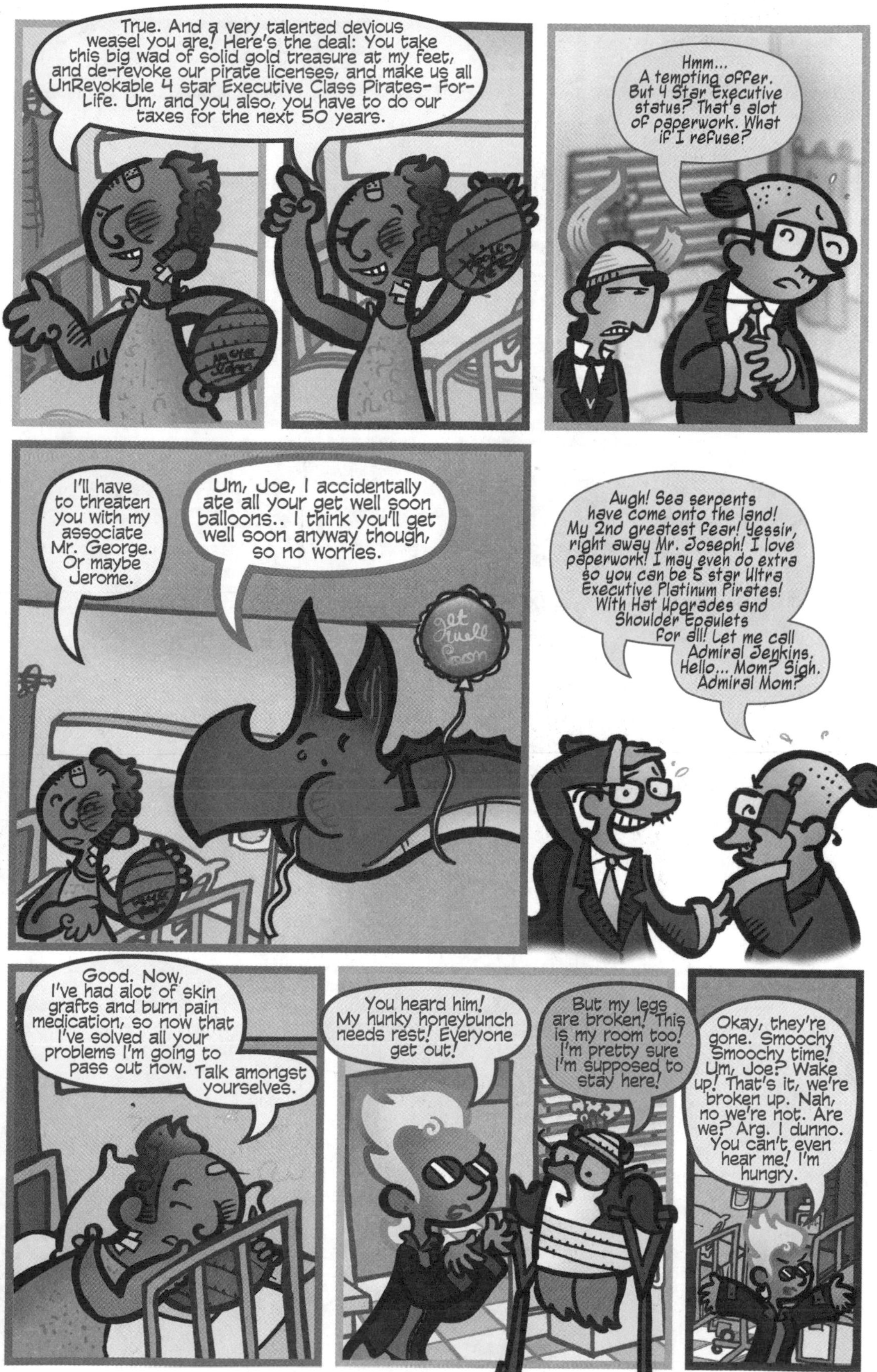
True. And a very talented devious weasel you are! Here's the deal: You take this big wad of solid gold treasure at my feet, and de-revoke our pirate licenses, and make us all UnRevokable 4 star Executive Class Pirates- For-Life. Um, and you also, you have to do our taxes for the next 50 years.
Hmm... A tempting offer. But 4 Star Executive status? That's alot of paperwork. What if I refuse?
I'll have to threaten you with my associate Mr. George. Or maybe Jerome.
Um, Joe, I accidentally ate all your get well soon balloons.. I think you'll get well soon anyway though, so no worries.
Augh! Sea serpents have come onto the land! My 2nd greatest fear! Yessir, right away Mr. Joseph! I love paperwork! I may even do extra so you can be 5 star Ultra Executive Platinum Pirates! With Hat Upgrades and Shoulder Epaulets for all! Let me call Admiral Jenkins. Hello... Mom? Sigh. Admiral Mom?
Good. Now, I've had alot of skin grafts and burn pain medication, so now that I've solved all your problems I'm going to pass out now. Talk amongst yourselves.
You heard him! My hunky honeybunch needs rest! Everyone get out!
But my legs are broken! This is my room too! I'm pretty sure I'm supposed to stay here!
Okay, they're gone. Smoochy Smoochy time! Um, Joe? Wake up! That's it, we're broken up. Nah, no we're not. Are we? Arg. I dunno. You can't even hear me! I'm hungry.

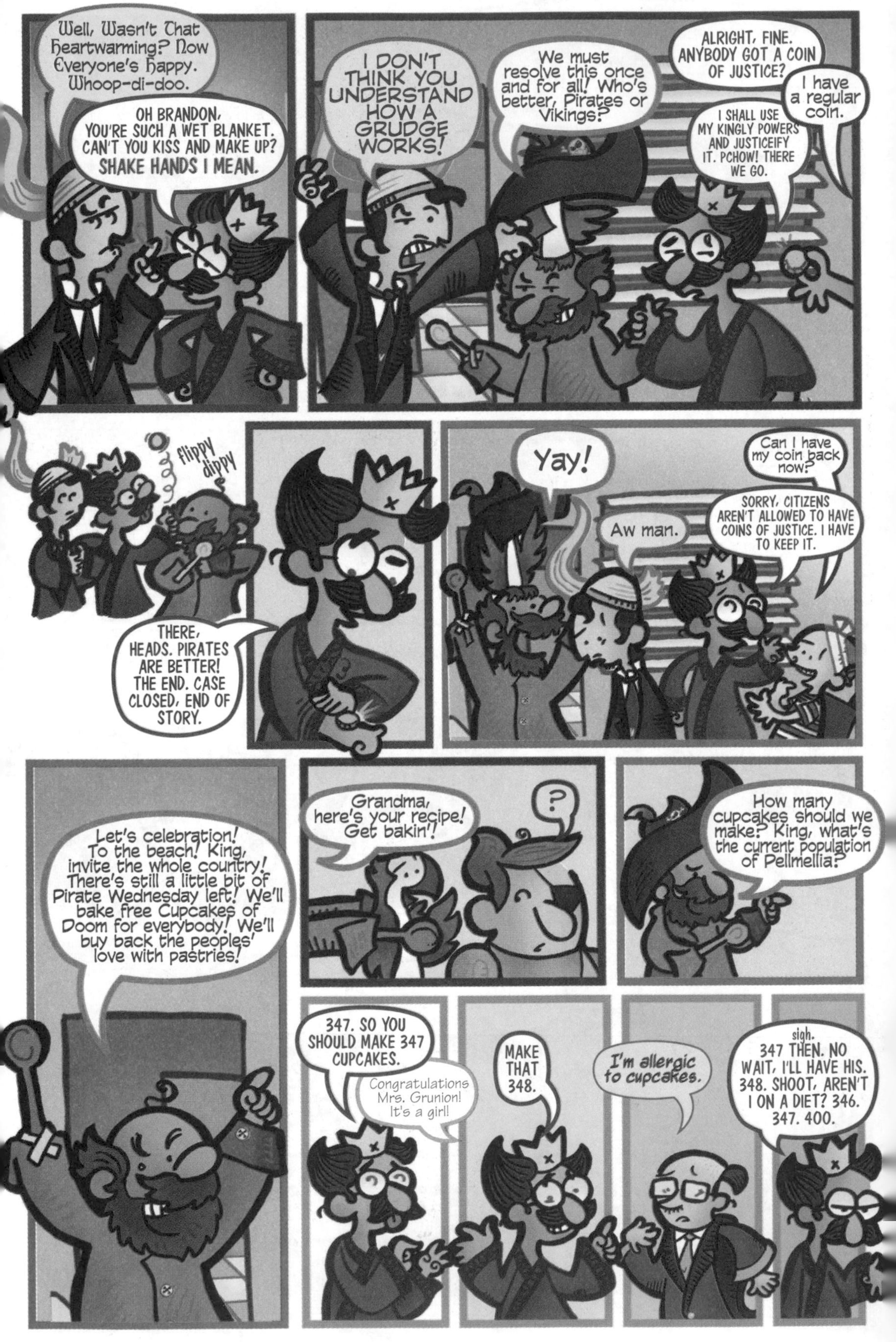
Well, Wasn't That Heartwarming? Now Everyone's Happy. Whoop-di-doo.
OH BRANDON, YOU'RE SUCH A WET BLANKET. CAN'T YOU KISS AND MAKE UP? SHAKE HANDS I MEAN.
I DON'T THINK YOU UNDERSTAND HOW A GRUDGE WORKS!
We must resolve this once and for all! Who's better, Pirates or Vikings?
ALRIGHT, FINE. ANYBODY GOT A COIN OF JUSTICE?
I have a regular coin.
I SHALL USE MY KINGLY POWERS AND JUSTICEIFY IT. PCHOW! THERE WE GO.
flippy dippy
THERE, HEADS. PIRATES ARE BETTER! THE END. CASE CLOSED, END OF STORY.
Yay!
Aw man.
Can I have my coin back now?
SORRY, CITIZENS AREN'T ALLOWED TO HAVE COINS OF JUSTICE. I HAVE TO KEEP IT.
Let's celebration! To the beach! King, invite the whole country! There's still a little bit of Pirate Wednesday left! We'll bake free Cupcakes of Doom for everybody! We'll buy back the peoples' love with pastries!
Grandma, here's your recipe! Get bakin'!
?
How many cupcakes should we make? King, what's the current population of Pellmellia?
347. SO YOU SHOULD MAKE 347 CUPCAKES.
Congratulations Mrs. Grunion! It's a girl!
MAKE THAT 348.
I'm allergic to cupcakes.
sigh. 347 THEN. NO WAIT, I'LL HAVE HIS. 348. SHOOT, AREN'T I ON A DIET? 346. 347. 400.

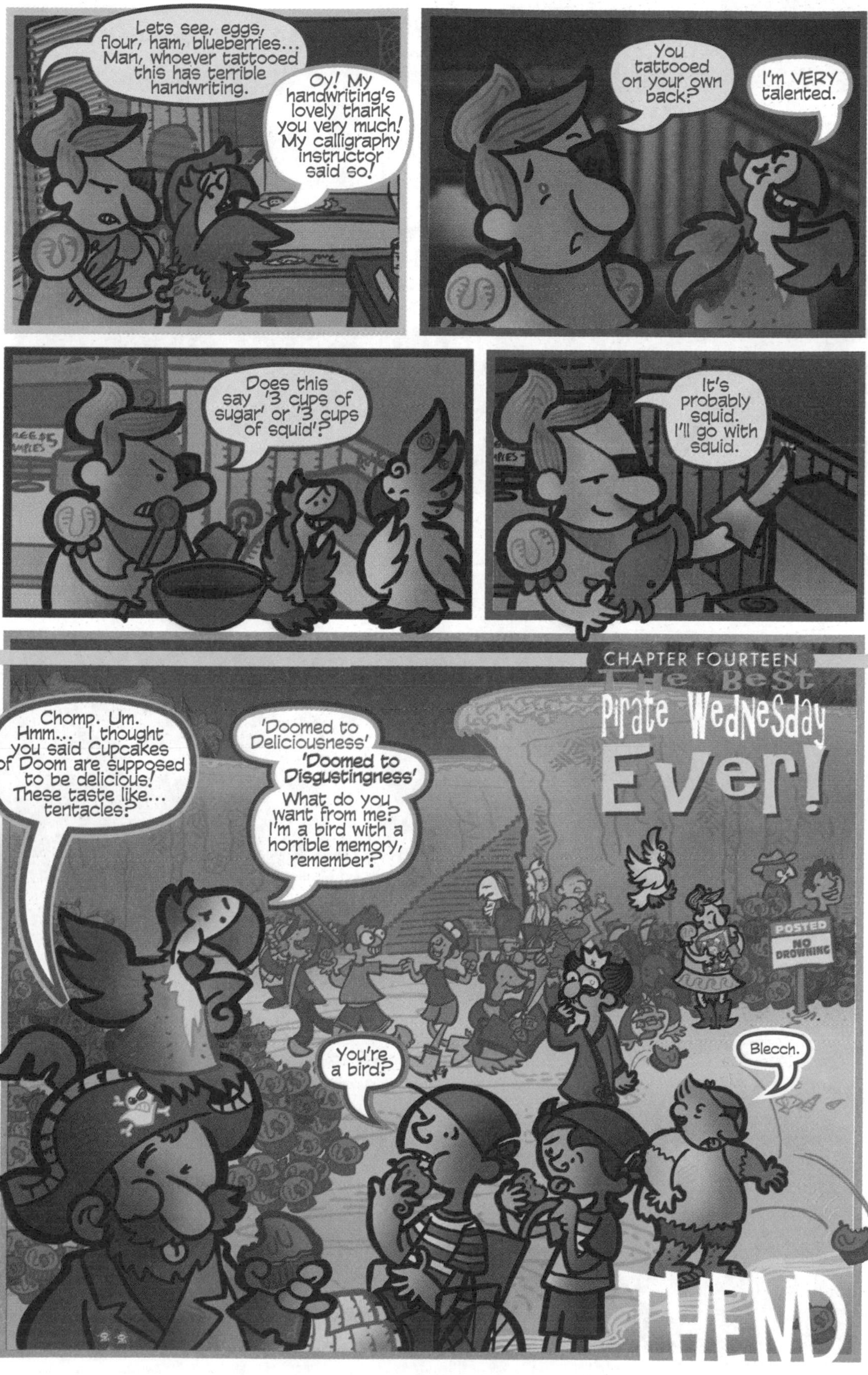
Lets see, eggs, flour, ham, blueberries... Man, whoever tattooed this has terrible handwriting.
Oy! My handwriting's lovely thank you very much! My calligraphy instructor said so!
You tattooed on your own back?
I'm VERY talented.
Does this say '3 cups of sugar' or '3 cups of squid'?
It's probably squid. I'll go with squid.
CHAPTER FOURTEEN
The Best Pirate Wednesday Ever!
Chomp. Um. Hmm... I thought you said Cupcakes of Doom are supposed to be delicious! These taste like... tentacles?
'Doomed to Deliciousness'
'Doomed to Disgustingness'
What do you want from me? I'm a bird with a horrible memory, remember?
POSTED NO DROWNING
You're a bird?
Blecch.
THE END

EPILOGUE

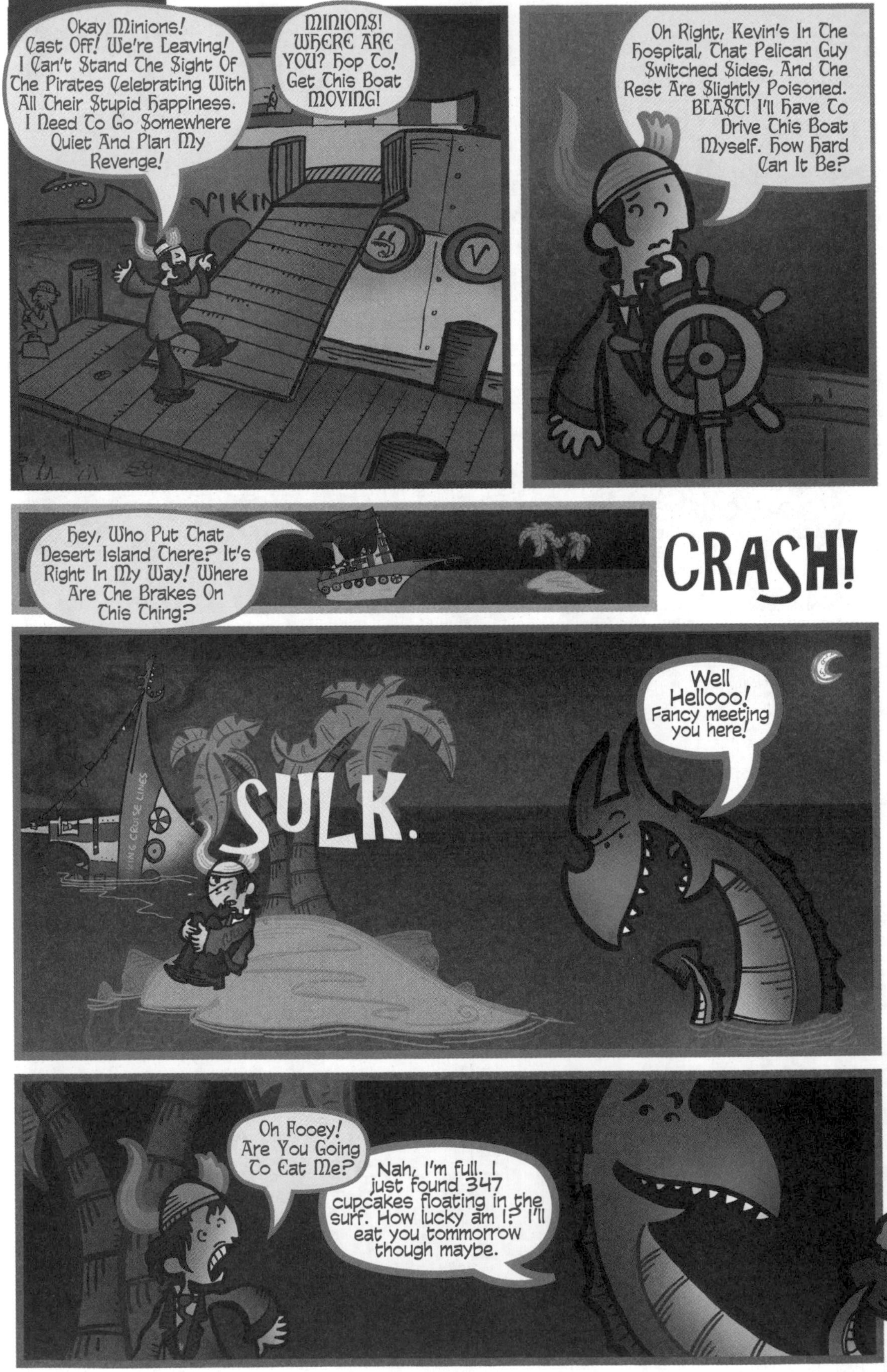
Okay Minions! Cast Off! We're Leaving! I Can't Stand The Sight Of The Pirates Celebrating With All Their Stupid Happiness. I Need To Go Somewhere Quiet And Plan My Revenge!
MINIONS! WHERE ARE YOU? Hop To! Get This Boat MOVING!
VIKIN
Oh Right, Kevin's In The Hospital, That Pelican Guy Switched Sides, And The Rest Are Slightly Poisoned. BLAST! I'll Have To Drive This Boat Myself. How Hard Can It Be?
Hey, Who Put That Desert Island There? It's Right In My Way! Where Are The Brakes On This Thing?
CRASH!
SULK.
Well Hellooo! Fancy meeting you here!
Oh Fooey! Are You Going To Eat Me?
Nah, I'm full. I just found 347 cupcakes floating in the surf. How lucky am I? I'll eat you tommorrow though maybe.

Eggs   Sugar   Squid   Flour   Blueberries   Ham

Outroduction by Ye Author

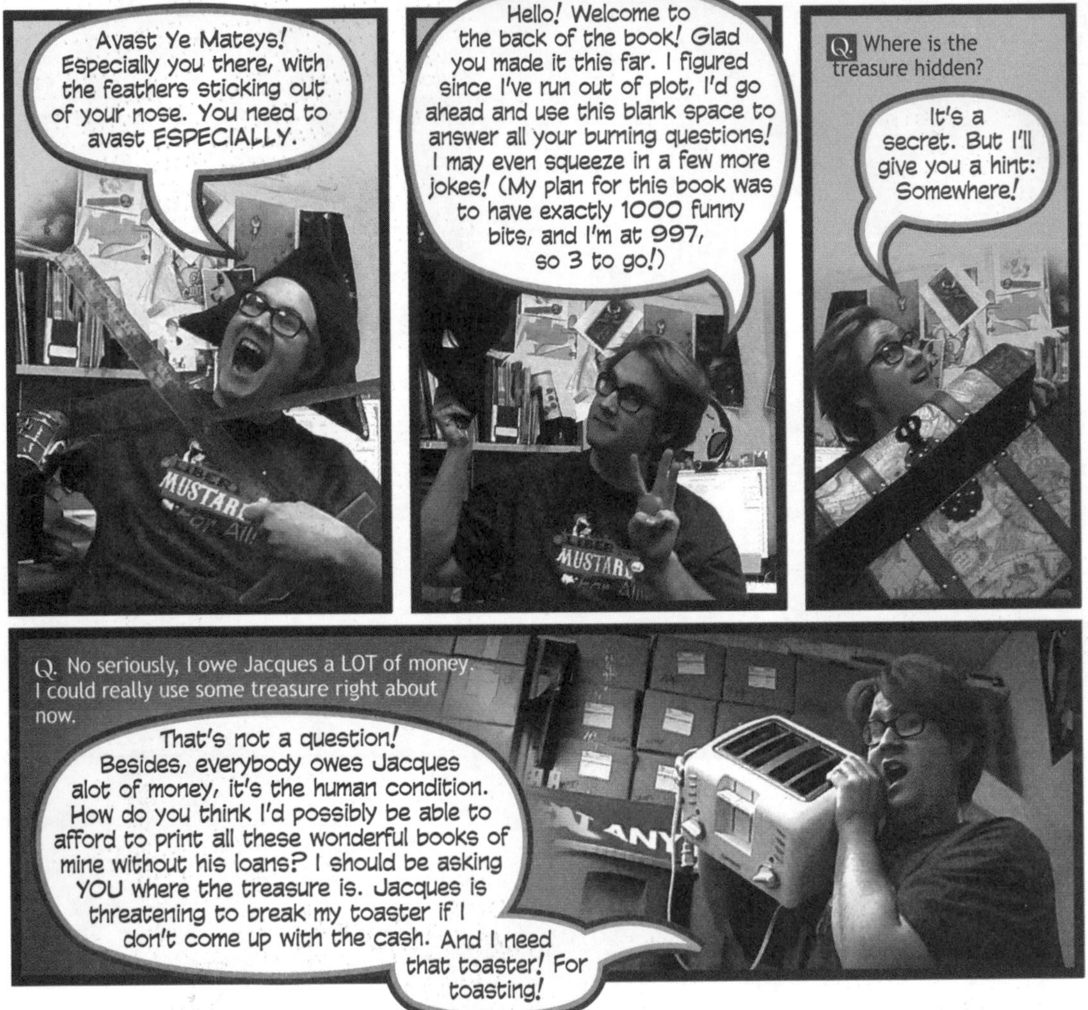
Avast Ye Mateys! Especially you there, with the feathers sticking out of your nose. You need to avast ESPECIALLY.
Hello! Welcome to the back of the book! Glad you made it this far. I figured since I've run out of plot, I'd go ahead and use this blank space to answer all your burning questions! I may even squeeze in a few more jokes! (My plan for this book was to have exactly 1000 funny bits, and I'm at 997, so 3 to go!)
Q. Where is the treasure hidden?
It's a secret. But I'll give you a hint: Somewhere!
Q. No seriously, I owe Jacques a LOT of money. I could really use some treasure right about now.
That's not a question! Besides, everybody owes Jacques alot of money, it's the human condition. How do you think I'd possibly be able to afford to print all these wonderful books of mine without his loans? I should be asking YOU where the treasure is. Jacques is threatening to break my toaster if I don't come up with the cash. And I need that toaster! For toasting!

Q. What's your deal, anyway?

Glad you asked that. My name is Ray Friesen, I am 6 foot 2ish inches tall, with fluffy hair and spectacles. I may or may not have a treasure map tattooed on my back. At the time of this publication I am 21, and so can now legally do ANYTHING I want! MWAHAHAHAHAHA! Within reason anyway. I'll need to get a piracy license if I want to do any robbing and stuff. Mentally, I'm much closer to 12 then 21. I've got one heckuva inner child, and the action figure collection to prove it!

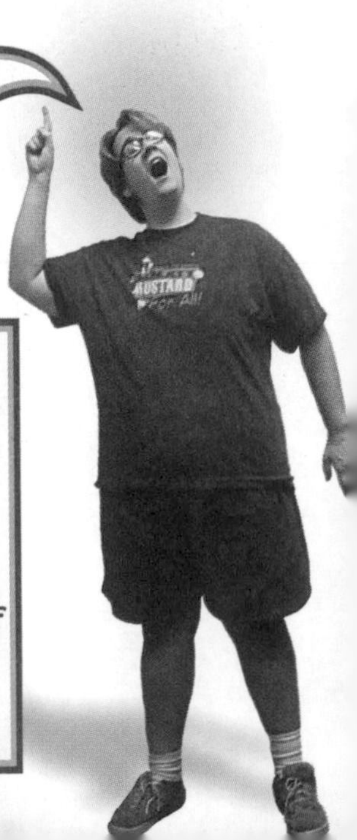

I've been drawing cartoons since practically forever. My mom still has the ones I did when I was 3. I published my first collection of comical strips when I was 11, thanks to the copy machines at Witts, my local office supply store. I convinced my local newspaper to start running my strip at age 12, and had my first pitch meeting with an animation studio when I was 13. At 16, I was nominated for my first award, an Ignatz for 'Most Promising New Talent'. At 18, I released my first full length graphic novel, 'A Cheese Related Mishap' and somehow figured out how to get it distributed to bookstores. It was one of the American Library Association's Top Ten Graphic Novels of the Year for kids! I've spent the intervening time drawing as much as possible to polish my craft, writing more books and coming up with ideas for LOTS more books, falling in love, worrying about whether I need a real job, and collecting more penguin toys.

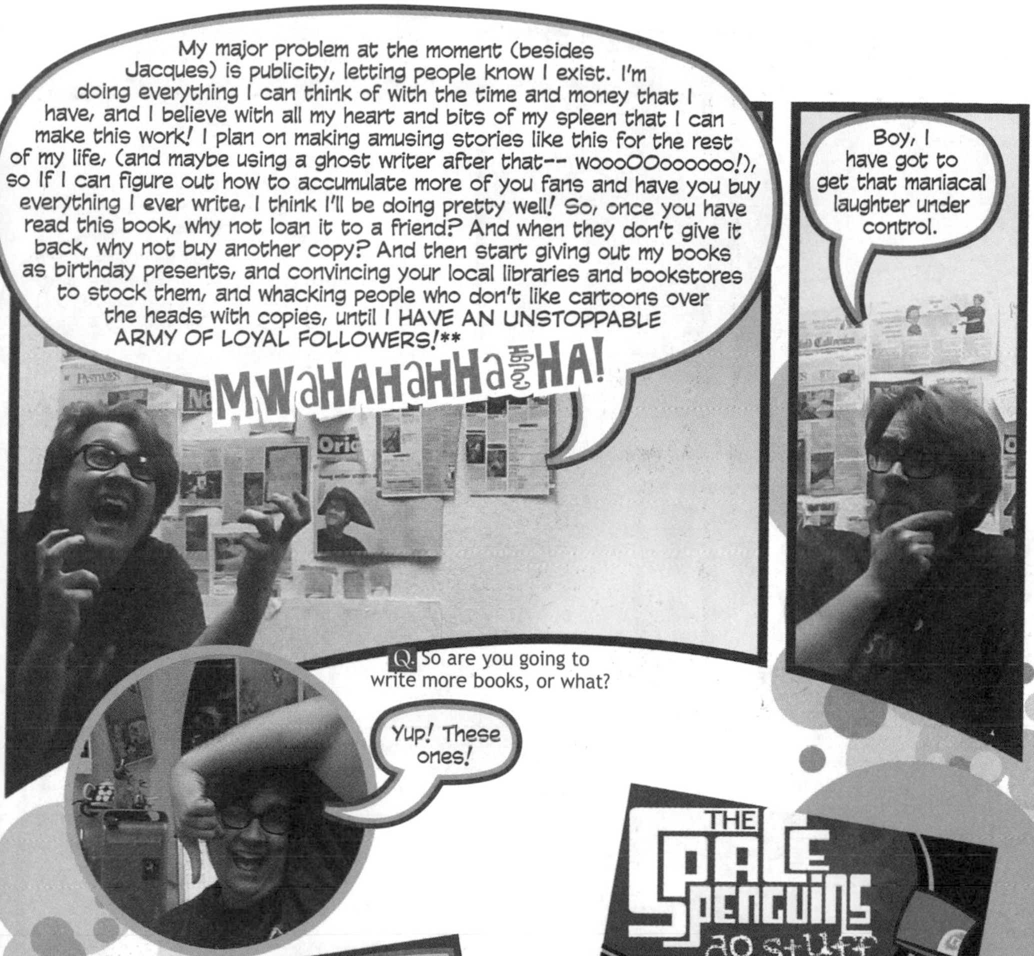
My major problem at the moment (besides Jacques) is publicity, letting people know I exist. I'm doing everything I can think of with the time and money that I have, and I believe with all my heart and bits of my spleen that I can make this work! I plan on making amusing stories like this for the rest of my life, (and maybe using a ghost writer after that-- woooOOoooooo!), so If I can figure out how to accumulate more of you fans and have you buy everything I ever write, I think I'll be doing pretty well! So, once you have read this book, why not loan it to a friend? And when they don't give it back, why not buy another copy? And then start giving out my books as birthday presents, and convincing your local libraries and bookstores to stock them, and whacking people who don't like cartoons over the heads with copies, until I HAVE AN UNSTOPPABLE ARMY OF LOYAL FOLLOWERS!**
MWAHAHAHHAHA!
Boy, I have got to get that maniacal laughter under control.
Q. So are you going to write more books, or what?
Yup! These ones!

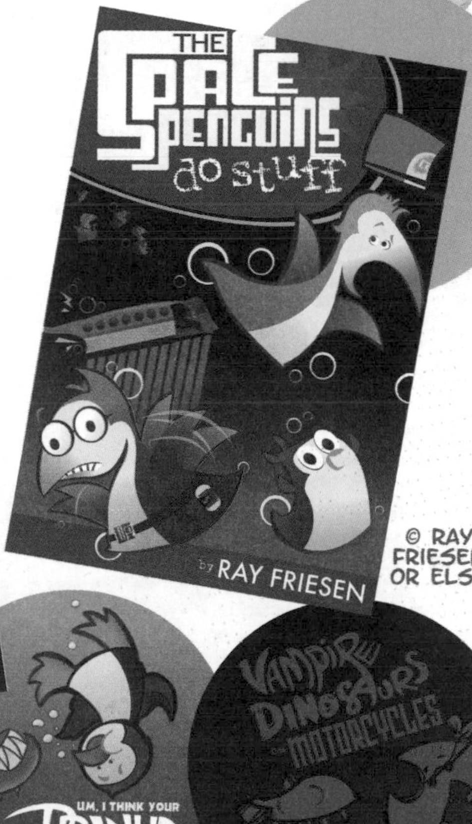
THE SPACE PENGUINS do stuff
by RAY FRIESEN

© RAY FRIESEN OR ELSE

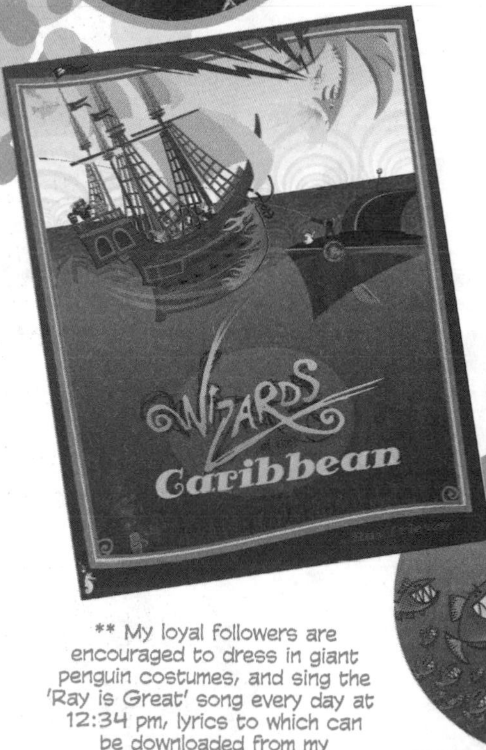
WIZARDS Caribbean

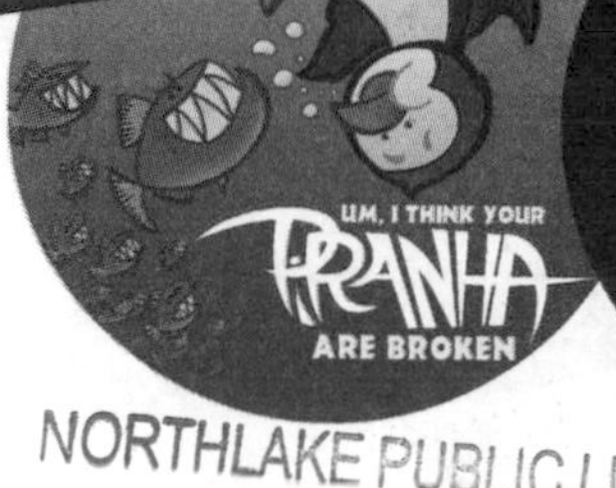
UM, I THINK YOUR PIRANHA ARE BROKEN

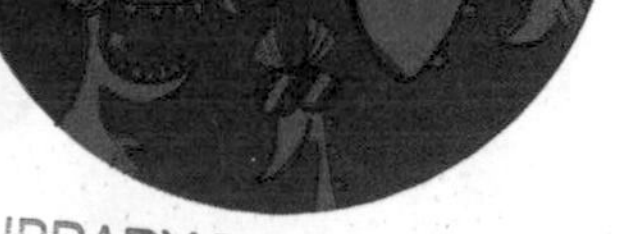
VAMPIRE DINOSAURS MOTORCYCLES

** My loyal followers are encouraged to dress in giant penguin costumes, and sing the 'Ray is Great' song every day at 12:34 pm, lyrics to which can be downloaded from my website.

Q. I can't wait that long. Have you written any other books?

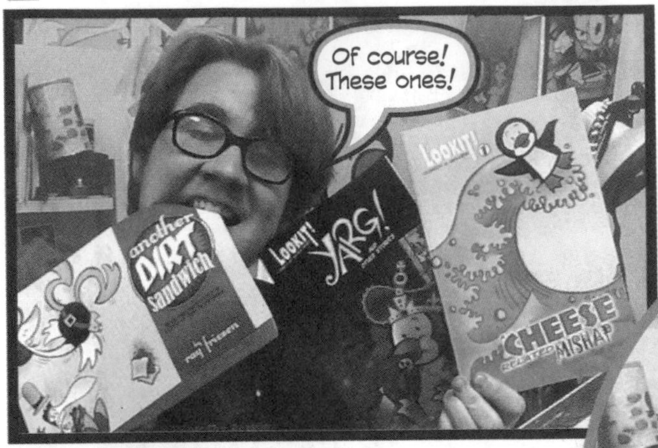

Of course! These ones!

Q. Wow! Those look awesome! I will definitely look for them. Are they in bookstores? And the Internets?

Of course they are! And even if they don't have them in stock, I'm sure they can order them for me.

Q. How come none of your other characters from those books were in this book?

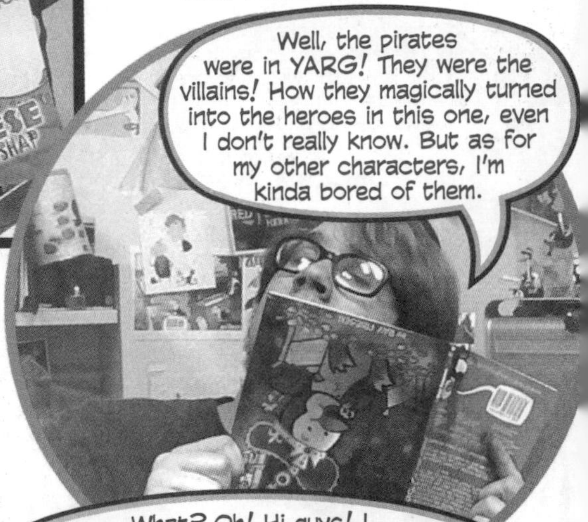

Well, the pirates were in YARG! They were the villains! How they magically turned into the heroes in this one, even I don't really know. But as for my other characters, I'm kinda bored of them.

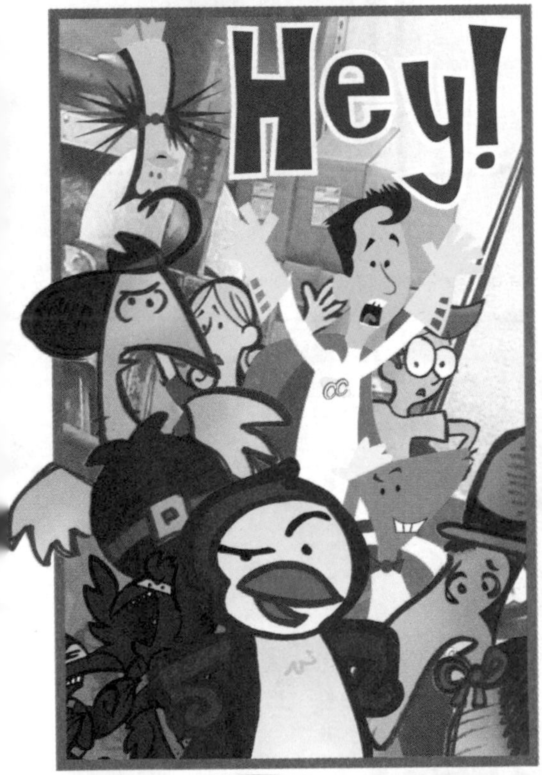

Hey!

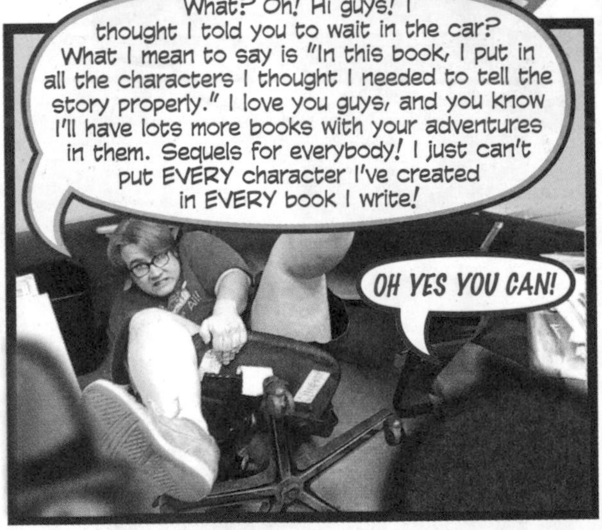

What? Oh! Hi guys! I thought I told you to wait in the car? What I mean to say is "In this book, I put in all the characters I thought I needed to tell the story properly." I love you guys, and you know I'll have lots more books with your adventures in them. Sequels for everybody! I just can't put EVERY character I've created in EVERY book I write!
OH YES YOU CAN!

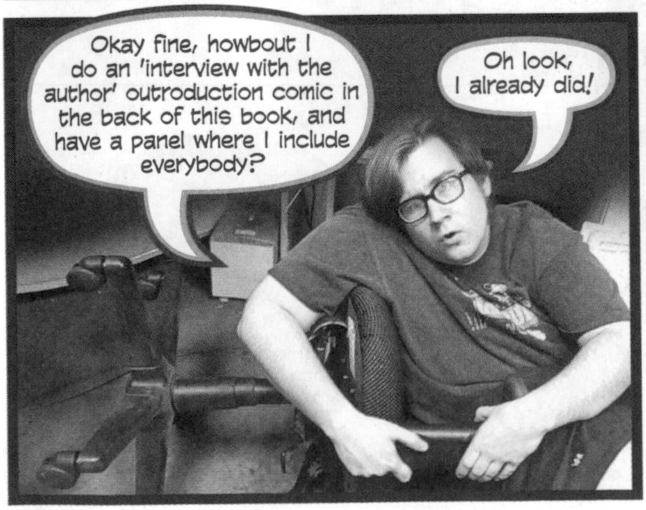

Okay fine, howbout I do an 'interview with the author' outroduction comic in the back of this book, and have a panel where I include everybody?
Oh look, I already did!

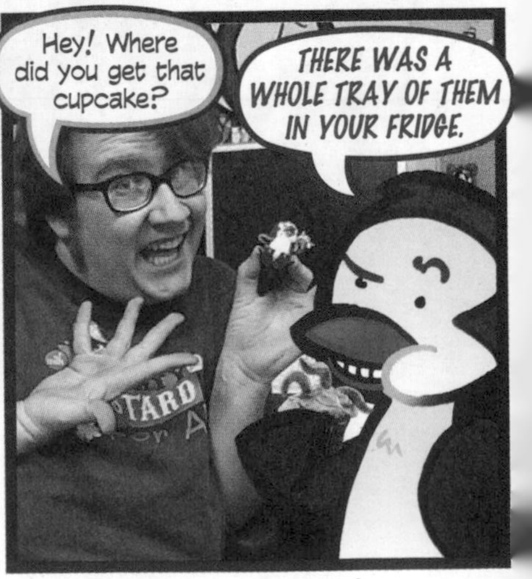

Hey! Where did you get that cupcake?
THERE WAS A WHOLE TRAY OF THEM IN YOUR FRIDGE.

Q. Where can we read more of your comics for free?

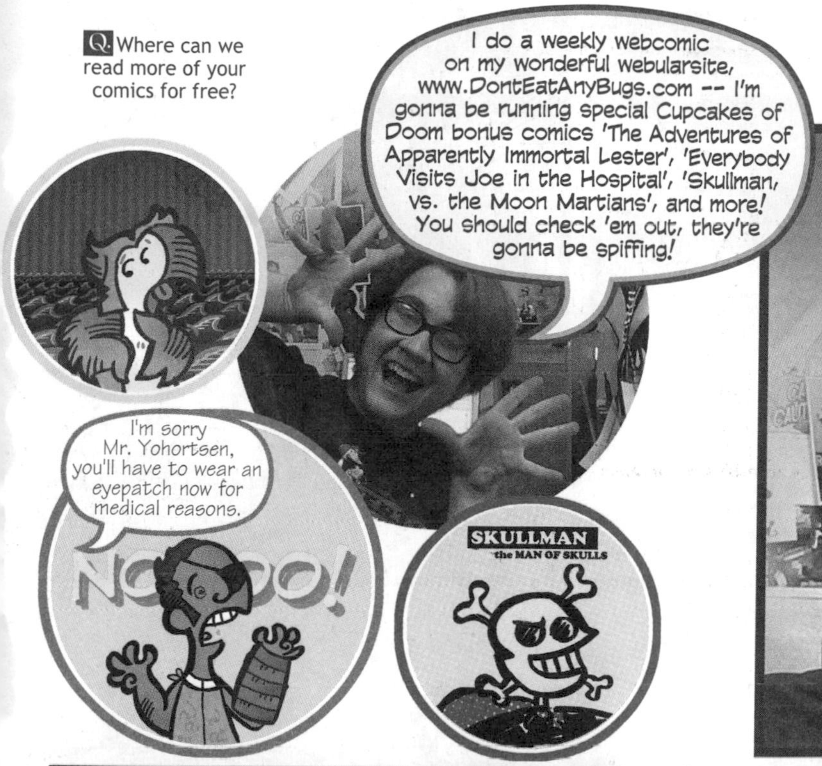
I do a weekly webcomic on my wonderful webularsite, www.DontEatAnyBugs.com -- I'm gonna be running special Cupcakes of Doom bonus comics 'The Adventures of Apparently Immortal Lester', 'Everybody Visits Joe in the Hospital', 'Skullman, vs. the Moon Martians', and more! You should check 'em out, they're gonna be spiffing!
I'm sorry Mr. Yohortsen, you'll have to wear an eyepatch now for medical reasons.
NOOOO!
SKULLMAN
the MAN OF SKULLS

Q. Do you sell any other merchandise on your fabulous website www.DontEatAnyBugs.com? Tshirts? Posters?

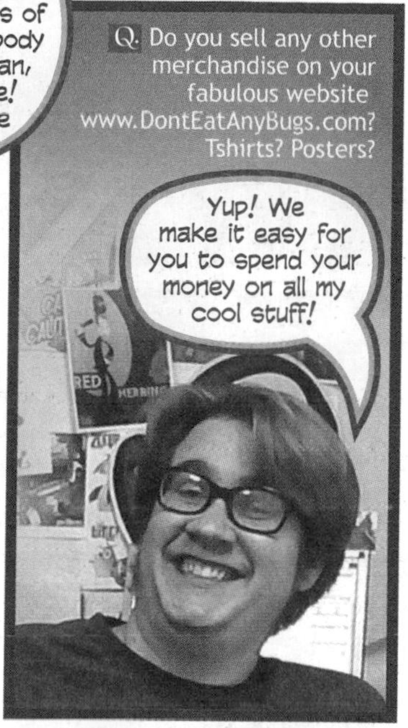
Yup! We make it easy for you to spend your money on all my cool stuff!

Q. I am a teacher, can you come to my school and teach my kids a cartooning lesson?

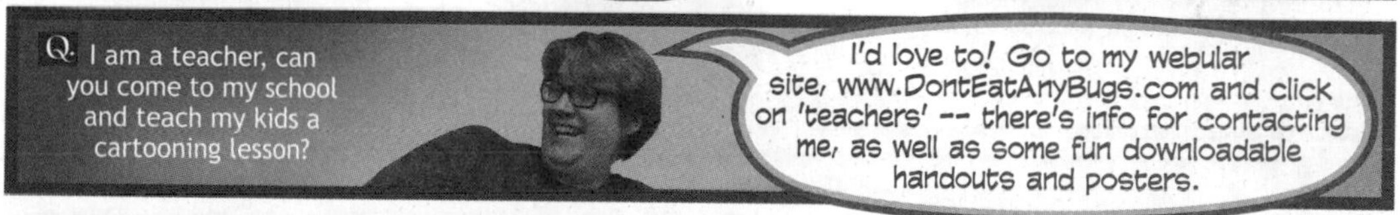
I'd love to! Go to my webular site, www.DontEatAnyBugs.com and click on 'teachers' -- there's info for contacting me, as well as some fun downloadable handouts and posters.

Q. I am a regular person, and also want you to come to my living room and teach me a cartooning lesson. It'll have to be after 5:00, because my favorite puppet show is on at 4:30. You're welcome to stay for dinner however, we're making cucumberburgers.

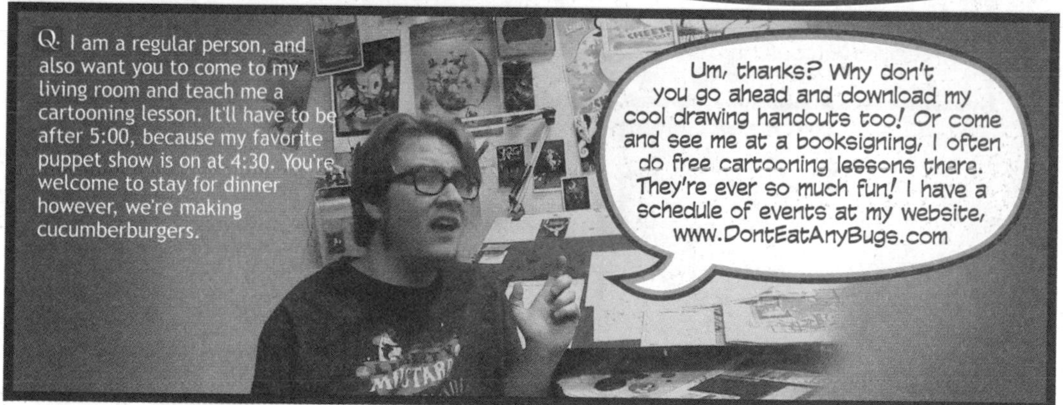
Um, thanks? Why don't you go ahead and download my cool drawing handouts too! Or come and see me at a booksigning, I often do free cartooning lessons there. They're ever so much fun! I have a schedule of events at my website, www.DontEatAnyBugs.com

Q. Why do you seem to like hats so much?

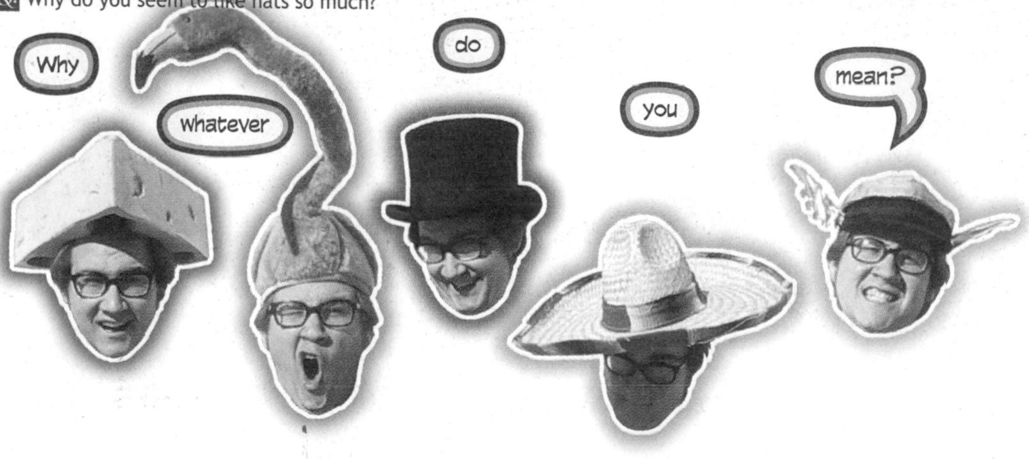
Why
whatever
do
you
mean?

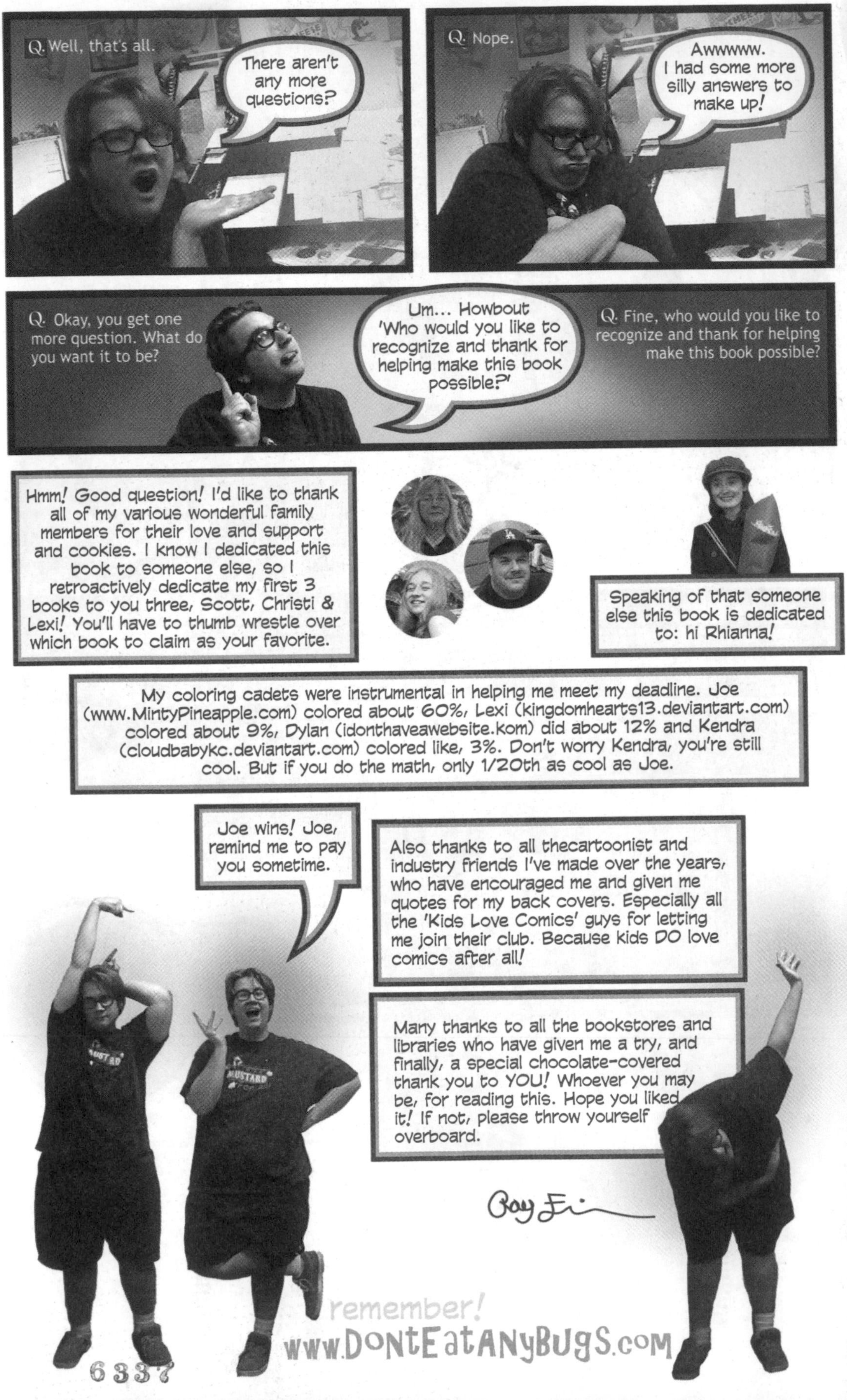
Q. Well, that's all.
There aren't any more questions?
Q. Nope.
Awwwww. I had some more silly answers to make up!
Q. Okay, you get one more question. What do you want it to be?
Um... Howbout 'Who would you like to recognize and thank for helping make this book possible?'
Q. Fine, who would you like to recognize and thank for helping make this book possible?
Hmm! Good question! I'd like to thank all of my various wonderful family members for their love and support and cookies. I know I dedicated this book to someone else, so I retroactively dedicate my first 3 books to you three, Scott, Christi & Lexi! You'll have to thumb wrestle over which book to claim as your favorite.
Speaking of that someone else this book is dedicated to: hi Rhianna!
My coloring cadets were instrumental in helping me meet my deadline. Joe (www.MintyPineapple.com) colored about 60%, Lexi (kingdomhearts13.deviantart.com) colored about 9%, Dylan (idonthaveawebsite.kom) did about 12% and Kendra (cloudbabykc.deviantart.com) colored like, 3%. Don't worry Kendra, you're still cool. But if you do the math, only 1/20th as cool as Joe.
Joe wins! Joe, remind me to pay you sometime.
Also thanks to all thecartoonist and industry friends I've made over the years, who have encouraged me and given me quotes for my back covers. Especially all the 'Kids Love Comics' guys for letting me join their club. Because kids DO love comics after all!
Many thanks to all the bookstores and libraries who have given me a try, and finally, a special chocolate-covered thank you to YOU! Whoever you may be, for reading this. Hope you liked it! If not, please throw yourself overboard.
remember!
www.DONtEatANyBUgS.com

6337